This edition, issued in 1956, is for members of The Companion Book Club, 8 Long Acre, London, W.C.2, from which address particulars of membership may be obtained. The book is published by arrangement with the original publishers, William Collins, Sons & Co. Ltd.

Also by
THOMAS ARMSTRONG
★

ADAM BRUNSKILL
KING COTTON
THE CROWTHERS OF BANKDAM
DOVER HARBOUR

PILLING ALWAYS PAYS

"A blessed companion is a book"—JERROLD

PILLING ALWAYS PAYS

★

THOMAS ARMSTRONG

THE COMPANION BOOK CLUB
LONDON

FOR THE BIG CHIEF
WITH A MOST HUMBLE APOLOGY FOR
DOVER HARBOUR

Made and printed in Great Britain
for The Companion Book Club (Odhams Press Ltd.)
by C. Tinling & Co. Limited
Liverpool, London and Prescot
S.356.UC

CHAPTER ONE

FRENZIED with frustration, traces of spittle frothing his mouth, the boy's vituperative torrent continued. Brought finally to understand that for perhaps the first time in his life he was being compelled to a course he did not wish to follow, his sole desire was to hurt in every way in his power.

"You . . ." he sneered. "And who the hell . . ."

The only other person in the small cabin was his father, a biggish-built man in the early forties wearing an expensive suit in Scotch tweed and a well-cut blue overcoat. Normally Sam Pilling had plenty of colour in his cheeks, but just now they were pallid; his eyes, too, usually good-humoured though keen, had an alien expression in them: that of wretchedness.

"Now, Gilbert," he said, "you're not short of intelligence by any means, so just ask yourself what's gained by carrying on as you are. Very shortly you'll be leaving Liverpool, which means you'll be away from England and from home for at least eighteen months—so the Line's Superintendent tells me. These being the circumstances, isn't it surely better for you to square your shoulders and face up to things——"

"Like a man, eh?" Gilbert Pilling jeered. "That's what you're going to say, isn't it? By God, you're real ingenious, aren't you?"

"Aye, like a man." Sam Pilling nodded. "Yes, like a man instead of acting like a spoilt child. Can't you think of this trip of yours as a real adventure? Of course, you're going to have to work at whatever jobs the Captain puts you on to, but you'll be seeing places you wouldn't ever visit on a luxury cruise, strange spots in South America, the West Coast of Africa, and all over, anywhere in fact where the company's agents can pick up cargoes for the ship to take or fetch. Why, there's thousands of lads would nearly give their ears for the opportunity."

Gilbert Pilling's eyes were glittering as he leaned forward. "Would they, indeed?" he said dangerously. "Go on, go bloody well on."

His father's lips momentarily tightened. "Yes, I've still another thing or two to say. And I'll begin by pointing out that the main reason I'm sending you off, the final straw so to

7

speak, is because you've been behaving as if you were years older than you are . . . not that I should excuse your sort of conduct even if you were half as old again. The fact is, however, that you're not eighteen yet, but instead of getting into scrapes lads of that age do if they've anything about 'em, clean and decent sort of scrapes——"

"I've done as I pleased, damn you," his son shouted.

"Yes, and now for once you're doing as I please," Sam Pilling growled.

Gilbert threw his head back to laugh. " 'Pilling who always pays' asserts himself. Ramsfield's leading turf accountant puts his foot down," he scoffed. "It's enough to make a——"

"That'll do," his father interposed.

"Ramsfield's card, the one and only Sam Pilling," Gilbert persisted noisily. "The chap who doesn't give a tinker's curse about anything or anybody, the chap who's always taken a delight in staggering people with what he did. But it doesn't cut any ice with me——"

Mr. Pilling's tone was firmer. "I've told you once already, Gilbert. You've said enough, and more than enough."

His son laughed again. "That warning would be sufficient for lots, I dare say, but it doesn't bloody well impress me. And it wouldn't impress Archie or Nancy either, for you see we've all lived too long with you not to know you aren't the tough customer you imagine yourself to be. Of course you've managed to deceive Mother——"

Sam Pilling, who was staring out of the open scuttle, rather unseeingly watching a crane at work on the opposite side of the dock, turned swiftly.

"You've hurt your mother enough, so keep her name out of this," he said angrily. "And if you don't, I'll do here and now what I ought to have done to all three of you years ago, and that's to give you a hiding when you needed it. Like them, you've been ruined——"

A hiss of fury escaping him, the gangling youth darted forward, his father involuntarily stepping back a pace under the suddenness of the attack. But if he escaped the wild swing to the face, he almost immediately suffered a most painful blow when Gilbert, lashing out with his right leg, kicked him violently on the shin.

Just then the cabin door opened to disclose on the threshold a man of middle height in uniform, who seemed to take in the scene at once, though he made no comment. Captain Crummock was of that not uncommon type of sea-going officer whose face tends to be a little fleshy, but his eyes and the set of his jaw more than hinted that here was a disciplinarian, a master mariner who would stand no nonsense, just but stern.

"Well, Mr. Pilling, I think you'd better be thinking of stepping ashore," he said. "So if you'll kindly bid good-bye to that young fellow I'll see you off."

"I think the last word has already been spoken," Sam Pilling said grimly.

Nevertheless, some pathetic quality of appeal revealing itself despite his anger, he looked towards his younger son, a youth he tried to believe was not as vicious as his conduct suggested. Indeed, had not Gilbert Pilling's features been distorted with the goading knowledge of impotence and hatred, even an impartial observer might have decided that there were plenty of faces less open and frank. At the final moment, however, Sam Pilling could recognize only the visible signs.

"Well, good-bye, lad," he said sadly.

On the deck outside, Captain Crummock pulled a bulky envelope from the breast pocket of his reefer jacket.

"There's no need for you to entrust me with this hundred pounds, Mr. Pilling," he began. "I appreciate your reasons, of course——"

"And I'll appreciate your keeping it on the off chance that it's needed," Sam Pilling said. "Right enough, I know that the Line takes care of its crews whether at sea or in port, but I'd feel happier if you had it. Supposing he'd to go into hospital, and needed treatment of a better sort? And then I wouldn't want the thought of expense to deter you from cabling me about anything which might crop up to do with him. Yes, you'll be doing me a favour if you shove that little wad of notes into your safe."

Thoroughly understanding the other's motives, although hardly sympathizing with a lack of parental control which had brought this situation about, Captain Crummock did not persist, and for the few moments they remained together before shaking hands, more general topics were discussed.

A quarter of an hour later, a very different figure from the brisk personality so well known in Ramsfield, Sam Pilling was walking dejectedly through the streets of Liverpool.

"Well, I suppose I'd better get some lunch," he muttered on entering Dale Street. "It's a damned nice beginning to nineteen thirty-six, by God!"

In the lavatory of the Adelphi he examined an ugly bruise on his shin, and then, with little appetite, endeavoured to simulate an interest in the meal he ordered in the restaurant.

Shortly after two o'clock he was sitting behind the wheel of his car, an exceptionally smart Bentley saloon in cream and black, which had been delivered to him by Thorntons' of Ramsfield less than two months before, as yet with less than a thousand miles on the clock.

When clear of the city, the long bonnet began to point easterly; to either side, as the car sped along, were the cotton towns of Lancashire, while ahead the gaunt lines of a mountain chain began to be more sharply drawn against the grey, wintry sky. Beyond the farther slopes of these stark hills was Ramsfield in the West Riding of Yorkshire, of world renown for woollens and worsteds, engineering goods and chemicals, for its two famous football teams, and for its wealth.

*   *   *

From the verge of the road on which the car was standing the prospect was extensive. To every hand, at the same height, was dun-coloured moorland; sparse grasses, stricken sedge, and stunted gorse, picked out here and there by the grey scars of outcropping stone. In the more remote distance were the smudges of smoke which represented other West Riding towns, and, given the best of eyesight, the tapering stacks of the factories of Halifax and Huddersfield could be discerned; perhaps also, on the clearest of days, the head-gear of a colliery close to Barnsley, or the spire of Wakefield's cathedral.

From Sam Pilling's feet, as on that cold January day he sat on the running-board of the Bentley, the Manchester Road started to drop into Ramsfield, dipping swiftly at times, often curving in snake-like bends, and occasionally passing from sight altogether.

"Ah, well," he sighed, shivering slightly, "I'd better be getting on. I've those proofs to check at the office, and then I want to get home to Milly as soon as I can."

But when he straightened he still continued to gaze at the town in which, with the exception of over four years of active service during the First World War, he had lived all his life. It was as familiar to him as the palm of his hand—from the smoke pall which hung over Ramsfield to the railroad, the canal, and the River Ram, which wound their way along the bottom of the valley in which the town nestled. Blindfold, he could have pointed out, at the more remote side, the clock tower distinguishing the great mills at Bankdam belonging to his kinsman, Simjoss Crowther, or farther to the west, higher up the valley at Scargate, two enormous enterprises controlled respectively by Watkinsons and Oldfields, to whom also he was distantly related, Northern Viscose, Ltd., artificial silk manufacturers, and Allan Oldfield, Ltd., tin box and canister makers.

Away to his left, six miles as the crow flies from Ramsfield Parish Church, was the village of Outham, where several of the wealthiest businessmen of the district, persuaded by their wives that the very select suburb of Moorheaton was no longer appropriate to their station, had built very large houses, in extensive, park-like grounds. The oldest of these, and by far the largest, was that of the late Sir Lancelot Handel Crowther, head of the senior branch of the Crowther family and known in his day as "the Major (Motor Volunteers) and Bart," who had created for himself—and for his son and his son's son he hoped—a big estate, with vast park, ornamental lake, carriage drive a mile long, and a mansion in keeping. Steeples Hall and its stabling and surroundings, however, were no longer maintained as once they had been, for Sir Lancelot Handel's son, with little liking for the industrial north, had sold to the junior branch of his family the interest he had inherited in the mills at Bankdam. Steeples Hall had become his sister's portion, and she resided there, married to a gentleman of considerable presence but little substance, who had hung up his hat—or rather Staff Captain's cap— somewhat disastrously as events proved.

"Yes," Sam Pilling reflected, knuckling his chin, "I wonder if Gainsway-Sinkinson sent his cheque this morning? Well, whatever my faults, and I've plenty as I've recently gathered, I've never lived above my means—or, worse still, gambled above 'em either."

He remained on those bleak heights a little longer, still gazing at a town which revealed so plainly commercial activity. The busy marshalling yards of the railway were implicit of this, and perhaps even more so was the evidence of "The Island," an immense acreage of hilly land confined by loops of the canal and the river. Here every inch of ground seemed to be occupied either by lengthy rows of houses or work-places, amongst these the mills at Dowling of Arthur Hirst and Son which, with their other large property, Moor-

11

cote Mills, made them second only to Simeon Crowther & Sons in the number of looms and setts of scribbling machines they possessed. And then, nearer the town, there were the far-ranging premises of an engineering firm, Murgatroyd Conveyors Ltd., a child which had outstripped its parent organization, itself a concern known all over the globe for textile machinery.

"This won't do," Sam Pilling remarked to himself suddenly. "Hanging about here looking as miserable as sin. . . ."

Snipping a prime Havana and lighting it, he at once climbed into the car, which soon, in third gear, his notion of prudence, was speeding down a steep hill, leaving the high moors behind.

Very shortly afterwards, cigar at a jaunty angle, Sam Pilling was responding with easy good-fellowship to the deferential salute of the commissionaire standing outside the offices of Charles Beaumont & Sons' Chemical Works, a gigantic enterprise whose retorts and towers covered sixty acres. And then came Ramsfield Bridge, at the far side of which were the business headquarters of his father-in-law, identified on the apex of the roof, in metal lettering, by the words: "Ezra Sykes—Tripedresser."

Next, Lowerhouse Street, Church Street and, the town's fashionable shopping thoroughfare, Teazle Street. Beyond this Market Approach, leading into Market Square, where Sam swung the Bentley around a taximan's shelter built in the form of a temple. He parked in the centre of the square between white lines painted in echelon on the wooden blocks of the road's surface to allow easy egress.

After imposing his will upon his younger son, Sam Pilling was nearly home.

Filling one side of Market Square was the grimy façade of the railway station; it faced the Town Hall at the other, a squat pile with a handsome, pillared portico. The buildings on the third side were distinctly varied, the outstanding of these being nearest the Town Hall: the exclusive County Club, a fine property; then the Baptist and the Methodist Chapels, factory-like buildings, and in the corner, abutting on to the station, there was a private house converted to commercial use, where old Ben Buckley, despite the keen rivalry of a younger man whose clientèle extended far beyond the boundaries of the town, nevertheless succeeded in preserving for himself a modestly satisfactory bookmaking connection.

On the farther and west side of Market Square, again beginning at the Town Hall end, the most noteworthy buildings were the Music Saloon, the George Hotel and, with frontage to both Market Approach and Market Square, a new erection, Neptune Buildings, on the first floor of which, spaced and designed to his own requirements on the strength of a lengthy and high-figured lease, were Sam Pilling's business premises. It was said in Ramsfield that the architect responsible for this project pulled every string imaginable when he learnt of a stipulation Mr. Pilling made before consenting to sign the lease. If so he lost, for on two sides of Neptune Buildings, Market Square and Market Approach, were immense signs which read:

PILLING ALWAYS PAYS

In Ramsfield this victory of Sam Pilling's, if such it were, was often cited, indignantly or with a chuckle as the case might be, among the many examples illustrating the methods he had used in advancing his ambitions in life.

When Sam was pushing back his seat to swing his legs out of the Bentley more comfortably, he sighted a Riley Kestrel saloon, his daughter Nancy's car. It was standing against the kerb outside the George Hotel.

"Mmm..." he grunted.

But, after a jovial word with the car-park attendant, he walked towards the fine entrance to Neptune Buildings where, scorning the lift, he passed through the large vestibule and climbed a flight of steps. At the top he turned into a long corridor, at the far end of which was a broad door, with frosted glass panels, marked: "Sam Pilling, Turf Accountant —Inquiries." A young lady was within, seated behind a walnut counter. She responded to his joking remark with a bright and welcoming smile; though he could be strict, Sam Pilling was both liked and admired by the young women he employed.

Behind this reception room with its adjacent waiting-room was another corridor, both sides of which were panelled in clear glass, so permitting a view of the activities taking place throughout the extensive suite of offices. It was the steeple-chasing season, and business would not begin to hum for a couple of months, until March came and the opening of the flat-racing season. Then the young ladies in the private exchange and the lengthy telephone room would have to forgo knitting, and on the settlement side duplicators, electrical adding machines and typewriters would be chattering away from morning until night.

Turning right, Sam stepped briskly along, seen by thirty or forty members of his staff as he proceeded into his private office, a room large enough to hold four leather-covered sofas and half a dozen luxurious club chairs. A massive flat-topped desk stood in the centre, upon it a Post Office telephone and an instrument with an array of push-switches for departmental connections. Near one end of the desk, on a stand, stood a dictaphone, while at the other, silent now, there was a tape machine. Elsewhere, across the expanse of carpet, were a craftsman-made mahogany cigar cabinet and a Sheraton bookcase, the lower part of which served for baser usage.

There were three windows in the office, one overlooking Market Approach, the others Market Square, and a second door, quite close to the corridor door, led into the room of Mr. Pilling's secretary, Hilda Schofield. Pierced through the wall on this side, near its extremities, were two openings provided with sliding, plate-glass panels. Through these, from the desk, blackboards could be seen in the Telephone Room and the Blower Room. These, on racing days, provided the observer with vital information, not the least important of this being the moment by moment change in the rates of betting on the course.

One other unusual feature in the office was displayed on the blank wall. This was a wooden board about twelve feet long on which was painted the slogan which had always been associated with the firm: PILLING ALWAYS PAYS, a slogan created by Elishah Pilling, Sam Pilling's father, under which he had traded until his death, when bankruptcy was upon him.

In surroundings so different from those in which his father drank away such profits as he might make, Sam hung up his overcoat on a stand and, as the door to his secretary's room opened, he tossed his hat towards one of the curved antlers. When the shot failed, he attempted it again, this time successfully.

"I'm still averaging one in two, Hilda," he said, laughing.

She smiled. "You've got such a good eye, Mr. Pilling," she said.

"Nay, I don't know about that," Sam demurred.

"But I do," she remarked, most seriously. "If you hadn't, you wouldn't have won so easily when Mr. Firth suggested a hat-throwing contest . . . you know, after the result had come

14

through for last year's Manchester November Handicap. Why, none of them could touch you at it."

Hilda Schofield was a woman somewhere between the late twenties and the early thirties, quietly but nicely dressed, tall and with a most attractive figure. Her chin was slightly pointed and she was very pale, though the pallor was not that of ill-health and served to emphasize the beauty of dark and large and very luminous eyes. In general her manner was restrained, although on occasion, when anything seemed likely to affect the comfort and well-being of her employer, she could be the very opposite, as was noticed by other members of the staff, especially the ladies, who drew their own gossipy conclusions.

Sam chuckled. "Anyhow, I relieved him of some of his winnings, didn't I?" Then, back to business and taking up the threads once more, he added: "Well, anything fresh?"

"Nothing really of importance," she replied. "But you've just missed Captain Gainsway-Sinkinson, who rang up a minute or two ago. He's catching the tea-time train to London, and said he was most frightfully annoyed because it wasn't until he'd left Steeples Hall that he remembered he'd forgotten to post us a cheque. What made it worse, he said, was that it's not the first time he's been so stupid."

"It isn't," Sam remarked noncommittally.

There was concern in her eyes, but this did not relate to financial matters. "What about a whisky, Mr. Pilling?" she inquired. "You've had a long drive and . . . and . . . well, shall I get one for you?"

Sam considered. "Yes, I think you might, Hilda."

Glad to be of service to him, she put down her notebook and turned towards the Sheraton bookcase as the internal corridor door was opened by Sam's trusted right-hand man. Fred Lumb, whose sixtieth birthday was not far away, had a solemnity of demeanour which could be most deceptive, and no one knew better than he the trials and tribulations through which the House of Pilling had passed. On settlement days for years on end he had cogitated with Elishah Pilling as to how the legitimate claims of winning clients could be met, and for years his own wage had been a most uncertain factor, depending on how much cash remained when the disbursements of honour had been made. Given such a background, and the immense changes which had taken place since then, it was hardly surprising he thought a great deal of Elishah Pilling's son. But it was characteristic

15

of him that, apart from means extremely indirect, he never permitted a word of approval to pass his lips.

Sam, seeing him, waggled a hand in cheery greeting. "Now then, Fred lad," he called out.

"Well?" said Fred Lumb.

His employer guffawed. "Yes, I've got the young devil off. He'll be getting a taste of the briny by now I should imagine, somewhere in the vicinity of the Mersey bar."

Fred Lumb's attention was elsewhere. "That's where he'll be, is it?" he remarked.

"Nothing like allowing youngsters enough band," Sam was asserting. "Then, when they go beyond reasonable limits . . ." his fist crashed down, "cut 'em short and show 'em who's the master."

Momentarily Mr. Lumb's expression was cynical. "Sounds all right," he commented, before once again giving his attention to Hilda Schofield, who was bending over the desk arranging syphon and decanter. Then he sighed. "By, but it must be grand," he murmured, "to have an angel of mercy administering to you when you're weary and heavy laden."

Sam Pilling's private secretary straightened abruptly. "And just what do you mean by that, Mr. Lumb?" she asked haughtily.

Fred Lumb's bushy eyebrows went up in surprise. "Just what I said, Hilda. It should be real pleasant when a comely hand-maiden——"

"Where the hell is Archie?" Sam demanded.

He had taken his drink into the window overlooking Market Approach, and was looking down at the extensive plate-glass front of Thornton's Garage, situated between the Vaults and the Theatre Royal. From this height he could see the bonnets of at least sixteen quality cars, an array which would not have been shamed by anything any London motor-showroom could have offered.

"Nay, he went out somewhere," said Fred Lumb.

"To try out a new bus with Frank Thornton, I expect," Sam said angrily. "Why do you let him go off idling, Fred? You're the boss here when I'm away, aren't you?"

"Aye, and he's the boss's son, Sam," Fred Lumb retorted.

Upon this Sam was guilty of a few extremely salty observations, and then, draining his glass, announced he was going home.

"I want to get back to Milly as soon as I can," he added.

16

"Women take things ridiculously to heart, and she's very upset about Gilbert. It's only natural for a mother, I suppose."

Fred Lumb moved his head sympathetically. "She'll feel it, so you be off to Glenfield as soon as possible," he agreed. "But if you could wait until the lad comes on from Wimpenny Eastwood's it would be helpful. They're sending on the proofs of our Sporting Handbook and Rules for this year, and I'd like you to scan through one or two of the items we've changed."

Sam appeared to be considering. "How long is he going to be?" he asked eventually.

"From what the printing office said he'll be on his way already," Fred Lumb replied.

"Right." Sam nodded. "Then I'll just pop across to the George for a minute or two."

Not long before, Fred Lumb had been at the far end of the offices, in the duplicating room, where a battery of machines turned out circulars and investment forms for clients' use. From there he, too, had noticed a dark blue Riley car.

At his employer's decision he again moved his head in acknowledgment, this time understandingly but far less sympathetically.

By comparison with great cities such as Birmingham, Manchester and Glasgow, Ramsfield was small indeed, a tenth or less of their size, but for all that visitors to the town, whether from London or elsewhere, were in complete accord about the George Hotel. In their opinion it was without question the finest hotel in the provinces, and if challenged they would dwell upon its fine furnishings and the quality of the dining-room and general service in support of their claims. In short, whether in reference to the appointments of the Ladies' Room or scrupulous cleanliness from roof to cellar, everything was first rate, and it is very certain that such an establishment could have existed only where it did, in the midst of a wealthy and free-spending community. Of course, pursuing the theory that the prophet is without honour in his own country, local residents were less effusive about its merits than strangers, but it was noticeable how, in the evenings, they flocked into the long bar or the American Bar, and the George's dinner dances never lacked patronage.

On that January afternoon, three well-known frequenters of the hotel were sitting together in the lounge, two men and a girl of about nineteen. The elder of the men, whose age was somewhat indeterminate, was definitely not regarded with overmuch favour in Ramsfield. This was on three counts: the first that Ram Valley manufacturers regarded with suspicion mid-European refugees who bought mills cheaply and settled amongst them; the second that, of those gentlemen, Josef Brozik had proved himself oversharp in his dealings; and the third, especially for those with daughters, Mr. Brozik had rapidly acquired an unsavoury reputation for his affairs with young women.

The same objections could not be advanced against the other man, but none the less he was disliked even more heartily, apart from by a section of the womenfolk. Rafe Bottomley—nowadays he spelt his Christian name this way and vehemently opposed the more usual regional pronunciation, Ralph—was a hook-nosed and scented exquisite of thirty-three or four. From his aunt, Madame Gladys Shires, he had inherited a gown shop in Teazle Street, and this, with his Spring and Autumn Collections and Mannequin Parades, he had transformed. He was, in fact, Ramsfield's *couturier*.

The girl with them, Sam Pilling's daughter Nancy, was laughingly bending over a flame which Mr. Brozik had produced with amazingly celerity from his gold lighter.

"My dear, no really," Rafe Bottomley was drawling in horror. "I simply couldn't consider a model . . ."

Truth to tell, his companions were not taking a great deal of notice of him. Cigarette lighting the excuse, they were gazing closely at each other, the yellow flickering flame reflected in the girl's lovely eyes and the man's dark, compelling ones. "Stare you out" was a game Nancy Pilling had often played in her youth and she had no intention of yielding. She did, however.

"Thanks, Josef," she said breathlessly.

Mr. Brozik smiled a little. "Enchanted," he murmured.

Just then, as she was adjusting the scarf over her head, Nancy encountered another pair of eyes, her father's.

"Good God, the patriarch's returned," she exclaimed. "Oh, Daddy darling," she called out to him, the bracelets on her wrists tinkling as she waved violently, "do come and join us. We'll be devastated to hear about poor Gilbert's final curtain, the sacrifice at the altar so to speak. Yes, *do* come."

Sam had been in the hotel quite a while already. On his arrival, as he was being greeted by the hall-porter with that enthusiasm hall-porters and head-waiters accord to successful bookmakers, he had been clapped on the shoulder by the son-in-law of the late "Major and Bart."

"Speak of the devil, what what," Captain Gainsway-Sinkinson exclaimed, guffawing heartily. "Just the chappie we want to meet. Eh, Entwistle, old man?"

Thereupon Sam was introduced to a Mr. Entwistle who, it appeared, was staying in Ramsfield with a couple of senior members of his staff until the middle of the following week for a series of conferences with the Borough Engineer, the Waterworks Committee, and other interested parties, to do with the provision of a new large dam in the vicinity of Lumbig Tarn, on Barntat Moor where Sam Pilling joined Septimus Firth's party each "Twelfth." The immediate reason for Captain Gainsway-Sinkinson's pleasure was that Mr. Entwistle believed a horse he favoured might be running in the White Lodge Chase at Haydock Park the next day, and it would be convenient for him if he could defer placing his bet until the last moment, which meant that a Ramsfield bookmaker rather than his own would be best.

"Delighted to oblige you to-morrow or any time," Sam Pilling said. "I'm going back to the office in a minute, and I'll arrange for an account to be opened for you."

Mr. Entwistle expressed voluble thanks, and then, after monopolizing the conversation, excused himself. Immediately he had gone, Captain Gainsway-Sinkinson, a gentleman almost shriekingly of the commonly accepted Army type, embarked on an explanation as to who his friend was—which in its essentials boiled down impressively enough. Peter Entwistle was the Chairman of Entwistle and Partners of Manchester, one of the largest firms of contractors in the north.

"I hear," Sam said after this, wondering if it might bring about some reference to that lapse of memory of which he had been told, "I hear you're off to London."

Captain Gainsway-Sinkinson's eyes lit up. "Yes, jolly old Town for a few days, and . . ." he winked, "as a gay bachelor, mark you. See my tailor and bootmaker in the morning, gunsmith in the afternoon, and wind up the evening at a Fifth Army Staff reunion, and then for a spot of fun, what. And, by George!"

A glance at his watch was responsible for the exclamation. With a hasty: "Cheerio, Pilling," he departed, accompanied by the luggage-porter of the George, who carried his gear.

A wintry smile momentarily illuminating his features, Sam wandered in the direction of the lounge.

When he perceived his daughter, who as yet was unaware of his presence, he was possessed by a most primitive urge. His desire was to march forward, to grasp the suave Mr. Brozik by the scruff of his neck, likewise the soft, white-handed Rafe Bottomley, and thereupon crack their heads together.

"Yes, and I might have done it at one time," he confessed to himself. "Moreover, even if I did," continued his unsmiling reverie, which significantly was not boastful as he contemplated escapades of other days about which he was secretly proud, "nobody would think so much of *me* doing it, because it would only be on a par with the unexpected things I have done."

Instead, he stood where he was, waiting to catch her eyes. The events of the past twelve months had taught him the lesson that the modern miss does not permit cave-man departures, or indeed any action she might deem to affect her rights and dignity.

He sighed faintly as he watched her, for even a father can occasionally consider his girl quite objectively. Nancy, he told himself, was still an exceptionally attractive creature, but she was not as pretty as she had been at eighteen, and that was wrong somehow. But he knew the reason for the hollowness in her cheeks, the shadows beneath her eyes.

"It's her rackety life," he thought. "Driving herself at this and that, until she's everlastingly quivering inside herself like a piece of elastic stretched too tight. And me, Ramsfield's star turn as Gilbert indirectly put it, can't do anything about it. Well, I'll damned well see about that from now onwards."

This resolve involved him in a tactical mistake within a few seconds of Nancy's temporarily abandoning her companions to join him.

"Poor Daddy," she mocked him, "to be beset by such terrible offspring. Why didn't you send Archie and me off with Gilbert?"

"I'd have preferred to ship off those two chaps you're with," Sam snapped. "God, what wouldn't I give to see 'em both scrubbing a deck."

"Oh, *really*," Nancy protested. "I mean, quite apart from their being friends of mine, one must be civilized."

Hitherto Sam had not contemplated grasping her by the scruff, but the temptation then arose. Wisely, however, he turned abruptly and left her, to proceed with enraged strides back to his office, where he speedily disposed of the Sporting Handbook with its rules, ready reckoner for odds of 11/10 to 100/6 On and Against, 2/6 Doubles for the same range, and, an innovation introduced successfully the previous season, details of conditions under which clients' own systems could be worked for them.

Then, after giving a few instructions to Fred Lumb and Hilda Schofield, he collected hat and overcoat and returned to the parking place in Market Square.

Traffic in the centre of Ramsfield moved in a clockwise direction, which meant that to return to Ramsfield Bridge from Market Square another route must be taken. And so Sam headed his car for the narrow gap between the Town Hall and the Country Club, which led into Sheepgate where, a little beyond the Mechanics' Institute and the Cloth Hall, he left the main road at a point just short of a signpost marked "To Wakefield and Leeds," and swung along Folly Street. This, at the far end, brought him to his father-in-law's works and Ramsfield Bridge, beneath which the dark body of the river flowed, steamy vapour rising from grease- and dye-polluted water.

Immediately on the other side of the bridge, at traffic lights, the road divided: Barnsley Road, which he followed, stretching straight ahead, and Manchester Road, by which he had entered the town earlier that day, bearing sharply to the right. Some three or four hundred yards up Barnsley Road the very pleasant suburb of Roydlea began. The change from industrial surroundings to a reasonably select residential area was quite sudden, heralded on one hand by the ornate memorials to the dead in the Cemetery, and the fine buildings and playing fields of Ramsfield College on the other. The Regal Cinema was beyond this, a discreet erection marred by the posters on its lofty tower, but the Tudor-style fish-and-chip shop, adjoining, was wholly of a superior description, and nothing could have been more elegant than the oval-shaped glass plaque in its window which drew attention to a salient fact: "Ezra's Tripe Sold Here." This notice, one of many hundreds which could be found within a radius of fifteen miles of the Cloth Hall, provided just another instance of a lifetime's hard work, care and devotion —subject to the demands of the Methodist Chapel in Market Square—which had earned for Mr. Sykes a very considerable fortune.

Then came the Hospital, its many windows glowing in the failing light; next a lavatory in the middle of the thoroughfare, opposite the entrance to Knowlbank Road, which ran into Moorheaton, and finally, a quarter of a mile higher up Barnsley Road, the turn into Penny Lane, an alternative way into Moorheaton, usually preferred by Sam.

Still retaining lamp standards, whose form was a supreme example of the iron-founder's art, from whose summits gas-mantles sent out a greenish-yellow light from dusk onwards, Moorheaton was the most exclusive locality in Ramsfield; and, of its exclusive tree-lined streets, none was more exclusive than Moorheaton Drive, in the middle of which Sam Pilling lived, at Glenfield, a large Victorian Gothic residence identical with the next house farther up, Stonewood, the home of Mrs. Clem Roebuck, Milly Pilling's sister.

By contrast with houses about them, however, Glenfield and Stonewood were pigmy places, and in the days before the Dawsons of Dowling Mills crashed, Sir John Edward Dawson had bitterly resented their being built. From The Turrets, an immense pile immediately below the site on which Glenfield was erected, he had watched the new foundations being dug, and was so infuriated that within four months he began to build himself, seven miles out up the Halifax Road, on Barntat Moor, setting up a mansion which put even his former house in the shade. Since then, as it was at present, The Turrets had often been unoccupied, and so, uncared for.

But despite this single blemish, Moorheaton Drive was a very notable stretch. The majority of the houses along it, sited well back from the road, would not have been out of place surrounded by appreciably sized parks; their grounds, averaging perhaps six or seven acres, were beautifully maintained; terraced walks were guarded by stone balustrading and statues on pedestals peeped out here and there. Approaches often had their own lamp-posts spaced at intervals; the pillars of main gateways were embellished with stone or bronze lions, eagles and griffins, their entrances being given an added importance by a lodge alongside, usually the perquisite of a gardener.

Yes, Moorheaton was indeed select, and, alarmed by the dire example offered by the late Sir John Edward Dawson and the equally defunct Sir Lancelot Handel Crowther, the wealthiest citizens of Ramsfield, for the most part, preferred to remain there.

Glenfield, Sam Pilling's house, and Stonewood, the residence of his best friend, Clem Roebuck, shared a semi-
circular driveway, the entrances in Moorheaton Drive being
about a hundred yards apart. The respective garages were
behind, reached after passing across the broad court which
separated the houses.

Sam, however, after slowing down on reaching the un-
curtained windows of The Turrets, turned into the lower
gateway, but stopped as soon as he drew level with the front
door of Glenfield, anxious to be with his wife as soon as possible. Unhappily this haste was responsible for a minor misfortune as, immediately on entering the small outer hall, his
feet shot from under him. By a supreme effort he prevented
himself from falling but could not prevent himself from kicking the umbrella stand every bit as violently as his son Gilbert
had kicked him in Liverpool. The umbrella stand was a
cherished trophy, a brightly gleaming shell-case in which
stood several walking-sticks, a putter and the like.

In these circumstances man is not always at his best. "God
damn it," he bellowed.

The almighty clatter had its repercussions. When he
entered the large inner hall the maid was there, and the cook
was gaping from a baize-covered door to the rear. The lady
of the house had also been drawn by the commotion, but she
was peeping over the banisters at the top of the broad staircase.

"Somebody's going to break a neck in this place one of
these days," he fumed as he handed his overcoat to the girl
waiting. Quite where this might be he did not specify, and it
would have been difficult to name anywhere apart from
bathrooms or kitchen quarters. Glenfield was a house of fitted
carpets everywhere—the staff sitting-room had one, too.

"And where's your mistress, Olga?" Sam was inquiring,
when he broke off to sniff. "Distemper, or I'm a Dutchman,"
he muttered, adding a pregnant: "Oh!" when he looked upwards and saw his wife. "And now what are you up to?" he
demanded.

"You'd better come up and see," Mrs. Sam Pilling retorted.

"I will," he promised.

Milly Pilling awaited him on the spacious landing at the
stair-head. She was slenderly built, not very tall, and though
she was far from appearing at her best she looked much too
youthful to have a grown-up family. Dressed more effectively

than at present she would be judged by strangers to be at least eight years younger than her years, which were close on thirty-nine, four less than her husband's. At the moment her eyes, normally very vivacious, were definitely red, and her cheeks had suspicious streaks as though recently she had been crying.

"The house has to be kept nice," she remarked when Sam joined her. "All that hullabaloo because you slipped."

"But can't the house be kept nice without the tiles out there being waxed and polished, waxed and polished, day and night?" he complained.

"You *do* exaggerate, Sam," Milly retorted.

Sam smiled, and then asked where renovation was taking place. This proved to be in the boxroom, to which she led him, shapely ankles showing below a loose, paint-grimed, distemper-coated garment which failed to hide altogether a very trim figure beneath.

Éau-de-nil, on the shade card issued by a firm of distemper manufacturers, had been her undoing. That, and the urgent need to do something which would soothe her nerves on what had been a dreadful day. Her husband knew this, just as he knew her passion was her home: she was absorbed in her family, her house, her plants and her garden.

"Very nice, love," Sam commented after inspecting her handiwork. "But there's one thing that worries me—don't you think that sooner or later folks will be saying that Sam Pilling can't afford to get a firm of decorators in?"

For a fleeting space she was her real self, smiling despite her grief.

"The moon will be made of green cheese before anybody gets that idea into their head," she said with emphasis. "*You've* taken care of that."

Sam chuckled. "Maybe so, love," he agreed.

There was an appreciable silence afterwards and then, quickly, she turned to him. And he, recognizing the signs, put a consoling arm around her.

"He's gone then?" she asked, her voice breaking.

"He has, love." Sam nodded. "And it went off a lot better than I expected, and I feel pretty sure I put it into his head that he'll be enjoying himself before very long. Moreover, I'm certain that we couldn't have bettered Captain Crummock as a man to trust him to."

"He won't be cruel to him?" she whispered.

"Of course he won't," Sam scoffed. "Not a bit of it, love.

Aye, it's hard I know, but in Gilbert's own interests I think we've done the right thing in sending him off."

Milly stirred. "*You* sent him off. I shouldn't have dreamed of taking such an awful step."

With a preliminary clearance of his throat, Sam began to speak somewhat pompously. "There's a time when a boy must learn the meaning of authority, Milly. The world isn't an easy place, and——"

"Cavalier." Milly gulped.

He gaped at her. "You what?"

"You don't care, that's all," she wailed. "It means nothing to you that he's all by himself."

"Now come, love," Sam said quietly.

Wisely he let her have her cry out, holding her head against his breast as she sobbed. And when she calmed down, and when he heard a final but not quite so desperate snivel, he pulled out his handkerchief to wipe her eyes. In the end, teasing her as much as he could contrive, he was rewarded by a very watery smile.

"Yes . . ." She nodded. "I know you're upset, Sam, and I didn't mean what I said."

Sam smiled. "Friends, love?" he inquired.

She looked up. "Friends, Sam darling," she said.

After kissing her again, he brought matters to a more mundane level by reminding her it was Friday, and that on Friday evenings for some years past they had had an outing together.

"Oh, I couldn't bear to go to the theatre to-night, Sam," she expostulated. "Not when Gilbert's——"

"By Jingo," he said, disgust displayed in every line of his face, "your opinion of him must be a lot worse than mine. Do you for a minute really think he'd deny you a pleasure because he'd had to leave home?"

"No, I don't, Sam, but——"

Sam was firm. "We're going, Milly. Do you good and it'll do me good, too. Damn it, you know how I always enjoy a decent play."

When they parted a little later it was on the understanding that their jaunt was on.

When the master of Glenfield was called by the maid for the evening meal, he was sitting in the study, behind a closed door. From a drawer in the roll-top desk he had taken out two letters, one of which was from the Headmaster of

Gilbert's school explaining, in cold, formal terms, why the boy had been expelled.

The second letter, from his son's housemaster, was a bitter pill for any father to swallow, but Sam nevertheless respected the writer for his frankness and honesty of purpose. Again and again he read a paragraph:

> "*Without being too optimistic about the outcome,*" it said, "*my view is that your son might benefit by a lengthy period in a more healthy and sterner environment than has been his lot when at home, where the mischief has undoubtedly occurred, to such a degree that even school could not remedy it. That the boy was expelled for a most distasteful liaison with a kitchen-maid on the domestic staff here is grave enough, but ...*"

Sam groaned as he recalled visits paid him by one of the Farrers and one of the Gledhills during the previous summer's holidays. Both gentlemen had complained vigorously of Gilbert's behaviour with their daughters.

"Why the hell didn't they give him a real hiding instead of running to me?" he muttered, ignoring the fact that seldom had his younger son suffered painful punishment at his own hands. "Did they imagine I should object?"

He glanced at the letter again, colouring a trifle at the bluntness of what followed:

> "*This tendency, this self-willed refusal to accept decent standards of conduct has arisen in the last few years only, and in my experience the boys at fault came from urban localities in which a vast amount of wealth was created as a result of the war. Possession of wealth involves responsibility, but in such cases as I have noticed, all too many, I fear that the parents in question have not reached such an understanding. To allow a boy of fifteen or sixteen the sum of five pounds a week for pocket-money—and I could substantiate such incredibly foolish examples—is to destroy the fibre of ...*"

"It's true, too." Sam Pilling sighed. "Well, I suppose I'm one of the new rich, but all the same the Crowthers were carriage folk and I've their blood in me. For that matter. . . ."

Suddenly he was impatient with himself, for he was as guilty as the rest about the main issue, paternal stupidity.

His hearing, good always, caught the first sound as the knob of the door turned, and swiftly he whipped the letters out of sight. "All right, Olga," he said as soon as he saw who it was. "I'll be in the dining-room in a minute or two." When she had gone he re-locked the letters away.

Seated already, his wife and daughter awaited him.

"And where's Archie?" he demanded.

"He rang up to say that as soon as the office closed he's running down to Leeds with Frank and Alec," Milly explained.

"The lad must be seriously considering buckling to," Sam observed ironically. "He wasn't there when I left, but this indicates he'll have popped back later to make sure all's well."

"*Bread,* Daddy," Nancy said loudly.

Startled, her father stared at her, but luckily he grasped her meaning. Nothing further was said about Archie's sins of omission or commission.

For the next quarter of an hour a running argument was in progress between mother and daughter on the subject of winter nights, hot rooms and flimsy undies.

"And what's all this about?" Sam inquired, rousing out of his preoccupation to slice himself more tongue. "You're both looking heated."

"She doesn't wear enough," Milly asserted.

"Of course I do, Mummy," Nancy countered.

"Anyway, where are *you* off to to-night, miss?" her father asked.

Certain functions, though high-spirited, were most respectable affairs. "It's a dance at the Masonic Hall," Milly told him, quick to protect her daughter whenever possible.

Nancy glanced at her wrist-watch, a tiny, diamond-studded gem of the jeweller's craft.

"Gracious, I must fly," she screamed. "And please, Mummy, darling," she went on as she jumped up and then bent to kiss her mother, "please don't fret any more, will you?"

"I'm not, not really," said Milly. "But you must remember, Nancy, that Gilbert isn't the child you bore."

Nancy giggled as she rumpled her father's hair. "Good lord, I should hope not," she said. "Apart from being some dreadful 'ism' it'd be a miracle, wouldn't it? Even if Daddy had had some fearful passion for me——"

"Nancy!" Milly's tone was severe.

"Anyway, why are you off so soon?" Sam asked.

Any objections he might have had were brushed aside. "Oh, I'm being called for early," his daughter shouted from the doorway. "We're having drinks at the George first and then going on. And sorry, Mummy, for my shocking suggestions."

"That girl!" Milly bewailed when she and her husband were alone. "She's never still a minute, here, there and everywhere. She doesn't eat half enough, either. And all that drinking young people go in for nowadays . . . I detest it. What do they get out of it anyhow?"

"It's just . . . er . . . a self-willed refusal to accept the . . . the standards we were used to," Sam observed. "Symptomatic of the age."

"I suppose so," Milly said, sounding a little uncertain.

But she was doing her utmost to be bright, and undoubtedly she had a very choice piece of news to impart.

"Laura came across this afternoon, Sam," she started off. "And do you know what? Estelle's going to divorce Philip Illingworth."

That really roused Sam. "But they haven't been married five minutes," he said. "What's happened?"

His wife's face clouded a little. "That's all Laura told me, and even that was in confidence to me only. They're keeping it strictly to themselves until something's decided. Anyhow, you know how she can be sometimes."

"Don't I?" Sam grunted. "But I think, love," his eyes were twinkling, "that when you're getting ready for the theatre I'll just slip in for a word with Clem."

Milly laughed outright. "You old gossip," she declared fondly.

And that was precisely what Sam Pilling did as soon as his wife went upstairs, after he had washed in the cloakroom and donned overcoat and hat so as to be in readiness on his return.

It was a cold but very starlight night, and he had no difficulty in seeing as he walked along the straight portion of the macadamized driveway which linked his own house and his neighbours'.

Their maid, Maggie Batten, had known Sam for fully eleven years, since she first entered service with the Roebucks as a girl of fourteen, when they lived in Roydlea, in Highthwaite Road. She was a plump and comely creature, with the softest and kindliest of brown eyes, and even her smart coffee-coloured cap and apron did nothing to offset the impression that her rightful place in the scheme of things was in her own home, with a husband to look after and as many children as they could afford.

Sam had always joked with her, and she beamed on opening the front door of Stonewood in response to his ring.

"No, I'm not taking my coat off, Maggie, but if Mr. Roebuck's in I'd like a word with him," he said. "And, by the way, I'm sorry I passed you without speaking the night before last. Of course," she was staring blankly at him as he continued to twit her, "of course you were otherwise engaged, weren't you?"

"Wednesday night!" she exclaimed. "But that isn't my night off, and I wasn't out."

Impassively Sam expressed surprise. "You were going into the Majestic Picture House arm-in-arm with a real Rudolph Valentino of a young fellow—black side-whiskers, pointed leather shoes, ear-rings, and the rest of it."

The picture was over-drawn, and his succeeding smile betrayed it. "You're stuffing me up again, Mr. Pilling," she giggled. "I ought to have known by now as soon as you went so solemn."

From the dining-room door-way, amusement playing about his lips, Mr. Roebuck was watching them. He was a little older than Sam, grey at the temples, his receding hair seeming in some queer sense to emphasize an air of gentleness which in his case was just as pronounced as kindliness in Maggie Batten's. This quietness of manner hardly seemed in keeping with the unquestioned reputation he enjoyed in the hazardous occupation he followed. He was a master steeplejack, of the fourth generation of a family of steeplejacks, proprietor of a business whose profits were ample enough to enable him to live comfortably had he not been overburdened by the expense of a house on Moorheaton Drive and the launching into the world of four children to a pattern beyond his means.

"Come in, Sam," he said, beckoning warmly. "In here, lad," he pointed, "there's a grand fire."

The close friendship of Sam Pilling and Clem Roebuck had ripened in days and weeks of pain and discomfort when, each sorely wounded, they had occupied adjoining beds as prisoners-of-war in a German hospital. Since then there had been few reservations between them, and so, with the sole exception of any reference to an ugly bruise on the narrator's leg, the story of Gilbert's departure from Liverpool was fully told.

"Aye, it's been a trying job for you, Sam," Clem Roebuck commented sympathetically. "Let's hope it does the trick."

Sam, after filling a pipe, had lobbed his tobacco pouch into the waiting hands of his companion.

"There's one thing that's sure, Clem," he grunted when sucking the match flame towards the bowl, "he can't come back any worse than he went away."

"They're a problem, aren't they?" Mr. Roebuck confessed. "Thanks, lad, I will."

"They're a problem all right," Sam agreed grimly. "But I've only myself to blame for my three getting out of hand. Well, I've dealt with one drastically and from now on I'm not giving much rope to the other two. Before long I'll teach both Archie and Nancy which side their bread's buttered on."

"Putting the screw on, eh?" said Clem.

"By God, aren't I?" his friend growled.

For a short time the two men were silent, until Sam, who undeniably had a certain weakness, made the opening towards satisfying his curiosity.

"I hear from Milly that you've got a nasty bit of trouble yourselves," he remarked quite casually. "Whatever's happened between Estelle and her husband to bring such a state of affairs about?"

Clem Roebuck, a little edgy, said he knew nothing more than one bare fact : that there was no hope whatsoever of a reconciliation between the young couple. This information he wryly supplemented, however, and was in the middle of remarking that his wife had never ceased to scold her eldest daughter since learning what was afoot, when Laura entered the dining-room. Flouncing behind her was the presumed culprit, Mrs. Philip Illingworth, a platinum blonde who at the moment looked extremely sulky.

Obviously a family wrangle was in prospect, and Sam was too sickeningly used to such disturbances to desire to be involved in one unnecessarily. He rose immediately, explaining the why and wherefore of his sudden departure.

"It won't hurt Milly to wait a minute longer, Sam," Mrs. Clem Roebuck asserted. "There's something I want to say to you, and it's this—will you be kind enough in future not to be so familiar with the servants."

In point of fact the Roebucks employed a maid and a charwoman.

"You're speaking about Maggie, I suppose, Laura," Sam said.

"Indeed I am," his sister-in-law replied stridently. "I heard you carrying on in the hall with her and I've warned you before, too."

Clem Roebuck, flushing deeply, ventured a word. "I heard as well, Laura," he said. "But even if we'd had company, which is what you're thinking of, what would it have mattered? Everybody knows Sam's a lively spark, and there's no harm in his pulling Maggie's leg."

"There's every harm," Laura retorted. "And I simply won't have it."

Eyeing his sister-in-law, Sam was thinking of several things, one that Laura's carefully cultivated speech, so different from the broadness of her father's, suffered a decline when she was angry. He was also thanking God that his fate had been the younger of the Sykes sisters.

"Poor Uncle Sam, doesn't he look crestfallen?" Estelle Illingworth said irritably. "Or does he?"

"This has nothing whatever to do with you, Estelle," her mother snapped.

It hardly seemed possible that any trace of the same blood flowed in the veins of Milly Pilling and Laura Roebuck, so different were they both in temperament and appearance, the elder dark, dominating, a thorough Junoesque, very conscious of her dignity. From girlhood Laura had always been acutely concerned about money; that trait distinguished the sisters also, but despite this blemish Sam recalled that in her early days, into young womanhood and newly married life, his sister-in-law had been capable of real kindness in so far as it did not incommode her own plans. But in recent years, so he reflected as he perceived the fury simmering in her, another facet of her character had strengthened, until now she was ambitious for herself and her children to an extent which conceivably could hold many dangers in the future.

"And neither have my private affairs to do with you, Mother," Estelle said, her eyes hardening.

"By Jove, I'd better shoot off," Sam said hurriedly. "And, Laura, I'll try to mend my bad ways. But the truth is," his attempt to smile was feeble, "the truth is that I can't forget that Maggie is the lass who used to slog my leg-breaks for sixes when we played cricket in your back garden in Highthwaite Road. That was in the days when all our youngsters took part in the game and you allowed Maggie out of the kitchen to join us."

"Those were other days, Sam," Laura Roebuck said stiffly.

"So it seems," Sam replied.

Rejecting Clem's attempt to escort him to the door, Sam went out to the hall by himself, and grabbing his hat from the stand, was hastening towards the glass inner door when one of his nieces called out to him. The two younger Roebuck girls were coming down the stairs, Lois, the spit and image of her mother, a most determined-looking young woman, and Cora, who took greatly after her eldest sister, Estelle, fair-haired and fluffy. The middle Roebuck girl was fourteen months older than her cousin Nancy, but Cora was much younger, and now permanently at home after acquiring at sixteen the *cachet* of a good boarding-school without involving her father in the expense of maintaining her there until a more accepted leaving age.

"Hallo, Uncle," said Lois.

"Well, girls," Sam said.

"But, Uncle Sam," protested Cora, "surely you're not going now? Don't you realize that the most excruciating dramatic scenes are taking place in the Roebuck *ménage?*"

"Perhaps so, but destiny awaits me," Sam said, laughing. "Meaning your Aunt Milly, of course."

With this, he escaped from a house in which nowadays he was seldom completely at ease. On returning to Glenfield he found Milly downstairs, dressed for the occasion, wearing a very fetching hat and a mink coat.

"Ready, are you?" he greeted her on entering. "Now come on, love, the car's still outside in the front drive, so we can start without a ha'porth of delay."

A few minutes later they were sliding through the lamp-lit streets of Moorheaton, and she was telling him that his sisters had been ringing up about Gilbert while he had been out. The Misses Emerald and Ruby Pilling were severe-minded spinsters, watchful from a distance of everything concerning their brother and his family.

After nodding and smiling to various acquaintances in the Theatre Royal, the Pillings settled themselves in their aisle seats in the middle of the second row of the stalls, Sam then devoting his attention to a large advertisement on the safety-curtain, sufficiently striking, he believed, to attract a fresh volume of custom when the flat-racing season began. It was being repeated in many other places of entertainment in a dozen more towns in the neighbourhood, and, as it was a new departure by his publicity department, he anticipated with zest his wife's reaction. It went:

THE BOOKMAKER WITH GENUINE NO-LIMIT

£493 15s. od. paid out on a 5s. Accumulator. Harry Wagstaffe, of 75 Swanroyd View, Holmluff, Nr. Spedding, was so gratified that he gladly granted permission for his name and address to be made known for verification purposes if needs be.

ENTRUST YOUR WAGERS TO THE ONE AND ONLY

PILLING WHO ALWAYS PAYS

Milly grimaced. "Still at it, Sam," she whispered. "When are you ever going to give up?"

His reply was most unexpected. "In a sense I'm starting taking things a bit easier this year, love," he said.

His wife's eyes widened. "Whatever do you mean?"

Sam winked. "Tell you to-night, dear."

They were thoroughly diverted by *Autumn Crocus*, which they had missed during all too brief jaunts to London, and were discussing the play animatedly when leaving the theatre. Arm-in-arm, they inspected a Phantom II Rolls-Royce in Thorntons' showroom, bade good night to the men in charge of the petrol pumps and the Taxi-Hire Service office, and then crossed Market Approach towards the corner of Neptune Buildings, against the main entrance to which the Bentley had been parked, the police not being too insistent about regulations at night.

A trifling mishap took place when they got into the car. On pressing the starter button there was a horribly protesting whine, and the Bentley, slowly but jerkily, moved forward.

"Whatever's the matter, Sam?" Milly was sitting upright.

"Damned if I know," Sam grunted. Then he guffawed. "I'd only left her in gear, that's all."

"What did you do that for?" Milly inquired.

"Oh, it's much the safest," he told her knowledgeably.

This was the prelude to a pleasant drive home which brought no mention of a severance in the family, and Sam, after dropping his passenger at the front door, was in a much less apprehensive mood as he swung the car across the paved courtyard between his own house and Stonewood. Brightened by this, he rolled back one of the doors of a coach-house converted into a four-car garage, and then drove in, drawing alongside the Riley. Archie's space was as yet unoccupied, but a car stood at the extreme end, its bonnet pointed towards a heap of junk which should long ago have been removed: broken chairs, a derelict perambulator, and several trunks.

The M.G. Magnette, presented to Gilbert on the morning of his seventeenth birthday, was a sharp reminder of that family severance.

"I wonder if I ought to have that stored elsewhere, out of Milly's sight?" Sam muttered. "Anyhow, I'd better see how she goes on."

Closing up the garage, he walked briskly towards the back door, skirting the one-storied billiards room he had had built on to the side of the house some years before.

When Sam went into the drawing-room, tea and sandwiches had already been wheeled in, and Milly, just downstairs, was leaning over the arm of her chair to reach the silver teapot. He felt a radiator, glanced at the cheerful fire, and rubbed his hands.

"Well, I'm like you, love," he announced. "It's grand to go out for a change, but there's nothing like your own fireside in wintry weather."

She nodded. "Two only from now on for you, Sam," she remarked rather inexplicably. "Lumps of sugar," she added. "It's fattening, and I've an idea you're putting on weight."

Sam grinned. "You're the boss here, Milly, but if I discover weakness growing on me I'll stoke up a bit extra when I have tea at the office."

"Will you?" she retorted. "I shall make sure about it by telling Miss Schofield you're *not* to have more."

He smiled but let it go at that, allowing his thoughts to wander into very delectable channels. For the past five years, as his wife knew, it had been his dream to own a modest string of horses, and the disturbances at home had made him believe that this desire would be of immense benefit and enjoyment to both Milly and himself. The business, with an efficient and highly paid staff, ran like clockwork in his absence, and he would not be missed for a day or so every week. It would have the effect, besides, of compelling Milly to live her own life more, and not to live it in that of the children as she was prone to do. Excitedly he started to discuss the project.

"I should, Sam, this year, not next, and no putting off, and why shouldn't you?" she said, when he had run out of words. "You've worked hard and you deserve it. And of course I'll go off with you to Mr. What-do-you-call-him's at Malton, to look at the two-year-olds he's got. It would be a real nice week-end's outing for us, wouldn't it?"

"It's fixed, love."

She watched him affectionately when, too thrilled to remain still, he began to pace quarter-deck fashion in the big room.

"Sam," she said, a little while later, eyes a trifle misty, "isn't it wonderful to think that you can contemplate buying bloodstock without even a qualm. When you consider that only fifteen or so years ago, in 1920, when . . ." She turned a little. "We can afford it, can't we?"

"Just, love," Sam told her, poker-faced. "You must bear in mind I'm not intending to lay out a fortune."

She had strayed into memories of the past. "We'd a hard time to begin with, hadn't we? And do you know, Sam, I suspect that's the reason we've over-spoilt the children."

"Yes, I dare say, love," Sam agreed.

He began to reminisce. "Do you remember that poky little office of my father's, and how you used to come down, with all the children and none of 'em more than tots, to answer the telephone?"

She nodded. "While you and Fred Lumb were out with home-made sandwich-boards on your backs with advertisements on them that we used to do on the kitchen table at night. You drew the outline of the lettering and I filled in with a camel-hair brush."

Ruefully Sam shook his head. "And how we used to puzzle to find words without s's. I never could make the two loops look alike."

She screwed up her face. "And those bets I used to book down when anybody rang up—2s. 6d. on that and 5s. on something else, and all to comes, and ups and downs, and each way trebles, and to begin with I didn't know what on earth they meant, for all the coaching you'd given me. And I shall never forget that morning of the Ascot meeting when somebody I'd only heard of through you wanted to bet *fifty* pounds each way on Square Measure for the Royal Hunt Cup. I wouldn't believe he meant it, and he nearly laughed his head off when I said it was too much for anyone to risk, and that it wasn't on anyhow until I'd seen you. I was trembling so much I could hardly put the receiver back."

"Aye, that was Dale Watkinson, and it was the turning point when he began to give us his commissions regularly, for lots of his friends followed him," Sam said soberly. "Truth to tell I think he was so surprised to get my cheque on settlement day—altogether it came to over seven hundred pounds, almost twenty times as much as I'd paid anybody up to then —that he blazoned my name from the roof-tops. Yes, love, here we are only at the beginning of 1936, so I think we can congratulate ourselves on what we've done, by heck I do."

In this vein Sam and Milly Pilling continued to talk. It was long past their usual bedtime when they climbed the broad stairs.

Her head filled with harrowing conceptions about brutal bosuns, the perils of the sea, and the heartbreak her youngest child must be undergoing, Milly had not slept at all, but towards four o'clock in the morning she was slipping into a fitful doze when startled by a car which roared into the drive-way and then, tyres screeching, braked cruelly to pull up at the door.

"Nancy's back," she murmured, listening to her husband's steady breathing. "I hope there isn't going to be the noise there was after the Bachelors' Dance last week, when those three boys came tearing up and then back again time after time, and it seemed as if scores of them were rushing to kiss her good-night."

Certain of the more sought-after young women of the town had recently evolved a technique which provided them with much amusement. Having consented to allowing one young man to drive them home they would then be gracious enough to hint to another suppliant, and sometimes a third, that if he followed behind at a reasonable distance his predecessor would be disposed of fairly quickly. So far so good, but Rams-field's young men, despite appearances to the contrary, still retained in them echoes of the gumption and shrewdness of their grandfathers, and soon became suspicious. The result was that, after bidding a girl a fond farewell, they lurked not too far away, watched closely, and moved in rapidly again when the rival, after *his* fond farewell, drove off. This sport, providing great fun for all parties, was nevertheless not popular with householders in the neighbourhood in which it took place.

As a booming exhaust did its damnedest, there was an upheaval alongside Milly, and an irate voice growled: "God damn it." The bedside light went on, and Sam, eyes screwed up tightly, thrust out an empurpled face, before padding barefoot to the window.

"Don't say anything, Sam," she begged him. "I think that's the end, and though it's awfully inconsiderate they only think of it as fun."

Slowly Sam closed the curtain he had started to pull back. "Yes, they're young and silly, but there's no great harm in that sort of thing really," he said reflectively, as he shoved his feet into slippers and picked up a dressing-gown. "So long as Nancy doesn't develop any worse tendencies I shan't be bothering myself."

"Oh, she won't, Sam," Milly said. "And what do *you* propose doing?"

Sam jabbed a stern finger towards her. "I'm going down to make you a cup of tea. If you've slept half an hour so far that'll be the limit."

"Nonsense, dear," she protested. "I was wakened just like you were, that's all."

"H'mph," Sam snorted.

There was a slight contretemps when, on the landing outside, he pushed down the switch. A light appeared fleetingly, but returned again in a series of flashes. This sort of thing does happen when two people at the opposite ends of a two-way system attempt to operate it simultaneously. Nancy was in the hall.

As soon as permanent lighting became available, Sam descended the stairs.

"What's the matter, Daddy?" Nancy asked, on the defensive immediately.

"I'm making a cup of tea for your mother and myself," he told her.

She looked very lovely, her fur coat loosened, an exquisite but daringly-cut black lace evening frock beneath. But she was a little too flushed, and her speech was a little too slurred.

"No, let me do it, Daddy," she said. "I'll have it up to your room in a tic-tac."

Sam jerked his thumb. "You get off upstairs and into bed," he said. "And *don't* go in to see your mother."

Head high and colour more vivid, she walked past him, disdainfully holding her skirts aside. Grasping the gleaming banister rail, she began to mount the stairs, with dignity and with care.

In the kitchen, Sam speedily boiled a small kettle of water on the gas-stove, took milk out of the refrigerator, and rummaged in a cupboard for biscuits.

On his return to the bedroom with a tray, Milly was sitting up in bed, a peach-pink bed-jacket round her shoulders. She expressed gratification about his endeavours, complimented him upon remembering to bring biscuits, but made no comment about his selection of crockery, one cup being of egg-shell china and the other, Johnson the gardener's, of thick white porcelain. As she started cautiously to sip, however, she remarked that Nancy had looked in, as cautiously watching him over the rim of her cup.

"She's having a bath now," she added. "It'll freshen her up when she's so tired. She's really quite worn out, Sam, almost reeling on her feet."

"The hot-water cylinder thumping for half an hour and then the waste guggling its neck out for another bit," Sam commented sourly. "Well, there's nothing like a Bohemian atmosphere, so they say."

"Archie's in, surely?" said Milly.

"Snoring like a hoodlum," Sam retorted.

These observations were not without effect upon her. She decided against the second biscuit she had taken from the plate.

"Nancy's never been the same since just before Estelle got engaged," she said. "She was a minx even then, admittedly, but she never was wild as she is now."

His mind jumping to an impending divorce, Sam turned, aghast. "You don't mean there was once something serious between Philip Illingworth and Nancy, do you? Oh, he used to come here often enough, I know, but so do lots of young fellows."

Milly hesitated. "I feel fairly sure there was nothing *definite*, because she'd have told me if there had been."

"Good God!" Sam ejaculated.

Milly shook her head. "No, no, Sam," she said. "To begin with, you must remember that Nancy was only seventeen when she first met him, and though she might have been attracted—well, young girls do take violent fancies, but they soon forget. And since then I've seen her talking to him many a time over at Laura's, and she was just her usual self."

"Maybe so, Milly," said Sam. "But if she went off the deep end because of him, why is she still carrying on like she is, if young girls soon forget, as you say they do?"

Milly's lips were beginning to quiver. "Because it's become a habit with her . . . and . . . and it's making me so unhappy. What with that and . . . Archie drinking . . . and Gilbert having to be sent away. . . ."

It was time for stern action. Throughout his career as a bookmaker Sam Pilling had been a fervent believer in the merits of novel measures. It was a policy which had paid him magnificent dividends. He adopted one now.

"You can stop worrying about them," he said, speaking with the conviction of a businessman in conference. "Because I'm as sure as I'm here that when they've sown their wild oats they'll settle down all right, and we'll be proud of 'em."

"Do you think so, Sam?" she said wistfully.

"I do, but that isn't what I want to talk to you about," he resumed. "What I would like to discuss is a matter I've been chewing over for a longish while. Now, to begin with, there's no argument that if we'd our time to go over again we wouldn't make the same mistakes in bringing up the children, would we?"

She sniffed. "No, we wouldn't dear."

"Right then," said Sam, clapping his hands together. "Then what about having a fresh go and making a better job of it this time? We're both young enough yet."

There was no question now as to whether he had captured her interest. Wide-eyed, she stared at him.

"You . . . you don't mean . . ." she gasped.

"I do," Sam declared. "Let's have, say, a couple of additions to the family. It needn't make all that difference to us. We could have the best of nurses so that you could go off racing with me now and then. . ." Milly, troubles forgotten, was giggling uncontrollably. "And what's the matter now?" he demanded.

Weakened with laughter, her reply was delayed. "You silly old coughdrop," she gurgled at last, adding: "And do you know, I'm feeling quite drowsy now," so bringing the conversation back to a more sensible plane.

"Oh!" said Sam.

Disgruntled, he climbed into bed and switched off the light. Rarely had his bluff been called so effectively, and, though the immediate objective had been achieved, her failure to take him seriously rankled. True, he had been joking, but she was not supposed to know that.

"Well," he decided with some grimness, "the joke's going on, and before long I'll have her wondering whether I *am* kidding her. If I can't put it into her noddle that I'm clamorous for another youngster or two—well, I'm not the chap I reckon I am."

Hotly resolved on this course, he speedily slipped into profound slumber.

CHAPTER TWO

PALE after a most inadequate night's rest, but cares for the moment forgotten in the pleasure of what she was doing, Milly Pilling glanced once more at the mass of pink azaleas in the conservatory. Then she picked up a pot she had selected and, returning through the drawing-room left it on a table in the hall. Her next task was even more inviting, and she happily rummaged for her own trowel in a box kept in the kitchen.

"Oh, Cook," she said, before starting down the garden, "I think Miss Nancy's stirring, and though I don't suppose she'll be getting up I'm sure some tea and just a little toast will help to bring her to life. It was the Masons' Dance last night, and you know what Masonic hospitality is."

Her cook, an ample body who each year in a courtship now extending to twenty years had been proclaiming marriage to be imminent—and did not appear in the least thwarted about the delay—wrinkled her nose understandingly.

"Gallons of champagne and chocolate and what not, I know," she said. "Yes, I'll do it right away, ma'am, and send Olga up with it."

"Yes, if you will," said Mrs. Pilling, smiling as she left by the back door.

Since the day Sam Pilling and Clem Roebuck had bought Glenfield and Stonewood, they had enthusiastically made changes in the big gardens which would seriously compromise the value of either property if it were offered for sale and, a laughable contingency they knew, could cause embarrassment if ever the two families quarrelled. A former dividing wall had been torn down and now, beyond the stone-paved expanse which stretched across the backs of the houses, a lengthy terrace extended. At each end of this a short flight of steps descended to a lawn sufficiently large for two tennis courts, and, if anyone fancied bowls, a bowling green, play on all these being possible simultaneously.

This opening-out had immeasurably improved the vistas in the formal part of the gardens, but the kitchen gardens were still separate, the Pillings' being reached through a ravine at the side which no doubt had influenced the first owners of the house in their selection of its name.

This narrow little valley sloped rapidly, and was almost twenty feet below the lawn before it opened out into the kitchen garden. The sides were thickly wooded and steep, but Milly climbed to the top of the east side as far as the boundary wall of The Turrets, the vacant mansion below. There, at the foot of the wall, she dug up a clump of snow-drops, wrapping it carefully in the sheets of paper she had brought for the purpose. Armed with this she returned home, where she went upstairs to wash and put on her outdoor things.

Sam had finished with the morning paper and the weekly edition of the *Ramsfield Reporter,* and was coming out of the dining-room when she reached the hall again.

"I'm just going for the car, dear," he said. "Now I can quite easily wait for you at Mrs. Crabtree's, and then run you on to town. And if you'll pop into the office when you've done your shopping, you might just as well ride home with me."

Milly smiled. "I'll be home long before then, Sam. You see I haven't much to do, so I'll catch a bus to Penny Lane. And as for you waiting for me at Highthwaite Road. . . ."

He took her point. "Aye, I need only quote Walter Crab-tree's despairing words: 'When your wife and mine begin to discuss matters horticultural, well, time's nothing, Sam.' Yes, that's what he vows."

She dimpled. "We're not as bad as that. But just look at this azalea. Isn't it beautiful?"

"It is, indeed," Sam agreed. "Yes, I think you've surpassed yourself this year."

A few more professional observations by the grower, and then they started out.

Highthwaite Road was a quiet, pleasant street, in Roydlea, facing the tall, iron railings which surrounded the spacious football and cricket grounds of Ramsfield College. Along it were reasonably sized family dwellings, for the most part well kept, the one glaring exception being that of Sam Pilling's brother-in-law, which sadly lacked a coat of paint, although the curtains were clean enough.

"It's getting worse," Sam said as he stopped at Mr. Crabtree's, next door. "But Alonso won't hear of me doing anything, though I've told him the woodwork will go rotten if something isn't attended to soon."

"Whatever possessed him?" said Milly, referring to one of Ramsfield's mysteries, as she collected the plant and the little bundle containing the snowdrop roots. "I don't even understand to this day, for in some respects Alonso isn't what you might term really religious."

"He's doing grand work even though he's not so very orthodox in the way he sometimes sets about it," Sam remarked. "But why he did what he did . . . some urge stronger than himself, that's all it could have been."

"When I leave Mrs. Crabtree I'll call to see if Kate's at home. She shouldn't be at the High School this morning."

Sam had a very soft spot for his fifteen-year-old niece, and considerable respect, too, for she managed house, brother, and eccentric father admirably on abysmally scanty means.

"Yes, do, love," he shouted out as his wife walked up the Crabtrees' path. "And I shan't be late—the Hornets are playing at Swanroyd this afternoon, and we're having a bit of a directors' pow-wow before the match begins."

Milly waved, nodded, and then rang the bell.

Heading for Barnsley Road and the run down to Ramsfield Bridge, Sam continued to reflect about his brother-in-law, who in middle age, immediately after the death of his wife, Sam's eldest sister, had thrown up his profession to become a parson. The Reverend Alonso Dyson was now a curate at the Parish Church, and very often a thorn in the flesh of the Vicar of Ramsfield and others. Four years before he had been a partner in the town's leading firm of solicitors, Ramsden Lister and Wainwright, with a reputation for acuteness—and perhaps guile—which made him sought after from far outside the neighbourhood in which the firm practised.

"But it's been hard on Scipio and Kate," Sam was soliloquizing as he swung into Teazle Street, now filling up with ladies who, on Saturday morning's parade, vied with one another in the smartness of their attire.

At the far end of the street there was space available against the fine new premises of the Ramsfield Commercial Bank, and so he pulled the car alongside the kerb. Then he crossed to a sports' goods shop on the corner, Pilling's, and there examined a catalogue with John Arthur Pilling, who, incidentally, was not related to him. The outcome of this was an order for a rowing-machine, delivery of which would be made as soon as possible.

Delighted with the first move he had taken towards vindicating himself as a man who would never jest upon such an important step as increasing his family, Sam, grinning broadly, had just left John Arthur Pilling's establishment when, on the pavement, he bumped into a stout, elderly man.

"You're looking pleased with yourself, lad," Ben Buckley remarked.

"Yes, I've learnt that when flat-racing starts again I shall be taking about a dozen of your best clients, Ben," Sam replied.

Mr. Buckley rumbled with laughter and, responding appropriately, the conversation continued on these lines awhile. Bookmakers, in the heat of trade warfare, think nothing of slitting one another's throats, but outside competitive stress they are boon companions.

Later the talk became more serious, when the older man confided that at the end of the season he would probably sell out and retire to Blackpool. In addition he made no bones about inquiring if the other would be interested in buying the business.

"I'd be obliged for the promise of the first offer, Ben," Sam said at once.

Ben Buckley held out his hand. "You've got it, Sam."

"Just let me know when you're ready," Sam nodded.

Well satisfied, he drove his car into Market Square. Though not large, Ben Buckley's was a tidy and sound concern, and he was already looking forward to the prospect of acquiring it.

When Sam had dictated nine or ten letters he remarked: "That'll do for now," and promptly thumbed down a button on the internal communication system which connected him with the Settlement Room.

"Tell Mr. Archie I want him," he said.

The next few minutes were taken up by a chat with a fellow director of Ramsfield Hornets, one of the finest sides in the Rugby League, who had telephoned to say that the directors' deliberations were to take place after and not before the game with Warrington. This conversation was still in progress when his son arived, a powerful, broad-shouldered young fellow, with sandy-coloured hair and grey eyes which regrettably were not as clear as they might have been. It seemed the hour for the subject of rugby football, professional or amateur, and when his father replaced the telephone receiver, Archie began to discuss Ramsfield Rugger's away match, for which very shortly he would be setting out to join his colleagues of the First XV. Among the playing strength of the Ramsfield Rugby Union Football Club, which ran four teams, there were a limited number of members without cars, and, partly for democratic reasons, partly because it made a good party, a privately hired bus was frequently used for transport.

"And who gave you permission to leave the office early?" Sam asked.

Archie was too taken aback to do more than stutter: "Why, nobody, of course."

"No 'of course' about it," his father declared, glowering. "In future you see either me or Fred Lumb before you take any time off whatsoever. Mind you, no reasonable request will be refused."

"Thanks." Archie, pillar-box red with surprise and anger, was recovering quickly. "Thanks a million. And while you're about it you might as well tell me why all of a sudden——"

"Because you're not damned well framing to be of any assistance or use to me," Sam bawled. "You're about worth as much——"

Just as he started shouting, the smaller door into his room had been opened and Hilda Schofield stood hesitatingly on the threshold, her expression very betraying as she looked at father and then son. Her dark eyes were full of sympathy as fleetingly she glanced at the older man, and there was no mistaking her indignation and censure as her gaze switched to Archie.

"I'm . . . I'm sorry," she faltered.

Sam Pilling nodded at his desk, and waited until she placed a sheaf of letters at his elbow, to which she drew attention with a few whispered words.

"That's all right, Hilda," Sam muttered when she apologized again. "But don't come in any more until I ring."

Meantime Archie was rapidly mustering his forces, and, square jaw pugnacious, he was fully prepared when his father's secretary withdrew.

"You're hardly ever in the office," Sam resumed scathingly. "Eternally popping across to the Vaults, nipping into the George, and hanging about the Thorntons' place. What do you want to be, a motor salesman?"

"You know damn well what I *wanted* to be," Archie growled.

Sam's hand moved impatiently. "Oh, we've gone into all that bunkum before."

Furiously Archie leaned across the desk. "So we did, but do you still remember how I warned you?"

"Be that as it may, it's me who's warning you now, and I'm doing it no more," his father snapped. "Instead, I'm informing you about one thing only, and then you can get out."

"And what's that?" Archie demanded.

"Your salary, which from next month is going to be a wage," Sam said crisply. "At present you're drawing six hundred a year, but I'm cutting you down to three pounds a week. I'll reconsider the question every quarter, and if there's any real sign of improvement I'll keep giving you a rise, ten shillings or so at——"

"How the bloody hell do you think I can make do on three quid a week?" Archie bellowed.

Impetuously Sam jumped up. Palms resting on the morocco leather of the desk, he bent forward until two inflamed faces were almost touching.

"How the bloody hell do you think a clerk manages to keep a wife and a youngster or two on the same amount?" he roared. "And there's plenty earning no more."

"How the hell do I know?" Archie retorted.

Sam laughed unpleasantly. "They do it by making the pennies spin out. And from now on, to a lesser degree, you're going to have to learn to do the same thing."

"I'm getting out." Archie was almost choking.

"One thing, if it keeps you off the beer, you'll be a better man in the pack," his father jeered. "Not twenty-one yet, and you're blowing like a grampus."

Face thunderous, Archie darted to pick up a battered Gladstone bag dangling from which was a sleeve, striped in purple and gold, Ramsfield Rugger's colours. In his swift passage he collided with the antlered coat-stand, his further retreat being marked by a furiously slammed door and the quick tread of angry feet.

Sitting down again, Sam felt for the handkerchief in his

breast pocket. Shaking out the folds, he began to mop his brow.

"Well, that's the first time in my life I've ever been really nasty to one of my own," he reflected. "But I'll let him see I'm not carrying any grudge, and then maybe it'll be all the easier for him to realize that what I'm doing is only in his own interests."

For a little while longer he remained as he was, still upset by what he had had to do. But then, stretching out, he pressed a button and sent out a demand to all departments for the senior employee's immediate attendance.

When Fred Lumb joined him, the change in Archie's pay, with effect from the first of February, was dealt with at once.

"I'm bringing him to heel, in fact I'm bringing 'em all to heel now I've started, Fred," he explained. "Yes, he and Nancy, with the example before them of how I've walloped down on Gilbert, will soon be toeing the line. Of course, they'd never have got as they have if I hadn't been so pre-occupied in building up the business. When all's said and done, youngsters need a man's hand, and I've left things too much to Milly."

Fred Lumb, who had a monk-like tonsure surrounded by coarse grey hair, was thoughtfully stroking his bald patch.

"Aye," he murmured noncommittally.

A thought struck Sam. There had been occasions, he recalled, when his elder son had drawn advances of salary.

"Yes, he's in the firm's ribs very nicely," his manager replied when questioned. "Strictly speaking, there's nothing due to him until April."

Sam's face expressed acute disgust. "All right, then," he said, "I'll give you my personal cheque to make it up so that he starts all square in the new arrangement. But what the devil have you been thinking of, Fred, to allow him to sub to that extent?"

In workaday life Fred Lumb sometimes gave the impression that he was acting a supporting role in a play. On this occasion he was a delightful but very stubborn servitor privileged to speak his mind in his own inimitable fashion.

"Hey! Hold on," he observed austerely. "You see I've just happened to recall a time when Archie tried to touch me for some brass he hadn't as yet earned, and I refused—so his nibs had a word with you, and you instructed me to let him have it. In a sense you went over my head—but of course I'm just a menial, and far be it from me to presume to——"

"Ah, well, let's forget about it, Fred," Sam said in some haste. "I've other things I want to go into with you before I'm off. There's that fresh advertising stunt for March—I've got the motor-wagon arranged for, and I've seen the chap who can fix up for the men who'll act as the bookies on it."

Beyond an almost imperceptible glint of delight, no other indication revealed how very much Fred Lumb was enjoying himself.

"And then there was another occasion," he resumed inexorably. "I'd better give you full chapter and verse, knowing——"

"Another infernal word on the subject and I'll crown you," Sam interposed. "Damn it, I haven't all the morning."

Fred Lumb's face was slightly reproachful. "I nobbut felt it my duty to make my own position clear."

"And you have," Sam groaned. "Make no mistake on it, you've done that, Fred, to full and overflowing."

"I like matters straight," Fred observed complacently.

This little breeze dying down, they dealt with a few outstanding matters, Sam signing his letters and ringing for his secretary as the last of these was disposed of.

"There you are, Hilda," he said, looking at her as she bent to blot the final signature. "That's the lot, so when they're made up you get off home. Anything special on this week-end?"

Smilingly she turned to him. "Of *course* I have, Mr. Pilling, and just imagine, you a director of the Club and not knowing what it is. Have you forgotten the Hornets are playing Warrington this afternoon?"

Sam grinned. "I haven't forgotten *that*, lass," he said. "But I had forgotten that you'd become an ardent patron at Swanroyd this season."

"Oh, I am," she agreed, pale cheeks flushing slightly. "And don't I just get excited."

"You're not the only one, Hilda," Sam confessed, laughing.

When she had gone, he turned to Fred Lumb. "She's a real fan, but I must say I'm still surprised about it. She hardly strikes you as the sort who'd get wild about a game like football, does she?"

Fred crossed his legs more comfortably. "Women are queer cattle, lad," he remarked. "For myself, I should have thought she was a sight too moony."

"Moony!" Sam ejaculated. "Nay, she's never that. Why, she's the most efficient secretary I've ever had."

47

"No gainsaying that," Fred Lumb admitted. "But all the same she can look very dreamy when she's cleared up her work. I've spotted her more than once gazing into the far spaces, as you might say."

Sam chuckled. "You're developing a rare imagination, Fred," he said. "Anyhow, what about you this week-end? Have you a suitable star in prospect to sit under to-morrow?"

It was the pleasure of Fred Lumb and his wife on Sunday evenings to attend whatever place of worship, irrespective of denomination, promised the best preacher. For the next few minutes, master and man debated most seriously the respective merits of the Bishop of Wakefield, at St. Paul's, and an evangelist minister who could be heard at Outham Chapel.

The combination of dawdling over coffee in Wood's Café, and a further bout of gossip with friends in Teazle Street, made Milly much later than she had thought, and so, with a pleasant run home to Moorheaton in mind, she walked along to Neptune Buildings. As she turned round the end of Market Approach she saw, to her mortification, a cream and black car nose out of the parking-place to join the flow of traffic towards Sheepgate. Her frantic cry of "Sam!" made no impression as she started to run, nor did the kindly efforts of a man and a youth who guessed her reason as she pointed, the former bawling a stentorian: "Whoa, lad!" to Sam, the latter emitting a piercing whistle with two fingers.

It was hopeless from the beginning, and she was standing ruefully a little below the taxi-men's shelter, thanking her would-be helpers, when she noticed the Bentley had pulled up between the County Club and the Mechanics' Institute. Again she raced off, but got no farther than the low side of the Baptist Chapel before the car set off again. In the interval, however, she had seen a smiling and sprightly woman get in.

"So Carrie Gee, or Carrie Calverley, or whatever her present name is, has asked him for a lift," she remarked breathlessly to herself.

As nothing could be done about it, she gathered her parcels together a little more securely, and hurried towards the nearest bus stop, opposite Ben Buckley's.

"And to think of me standing here while she's lolling at ease and making eyes at Sam," she reflected indignantly. All of which was distinctly unfair.

Meantime Sam was being highly amused by Mrs. Dale

Watkinson, who was describing how she had come to grief in her own car the previous evening.

The daughter of Mr. William Pobjoy, the stockbroker, Carrie Watkinson, though only in the middle thirties, had been divorced twice already, and was now the wife of Dale Watkinson, joint managing director of Northern Viscose. As was to be expected, she was regarded warily by married ladies of the town.

The Watkinsons lived at the top of Moorheaton Drive and, on arrival there, Carrie invited her benefactor in for a drink. Her husband had just reached home from his firm's vast works at Scargate, and he and Sam, good friends for years, enjoyed themselves swopping yarns. Dale Watkinson was a very different individual from his pompous brother Law, though they were twins.

The result of all this was that the master of Glenfield, full of good fellowship with the world at large, arrived home a good deal later than he had said.

"Sorry I'm a bit behindhand, love," he said to his wife breezily. "Nothing's spoilt, is it? Or have I to go into the kitchen to make my peace with Cook?"

Quite ignoring this persiflage, Milly nodded to the maid. "You can serve lunch now, Olga," she said.

Nancy was yawning and liverish, and some time later, after a dispute about the amount of leavings on her daughter's plate, Milly took up a matter which she felt should have been broached by her husband. She went about it indirectly, nevertheless.

"I thought you wanted to be at Swanroyd sooner than usual," she said.

"No, the meeting's to be after the match," Sam said. Fortified slightly, he was in an expansive mood, and promptly proceeded to give her full details of the reason for the gathering.

"You see, love, at Swanroyd it's Rugby League football," he said, heavily humorous. "In other words we pay wages to our players, and if we don't think we're getting value out of a man . . . well, we don't want to keep him." From this beginning he went on to explain that at this time of the year it was customary for clubs of the professional rugby football code to weed out their players. "Those we don't wish to retain are put on the transfer list, with a price on each man. It's a sort of . . ." he guffawed loudly, "a sort of 'end of season' bargain sale."

"More Eve's pudding?" Milly asked him coldly.

Inwardly seething at what she considered to be his secretiveness, she subsequently adopted more direct measures. These were quite effective.

"Yes, I've been up the road, and me and Dale have been putting away one or two," Sam admitted. "But," he asked, astonished, "how did you know? I haven't mentioned it, have I?"

Milly smiled sweetly. "You haven't, dear. But I happened to see Carrie Watkinson getting into the car, after I'd made an exhibition of myself trying to catch you."

"I wish I'd seen you," Sam said, contrite. "But Market Square's pretty busy around noon on Saturdays."

"And the funny thing is that half Market Square was trying to attract your attention for me," Milly informed him, laughing lightly.

"Oh God," said Nancy. Hand clasped to her forehead, she rose from the table, and left the dining-room.

The match at Swanroyd did not by any means rank with the best the season had produced, and the result, a draw, was most disappointing to the spectators.

After the meeting, several of the directors, among them Sam Pilling, drove into the town, with the County Club as their rendezvous, where they enjoyed a convivial half-hour together. As so happens, the small party paused again outside the club entrance for a last few words before separating. Their final exchanges, however, terminated abruptly when a religious procession was observed marching through Market Square. The leader, a little ahead of two young men supporting a large Crucifix, was a gaunt, saturnine-looking clergyman, and already, in consequence of haranguing everyone in sight at various halting-places, he had gathered in his train eighty or ninety people—working-class couples, women carrying laden shopping-baskets and string bags, men with children in their arms or on their shoulders, young women in week-end finery and youths in their best clothes . . . every sort and condition, of virtue and little virtue, solemn, embarrassed, grinning broadly. In due course a congregation possibly more than two hundred strong would file nervously into the Parish Church, for a service in which singing to the swell of the organ would predominate—the Rev. Alonso Dyson knew his people, Ram Valley folk in whom the love of music was bred in the bone.

50

A gentleman at Sam's elbow suddenly yelped: "Look what's coming. I'm off."

His colleagues were no more courageous. Nothing would have better delighted the Rev. Alonso Dyson than to stay his disciples while he vitriolically addressed that small cluster of some of the town's best known and most prosperous personalities with all the undoubted eloquence at his command, with all the intimate knowledge he possessed of their frailties and foibles.

Sam was in the forefront of retreat, darting across the Square towards the parking-place. Firm friends though he and his brother-in-law were, he had no delusions as to who might suffer the most severe castigation of all if he remained there.

"A narrow squeak that." He was still chuckling as he drove past the Hospital in Barnsley Road. "By, but wouldn't Alonso just have relished giving me hell in public."

At home he put the car away, and was hurrying towards the house when, deciding that if Clem Roebuck could come across later for a game of billiards it would be very pleasant, he switched his direction to Stonewood. When close to the adjoining residence, he distinctly heard the sounds of scuffling and a woman's protesting cry, and promptly stopped to discover what was afoot. It was dark and it had started to drizzle, but in the light cast by the kitchen window he saw Maggie Batten against the side of the house, her expression both perturbed and annoyed. She was struggling with a passionate-looking, swarthy man he knew well enough: Clem Roebuck's senior steeplejack, Vincent Uttley.

"Oh, I'm sorry, Maggie," Sam said. "I was wondering what could be making a noise."

Her soft eyes were filling with tears. "Oh, it's all right, Mr. Pilling," she said, gulping. "I'm just going in anyway."

"And _I'm_ damned well off, too," Vincent Uttley said, his voice brusque with resentment. "And don't you fret yourself, Mr. Pilling, you've interrupted nothing that was worth interrupting. And you're not likely to again, either."

Swiftly he turned away, his footsteps drumming on the paving-stones between the two houses, leaving Sam devoutly wishing he had reached home much sooner or a good deal later. These sentiments he somewhat awkwardly expressed.

"If I hadn't turned up when I did, you might have settled matters between you, even if you'd gone on differing a bit longer, Maggie," he said.

51

She shook her head. "It wasn't one of those kind of quarrels you're thinking of, Mr. Pilling," she replied miserably. "Anyway, what's done is done, and I'm glad I've finished with him."

"Now come, lass, don't be so sure," Sam said.

"Oh, yes, it is," Maggie Batten declared with new-found resolution. "I'm not having anything to do with a chap who frightens me like he has done lately. I've only walked out with him five or six times, but already. . . ." Her words died away.

"But you must have liked him well enough to go out with him, Maggie," Sam pointed out.

"Oh, I liked him all right to begin with," she said, nodding. "But since then he's got that impetuous and . . ." there was a shaky dignity about her, "and I'm the sort who prefers to give instead of being rushed into. . . ."

She faltered, painfully confused, quite unable to continue, rich colour mantling her cheeks.

Convinced she would be happier if she were left alone, Sam gave her a message for Clem Roebuck and, squeezing her arm comfortingly, left for home himself.

2

The drizzle of the previous evening had been replaced by a southerly breeze, and worshippers streaming from the Methodist Chapel in Market Square, after attending morning service, were able to pause outside for a chat with friends, in warm but most unseasonable conditions. Of these, while her husband stood a few paces back, Mrs. Clem Roebuck was engaged in a long and apparently interminable conversation with a lady who held one of the leading positions in Ramsfield society.

Some distance away, Sam Pilling scowled indiscriminately at his sister-in-law, and at the owner of an opulent, chauffeur-driven limousine, who was inclining her head graciously every now and then at certain of Mrs. Roebuck's observations.

"Well, Milly, how much longer do you think Laura's going on gushing over Law Watkinson's wife?" he inquired.

Sam was there for one person's sake only, his own wife's, who knew full well that to cease chapel-going would mean the severance of the slender remaining link between herself and her father. Milly was as much out of sympathy with that father as was her husband, but she shrank from a step which would inevitably break up the family circle.

"Yes," she said, smiling wanly, "it does seem silly hanging about to talk to Laura and Clem when we live so near to them. But Father hasn't come out of Chapel yet."

That was the real crux of the matter. Ezra Sykes expected his daughters to await him. They had done so when their mother was alive, and now that he was alone, it should be even more their duty and pleasure to preserve the Sabbath reunion.

"Now look here," Sam said firmly. "We'll stay if you're going to be bothered."

"No, let's be off, dear," she said.

Milly was in low spirits. Her heart still ached about Gilbert, and now she had a further anxiety: the rift between her husband and their elder son, who that morning had been barely civil to his father. What the quarrel was about she could not discover—each had minimized it when questioned, Sam with a laughing: "Oh, I've just pulled him over the coals a bit," while Archie, referring to both his parents in terms she detested, merely winked before saying: "Oh, it's nothing, Ma. My views on office efficiency don't happen to coincide with the old man's, and so I'm letting him cool off."

In these circumstances, Milly was a most unhappy woman as her husband drove her home, where, on the lengthy driveway extending in front of Glenfield and Stonewood, they found a line of cars; there were more cars between the two houses, and the whole of the back as far as the Pillings' big garage, was packed with motor vehicles of every description, British and foreign, from a baby racer to a brand new Hispano Suiza.

"Seems to be our Sunday for the gang, Milly," Sam remarked. "Well, I'll have to leave the bus here for the time being, and you'll have to do the remainder on foot."

A surprisingly limited number of either drivers or passengers was visible, but from the glass-roofed car-washing-place beyond the garage there was every indication that a lively party was in progress, which recalled to Sam the arrival of several cases of bottled beer at the beginning of the week, carefully smuggled in by Archie and his two boon companions, all of whom were unaware there was a witness to their activities.

Smiling in a manner he felt must be ironical, Sam thought

with some satisfaction that lack of funds would soon end his son's capers.

Milly, wide-eyed, was staring at him. "*Whatever* are you sneering about?" she inquired.

"Sneering!" Sam blustered. "Why on earth, love, do you think——"

They had been picking a winding way through many thousand pounds' worth of vehicles, and, taking another step, he bumped an already tender shin against a far-extending exhaust pipe. His comment was hardly in keeping with the homily of the Minister to whom he had listened that morning.

"Ssssh . . ." his wife said. "Remember what day it is."

"Well, it's the second time I've cracked myself on the same spot," he complained.

"Oh," said Milly, nodding her head as if a problem had been solved. "So that's why you were twisting your mouth so queerly."

Sam smiled at her. "Sounds a reasonable explanation," he remarked, somewhat ambiguously.

The exodus started about half an hour later, led by Scipio Dyson, Kate's brother and Archie's cousin, in a battered seven-year-old Austin seven, owned by a partnership of four students, all of whom, in term time, travelled in it to the Medical School at Leeds; he was followed by a nine-year-old $6\frac{1}{2}$-litre Bentley whose driver began to practise racing changes, to the consternation of drivers immediately behind, who expressed disapproval by continued blowing of horns and klaxons. Dickeys of two-seaters and the seats of saloons and tourers were packed with young men and women, all of whom did whatever best appealed to increase the prevailing uproar.

As the bonnet of each car reached the gateway, it seemed a point of honour to stamp accelerators to the floorboards and spin over the steering wheels simultaneously, and the air was rent with pulsating sounds: the deep-bellied roar of big exhausts, the whine of superchargers, and the ear-piercing din when cut-outs were opened.

Seven or eight minutes of this commotion sufficed, however. Then the exclusive district of Moorheaton became Sunday-quiet again.

Sunday lunch at the Pillings had not been a cheerful meal, although Nancy did her best to bring about a better atmosphere, so talkative that her father began to regard her with a suspicion that proved to be justified.

As soon as possible afterwards Sam escaped to his study, taking with him a selection of suitable reading matter. He had skimmed through a couple of the more respectable Sunday papers, and was preparing to give his attention to the most lurid one of them all, when his daughter entered the room. She perched on the arm of his chair.

"Out with it," he observed without preamble.

"Cash," she replied succinctly.

"*Never*," said Sam.

Nancy sighed. "I'm afraid so, Daddy. Unless you can soften your heart to the tune of thirty of the best there's nothing left for me except to file my petition."

"But dammit, it's less than a fortnight since you had your cheque," Sam expostulated. "Were you already in debt to that amount?"

She sighed again. "Yes, it all had to go. Pilling always pays, you'll remember."

"Right!" said Sam. "Now you stop tweaking my hair and get off this chair. Go and sit down there facing me."

She eyed him, raised her eyebrows, and shrugged, but did as she was bidden. Her demeanour a trifle resigned, she seated herself carefully, smoothed out her dress, and demurely clasping her hands on her lap awaited his will.

"I'm going to give you the thirty pounds, but it's on one understanding, Nancy," he told her grimly. "And it's that I have your promise you won't exceed your allowance again. Is that understood?"

"Yes, Daddy," she said primly.

"Fully?" Sam persisted. "For I mean it."

"Yes, Daddy," she repeated.

"Very well then, that's that," Sam continued. "But it won't do any harm if I remind you how fortunate you are compared with some girls. You don't pay board and lodging here, do you? Lots of young women have to do, you know."

Nancy smiled sweetly. "You're not *really* wanting me to make a contribution to household expenses, are you, Daddy?"

Unsmilingly her father went on. "You know very well I'm not. I'm just trying to impress on you certain things. There are others yet, as I suppose you can guess."

She wriggled a little. "Oh, of course," she agreed.

"We'll tot 'em roughly," said Sam. "To begin with, you get fifty pounds a quarter pin money, don't you?"

"Yes, Daddy," she said.

"And in addition to that I pay for any big items you need, a fur coat say, don't I?"

"Yes."

"And on top of that I also pay all your bills for dresses and what not at Madame Gladys Shires', don't I? And whatever else there is about that Rafe Bottomley he knows how to charge. He's keen enough where money's concerned."

Nancy's eyes suddenly sparkled. "Rafe's built up a wonderful business as a gown maker, so why should you sneer at him? What harm has he done you?"

Sam laughed. "None, and he wouldn't do you much either," he said sarcastically. "But that other chap, Brozik, could. Why the devil do you mess about with men old enough to be your father?"

"But . . ." she smiled again, the first time for a while, "I shouldn't exactly call you *aged*, Daddy."

Sam leaned forward. "I'll tell you what you'd call me if I were angling after a girl of twenty or thereabouts, my lass . . . a dirty old man."

She went quite pale. "Is there anything else?" she asked.

"No," he told her.

Chin in the air, she swept past so arrogantly as to bring into flame the smouldering glow of anger that was in her father.

"Nancy!" His unaccustomed sharpness checked her. "You'd better understand this, too—in future you're going to behave yourself and not do things that worry your mother to the red wick. If you don't, I shall be on to you like a ton of bricks."

Quivering with temper, she retorted: "You seem to forget I'm no longer a child."

His usually good-humoured eyes hard, Sam glanced round the back of his chair. "Whatever I seem to forget is one thing, but I notice you don't carry your resentment to the extent of telling me you don't want the thirty pounds. Well, you shall have it before bed-time."

The hollows in her cheeks and the shadows beneath her eyes seemed more pronounced as she stared back as though hating him.

"You . . . you beast," she gasped.

When she had gone, Sam picked up one of the newspapers. For several minutes he gazed blankly at the same

56

paragraph, and then the sheets fell from his hands to the carpet. Motionless, he continued to look into the flames of the fire.

3

Within a few days of sadness and discord rising to a new peak in the Pilling household, the country and the Empire were anxiously disturbed by news of the King's serious bronchial attack. That this was the end a B.B.C. announcement made grievously clear one evening, when Sam and Milly were sitting in the drawing-room of Glenfield. Intently they listened to the announcer's solemn voice. *"This is London. The following bulletin was issued at 9.25."* And then came a few simple and inexpressibly touching words: *"The King's life is moving peacefully towards its close."*

Tears were trickling down Milly's cheeks as she switched off the radio.

"I knew there was no hope from the beginning, Sam," she said. "And won't it seem different?"

The familiar figure of the King had for so long been a constant, before and during the war, throughout the early troubles of peace, and into the messy era of Communism, Fascism, and Nazi-ism—from settled days of Edwardianism to the disturbed days of the present, whose influence, Sam was now telling himself not very convincingly, might be responsible in part for the revolt against authority of the younger people.

He sighed. "Yes, and I fancy it's the end of more than a reign, Milly."

"And millions of people besides ourselves will be miserable just now," she said, dabbing her eyes. "I'm sure Laura and Clem will. Shall we go over there, it's not really so very late? Of course . . ." she was sensitive to his reservations about her sister. "Of course, if you'd rather not, we won't. I'm not the least bothered."

Sam was glad to do anything to lighten his wife's load. "When was it that I didn't enjoy a change?" he asked, smiling. "No, let's be off, love. It was only that I couldn't fathom why you chose this particular moment to go visiting."

"Contemporaries," she said.

"*Contemporaries?*" Sam repeated in astonishment.

She seemed a little surprised. "You can be dense sometimes, dear," she said. "I mean that we four are more or less of the same generation, and we can understand each other

57

when we talk about all sort of things that happened while King George was king. If the children were here they'd only get bored if I explained why I wore a Cossack hat at the beginning of the war. It was only a very cheap one——"

"I'll bet it was, on a Tommy's allowance," Sam remarked grimly. "But I gather what you're getting at, love."

"You see with Russia being our ally, everybody wanted to do something as a mark of respect and so——" Wide-eyed she stared at him. "Good gracious, and I never thought of it before. That would be why Olga was called Olga—she'd be born about the same time."

Patiently Sam heard her out. Then they clothed themselves for the short walk from the most convenient source. Milly started out smothered beneath a heavy, pilot-cloth overcoat, belonging to her husband, which reached to her ankles.

To ring the bell of her sister's front door once might be good manners, but to repeat the summons twice more, without eliciting any response whatsoever, was quite another matter. Milly, merely remarking that "Maggie must be out," went in without further ado.

Not far beyond the inner door of the hall, she and her husband found themselves spectators of a passionate scene utterly at variance with what they expected in the light of news now flashed to every part of the world. It was in the drawing-room, where Estelle Illingworth, as if dissociating herself from the dispute in which her parents and brother were involved, was languidly turning over the pages of a fashion magazine.

"I tell you, Clem," Laura was shouting, "I won't allow it. I absolutely forbid you to do any such nonsensical thing."

Clem Roebuck, exemplifying the adage: More haste, less speed, was jabbing his hand towards an elusive arm-hole in a rubberized mackintosh he had only just taken off on returning home. There was on his face an expression of determination and restrained anger which at least his sister-in-law, Milly, had never seen before on his gentle face.

"I'm getting the Chrysler out, Laura," he said, a slight tremble in his voice. "And I'm going to try to catch that girl whatever you say. You've done a wrong and cruel thing——"

"I'm the mistress of this house, Clem," Laura replied savagely. "And what I did was the only thing to do."

Harshly her son interrupted. "That's a downright lie, Mother. Good God, this might be Alnwick Castle, and me the heir to the dukedom . . . except that people of their sort wouldn't be so damned snobbish."

"That'll do, Jim," his father reproved him.

Laura drew an outraged breath. "I should think so," she declared. "A son speaking to his mother—and you're not going, Clem." Her voice rose.

Shamefacedly the master-steeplejack was apologizing to his visitors. But at his wife's protesting tone he turned.

"Yes, I'm going, Laura," he said, quiet now. "I'm going because it's getting late, and because I have some sort of conscience. What do you think she's going to do at this hour? And you needn't tell me she's a full month's wages in her purse. Haven't we the responsibility of making sure she's in some decent lodging for the night?"

For once in their lives Sam and his wife saw Laura desperate.

"But I've told you Father's telephoned he's coming up," she said. "You *must* be here when he comes."

Steadily Clem Roebuck held her glance. "It may be better for you if I'm not here, if you deal with . . . with *that* matter in the way you insist you will. But I warn you once again, Laura, you'll be a fool if you do . . . and unwise," he said before turning away.

There was a brief silence, each of them instinctively waiting for the sound of a door closing, the signal that Clem had acted as he declared he would. Then Milly spoke.

"Whatever's happened, Laura?" she said. "I don't wish to butt in. . . ."

"I'll tell you what's the matter, Aunt Milly," Jim interposed heatedly. "Just listen to this."

She did so, meantime closely watching him, a fairly tall, thin, young fellow some ten months older than his cousin Archie, with dark hair and slightly sunken eyes. As a schoolboy, which he had been until three years before, Jim had been a normal-looking boy, but now, certainly in the opinion of a most compassionate aunt, he had lost more flesh than he could afford, and there were times when she imagined herself detecting in him most disquieting nervous mannerisms. But more than once, as she knew, Clem had packed him off to the doctor, and as the report had always been: "sound as a bell" she thought it would be needlessly interfering to suggest that a visit to a specialist might get to the root of the trouble.

"You mean Maggie's been turned out at a moment's

notice?" Sam said aghast. "A kindly lass like her, who's always been only too willing to do anything for any of you."

"Oh, it was for a very good reason, Uncle Sam, which I was going to tell you about if you'd have let me finish," Jim said furiously. "You see Mother caught us skylarking in the kitchen—it was about a cake-tin that I'd grabbed as a matter of fact—and whether she assumed the shoving each other we were doing was really the preliminary to a spot of push and tickle——"

Laura's arm flashed, her hand cracking against his cheek. "Now that'll teach you," she gasped. "You've never in your life been so insolent to me as you've been to-night, and never again——"

Something of defeat showed itself in his strained eyes. "You generally get your own way, don't you, Mother," he said wearily. "Now you'll be able to get another maid who'll mind her p's and q's and call me Mr. Jim, not Jim as Maggie did . . ."

Despite heaving bosom, Laura was once more in command of herself and of the situation. As if superbly sure her desires would be met, she told her son that when his grandfather came he was to keep out of the way.

"It's a very private matter I've to talk over with him," she added.

"Then I'll push off now," said Jim. Smiling twistedly, he wished his aunt and uncle good night as he passed them.

"Estelle!" Laura said.

That young woman, gazing into the mirror of a compact, was frowningly fingering a platinum blonde curl when her mother spoke to her. But she nodded immediately in reply and, with strange submissiveness, lost no time in leaving the room.

Milly's eyes were bright with indignation. "Well, I must say I think you've behaved abominably to Maggie, Laura," she started off. "I couldn't have been so unkind, no, not if——"

Her sister's Luncheon Club voice was returning. "My dear Milly," she said, "I don't want to be rude, but I must say that I'm not prepared to discuss this either with you or with my in-laws."

"I'm not begging," Sam grunted.

Milly could be a stubborn creature. "It's all right you being clever, Laura," she resumed. "But the truth is——"

Laura laughed. "The truth is, my dear, that if you'd been

60

more clever and less kind, your children wouldn't be as they are. I hope mine will do better for themselves."

Sam rose like a jack-in-a-box. "I think that after that we'll be off, love," he said.

"That . . . that was very uncalled for, Laura," Milly said tremulously.

Laura patted her arm. "Perhaps it was, Milly, and I'm sorry. But I've so much on my mind—oh, nothing to do with this stupid Maggie Batten affair. And I must get a few things done before Father comes, so if you'll excuse me. . . ."

"Yes, and we must get back ourselves," Sam observed with some feeling. "Come to think of it, I've one or two jobs to do at home myself."

If he hoped to avoid his father-in-law he was to be disappointed. As he and his wife and sister-in-law reached the hall, the knob of the outer door was rattled violently, the sole indication ever given by Mr. Sykes when entering the houses of either friends or relations. A moment later he entered, a white-bearded gentleman with a considerable briskness of movement. As was his habit, he was sombrely clad from head to foot: bowler, black coat, bootlace mourning tie, Oxford grey suit and black boots.

"Come in, Father dear," Mrs. Roebuck remarked somewhat unnecessarily. "Milly and Sam are just going, and so——"

"Milly and Sam are stopping," Mr. Sykes declared unequivocally.

For a woman who prided herself on poise, Laura was surprisingly dismayed, and fleetingly showed it.

"But they can't, Father," she said. "Sam's just been saying he's something special to do at home."

"Whether he has or not he's noan going." Ezra Sykes was quite inflexible. "What I've come about is a family matter, and as a member of the family he's got to hear what I've to say on a very grave affair. What do you reckon I've come out at this time of the night for—to half do my duty?"

Leaving no opportunity for further argument, he turned and led the way into the drawing-room, a vigorous man whose spritely gait spoke volumes for his condition at sixty-eight. Three years ago, when her mother died, his splendid state of health had, from one aspect, been a considerable source of apprehension to Laura Roebuck. Though she had no grounds at all for the notion, she had worried herself into thinking he might marry again. Instead, he had installed

61

an elderly housekeeper into his house in Barnsley Road, and life with him had continued very much as before.

There is a certain type of businessman, in the ranks of whom Mr. Sykes must have been listed high, who instinctively furthers his own designs by methods which are quite opposed: the direct assault or the evasive withdrawal, employing whichever best suits the situation. On this evening he selected the former.

"Where's Clement?" he demanded.

"He's out at the moment, Father," Laura replied.

"Anyroad, you lot will do for a start," Mr. Sykes observed. "But where's Estelle? I want her here. And what's she doing staying so long at home—she's wed, isn't she? And how is it her husband is supposed to be up in London at t' Wool Sales, and the Sales isn't on? And is there any truth in a rumour that came to my ears to-night that her and Philip Illingworth are contemplating the sinful act of divorce? Now let's have your answers, Laura."

The barrage of questions had had their effect upon his elder daughter, who was extremely pale.

"I've . . . I've been trying to keep things from you, Father," she faltered. "In . . . in the hope that Estelle and Philip might patch matters up . . . even though in my heart I knew they could never again live together as man and wife. I . . . I haven't said anything to you because I was clinging to a slender hope that by some miracle I could avoid hurting you."

Ezra Sykes found the hub, and dealt with it. "I'm permitting no divorce, Laura," he asserted.

"There has to be, Father," Laura replied.

During a short interlude, Mr. Sykes placed his bowler hat on the upper edge of a picture frame and draped his overcoat over a china cabinet. Then, hands behind his back, he straddled his legs across the fireplace.

"I'm bowed enough with humiliation as it is," he began, sternly eyeing his son-in-law and younger daughter. "No, I'm not going back as far as I might——"

"You'd better not," Sam snapped. "I've no desire to be listening to all this——"

"Yes, I think it really would be better if you and Milly left," Laura urged. "It can't be very nice for you——"

Ezra Sykes stared at her from beneath bushy eyebrows. "Are you deaf or summat, Laura?" he inquired. "They're remaining here until I've done."

While the father rebuked one daughter, the other was whispering to her husband. "Don't let him goad you, Sam dear. Just stay calm and it'll be over all the more quickly."

"You might keep that as your motto, love," Sam replied. "I'm pretty sure you and me are going to be the target before very long."

Ezra Sykes was coldly eyeing the couple. "If you two have finished I'll go on," he remarked. "As I were saying, I've a grandson who's had to be sent away to sea, and another one, his brother Archibald, who's known for the toss-pot he is all over the town. Then there's my granddaughter, Nancy, as flighty a piece——"

"Father," Milly broke in, "I will not allow you or——"

Sam was clicking his teeth. "Nay, dear, just stay calm. It'll be . . . er . . . over all the more quickly."

Flashingly Milly turned on him. "You imitating thing!" she said.

This respite had given Laura the breathing space she needed. She was too well versed about her father's nature not to realize that whatever he considered necessary would be pursued to the bitter end. Difficult though it were, it was preferable for her to take the lead herself. She began by describing her eldest daughter as a good girl, a pure-minded young woman striving to be as devout and decent-living as her grandfather.

"Maybe so and maybe not," Mr. Sykes said. "But if there's any more of this talk of divorce I shall get out my big Bible, and I shall strike out her name, and yours for encouraging her, Laura. And . . ." he ended, "you'll guess what I mean by that."

"There's nothing left but divorce, Father, and I shan't do anything to prevent her, because I won't allow her to be treated so cruelly," Laura said in a rush. "And if I'm any judge of you, you'll put aside your scruples about divorce as soon as you hear about the terrible ordeals she has had to submit to at the hands of her husband."

Ezra Sykes eyed her. "And what does Philip Illingworth do to her?"

"He thrashes her," Laura said defiantly.

Thoughtfully Mr. Sykes plucked his beard. "Thrashes her, does he? Well, I don't reckon there's anything in the Scriptures that forbids a man to chastise his wife when she's been wayward and naughty."

"It . . . it isn't that sort of thrashing, Father."

Mr. Sykes had become fretful. "Now let's have a less of going round the corner, Laura," he said. "There's only one kind of thrashing as I know of, so what are you being so mysterious about?"

"I'm not being mysterious," his elder daughter replied, her voice rising with nervous tension. "Only there's some things you can't talk about so easily, even to your own father, and. . . ."

Startled, Ezra Sykes stared. "Are you meaning to insinuate ——"

"All I'm trying to say is that her health will break down if she lives with him any more," Laura Roebuck interposed with desperation. "And that's why there's *got* to be a divorce."

For a brief spell the silence in the room was nearly absolute, broken only by the sound of Laura's tumultuous breathing. Then Sam, his face very grave, whistled a soft: "Phew!" and his father-in-law groaned discordantly.

"So that's what's been happening," Ezra Sykes said, stricken, his eyes tightly closed. "Philip Illingworth's that sort, is he? Aye, I've heard of 'em, but I never dreamed that any o' mine would be sullied through one."

Sam got up from the sofa and, holding out a hand, pulled his wife to her feet. They said good night; meanwhile Laura, a shaky-looking woman indeed, talked feverishly about providing tea for her father and arranging for Jim to run him home in the little car.

"There's going to be a reckoning about this," Mr. Sykes said venomously, unheeding both of farewells and his daughter's forethought. "As God's above, there's going to be a reckoning."

"What do you mean, Father?" Laura asked.

"The Illingworths are folk of many possessions and great wealth, but I shall tumble them into the dust for this," Ezra Sykes soliloquized. "I'll publish their misbegotten son's infamy from the housetops and——"

"Father, you mustn't do any such thing or breathe a word about what I've told you," Laura implored him. "We've to consider what's best for Estelle."

Her father's mouth was implacable. "An eye for an eye and a tooth for a tooth," he said. "Wrong's been done to my granddaughter, but you bide awhile. Afore I've done, the name of Philip Illingworth shall stink in the godly's nostrils."

"Come on, Milly," Sam said.

The paramount impression he carried from that house was of fear, on Laura Roebuck's face.

When a household does not generally retire for the night very early, it is not the easiest of matters to change that routine, nor can one deal with a girl of nineteen and a boy of almost twenty-one as one might have done a few years before. Milly, quite unsatisfied with the talk she had had with her husband on the short walk home from Stonewood, and bursting with impatience to resume, had found Archie and Nancy impervious to her hints. Brother and sister were at the Steinway grand, hugely amusing themselves, Nancy playing and singing, Archie singing only, in a voice he deluded himself was not without quality. At their third rendering of "Thora," with pathetic effects, Milly bestirred herself, at last recognizing how vain for the present was her hope of getting them out of the drawing-room. She did succeed, however, in catching her husband's eye, and, her lips framing the words, soundlessly endeavoured to pass a message to him.

"Well," she said, after a final effort, tapping her mouth with the backs of her fingers as she yawned alarmingly, "I can't say for you others, but speaking for myself——"

"Oh, you hop off to bed, Mother," Archie grinned. "My tonsils aren't free yet."

Nancy giggled. "If they're much freer, my lad, we shall be looking for them. And good night, Mummy. Sleep well."

"Good night," their mother remarked with dignity.

A quarter of an hour later, with a few pages of an exciting chapter still to read, Sam reluctantly closed his novel.

"Yes, I think I'll be off myself," he declared. "Good night, love . . . good night, Archie."

"Good night," Nancy replied distantly.

"Night." Her brother was no more forthcoming.

With their frigid valedictions in his thoughts, Sam climbed the stairs. But any tendency to melancholia he might have had was short-lived, for Milly chattered away until late into the night. Everything that had occurred at the Roebucks' was discussed again and again.

"Well, have you about done?" he inquired as the grandfather clock on the half-landing struck once more. "Mind you, I'm as fresh as a daisy yet."

"Don't try to be funny," Milly said. "Who else can I talk to about it if I can't talk to you? I mean it's been such an evening if you come to think of it . . . oh, and I'd forgotten

. . . . what about Jim going on at his mother? I've never seen him like that before."

"For that matter I've never known Clem carry on with Laura to anything like that extent before. But we've gone into this several times already."

She ignored that. "You know, dear, Jim doesn't look all he should."

"He's a bit fine-drawn certainly," Sam agreed. "But for all his lightish build this is his second season as Ramsfield Rugger's centre three-quarter, and he's a grand bat, a fine cricketer all round. When a young fellow is as good an athlete as that he can't ail overmuch."

She nodded. "Laura's always been inclined to skimp the table."

"Tries to do too much in other directions," Sam grunted. "If you're not over well blessed you can't keep pace with monied folk unless you go short somewhere else."

"I wasn't hinting at Laura's social carryings-on," Milly remarked aloofly.

Sam groaned. "For the Lord's sake don't let's go into that."

Milly relapsed into a somewhat injured silence. The truth was that she was conscious of bearing a grudge against her husband, who had been by no means forthright on any of the many occasions she had brought up the evening's most titillating disclosure, Estelle's relations with Philip Illingworth. She made another effort.

Sorely tried, Sam was more unguarded than he had intended. "If you want my opinion, I think there's something very fishy about that business, and I'll bet Clem's a very worried man when he hears of it, especially about your father going on the rampage, crusading against Ernest Illingworth's son."

By now Milly was sitting upright in bed. "But why ever has such an idea entered your head, about it being a fishy business?" she demanded, jogging his shoulder.

Recklessly Sam continued. "For one thing, I've seen a fair amount of Philip Illingworth, and though you can always be deceived, I don't size him up as a chap who would go in for queer stuff with his wife. Then there was Laura, trying her best to get us out of the way—I suspect because she was after telling your father the tale when only the two of them were together. And, by Jingo, for all the front she put on, she was nervous enough—though that was nothing to what she was later, when your father let us all know he was going to make a public issue of the affair. Why, she was plumb scared to death then."

"Yes, I noticed that," Milly gulped. "But . . . but why should Estelle make up such a story . . . and Laura support her in it, say? What on earth would be the purpose?"

"Listen, I'm only surmising," Sam warned her. "But supposing Philip Illingworth's caught her going off the rails—I've seen her myself in that flash car of Tony Flassati's—you know, the owner of the Palais and a score of soft-drinks, ice-cream bars. Well, what would your father do if that happened to be the truth—why, he wouldn't lose a minute in cutting Estelle out of his will. Maybe even Laura would suffer, too. What you should remember, Milly, is something that Laura never forgets. And it's that your father has made a lot of money—nicely into six figures I should say."

"But what . . . I don't understand, Sam," Milly croaked.

"The whole thing might be concocted, as a kind of . . . kind of counter weapon to frighten young Illingworth from going in for a divorce," said Sam. "And if it failed, to provide an excuse for Estelle for your father's benefit—that she'd only done wrong herself because she'd been driven to it by her husband's terrible conduct."

Milly released pent breath. "So that's it, is it?"

"No, it isn't," he replied in exasperation. "It's only a wild shot in the dark."

"It makes you wonder," Milly mused.

"It's damned well not making me wonder any longer," Sam observed, "because I'm off to sleep."

A massive body burrowed lower, and a fold of bed-clothing flew up. With some distaste Milly stared at the hump beside her.

"Well, really!" she exclaimed. Now she caught sight of the bedside clock. "Sam," she squeaked, "do you know what time it is?"

His reply was muffled. "Nearly breakfast time, I should think."

The sonorous snoring, which followed immediately, could hardly have been described as faithful or artistic. But it definitely served its purpose.

*   *   *

Ramsfield and the West Riding were, after all, robbed of a *cause célèbre,* and the remainder of the country denied a

67

very spicy story. The sequence of events bringing this about were as follows:

On the afternoon following Sam and Milly Pilling's dramatic visit next door, the day of the Prince of Wales's Proclamation as Edward VIII it was, Clem Roebuck called at the offices of PILLING ALWAYS PAYS, where he had a short conversation with the principal. More than once during that conversation Sam considered he might be disloyal in wondering if his friend were concealing something, for if so it would be the first time in their long association; on the other hand he more than once came to the conclusion that Clem was no better informed than himself about the real truth of the Estelle-Philip Illingworth affair.

But there could be no doubt that the master steeplejack was a very troubled man, fearful about the consequences if his father-in-law carried out the threats he had made.

"If the Illingworths get even a whiff that it's got outside the family circle, they'll spend a fortune trying to disprove Estelle's allegations," he said. "And if they sue—and anyhow, I mean," he amended hastily, "just imagine the harm it would do her if she had to appear in court on a muck-raking issue such as this would be—which I reckon is what will happen unless Laura's father shuts his mouth. How the devil can *I* make sure of that?"

Sam made no reference to a damaging slip. "You can't do anything, lad, and neither can I, for the tripe king would take no notice of either of us. But there's one chap who might work the oracle, if he would—and that's Alonso. And not as a man of God, either, but as an ex-solicitor who is still spoken of with bated breath for opinions which have turned out sounder than K.C.s'. If he'd drop a hint to the old fool to the effect that meddling might land him in for big damages . . . well, I think that would do the trick. I needn't tell *you* that for all Ezra's money-bags he'd tumble over backwards rather than part unnecessarily with a cent."

There was admiration on Clem Roebuck's tired face. "You're a cute 'un, Sam. But would you think Alonso will do it?"

"I'll find out quickly enough," Sam promised.

Then he inquired about Maggie Batten. Clem was reserved on that, too, though he said he had seen her safe for the night. By now, he added, she would have left Ramsfield.

"And now I'll be off to our spot myself," he said, getting

up from one of the deep club chairs on the edge of which he had been anxiously perched. "And thanks, Sam."

"I'll call round Alonso's way when I'm going home, Clem," Sam nodded. "And all being well you'll hear before six o'clock whether it's yes or no."

It was "yes." Moreover the Rev. Alonso Dyson acted so speedily that long before the streets of the kingdom paid regal homage in crape, Mr. Sykes had washed his hands of the whole affair, much though he continued to deplore it, in terms heavily salted with biblical woe. It was understood by the Pillings, however, that in the circumstances as known to him he would offer no further objection to his granddaughter, who had left Ramsfield for an indefinite period, *seeking* a divorce.

That word "seeking" provided Sam and Milly with an amplitude of food for thought. From it they gathered that, as soon as such a dubious matter could be arranged, Philip Illingworth was to take the honourable course of providing his wife with appropriate evidence.

CHAPTER THREE

BETWEEN themselves, the inhabitants of Ramsfield had always regarded the town as a "rum spot," though this criticism was made with a mixture of amusement and kindly tolerance which would not have been accorded to any outsider guilty of similar sentiments. This feeling was perhaps expressed first in Victorian times, when Ram Valley manufacturers, as an easement of their pursuit of wealth, vied hotly with one another in whatever form tickled their lively fancies; it might be in the size and appointments of mansions, the splendour of carriages and the quality of horses, the dimensions of factory chimneys, or, occasionally, the proportions of stone towers, aggravatingly planned to overlook a neighbour's extensive gardens, towers which were heightened again and again to offset any counter measures carried out or proposed: the raising of boundary walls or the preparation of great pits for the introduction of full-grown trees as screens. It is almost superfluous to add that in such a community feuds were frequent, skeletons in cupboards many, and testators' dispositions more often than not the prelude to violent battles, personal and legal.

With the passage of the years, this pattern of individualism in the well-to-do had become less pronounced, though it still existed. The competition nowadays was in luxurious and/or fast cars, and in the ownership of racehorses, which were sometimes fast. A new factor had also appeared: the competition for women, for a rigid adherence to marriage vows no longer applied quite so harshly. But people still did the unexpected; there was the case of a man who picked a girl out of a back street in Scargate and sent her away to be educated for three years before marrying her; and that of the two daughters of a very "warm" family, one of whom went to a finishing school and the other into a noisy weaving-shed of her father's mill, nobody thinking very much about it, with the exception of the very refined mother.

There were still queer households about which many tales were told, and of these the Oldfields' in Moorheaton Drive had been responsible for much speculation since the death of Allan Oldfield, Chairman of Allan Oldfield, Ltd., tin-box and canister manufacturers, whose immense works were situated three miles up the valley, at Scargate.

For The Towers, Moorheaton, had been and still was a house of hatred. By his first wife Allan Oldfield had left a son, who had hated him for the treatment his mother had received; and Allan Oldfield had come to hate his second wife with a hatred equalled only by the hatred his son had for her.

But they continued to live beneath the same roof, Jim Oldfield around fifty, successor to his father as Chairman of the company from which the Oldfield fortune had sprung, and Phyllis Oldfield, his step-mother, an attractive woman in her forties, five or six years younger than he.

It was freezingly cold one Tuesday morning in late February when Sam ran his wife down to town. The day had begun badly, the postman bringing a letter from Captain Crummock merely reporting that his charge was in good health. Gilbert had not written, and in consequence his mother was very upset.

In Teazle Street, while passing between the crowded shop-front of Iredale Mallinson's departmental store on the right and Madame Gladys Shires's severely chaste windows on the left, Sam, with the idea of cheering his wife up, suggested he should join her in a cup of coffee at Wood's Café where, of course, she was going first.

"Oh do, Sam," Milly said, brightening. "To tell you the truth I don't feel like doing a lot of talking about something and nothing this morning."

In Wood's Café, beyond a cabinet, displaying home-made chocolates, they climbed a flight of stairs to an L-shaped room above, from the window-tables of which there was a commanding view of Teazle Street. Unfortunately, not only were these prized seats taken but the place was so full that they were compelled to share a table with a lady who, to a surprising degree, looked babyish—big blue eyes, pink and white complexion, moist red lips, with also, not wholly in agreement with that childishness, some quality of breathless, tantalizing stillness, as if in her innocence she had heard rumours of what men do but, nevertheless, was too petrified to run.

"Do you mind, Mrs. Oldfield?" Milly inquired, pointing to a vacant chair.

"Morning, Phyllis," said Sam. "It's icy enough for skating to-day. Remember when we used to?"

As Mrs. Oldfield had just received her check from the waitress, the conversation was not prolonged. Immediately the Pillings were alone Milly leaned across the table, a precaution hardly demanded in view of the noisy hum about them, no doubt much of it scandalous.

"Did you see the way she smiled at those men going through into the smoke-room?" she asked. "Hasn't she languishing ways?"

Sam chuckled. "She always had, but there wasn't anything at the end of it, as Allan Oldfield found out for himself when he'd married her. He was in his forties then and she was seventeen or eighteen, and he never got over it. It's always assumed that that was why, long before he died, he turned everything over to Jim, so that whatever the lawyers tried out for her she could never claim a penny-piece."

At this, Milly glanced cautiously about her, but, reassured that no one was listening, did her part to keep the topic in being.

"All the same, it wasn't fair leaving her entirely dependent on her stepson, was it?"

"On the face of it, no," Sam said. "But Allan Oldfield thought a lot of himself and he couldn't stand the kidding he got. Somehow or other it became known that his second wife

71

wouldn't — well refused to be a proper wife to him."

"Well . . ." Milly gasped. "Go on, Sam, I've never heard this before."

As they left the café, he had been prodded into recalling a remark made by Dr. Lister Fox, that Mrs. Oldfield was a pathological case.

"Or something like that," Sam remarked, eyeing a railway dray-horse. "By Jove, but he's a grand 'un."

Indifferent to the scarcely veiled surprise of a number of people and to the amusement of his wife, he approached the animal, which was perfectly placid while he ran a hand down its foreleg in a most professional manner.

"This chap seems likely to come early to hand," he observed in the jargon of the racing stable. "Aye, a fine piece of bloodstock." Then he winked. "Any idea where you and me are off to soon?"

Milly laughed. "There's something vaguely at the back of my head," she said.

"There'd better be," Sam said.

In high humour he left her, and then drove round to Thorntons' to fill up with petrol, where his blitheness of spirit was rapidly dissipated when he chanced to glance ahead, in the direction of an old horse trough recessed into the wall between the Vaults and the station. Against it a couple, his daughter and a rather precise-looking young man, in horn-rimmed glasses, were engaged in earnest conversation.

"Dammit, hasn't that girl any gumption at all?" he growled. "Doesn't she realize it's inadvisable for an unmarried young woman to be seen — of course, it's not very likely she'll know about the divorce yet. Anyway. . . ."

Abruptly giving instructions for the oil-level to be checked, he left Thorntons' with one purpose in mind: to part the pair before too many people saw them.

"Good morning, Illingworth," he said from at least ten paces distant.

"Good morning, sir," Philip Illingworth replied.

"Nancy, I want you to come across with me to the office straight off," Sam resumed. "I've left your mother in Teazle Street and she's forgotten her bag and hasn't any money. You can take some on to her—she's somewhere between Wood's Café and Hoyle's fish shop. She mustn't hang about on a morning like this so we'd better hurry."

Nancy, colouring unmistakably, stared at him before turning to her companion.

"Well, I suppose I'll have to rush off on my errand of mercy," she said as if the words choked her. "So, good-bye, Philip."

"Good-bye." Philip Illingworth raised his hat. "And good morning, Mr. Pilling."

"Aye, good morning," Sam said shortly.

The row between father and daughter started in the middle of Market Square.

"Even if Mother were without money, and even if you for once hadn't had wads on you, everybody knows who Mother is, and it wouldn't have mattered," she said furiously. "You just wanted to get me away from Philip, that's all, and your excuse was as transparent as glass."

"Maybe, but it served its purpose," Sam said, riled by her manner. "Now I don't want to go into details, but there's a sound reason why you shouldn't——"

Nancy's lips curled. "Oh, I guessed what you were being so stupid about . . . Philip's divorce, because he'd just been telling me about it. But this isn't the dark ages, and a girl isn't ruined if she chats to a man——"

"Shut up, you little fool," Sam shouted.

"Thank you," she said, spun on her heel and swished away.

Sam set off towards Neptune Buildings before remembering to face about. "By God!" he muttered, but this was nothing to do with collecting his car.

The young lady in the inquiry place at the office ventured nothing more than a squeaky "Good morning, Mr. Pilling," when she perceived the expression on his face as he stormed in ten minutes afterwards.

Later on that morning, as the Town Hall clock boomed out the last stroke of twelve, Hilda Schofield, who only a few minutes before had left the private office with note-book and pencil, returned to say that Mr. Illingworth sent his compliments and would be grateful for a few words.

"Which Mr. Illingworth?" Sam snapped, his mouth hardening.

"Mr. Ernest Illingworth," she replied, pointed chin quivering.

Sam nodded. "Oh, in that case get another glass out, and then fetch him in."

Hurt by his sharp tone, she carried out these instructions,

averting her head so that he did not see the moisture which had sprung into her eyes.

Mr. Illingworth, Philip Illingworth's father, was a portly gentleman of outstanding commercial prominence: Chairman of Illingworth, Cawthra & Foster, Woolcombers, Bradford, with a finger in the pie of other staple industries of that city: wool-merchanting, top-making, worsted spinning and manufacturing. Ostensibly he had called to discuss a sizeable investment in the Spring Double, the weights for which had been announced more than three weeks before. For the second leg he had a strong conviction that a difference of twelve pounds would not prevent Reynoldstown from repeating his victory of the previous year, in the fastest time on record over the Grand National course.

Later, without finessing, he referred to his son's troubles.

"Yes, I'm aware of them, and so is my wife," said Sam in response to a direct question. "But you can take it from me, Ernest, that we shall both keep mum. Mark you, we haven't much to be quiet about, for all we've been told was a bare outline . . . in fact nothing more than a broad hint about what your lad was supposed to have been up to."

Whisky splashed out of Ernest Illingworth's glass as he set it down.

"That bitch, Philip's wife, and with all due respect I must say I'm positive your sister-in-law was in it, too—they've done their damnedest with this monstrous story of whipping to stop Philip going in for a divorce, even though he'd caught his wife red-handed. And, by God, they weren't without cunning, either. You see a month or so earlier Philip discovered something of his wife's doings—nothing particularly bad, but all the same not so pleasant for a young married man to find out—and when they got upstairs he suddenly lost his temper and gave her a sound spanking."

"Did he?" murmured Sam.

A smile of pride crossed Mr. Illingworth's face. "Philip's deceptive, Sam. You take him for a quiet customer, which generally speaking he is, but there's more to him than that. Anyway . . ." he waved his hand as if impatient with himself for the tribute he had paid his son, "anyway, Estelle yelled blue murder, and shot out of the bedroom in a flimsy, torn nightgown. That's where the rub comes, for one of the maids both heard and saw, and all this later on was hotted up as the foundation for an allegation of much worse goings-on."

"It's a nasty pickle altogether," Sam mused. "All the same,

washing dirty linen in public doesn't help, and I reckon that what has been decided is the wisest . . . I more or less make out it's something on the lines that if your boy gives her the usual hotel bills, etc., she for her part will drop all the other business."

Ernest Illingworth licked his lips as though he had a foul taste in his mouth.

"That's it," he said resentfully. "But if it hadn't been that Philip, win or lose, would have been smeared for his lifetime, he'd have fought through every court in the land. I'd hell's own job to make him see sense. Of course, the mistake was in his ever marrying her, for anybody could realize they're poles apart. But he got engaged in a twinkling, and I'm hanged if I know why."

Sam chuckled. "If you're going to try to work out why misfits do get wed you've a job on, for there's plenty about, Ernest."

Mr. Illingworth took his overcoat off the stand. "It's the only time I've known Philip do something without carefully studying it over, in major matters I mean. Mind you," he chuckled, too, "I'm not referring to motor-car driving."

Sam nodded. "I've heard he's a bit of a speed merchant."

"I wish you could look at the trophies and cups he's won," Mr. Illingworth boasted. "Well, we'll soon be having them with us again. He'll be selling his Bradford house and coming home to live with us in Wharfedale. And now I'd better be off, Sam. It's done me good to let off steam."

"Yes, it does now and then, Ernest," said Sam, not very happily.

Until Clem Roebuck rang him up about half an hour after his visitor's departure he sat hunched over his desk. During that interval he came to the conclusion that, more and more wearied by his son's and daughter's conduct, the pressure in his own boiler was rising to a dangerous height.

* * *

The High School was at the far side of the town from Roydlea, about mid-way between Market Square and the big stands and terraces of the Ramsfield Town Association Football Club a mile out at Garth End.

When, at the end of the last period of the morning, it was seen that the games mistress had pinned up a notice cancelling hockey owing to frost, many of the girls who crowded to read it dallied afterwards, in no particular hurry to leave.

Others, regarding the prospect of a completely free afternoon differently, jostled to reach dark blue, belted coats from pegs in the cloakroom; still pulling on dark blue felt hats with Cambridge blue bands, they raced joyously off to the nearest bus stop.

As a threepenny ticket was an item worth saving in the Dysons' budget, Kate, slipping her arms into the strap of her school-bag, decided to walk home. Shortly afterwards she was swinging down the main road, her cheeks more and more rosily mantled by the exercise and the keen nip in the air.

The summer before, at an East Coast resort, while near-by the younger element enjoyed themselves in the bathing-pool, an hotel acquaintance in a neighbouring deck-chair had forecast to Mrs. Sam Pilling that when Kate Dyson grew a little older she would have a "perfect figure." The two ladies were among a group occupied in chattering about sons and daughters and others dear, and during the course of the conversation Kate's aunt described her very warmly as "a girl who grows on you." By this Milly was referring both to Kate's appearance and nature, and she could not have hit the nail on the head more happily.

True, although her expression was very sweet, Kate could lay claim neither to beauty nor prettiness as these are understood. Her eyes were too strikingly intelligent, her mouth too wide, and her forehead too broad—although as compensation the eyes were large and luminous; her mouth, when opened in the infectious laughter so characteristic of her, disclosed white and lovely teeth; and that brow was framed by soft, wavy hair glinting with a thousand lights.

She quickly reached the end of Sheepgate, and was compelled to wait there until the traffic lights changed before darting across to Folly Street. Just as green replaced amber she noticed a lengthy cream and black car.

"Uncle Sam!" she called out.

Sam, who was letting the clutch in and spinning the wheel to cross into Folly Street, came out of his reverie with a jar when she banged the window. Leaning over, he pushed down the door handle and, while the driver of an overtaking vehicle stood on his brakes to avert a collision, she scrambled in.

"Just in time, love," Sam said, laughing. "Another two seconds. . . ." His attention was diverted by the gesticulations of the irate driver of a gravel wagon. "Whatever's up with that chap?" he marvelled. "I put my indicator out to show I was turning . . . I think."

Between there and Ezra Sykes's commodious but not very hygienic-looking tripe works flanking Ramsfield Bridge, he learned that his niece would not be returning to school that afternoon.

"Well, what about a trip out with me to Bankdam Mills instead of washing your father's surplice and Scipio's laboratory coats, or something of that nature, which I suppose is what you'll be doing? Jim and his father are on with the big chimney there, and it'll be worth watching."

"No!" Kate's refusal was so sharp that he turned to eye her in astonishment. "Oh, but thank you for offering to take me, Uncle," she continued hastily, conscious of being abrupt.

"That's all right," Sam smiled. "I was only thinking you might be interested. After the Chemical Works, Bankdam's the tallest chimney in Ramsfield, and you won't often have the opportunity of seeing a chimney of that size being felled."

"They're *felling* it?" Kate's tone was quite different.

"Yes, and it's a very tricky job," said Sam. "The lower part has to drop between two six-storey buildings, and the top into a narrow lane with cottages on each side. Of course they're evacuating the houses as a precautionary measure."

Kate eyed him. "Could I come with you after all, Uncle? It sounds so thrilling."

Sam sighed. "Women!" he remarked. "They'll change their minds from one minute to another. All right, Kate, I'll pick you up about two-fifteen."

Beyond the Cemetery and the Regal Cinema he left Barnsley Road, to enter Highthwaite Road, tooting the horn immediately when, seventy or eighty yards ahead, he saw a clergyman stooping to open a gate.

"I want a word with your father, Kate," he explained.

"And I want a word with him, too," the Rev. Alonso Dyson's daughter remarked ominously. "He told me he wouldn't be home for lunch to-day."

As he slowed down, Sam wound down the window at his side. On the telephone he had previously thanked his brother-in-law for those good offices whose effect had been to alarm Mr. Sykes considerably, but now he wished to express gratitude in person, and did so as soon as his niece went indoors.

"It was a pleasure, my dear Sam." Alonso Dyson was

77

smiling broadly. "Although one of my outstanding regrets is that neither you nor Clem Roebuck was present to view the consternation on the old devil's face when, with artistry, no small imagination, and some palpable misinterpretation of the law, I outlined the scale of damages for which he might be mulcted if he proceeded with his avowed purpose. My other regret is that I am denied the pleasure of debating with my singularly narrow-minded colleagues of the cloth the ethics of my conduct in the matter. But don't misunderstand me, my dear Sam . . . I share with them much of their prejudice against divorce. Where I differ is in that I hold divorce is not only permissible but strongly to be advocated in certain cases, of which young Illingworth's was one. There, in my opinion, the somewhat unconventional means I applied wholly justified the ends I was seeking."

Sam was grinning. "Before long, Alonso, you'll be forced to seek a third profession."

This remark had an uncommon effect upon the Rev. Alonso Dyson. The rather saturnine smile which had been playing about his lips vanished. His eyes began to glow hotly and, had he been clad appropriately, he would have represented a militant Savonarola as he extended his arm skywards.

"My superior in God, the Vicar of Ramsfield, joined by the Bishop's chaplain, has already hinted it might be expedient if I sought pastures new," he said. "Oh, most friendly they were, my dear Sam. But I was less so, and unless I am grievously mistaken these gentlemen are now thoroughly convinced that they will have the fight of a lifetime on their hands should any attempt be concerted to tamper with either my priesthood or the place in which I exercise my curacy. Before they withdrew I allowed them to become cognisant that my knowledge of ecclesiastical law —which as a precautionary measure I have been studying of late—is fully comprehensive now as that of common, in which I have not been without my triumphs."

Sam burst into laughter. "You're a Tartar, Alonso, but you're doing a grand job. There's plenty of people have lots to thank you for by all I hear, and you can add Clem Roebuck to the list. He's very grateful indeed to you."

Fixing his brother-in-law with an unwavering eye, the Rev. Alonso Dyson referred to one "job" he was at present engaged upon, the fitting-out of a girls' room at the Parish Church Mission on the Island. With gifts already received,

78

this project could be completed if further funds were available to buy a sewing-machine, ping-pong table, and certain laundry equipment. The cost of these would not exceed forty pounds.

Perceiving the trend, Sam's jaw dropped. "Nay dammit, Alonso," he expostulated, "I'm not wanting to shove anything unfairly on to Clem, but if you're demanding forty quid for what you've done, surely he's the chap you should tackle."

"I prefer to relieve rich men of their ill-gotten gains," his brother-in-law observed blandly. "And I prefer also to deal with principals."

"Hey!" Sam pointed. "You get the idea out of your noddle that I'm all that rich, and not so much of the 'ill-gotten gains' stuff, either. And how the deuce am I a principal?"

"Who instructed me?" the Rev. Alonso Dyson barked.

"Well, I did," Sam admitted. "But——"

The curate rubbed finger and thumb together. "Forty pounds, my dear Sam, or . . . or I might be compelled to review the advice I have recently given."

Sam snorted as he pulled out his wallet. But the expression of outrage on his face was entirely assumed for, apart from being extremely fond of his eccentric brother-in-law, he could not but admire a man who had sacrificed so much for his beliefs. He was due, anyhow, for another charitable donation.

"I've made a mistake," he growled. "Before long you'll be in quod, Alonso. That's what's in your cards for the future."

Smiling sunnily, the Rev. Alonso Dyson folded four ten-pound Bank of England notes into a tight wad. These he placed carefully into an ancient leather purse which he stowed away in the trousers pocket of a shiny and threadbare, but neatly patched, suit. As he did so he remarked with overwhelming satisfaction that now he had twenty-five pounds in hand to launch a fund for ailing mothers.

"Clem Roebuck was kind enough," he explained, "to write out a cheque for fifteen pounds when I approached him earlier this morning."

Sam swallowed. "You'd got fifteen pounds out of Clem before you spoke to me? If you have, it's false pretences, you blasted twister. And where did you get the other ten pounds from?" He named the least likely source he could think of: "Ezra Sykes?"

79

The Rev. Alonso Dyson inclined his head. "As a matter of fact, yes," he said calmly. "Unhappily, my dear Sam, through some confusion of thought, Mr. Sykes erroneously believed I deemed it my duty to acquaint the Illingworths with the charge he had passed on to me about their son."

"You got ten pounds out of *him*?" Sam said with awe.

His brother-in-law's face clouded. "Trifling, I realize. But I felt that that represented the limit to which I could push my man, knowing him and having regard to the insecurity of my position."

Sam shook his head. "Well, Alonso lad, cheat and swindler though you are, there's a sublime touch about you."

Before the brothers-in-law parted, Mr. Dyson expressed the opinion that the forty pounds so generously subscribed would bring the donor a step forward on the difficult track rich men must follow if they desired to attain the gates of heaven. He added that, in so far as it was within his power, Sam should be granted further opportunities to insure for the hereafter.

At the Market Approach end of Teazle Street, his niece Kate sitting alongside him, Sam turned left past the statue of Queen Victoria instead of to the more familiar right. They were then in Huddersfield Road, a few hundred yards along which, just short of the long humped rise crossing over the railway, were the yard and store-places of Matthew Roebuck & Son, Ltd., Steeplejacks. From the middle of the railway bridge beyond, the Huddersfield road stretched out before them, less built up for the moment until it approached Scargate, while away to the left was the Island, between the canal and the river, its hills and little valleys so close-packed with dirt-grimed erections, dwellings, factories and workshops, that hardly a square yard of open space was visible.

"Oh, your Aunt Milly wouldn't miss the Royal this week for anything, love," Sam was laughing. "But that's what I think about amateurs—you go mainly to watch how people you know can act and sing."

The Ramsfield Amateurs had chosen *The Quaker Girl* that year, with Lois Roebuck in the leading part, and he was taking his wife that evening.

"Oh, but I don't think it's all curiosity, Uncle Sam," Kate demurred.

Ahead were cross-roads, from opposite sides of which two very large public houses faced each other, the Stag and the

Knur and Spell. Here, slowing, he swung right and then sharply left, up a steep private road leading to the immense properties of Simeon Crowther & Sons, Ltd. The chimney to be felled stretched upwards so far that its top projected beyond the stark line of rising ground extending far behind the mills; some distance from this chimney was a new one, short by comparison.

"After to-day, that new one is all that Bankdam Mills will have, Kate," Sam said. "Since they've electrified they only use steam now for dyeing, finishing, heating and so on."

Instructions must have been left regarding the visitor, for, outside the block of offices, a commissionaire saluted smartly and, without inquiring into the callers' business, opened the end section of a lofty iron gate and led them through a brightly illuminated tunnel.

"Go straight over yonder, Mr. Pilling," he said. "And if the young lady wants a real ring-side view of it when it tumbles she can get it if she can manage to do a bit of scrambling up there, well over to the right, up the hill."

"She's young enough," Sam laughed.

The mill-yard beyond was tidy and clean. Overhead, from the ventilators of single-storied buildings, steamy vapour was escaping, and the air was filled with sound, the clatter made by hundreds of looms and the continuous hum of rather more silent machinery.

As Sam and his niece, following the directions received, walked along a narrow canyon between two six-storied buildings, one of which was crowned by a massive clock-tower, they were hailed by Jim Roebuck, who was wearing a very soiled boiler suit.

"I see you've got here, Uncle Sam," he said cheerfully. 'And brought the young 'un with you."

"When you're older yourself, Jim," Kate remarked with dignity, "you'll realize that a girl is years and years older than her actual age by comparison with a boy."

Jim, greatly amused, would have ruffled her hair had he not remembered his hands were filthy. Instead he contented himself by winking at his uncle.

"Anyway, let's get on," he said. "It's just round the corner here, and we shan't be long now."

The chimney of Bankdam Mills was of brick, round, and tapered towards its far-away summit. At its base the brick-work was five feet in thickness, and a whole half-circle, to a height of six feet, had been cut out on the side to which the chimney was destined to fall. The gap was filled with stout timbering, which for the moment supported the chimney.

"No, it doesn't particularly matter what kind of wood we use so long as it's sound," Jim was explaining to Kate. "You can understand why it must burn absolutely evenly . . . if we used different kinds of wood, say ash *and* pine, it could topple anyhow."

Mr. Roebuck and a cluster of his men were there. The master steeplejack was carrying an immense burden of responsibility, for only a few feet of error in the line along which the chimney should fall would cause damage to the extent of tens of thousands of pounds. But he was perfectly calm, issuing his orders quietly and very clearly. Indeed, no doubt recently relieved about the course his daughter's divorce would now take, he walked over to Sam for a few light-hearted words while his men were piling kindling and old and greasy weft bobbins around the foot of the timbering. It spoke much for his improved state of mind that he, a rabid supporter of Ramsfield Town, spoke jokingly about the team's away defeat at Maine Road the previous Saturday, which had knocked them out of the Cup.

"Of course the ground was hard," he went on, much more seriously. "And we're at our best when——"

"Come down to Swanroyd with me some time, Clem, and I'll show you what real football is," said Sam. "Soccer, ugh! Now me to you and then you to me. Pirouetting about like ballet dancers——"

"What about rugger?" the master steeplejack demanded. "All brute force and ignorance."

Both passionate protagonists, the argument might have proceeded for some time. But Vincent Uttley, throwing aside an empty five-gallon kerosene tin with whose contents he had been soaking the already highly combustible material which would soon be lighted, caught his employer's eye, and nodded.

Mr. Roebuck at once spoke to a gentleman who was standing a dozen paces away, a man of middle height whose dark hair was streaked with grey.

"We're ready, Mr. Crowther," he said.

Simjoss Crowther, who four years before had succeeded his father as Master of Bankdam, raised his hand in response and, in turn, signalled to an engineer waiting in readiness across the stone-setted yard. Two minutes later the mill's syren blew piercingly and, as the buzz of machinery died down, many hundreds of workpeople streamed out.

The fire round the timbering was blazing fiercely; close to the foot of the chimney, within two or three feet of which they would remain until the last moment, were Clem Roebuck and his foreman steeplejack, their heads craned back to watch for any indication of a crack in the old brickwork stretching above them, their ears alert for the sound of the first creak.

"There!" said Clem, unhurriedly examining his watch before looking round. "Ten to fifteen minutes from now, Mr. Crowther," he called out. "And everybody away from here, please."

Sam's shoulder was touched. "Well, how are you, Sam?" Simjoss Crowther asked. "And what about our seeking a good vantage point? It seems appropriate we should watch it fall together, doesn't it?"

"Perhaps," Sam murmured.

He looked round for Kate. She was still with Jim, smiling up at him as he made some remark. As for Jim, who seemed for the moment to have lost his occasional facial twitch, he had in his sunken eyes that indulgent twinkle which grown-up young men reserve for young schoolgirls they like, creatures it pleases them to tease. "Right you are, Simjoss," said Sam, satisfied his niece was in safe hands.

"This way then," said Simjoss Crowther.

Together they climbed a steep scar at the back of the mill, one a successful bookmaker and the other the most influential man in Ramsfield, the richest manufacturer of the district, and richer still through his marriage with the only daughter of the owner of the vast Chemical Works on the Manchester Road side of the town.

"How will this do?" Mr. Crowther inquired.

"A fine bird's eye view," Sam replied, a shade stiltedly.

They were well disposed towards each other, these two, but between them there would always be a barrier not of their own making. It was the old, old story of a will. Simjoss Crowther and Sam Pilling were both great-grandsons of Simeon Crowther, the founder of Bankdam, and each of them shared the same grandmother, old Simeon's daughter, Mary. Their grandmother had two children: Simjoss Crowther's mother and Sam Pilling's father, and Mary Pilling, because her son had married against her wishes, left her fortune of a hundred and twenty thousand pounds to her daughter and not a penny-piece to her son. Even then this gross injustice might have been subsequently remedied by a friendly arrangement, but Sam's mother, furious that her husband had been disinherited, had been sufficiently foolish, as Sam had often heard, to use the fatal words "undue influence" in the presence of the Crowthers. After that no accommodation was possible.

"It's strange, isn't it, Simjoss, to reflect on what might have happened if my father had buckled to when he was put into the mill in my great-grandfather's day," Sam started off again. "I could have been here as co-chairman, equal with you, instead of being Pilling who always pays."

Simjoss Crowther nodded. "I've often thought that when I've seen you, Sam," he said.

"Not that I've any regrets," Sam insisted.

Simjoss Crowther's dark eyes were on him. "Of course not, Sam. You've done magnificently, and entirely on your own."

"No, I can't complain," Sam agreed.

Steadfastly he stared ahead. No one on earth could have been more proud of his success than he, and occasionally he feared he did not quite conceal it. But as he remembered many things . . . family makeshifts of his youth, the sorry schooling he had had, and above all the fact that here he was with his cousin, a Crowther of Bankdam, a family of power and probity respectfully regarded by everyone—as opposed to the hail-fellow-well-met attitude which is the bookie's lot from all classes . . . his eyes began to mist.

This weakness was a damned silly one, as he told himself fiercely a few moments afterwards.

Bankdam Mills were in the angle between the Huddersfield road and the Bradford road, both of which were black with spectators. As the tall chimney began to sway cries went up, and then there was silence as the inexorable movement gradually increased, a motion which nothing could halt, which would lay a thousand or more tons of rubble on the ground. From the top of the stack, as it leaned farther, a dark cloud eddied out as though coal dust had been shovelled on to a still living furnace below; for a while, through thirty degrees perhaps, the chimney remained whole, a slender cigarette toppling, and then it broke in three parts: amid a thunderous roar the base telescoped almost on itself; the middle portion dropped neatly between dye-houses and wool-sheds; the top, with massive overhanging cornice, flew through the air, to land between trim rows of cottages with no more hurt to them that what was done to the paintwork of garden gates by splinters of mortar and brick.

About a quarter of an hour later, Kate, eyes radiant, found her uncle.

"Uncle Sam, would you mind very much if I didn't ride back with you?" she said. "You see Jim says I can stay here a bit longer if I like, and he'll run me on to their office then. And afterwards to home."

Sam laughed. "As a matter of fact I've been wondering what to do with you, love. Mr. Crowther's asked me in, and if we get yarning together. . . ."

She blushed as soon as she realized what she had said. "Then it'll be nice for both of us, won't it?"

"Mmm," Sam murmured as, making a not too convincing excuse, she ran away, to hide her confusion he suspected. "Well, I'm hanged," he thought.

Within thirty seconds he saw embarrassment elsewhere, in the swarthy face of Vincent Uttley, who intercepted him. But, however awkward he might have felt, the steeplejack's resolute mouth was indicative that he meant to say what he had to say.

"Mr. Pilling," he blurted out, "you wouldn't have any idea where Maggie Batten might be, would you? I've found out she's never gone back to where her married sister lives in Castleford, and the boss hasn't any inkling of where she could be."

"I haven't a notion, Vincent," Sam replied.

Vincent Uttley nodded dejectedly. "Nay, I just wondered, Mr. Pilling, whether she'd ever talked to you about friends or relatives elsewhere. She'd always a very soft spot for you, and that being so she might have done."

"No," said Sam, tugging an ear-lobe. "Of course she always thought of Stonewood as being her home more than anywhere else."

The foreman steeplejack's passionate eyes darkened. "Aye," he snapped. "No," he continued at once, anticipating a protest, "I'm not blaming the boss. Anyroad, I'd better be off to see my chaps have got all our gear together."

Abruptly he turned away. Sam again murmured: "Mmm," before starting off for Simeon Crowther & Sons' range of offices.

* * *

One of the latest scandals in Ramsfield concerned another cousin of Sam Pilling, James Wainwright, senior partner of Ramsden Lister and Wainwright, solicitors, and the principal shareholder in Wimpenny Eastwood, Ltd., printers and bookbinders, a considerable business which had become Wainwright property through his grandmother, an Eastwood.

More than six months before there had been vague rumours linking the name of the plump, short and middle-aged Mr. Wainwright, who had always been regarded as a typical bachelor, with a willowy, extremely intricately-coiffeured mannequin employed by Rafe Bottomley at Madame Gladys Shire's. The origins of the young woman were well known—before taking up the post she had been a winder at Northern Viscose, Ltd.

Since then there had been rapid and quite startling developments. Hildred Pickersgill, a nondescript individual on a weekly wage in the despatching department of Wimpenny Eastwood, Ltd., had suddenly blossomed out as a director of that company. Simultaneously he had married the striking gown-modeller, the couple taking up residence in one of the best houses in Roydlea. From that time it was noticed that wherever Mr. and Mrs. Hildred Pickersgill might be, there also was James Wainwright. With complete unanimity Ramsfield now held that Mrs. Pickersgill was the solicitor's mistress, and that her husband was complacent about the situation.

As yet the liaison was something of a novelty, and it was therefore natural, on the Amateurs' Tuesday night performance at the Theatre Royal, that the eyes of a large crowd should be turned towards the trio as an attendant found them their seats in the stalls. Unfortunately Milly Pilling missed this, as she was still in the foyer with Sam, who had paused to discuss a flutter in armament shares with Mr. William Pobjoy, the stockbroker, a debonair spark who had passed on many of his qualities to his much-married daughter Carrie, now Mrs. Dale Watkinson.

The Quaker Girl was put over with the usual competence of the Ramsfield Amateurs, and with the final curtain the audience rose to pay enthusiastic tribute. Lois Roebuck received three bouquets, and, to her Aunt Milly at least, it seemed that the least expensive of these gave her the greatest delight.

"Sam, who is Lois laughing and nodding at?" Milly hissed. "I can't see."

"Neither can I, love."

"Well, stand on your toes," Milly said. "Oh, do be quick, dear."

Sam made an effort. "No," he announced. "Why don't you climb on your seat?"

Wondering if he had been heard, Milly looked about her. "Of *all* the things to say," she said.

As she began to edge along the line of stalls in the train of others, she continued to gaze in the same general direction in which, as she now recalled, Lois had glanced quite frequently during the performance. To her chagrin she was not rewarded with even a suspicion as to who the giver of the bouquet might be, and all she could conclude was that it must be someone of limited means.

When Sam rejoined her after struggling into his overcoat in the crush round the cloakroom, they bumped into his cousin James.

"Ah, Sam and . . . er . . . Milly," James Wainwright said, button-holing them. "And how are you both keeping? Well, I trust. And, by the way . . ." smilingly he drew his companions into the tight little circle, "have you . . . er . . . met Mr. and Mrs. Pickersgill? Hildred is now one of my directors at the printing works and is making immense improvements there."

"No, I don't think we've met before." Milly acknowledged the couple distantly.

"How do you do," said Sam. "I've seen Mrs. Pickersgill before, of course, knocking about the town, but I don't think her husband."

Hearing his "of course," Milly quivered. Previous to that she had been examining with ill-concealed distaste thin, black-pencilled lines used by Mrs. Pickersgill in lieu of eyebrows, and had decided that if ever Nancy's proneness to over-lavish make-up extended to plucking there would be the father and mother of a row.

"And how did you enjoy the show, Mrs. Pilling?" Mrs. Pickersgill inquired.

"Oh, quite good," Milly replied.

The late Herman Wainwright had, by his astuteness, prised the Ramsden Listers out of the dominant interest in a firm founded by them four generations before. James Wainwright was far from being the man his father had been but he could recognize storm signals.

"Well, I think we must leave you, Sam," he said. "Mrs. Pickersgill is kindness itself to me and . . ." he licked his lips

87

appreciatively, "and there has been a hint that I may be invited to partake in an agreeable supper."

Milly, on her husband's arm, was responsible for a most extraordinary observation as they walked through the crowded vestibule, which made him chuckle.

"If I'd any disinfectant," she said, "I'd like to wash out my mouth."

Driving down to the theatre, the conversation of the Pillings had exclusively concerned Archie's twenty-first, which was to be celebrated in the middle of the following month by a big affair at the George. On the way home the talk was exclusively about James Wainwright and the Hildred Pickersgills, with Mrs. Pickersgill in the forefront.

"Of course she's awfully smart and terribly good-looking," said Milly, when the car was held up against the Manchester Road traffic lights. "Don't you think so, dear?"

Sam was staring to his left, into the open doorway of a mill in which he could see gleaming textile machinery in motion.

"Yes, I suppose she is," he murmured.

"Oh, come, Sam," Milly protested, somehow sounding disappointed. "Surely you know a well-groomed woman, don't you?"

Moving off, he gave her more attention. "To tell you the truth," he said, "I didn't take all that notice of her. What I had in my mind's eye was a picture of James making love to her while that milk-and-water chap Pickersgill was washing up the pots."

Between the Tudor-style fish-and-chip shop, briskly trading, and the gentlemen's lavatory opposite the entrance to Knowlbank Road, Milly tried again

"No, seriously, Sam," she said. "There's something very . . . very distinguished about her, isn't there?"

Sam smiled. "There's that slinky walk to begin with."

"So you *did* notice that?" Milly asked sharply.

"I should have had to be blind not to," Sam grinned. "And more chaps besides me, if the number of necks I spotted being twisted round was any criterion."

Milly was guilty of a most unladylike snort. "Polygamous!" she announced. "That's what it's in the nature of all men to be, even when they're decrepit."

"You know, love," his voice was solemn, "you know I don't think you've taken to Mrs. Hildred Pickersgill. She wasn't swivelling come-hither eyes at me, was she?"

There was a silvery laugh. "It wouldn't have worried me

if she had," Milly said. "Thank goodness, I'm not one of those silly creatures who are jealous if another woman so much as looks at her husband. Isn't it *ridiculous*, Sam, when they're that way?"

His thoughts on another remark she had made, Sam did not reply about that. To begin with he hummed a phrase from the *Gondoliers* and then said: "If you're referring to me as decrepit, Milly, you'll do well to withhold any criticism until I've had a few more weeks' exercising on my rowing-machine. Between ourselves I'm improving very nicely lately."

"Oh, I didn't mean you, Sam."

"Mind you," Sam admitted judicially, "I'm not yet in the same state of fitness as I was when you and I regularly brought youngsters into the world. But, by Jingo, I feel it in my bones that I shan't be long before I am."

As far as the bus stop in Penny Lane, the sounds in the car were only those made by the driver's spirited humming, the purr of the engine, and the hiss of the tyres. Very carefully Milly moved, and, taking advantage of the greenish-yellow glow from several lamp-posts, surreptitiously surveyed her husband's face. Reassured eventually, she broke into his blithesome carolling to speak about Nancy, who had gone to a dinner dance in Huddersfield with a young man from Heckmondwike, or it might have been Wakefield. She was anxious about the roads, whether there might be ice on them.

"No, they'll be all right," Sam said as he swung in home, but on the heels of this comforting observation swore furiously, slamming down the brake pedal. "What damned fool's left his car there, bang across the gates? Oh, it's Alec Murgatroyd's . . . wait till I see the young idiot."

Fuming, he backed away from the Mercedes Benz drophead coupé, and then ran slowly up Moorheaton Drive to the top gateway, where he turned in. After passing the front of Stonewood, he drove across the paved court between the two houses, and then headed towards the garage. His headlights lit up the unsteady legs of Frank Thornton, who had just erratically garaged Archie Pilling's sports convertible; the brilliant white beam also illuminated the dried blood on the face of the vehicle's owner, who was leaning against another friend, Alec Murgatroyd. All three young men had had a glass too many.

"It's all right, Mother," Archie shouted. "A wash and a couple of pieces of sticking plaster will——"

"Archie!" Milly cried, scrambling out so anxiously that Frank Thornton, who would never have dreamed of doing such a thing in his normal state, whistled appreciatively on sighting a pair of very pretty legs. "Come indoors with me at once, Archie," his mother continued. "Whatever have you been doing?"

"Just an alter . . . a row with a gentleman who was insane enough to dot me one on the boko. But . . ." he went off into a vinous chuckle, "but you should have seen him when I'd finished with him. Done your heart good, Ma."

Milly was inspecting her son's injuries. "Where is he?"

"The mortuary, I expect," Archie replied.

"What!" Milly gasped.

Archie waved a negligent hand. "We left him for dead, Ma. Poor chap."

So far Sam had not spoken, but now he intervened decisively.

"You and Archie go into the house, Frank," he said. "That way you'll both be able to help each other to stand up. As for you, Alec, I think you're more the master of yourself than the other two—fetch Archie's bus out again and put it back so that I can get in."

The various parties went their several ways. When the garage door was rolled back again, Sam had a further few words with the son of Walter Murgatroyd, head of Murgatroyd Conveyors Ltd., and a fellow director of the Hornets.

"And now you'd better let me know where you three have been, and how it comes about that Archie's been scrapping," he snapped.

Additional lights flicked on at the back of Glenfield, from landing window, a bathroom and a bedroom. In the suffused glow the old and the younger man were able to see each other clearly.

"Well, sir, the trouble started in the Vaults——"

"And finished in Market Square, I suppose," Sam growled. "Where were the police?"

"They were about somewhere, I believe," Alec Murgatroyd said with some delicacy. "But thanks to friendly co-operation we were all hidden in the taximen's shelter, Archie's opponent—a new House Surgeon at the Hospital—and his associates included."

Sam was struggling not to grin. "What was it all about?"

As strongly built as Archie Pilling, Alec Murgatroyd had

a cherubic, choir boy-like face, which was largely responsible for his parents' firm belief that when he sinned he had always been led into it by others. Nevertheless he was Captain of Ramsfield Rugger's First XV, and as such was both respected by his team mates and feared by them whenever their play fell below the standard he desired.

Almost an hour later, after supper, when the first-born of the Pillings had been tucked into bed by his mother, with two hot-water bottles outside him and aspirin and hot milk inside him, Milly, who had been for the same length of time apprehensive as to what her husband would say, was startled when he suddenly chortled.

"Do you know what Archie and the young doctor had the fight about, love?" he asked. "Whether or not a try scored by England against Scotland was offside."

Milly was in the middle of discreetly pulling up her dress to warm her knees at the drawing-room fire. The house was cosy but she had got thoroughly chilled at the theatre.

"I don't see why that's so funny, Sam," she said. "Archie's been both to Twickenham and Murrayfield, and they might have been there at the same time."

Tears streaming, Sam doubled with joy. "Not on this occasion, love. The match they were arguing about was in 1881. Can you beat it?"

"I hope," Milly said severely, "you'll not let Archie know how amused you are by his brawling in public. Degrading, I call it."

"I presume you've told him so," Sam said.

Lips slightly compressed, Milly slowly nodded. "He'll not forget in a hurry the scolding I've given him," she said.

Sam picked up the evening paper, which he had not read. It served also as a most convenient screen.

CHAPTER FOUR

An **important** anniversary in a young man's life for which a very gay gathering is to be held, should banish animosity from his home, and in the past few days this had been so at the Pillings.

On the Friday morning of her elder son's twenty-first birthday, Milly rose more lightheartedly and, pulling back the bedroom curtains, announced to her husband that there was a covering of snow.

"It's only a dusting, though, and it won't affect anybody who's a longish way to drive. And," she definitely giggled, "it certainly won't prevent Laura's guests turning up for the smart bridge-party she's giving this afternoon. Oh, and isn't she cock-a-hoop. Do you know, Sam, she's done it at last. Mrs. Law Watkinson is coming down from Outham for it."

"What a triumph," Sam grunted.

"Well, it's not exactly the sort of thing I'd fret about," Milly said. "All the same Mrs. Law Watkinson *is* somebody."

Sam had designs of his own, and referred to the week-end outing to a racing establishment he had for so long ardently contemplated.

"The days are lengthening now, Milly," he went on. "What about us going a fortnight to-morrow? The Hornets are playing away at Hull and I thought we might watch the match and then drive up to Bridlington. We could stay at that nice old-fashioned hotel near the harbour you've always liked."

"I'd love to, dear."

Sam rubbed his hands. "On the Sunday morning we could potter about and enjoy the sea breezes before driving over to Malton—I already know the chap there will want us to have lunch at his place. That suit, love?"

Milly was too busy checking through a pile of peach-coloured underclothing in a drawer to do other than smile and nod, but nevertheless she was not too preoccupied to notice her husband's activities. When he left the bedroom a couple of minutes later, naked except for gym shoes and a pair of white shorts, she frowned slightly, as if perplexed. Shortly after that the now familiar thump-thump, in-out, started in the boxroom.

Family breakfast that morning was lively, very much as it might have been a year or so ago, excepting that the mistress of the house every now and then went off into a brown study. Archie was pleased with his presents: a 35-mm. camera, dress studs, and a gold wrist-watch on an expanding gold bracelet.

Milly sought out her husband when her son had left for the office, and Nancy was in the drawing-room playing Noel Gay's:

> *The sun has got his hat on,*
> *He's coming out to-day.*

As was his custom, Sam was scanning the morning papers before leaving for business.

"You know how you can get the most fantastic ideas, dear," she said brightly. "Well . . . well, I've had such a silly one. And it's all because of this exercising you're doing."

Sam gave her his gravest attention. "Yes, Milly dear."

Now that a start had been made, she should have proceeded more easily. It proved the reverse.

"Sometimes," she faltered, "well . . . well, you've made what I thought were quite queer remarks. And then there's this training you're doing here—and that heel-and-toe walking for a mile you mentioned once, whatever it may be, after you've done eighteen holes at golf . . . well . . ."

"Sit down, dear," Sam said very considerately. "Aye," he sighed, "I thought I'd kept it dark better than I have. You see I didn't want to bring up the subject again until I was in prime condition."

Milly's mouth was dry. "What subject?" she croaked.

"Starting another family, you remember?" Sam said, smiling at her with deep affection. "To tell you the truth, I'm . . ." He grabbed his handkerchief, prelude to a bout of ferocious coughing which reverberated in the room and left him to emerge with streaming eyes. "Excuse me, I don't know what the devil caused that . . . a crumb, maybe. But as I was saying, dear . . . to tell you the truth, I'm aching now to hear little feet pattering about the house."

His proposed partner in this venture had risen abruptly. "You're trying to stuff me up, I know. But it's not nice and it's horrible when you talk about 'prime condition,' as if we were animals at stud. And it's all nonsense anyway."

Regretfully Sam shook his head, as if upset about her wild outburst. "Now calm yourself, dear," he soothed her. "And let me tell you I agree that it isn't pleasant to deal with the situation as if we were beasts of the field. But if you'll forgive me dwelling on it a second or two more, the fact is that no vet. would pass me as capable of producing first-rate stock, not yet. For that matter, after all the anxiety you've had . . ." he stared hard at her, "I think you'd do with toning up yourself. What about Burgundy regularly?"

"Why . . . why, it's ludicrous," Milly gasped.

Smiling benignly, Sam rose to chuck her under the chin. "Tell you what, let's leave it for the moment like that," he said, humouring her. "Just that I'm stuffing you up. Then later on——"

93

Cheeks flaming, Milly faced him resolutely from the door. "There's going to be no 'later on.' And anyhow you don't mean it."

Slowly Sam smiled. "I'm not arguing, dear. Not *now*."

Afterwards, in so far as he was able, he kissed her good-bye exactly in the same manner as always in the morning. But as he walked across to the garage, and as he drove out, he kept the closest guard on his expression, suspecting—quite rightly as it happened—that he was under observation from the house throughout. Lower down Moorheaton Drive, however, this iron control was not necessary, and he laughed himself silly.

After parking the Bentley in Market Square, Sam headed towards the Town Hall and into Lowerhouse Street, where the grin which had been continually on his face since his laughter exhausted itself was displaced by unease. Midway along Lowerhouse Street, previously glancing fore and aft, he dived into a dingy shop whose windows were packed with specifics and appliances of special appeal to ladies who wished either to avoid distress or dispel it, or to gentlemen suffering from kidney complaints or—in two very dissimilar forms, the medical and the vulgar—the itch.

On emerging, sweating freely, he bent to fumble with his shoelace while reconnoitring the street, and then with long strides tore away from the unsavoury place.

With some natures the memory of the shoddy and squalid can linger surprisingly long, and Sam, with Fred Lumb and Hilda Schofield in succession, had done an hour's hard work at the office before he had completely shaken off the depressing effects of that call in Lowerhouse Street. But then he began to enjoy himself. For almost ten minutes he talked on the telephone with most gratifying results to a horse-breeding and training establishment at Malton, and then rang up to Bridlington to book accommodation for himself and his wife.

"And now for that business of keeping Milly wondering," he thought, chuckling to himself. "And, by Christopher, it's working, for she hasn't been bringing Gilbert up every minute lately as she was prone to do."

From his jacket pocket he took out a bottle filled with white tablets. The label on it was all that he could have desired and, laughter creases round his eyes, he read the claims made for:

94

WONDER SHOTS—FOR GENTLEMEN

The Miracle Worker
Restore Youthful Impulses
Recommended by the Medical Profession
Prepared in our own Laboratories
To the secret formula of
Dr. Oleg Wassiheimer
Whatever your Age

YOU CAN BE VITAL AGAIN WITH WONDER SHOTS

"These are going to rattle her when she finds 'em," he said, grinning. "When the time is ripe I'll leave them about somewhere . . . maybe in my handkerchief drawer. Aye. . . ."

A further refinement suggested itself to him. In the private lavatory off his office he flushed away half the tablets to prove he had been dipping into them extensively, corking up the remainder. He also decided that, before going home for lunch, he would pop into Ainleys' the Chemists in Teazle Street. There he intended to buy a few small lozenges of a very innocent nature, for consumption when appropriate.

*   *   *

Archie Pilling's twenty-first party was going with that unmistakable swing attained only when a number of people are really having a good time.

Wearing an exquisite, ivory lace dress which revealed soft, rounded arms and smooth, satiny shoulders, the mother of the most important person of the evening stood holding her husband's arm in the doorway of the ballroom.

"Here are Lois and Cora, Sam," she said, as, to the strains of a first-rate band imported from Manchester, her nieces glided past in the arms of two young men. "And doesn't Kate look pretty to-night? She's over there, dancing with Jim."

"Ah!" Sam grinned. "Wait until she passes."

With an exuberance a shade overdone, Milly was waving to Alderman Hirst's daughter, a somewhat tight-faced young woman who was dancing with her *fiancé*, Augustus Firth. Bee Hirst was Nancy's best friend, and the truth was that neither Sam nor his wife cared greatly for her. To make amends for what she could not help, Milly tended to be a little fulsome whenever she saw her.

Now she had to confide again. "I don't think Nancy would ever have been like she has if Bee hadn't got engaged," she said. "Of course Bee naturally wants to be with Augustus as often as possible."

"I suppose so," nodded Sam, eyeing the circling couples.

Milly guessed what he was looking for. "Now, dear," she said, an air of wifely sternness about her, "there's to be no more of your elephantine teasing of Kate about Jim. I've known for ages she'd a crush on him, but I'd enough sense to pretend not to notice. Girls of her age are very sensitive, and though she laughs at what you say I think she'd nearly drop if Jim heard you—you see he just regards her as . . . as a child almost . . . and that would make it so much worse for her."

"I'll stop it then," said Sam, crestfallen, although a moment later he recovered a little. "But, hold on, Kate isn't exactly a child in arms, is she?"

"She's not sixteen yet."

Sam's tone was sly. "Aye, but you see I can remember you very well when you were only seventeen. That was when we got married."

The triple row of pearls on his wife's bosom, hitherto backed to perfection by creamy-white skin, began to stand out boldly as that background changed to scarlet.

Sam smiled at her confusion. "I can remember those days as if they were yesterday, love," he said, in the mood to reminisce. "Just before the war it was, and not long afterwards I was one of Kitchener's men, in a slouch hat from the Boer War, a blue dress jacket, khaki trousers, and black boots too little for me. Didn't we look guys until there was enough proper clothing to go round? No wonder we called ourselves Fred Karno's Army."

That reminded her of the broken catch on her husband's Victory Medal, which he would wear on the breast of his lounge suit at the forthcoming annual reunion of the King's Own Yorkshire Light Infantry.

"Yes, so it is—a week on Wednesday," said Sam. "And if you'll leave it somewhere to be repaired. . . ."

"I'll try a jeweller," said Milly.

"Yes, you were only seventeen then, love," Sam repeated, fondly eyeing her up and down.

In return Milly eyed him stonily. Since morning she had

been a trifle *distraite,* and now, the more he insisted upon her youthfulness, the more suspicious she was becoming about his motives.

*   *   *

The office of PILLING ALWAYS PAYS had been very busy on the day on which two important events took place, the departure to Greenock of the *Queen Mary* from the ship-builder's yard and, on this the third day of the new flat-racing season, the running of the Lincolnshire Handicap, won by Overcoat at 10/1. There was the usual convivial gathering of customers in Sam's big room, and it was not until close upon five o'clock that these guests began to disperse. Then he and Fred Lumb thoroughly checked over the Doubles List for those clients who, with Overcoat's victory, had pulled off the first leg of the Spring Double.

This left him with reasonable time for a light meal before starting out for the annual getting together of the K.O.Y.L.I.s.

Regimental reunions can become tedious at the stage when the soaks group noisily to make a night of it, and others, whose special comrades may not have been able to be present, begin to drift away. Among the latter was Sam Pilling, and as a result he was in sight of home quite early. Shortly before half-past ten he had reached the town boundary beyond Spedding and there, to save himself nearly three miles, he left the main road, turning down to the grey bridge spanning the Ram at Holmluff. This brought him into a countrified lane on the south side of the river which, by way of the Ramsfield Golf Club, led to Swanroyd and Knowl-bank Road.

About three-quarters of a mile farther along, around the bend near the tenth hole, he came suddenly upon a car standing partly on the verge and partly on the lane.

"That's Nancy's," he ejaculated, slowing down. "I wonder if she's broken down." Just then he noticed another vehicle ahead of his daughter's, a low, powerful-looking sports car with canvas hood and mica side curtains. "Well," he muttered, as he stopped, "I don't like to interfere with a young woman's legitimate fun, but if the chap she's with happens to be that Brozik fellow, the fur's going to fly."

Leaving only his side-lights on, he began to walk forward as blazing headlamps approached. They were as yet a couple of hundred yards distant, but aided by the dipping beam, he clearly saw that the Riley was unoccupied. Shading his eyes against the oncoming lights he stepped forward again, reaching the sports car as the two persons in it were brilliantly illuminated.

In that fleeting second or so Sam perceived a great deal that any father, however much a man of the world, must take instant measures about.

Nancy's head nestled on Philip Illingworth's shoulder, his arm cradling her tightly; her topcoat was loose and, blouse partly open, her breasts were visible.

"By God!" roared Sam, wrenching open the car door with an enraged pull. "What the devil do you think you're up to, you little trollop? Out of it!"

"Daddy!" she said faintly.

The events of the next minute were confused. Nancy was bundled out of the car and Philip Illingworth, scrambling out behind her, received a smash between the eyes which sent him cartwheeling through the darkness into a ditch.

"Now get yourself buttoned up and decent—as outwardly decent as you can be," Sam growled at his daughter.

When Philip Illingworth appeared again he was holding a pair of spectacles in which both lenses had been broken. In the dim gleam from the side-lamps and the ruby glow from a rear light, it was just possible to discern in his eyes the myopic look, a little helpless and pathetic, of one denuded of much of the means of sight. But his voice was resolute enough.

"I'm sorry for this, Mr. Pilling, but——"

"Another whisper out of you and I'll crack you another one," Sam snapped.

"I shouldn't blame you if you did," Philip Illingworth admitted. "But I must say two things to you, sir. The first is that I fully realize that in my present situation I've been wantonly foolish with Nancy . . . in risking anyone's having even an inkling she was here with me."

Sam exploded. "That's it, you damned fool."

"I know, Mr. Pilling." Philip Illingworth nodded. "But if you'll allow me to go on. You see I want you to understand that it's my fault entirely."

"That's not true," Nancy said passionately. "I made him bring me."

"And now *I'm* taking you back, miss," Sam said.

"Just another thing, Mr. Pilling," Philip Illingworth persisted. "I don't know what you saw when you looked into the car . . . and I'm not making excuses. But I've got to tell you that we've been in love for a long while, really in love, sir, and this was the first time for ages we'd been alone. I think it went to our heads—it did to mine."

Sam grabbed his daughter's wrist. "If I listen to this sea-lawyer much longer I'll soon be believing I'm in the wrong. Now come on, you, or I'll damned well carry you."

Desperately Nancy resisted him. "Daddy," she cried out. "There isn't any need for you to drag me. But if you treat me as if . . . as if I were a slave, I'll kick you and scratch you and bite you every inch of the way. And I'll scream in the car every second I'm in it."

"Well, we might as well see if your word's worth anything," said Sam. "Right, then, it's a bargain."

She turned from him, and lifted her face to Philip. "Good night, darling," she said, lips quivering.

Philip Illingworth shook his head. "We'd better not, my sweet."

"All . . . all right," she said.

That was the end. Father and daughter walked back to the Bentley, not a word passing between them. Then silence was broken twice, when Sam, recalling how he would be compelled after all to return home by the long way round, was responsible for a heartfelt: "Done it," on succeeding in manoeuvring the car to face the opposite direction. And Nancy spoke shortly afterwards when, her father driving much too quickly in his temper, they sped by an Alfa Romeo in battleship grey.

"I suppose you realize Philip can't see at all well without his glasses," she said icily.

"He can drive over the side of Holmluff Bridge for all I care."

"Oh, he won't do that," she countered proudly.

On reaching the town, Sam called in at Thorntons' garage in Market Approach, which boasted a twenty-four-hour service. There he gave instructions for the Riley to be sent for.

"I don't think there's anything wrong with it," he remarked with some cunning and more or less smilingly. "I rather suspect my daughter has overflooded the carburettor, and I dare say that after this interval she'll start up with the first touch on the button."

At Glenfield, Nancy went in at the front door, her heels madly drumming. Her father drove round to the back, where he garaged the car.

Milly's face was white when her husband entered the drawing-room. Nancy, still in her outdoor things, was sitting on a straight-backed chair near the radiogram.

"Oh, Sam," said Milly. "Whatever's the matter? Nancy told me you've caught her with——"

"I didn't say *caught*, Mummy." Her daughter contradicted her very clearly. "I said I was with Philip."

"And you're going to be with him no more, my girl," Sam announced.

Nancy's cheeks flamed. "Yes, I am, and that's why I've waited until you came in. Because I want you both to know that as soon as Philip is divorced we're going to be married."

"Nancy!" Milly wailed.

"You'll marry when you've my consent," said Sam. "After you're twenty-one you can do as you please, but in the meantime you can't."

"And another thing," his daughter said feverishly, "I'm going to help him with his divorce."

Sam's eyes narrowed. "And just what do you mean by that?"

Her lips curled. "Do you imagine I shall let Philip go through one of those dreadful things lawyers arrange? With some horrible stranger in a hotel bedroom when a waiter brings tea in the morning. Of *course* I shan't. I shall be the woman Estelle cites."

Aghast, Milly had been standing, staring from husband to daughter. But at this, as though her limbs were fluid, she sank into a chair.

"Nancy, love, you mustn't talk that crazy way," she begged.

Sam jerked his head. "I think you'd better go upstairs, Nancy," he said. "For your mother's sake if not for mine."

Gathering her coat about her, and picking up her bag, Nancy stooped to her mother.

"Don't worry, Mummy, because everything will be all right," she said, kissing her affectionately. "It's only because you're a little old-fashioned, darling. But I thought it was only fair to let you both know."

That hardly improved Sam's chances of soothing his wife, but in just over twenty minutes she was slightly less distraught.

"I'll go up to her, Sam," she said, gallantly sniffing back her tears. "She looked so terribly desperate, didn't she?"

Sam was in mind to point out that their daughter, instead of being desperate, was in a desperate rage: because she was utterly spoilt and had been thwarted. But he said nothing of the kind.

As soon as he had satisfied himself that his wife was safely upstairs, he went into the hall and rang up a Wharfedale number, leaving a message. Happily the call came through while he was still alone. A conversation followed, brusque at one end and crisp at the other. The appointment with Philip Illingworth was arranged for the following afternoon.

Frills were entirely missing at that meeting in Bradford. Sam, still wearing his overcoat, sat in the middle of the longer side of the massive, rectangular table in the Board Room, Philip Illingworth facing him from the other.

"Isn't your father here?" Sam demanded.

"He's in London, Mr. Pilling," Philip replied. "But with all due respect I can't conceive that he has anything to do with this. Of course, if you would prefer to discuss everything with him later on I have no objection."

Level-eyed, Sam weighed up his man. "No, I think this is sufficient, Illingworth," he said, after deciding. "All I'm here for is to make you understand you are not to meet my girl again."

Philip Illingworth nodded. "Yes," he agreed.

Sam meant to tie up all the corners. "And you'll not deliberately set yourself so that—well, to meet her as if it were by accident?"

His tone sharper, the younger man replied to that: "Both in the spirit and in the deed, I'll strictly adhere to what I have undertaken, sir."

Unruffled, Sam continued: "And, saving one exception, you'll neither write nor telephone her?"

A bookmaker, though he has other powerful weapons of persuasion at hand, cannot collect through the medium of the court book debts owed him by clients. This quite frequently brings him into contact with the recalcitrant, the majority of whom rely upon bluff, frank admission or ambiguous promises temporarily to ward off the evil day, that of "warning off" and black-listing. In the present instance, if his judgment were sound, the conciliatory answers he was receiving came from strength, not weakness. But the manner in which this last demand had been framed might well demonstrate this. So it proved.

"I'd like to know what that exception is," he was asked.

"That you post off a letter to Nancy to-night, bluntly setting out all this," said Sam.

Philip adjusted his spectacles, above the bridge of which was a livid bruise.

"I'll do that quite faithfully, sir," he said. "But . . ." his eyes glinted, "I'd better tell you now that it will be far more than a stiff and formal business communication."

"So long as it contains the salient points, that'll do for me," Sam snapped. "But I've still one more question, although in view of what has gone before I hardly think it's necessary. All the same I'm putting it—has there been any suggestion that Nancy should be the woman in the case? She informed me and her mother that that was her intention."

Patently astonished, Philip Illingworth stared. "It's the first I've heard of it, Mr. Pilling, and I hope you'll believe I'd have quashed it damned hard if it had been made to me. And so," he went on, his face lighting up as he mused, "that's what she was proposing, was it?"

"It was," Sam said, reaching for his hat.

Philip Illingworth had risen, too. "Just a minute, sir," he said. "I'd like to say something now. And it's that I am assuming throughout that the promises I have made cover only the period it will take for me to be divorced. After that, if Nancy hasn't changed, I hope some time to make her my wife."

Sam, bowler hat already on, turned impatiently. "Then I'd better tell you plainly that I don't want a son-in-law who's no more respect for the girl he wishes to marry than to maul her about in a car on a public highway."

Philip Illingworth coloured and then became quite white. "I tried to tell you last night how that came about, sir," he said.

"Then that finishes us except for an afterthought of mine," Sam resumed inexorably. "If you are as fond of my daughter as you also told me last night, how was it you married Estelle five minutes after you stopped coming to our place?"

"Because Nancy and I had a row," Philip replied. "I went crack off the rails . . ." he smiled faintly, "and, well Nancy can be a haughty little dev—creature. Bad became worse, sir, and it ended by each telling the other that if we never saw each other again it wouldn't be too soon. And I . . . I got engaged to Estelle, that's all."

"I see," said Sam.

Philip escorted him along a broad passage, hanging in which were the portraits, four generations of them, of men who had in turn steadily enlarged a family business until it

102

had become a commercial dynasty . . . Mark Illingworth, who as a young man had set up for himself during the months following the Peace of Amiens, in Napoleon's days; next, his nephew Matthew and in direct descent from him, Saul, and then Stephen, the present Ernest Illingworth's father. As with the junior branch of the Crowthers of Bankdam, these men were content with the district and the sphere into which they had been born. For them there were none of the social excursions which had ruined others.

The building, in the heart of Bradford, was the control centre of the Illingworths' interests, many of which were defined on bronze plaques flanking the doorway of the outer lobby.

There Philip Illingworth and his caller said good-bye, a nod from each other, nothing more.

With little appetite, Sam next toyed with a tender steak and choice chops at the Midland Hotel. By then he had decided that he had not been entirely fair with Philip Illingworth, this merely adding to his gloom. Nor was he brightened when, outside the hotel, he noticed the crowd surging round a six-wheeler wagon which had been touring the streets of Ramsfield that day. On it was a very living tableau whose invention had caused him a great deal of fun— beneath floodlights of the fairground type were six bookmaker's stands, each attended by a bookmaker busy with chalk and sponge while bawling the odds; with them were tic-tac men, white gloves flashing as in their peculiar code they passed messages to and from unseen colleagues, and there were as many bookies' runners, deliberately over-vociferous for this purpose, which was to give an impression of babel and confusion.

Along the side of the wagon, painted in prominent lettering, was this query:

Why struggle to place your bets
When you can do so in comfort at home
By Telephone, Telegraph and Letter
WITH PILLING *who* **ALWAYS PAYS**

This exhibit, before moving away to fresh fields, was to travel Bradford and its suburbs for the next seven days.

Sam sourly eyed the evidence of his ingenuity. "Humph!" he snorted. "I'd rather be living with Milly in a back-to-back house on the Island as long as we'd peace."

In this dejected state of mind he returned to Ramsfield, where he drove straight to the Hornets' ground at Swanroyd. It was Selection night, to pick Saturday's teams, but he took such a scanty part in his fellow-directors' deliberations that one of them commented upon his abstraction. Simeon Calverley, of Hirst & Calverley, Ltd., Dodthong Mills, was a good-natured individual but, as his father and grandfather before him, never held anything back.

"What about a few words of wisdom from you, Sam?" he demanded. "You're like a chap who's lost a florin and found a sixpence."

Sam bestirred himself. "I haven't found even a farthing towards it, Simeon. But surely a thinker is better than a jabber, and I've just come to the conclusion that we shouldn't change the three-quarter line for Hull. Admittedly they have been at sixes and sevens but they're settling down now."

Simeon Calverley chuckled. "The oracle has spoken. Well, there you are, gentlemen."

Only once before reaching home that evening did Sam feel less disquieted, when suddenly he muttered to himself:

"Well, thank God, Milly and I are getting away from everything this week-end. It'll do her good and it'll do me good—shan't I damn' well enjoy myself, and she will, too, I'm sure. Clear the cobwebs out of both of us."

Resolved to squeeze out of a couple of days all the pleasure he could for his wife, his anxiety about Nancy, and to a lesser degree about Archie, was momentarily forgotten.

*   *   *

The Grand National for 1936 had been run, and won, a few seconds before by Reynoldstown at 10/1 against. When the commentator's voice died away the twenty or so gentlemen in Sam Pilling's room began to talk, while his secretary again began to circulate hospitably with drinks and a box of cigars, more than one pair of eyes taking notice of her slender but very shapely figure.

"Well, Major Furlong's done it again," said Mr. Entwistle ruefully. Business had brought him over from Manchester, and he had taken an hour off from Barntat Moor, where two of his surveyors were working. "Yes, as I was saying——"

Hilda Schofield stooped lower. "Would you care——" she began.

Mr. Entwistle, who was inclined to be garrulous, waved her aside, a trifle impatiently.

"Aye, and Ernest Illingworth nearly pulled it off, too," said Jim Oldfield, a gaunt man who looked as though he might long have had the seeds of tuberculosis in him. "If his choice for the Lincolnshire Handicap hadn't swerved he'd have been drawing a rare packet. How much would he have won, Sam?"

Racing still continued at Liverpool, and Sam, from his desk, was keeping an eye on guests, the tape-machine alongside him and on the blackboard clerks in the Telephone Room and Blower Room respectively, whom he could watch through the port-holes in the opposite wall.

"Oh, just over twelve thousand, Jim," he replied.

"Would he?" said the tin-canister manufacturer. "I wonder why he isn't here to-day? Of course . . ." Mr. Oldfield laughed, "he wouldn't be all that interested, with going down on the first leg of the double, would he?"

"I shouldn't reckon so, Jim," agreed Sam.

Mr. Oldfield continued talkative. "A little bird told me that not so long ago you and your wife had coffee in Wood's with that baby-eyed step-mother of mine, the fair Phyllis. Why the hell didn't you drop a good pinch of hyoscine, or whatever it was Crippen used, in her cup?"

The buzz of conversation in the room was considerable, and so Septimus Firth, the wool merchant, removed a lengthy cigar from his mouth and held a hand at the side of his face the better to make himself heard.

"Jim," he bawled, "and why the hell don't you arrange a decent allowance for her and let her go? You wouldn't even miss it."

Dr. Lister Fox, a man in the late fifties, took a hand. "Half the pleasure would go out of his life, Septimus," he chuckled.

Jim Oldfield looked vicious. "Too true it would. What, not have dear Phyllis to glower at over the table every suppertime!"

"Oh, you," the wool-merchant jeered. "You're cracked."

Dale Watkinson, bosom friend still of Mr. Simeon Calverley, whose former wife he had married after her divorce, addressed his host.

"Saw your latest advertising dodge yesterday, Sam lad."

"So did I, Dale," said Mr. Walter Crabtree, a machinery merchant, whose wife and Milly Pilling shared the same hobby. "Very novel I thought it, but that's what we expect of Sam, isn't it? He's stirred us up many a time before now with his innovations."

This started off a discussion about a few of Sam Pilling's earlier projects to attract attention . . . the 50,000 faked copies of the *Ramsfield Reporter* he once sent out, which resulted in an action against him. And then there was the string of elephants, advertisements on each flank, which caused chaos at the peak hour of shopping late one Saturday afternoon, by jamming traffic at the junction of Church Street and Teazle Street, opposite the Parish Church.

Meanwhile the originator of these schemes was speaking on the departmental telephone. "All right, Fred, I'll come along," he said, and, excusing himself, left the company to their devices.

Fred Lumb's office was between the Blower Room and the General Correspondence Department, and though smaller than Sam's had the same facilities—through one end, a portion of the long glass-panelled passage, there was a view of the Telephone Room, and a port in the cross-wall looked on to the blackboard in the Blower Room.

"This has just been queried by the Ledger Room, Sam," he said, flourishing a flimsy. "It's a two hundred pound bet, a loser as it happens, by . . ." he jerked his head sideways, "by Mr. Entwistle in there."

"What of it, Fred?" Sam inquired.

Fred Lumb was running his fingers round his shining, tonsure-like bald patch.

"Well, it's a newish account, no figure for credit is stated, and references aren't completed," he replied. "All we know is that he was introduced by Captain Gainsway-Sinkinson, and if he's one of his kidney we'd be better without him."

Sam snapped finger and thumb. "It's my fault, Fred. I opened an account for him but I must have forgotten to transfer to Ledger Department. Mark him for a nominal thousand so they've something to work to . . . I know more about him now and his credit can be what he wants. Rolling in it, Fred."

In his precise manner, Fred Lumb entered particulars on a coloured slip, but glanced up to check his employer, who was leaving.

"Archie would like to see you specially when everybody's gone, Sam."

"What for?" Sam asked.

"Nay, he'll tell you himself," his manager answered.

"Oh," said Sam, pausing as if to demand details. "Oh, all right then, in my room."

This formal approach was by no means in character with his son. As he rejoined his guests, Sam could not help wondering whether more trouble was in store.

Before he saw Archie, however, he was confronted with another problem. When his secretary came into the room, to clear up last-minute correspondence now that the noisy company had left, she looked as though she had not been far from tears a little while before.

Sam stared. "What's been bothering you, Hilda?" he asked. "Anything wrong, lass?"

"Anything wrong!" she said, as though extremely surprised. "Why, there's nothing at all, Mr. Pilling."

"Now come on," Sam insisted. "Something's the matter, I'm sure, and I want to know what it is."

Neither her smile nor the way in which she attempted to arch her eyebrows quizzically was very convincing.

"Really, there's nothing, Mr. Pilling," she said stubbornly. "What could be the matter?"

"That's what I'm wanting to find out," Sam remarked.

After bringing considerable pressure to bear, he met with only partial success, learning that while serving drinks she had been very much embarrassed by one of the clients, who seemed unable to keep his hands to himself. But neither by bullying nor cajoling was he able to obtain the name of the culprit.

"But look here, lass," he expostulated. "Why should you cover up for this chap?"

Her eyes were shining. "Because I know what you'd do to anyone who behaved nastily," she said. "And even if he were a good client it wouldn't stop you either."

"Mmmm." Sam murmured. "But you can't have carryings-on like that, can you? Anyhow, the next time we've a convivial gathering," he continued, wagging a finger at her, "you keep out. They'll find their own way to the whisky, you'll see."

At once she showed distress. "Oh, please no, because I do like to help," she begged. "And it won't occur again. I'll take care not to go too near to—to him. It was only that you might have seen it, and ... and ..."

Sam, who was leafing through letters to pick out those to be dealt with that night, glanced up on hearing her hesitation.

"Only what, Hilda?" he inquired.

Painfully confused, she swallowed before speaking. "I . . .

I didn't want you to think that I'd . . . I'd encouraged it."

"Of course I shouldn't," Sam scoffed. "And you forget all about it because it just isn't worth worrying about. And now let's tackle this lot."

Three-quarters of an hour of concentrated effort sufficed for that, and then Hilda Schofield, collecting together notebook, pencils and correspondence, left the big and comfortable room. By that time she was so much more herself that her tone was quietly disdainful when she told Archie that his father now awaited him.

Just before the menfolk were due back from the office, Milly sought a few minutes' solace in the conservatory, amid a display of pelargoniums, their purplish-pink her brightest ever, she sincerely believed. It had been a dreadful day, even though Nancy had never been more helpful or considerate. But the girl looked like a ghost, if a ghost can be supposed to simmer underneath with fury.

"I don't know whatever we're coming to," she murmured.

When Sam arrived, she made a wonderful effort to be cheerful, but as soon as he entered the hall she felt sure the end of the day was going to be even worse than the earlier part.

The storm began towards the close of the meal, just after Olga had left the dining-room for the last time. Nancy had gone, too, frozenly remarking that she was driving up to Bee Hirst's.

"Well, you'd better get on with it now, Dad," Archie said resentfully. "Though why the dickens you're making such a commotion is beyond me."

"Get on with what?" his mother asked.

"Oh, nothing, Mother." Archie shrugged, which seemed, and was, foreign to a young man with very wide shoulders. "Just a matter Dad got het up about, that's all, but I think it'll be less nuisance to everyone else if we two go into the study to argue the toss. What say you, Dad?"

Nodding approval, Sam's grimly clamped jaw became less set at this sign of forethought in his son.

Milly rose a split-second after her husband. "No, you're not," she declared. "*I'm* going to know what all this is about."

Archie tweaked her hair. "Listen to her, Dad," he said, smiling. "Now come, Ma, a couple of chaps going into conference don't want a skirt about."

"Don't think I'm swallowing any of your blarney, Archie," Milly said. "And don't let me hear you using such common expressions again."

"Archie's right, after all, dear," Sam said. "We've a bit of a business chat to do, and we'll get on quickest by ourselves."

There was a rare determination on Milly's face as she answered. Her words fell as though they were separate units, each accompanied by a momentous little tap on the back of a chair.

"I'm . . . going . . . to . . . know . . . what . . . it's . . . all . . . about," she said.

"All right, then." Archie laughed. "Here goes . . . I'll make a dock confession."

His story began with an account of how he had removed fifty pounds from the safe in the Settlement Room, leaving an I O U in its place; it ended with an admission that the money was needed to settle a poker debt.

"You treat it very lightly," said Sam angrily. "But what sort of a tale is it going to make when it gets round the office? And it will. A nice example for you to set, isn't it?"

"When did I ever care about the office?" Archie retorted. "Who pushed me into it?"

"Anyway, you've no business to be playing poker for amounts you can't afford," said his mother. "How much had you lost?"

Archie was evasive. "A fairish amount, Mother. But as I've been caning the gang for several weeks I can't complain. As a matter of fact I shouldn't have got into this hole . . ." he eyed his father, "if my resources hadn't been limited recently."

"Limited!" Milly was indignant. "With all the salary you get!"

"With all the . . ." Archie spluttered as far as that when he switched into: "I have been making it fly a bit lately, yes, I fear I have, Mother. Regrettable, but there it is."

Sam gathered renewed voice. "What *is* regrettable is that you don't appreciate you've done something that if it had been done by any of my clerks he'd have been called a thief."

Impatiently Archie turned on his father. "Oh, but dammit, this is different."

"Could you have honoured that I O U on demand?" Sam thundered.

Archie considered. "Not exactly, but given a little time. . . ."

"That's the sort of optimism which has landed many a man for years of penal servitude."

Archie sighed as he extended his wrists. "I'll come quietly. Put the handcuffs on. And kiss my brow, Mother dear."

"Of all the damned fools," Sam said bitterly.

"Anything else?" Archie inquired.

"No," said Sam. "*That* covers it precisely."

"Then I'm off out," shouted his son. "And good night."

Quite often Friday nights were spent by the Pillings at the theatre, but the reports on the company at the Royal that week were so bad that they had decided not to go. And so, when their son stormed out of the house, they went into the drawing-room, and sat there for the best part of an hour. By then Milly's tears had dried, and she was sufficiently recovered to consider paying a call on her sister.

"I shan't breathe a word about Archie, naturally," she explained. "And of course I never told Laura a thing to do with Nancy and . . . and that young man . . . I mean, whatever would she say? Because I know that at the bottom of her she's seething about Estelle's divorce, after she'd married her off so well. It is awkward, isn't it, Sam?"

"Oh, I've put paid to that, love," Sam said. "So don't let it enter your head again."

The front door slammed violently as Nancy left, hard enough to make them wince.

"She can be a bad girl sometimes," Milly murmured.

"Never mind about her," Sam said briskly. "You slip over to Laura's and have a good old gossip. Hang it, she rang up asking you."

"I think I will," said Milly. "Sam, do I look awful?"

Sam smiled. "You look champion, love, and nobody'll suspect a thing."

Nevertheless she went upstairs, and spent a few careful minutes in the bathroom and at her dressing-table before leaving.

When Milly had gone it took Sam little more than five minutes to change his shoes for a pair of soft and shapeless leather slippers, return to the drawing-room, light a cigar, and sit down in his own chair. In bodily peace whatever else, he had barely completed preliminaries with the evening edition of the *Ramsfield Reporter*—by opening it out from the tight wad the newsboy had thrust through the letter-box, a duty Olga forgot more often than not—when his daughter came in. She was wearing a camel coat and a tight-fitting hat.

"I've been sitting in the car waiting to see if Mummy would go over to Aunt Laura's," she started off, hostility in every note. "Because before I leave for Bee's, I'm going to talk to you, do you hear?"

"I'm stone deaf if I don't," Sam commented. "Well, you had a letter this morning and I suppose it was from Illingworth and it's about that. Now there's no need for me to dwell on what I think about it, but——"

"Don't you say a wrong word about Philip," Nancy broke in furiously.

Her father sighed. "All I intended saying was that he genuinely realized that as a man whose impending divorce will be on everybody's tongue shortly, there could easily be a slur on your name if anyone had spotted you last night. He's been pretty plain, has he?"

Defences broken, Nancy's lips quivered. "Yes, horribly . . . and lovely, too. But . . . but why couldn't he have come here now and then?"

"What, as Archie's new pal?" scoffed her father. "Nay, for the Lord's sake do have a bit of sense, girl. What about your Aunt Laura and Estelle next door? Besides I wouldn't have him."

The change of inflection at the end brought her in a flash to the offensive. "Why . . . what other reason have you?"

"Just this," Sam replied very slowly. "I will not harbour a man who handles my daughter as if she were a pick-up."

Nancy flamed. "There wasn't anything wrong in anything we did. It can't be wrong when people love each other as Philip and I do."

"Opinions differ," Sam snapped.

She drew back. "You . . . you beastly hypocrite!"

Sam turned. "What do you mean exactly by that, Nancy?"

"Oh, nothing," she said. "But are you still going to refuse to let me see Philip?"

"I am," said Sam.

"I shall only ask you once again."

"You can ask me a thousand times and it won't make any difference," Sam growled.

Nancy was walking towards the door, but, skirts whirling, she faced about.

"God, that anyone living could have so little understanding."

Frenziedly she was dashing away when he checked her.

"Nancy, why did you call me a hypocrite?" he asked.

She stared at him across the big room. "Will you change your mind about Philip?"

Sam shook his head. "Never," he said.

"Then I'll tell you why you're a hypocrite," she screamed. "Because you and Mummy have done a lot worse things than we did last night—not that I should call them worse, but you would nowadays."

Every vista of colour drained from Sam's face.

"Do you fully realize what you're saying, Nancy?" he asked sternly.

Beyond self-control, she retorted: "Yes, I do. You and Mummy *had* to get married, and I've known it for quite a long time and so has Archie. We couldn't help knowing because of grandfather throwing out hints every time he was annoyed with you or Mummy. Of course I don't blame you and Mummy. . . ."

Plainly visible, a pulse was beating in Sam's temple as, jumping up, he bore down on her, his rage such that she recoiled from him.

"Get out," he shouted, pointing.

"All right then, I will," she said. "*All right.*"

Again there was the sickening crash of a door, three times: first that of the drawing-room, then the inner glass door of the hall, and after that the front door. As the engine of his daughter's car revved into speedy life, Sam wearily walked to his chair.

"You bring children into the world, do every damned thing you can for 'em, and as a reward you get a thing like that chucked in your face," he muttered, wiping beads of perspiration off his forehead. "And by a lass who hasn't a tenth of the guts of her mother. No, Nancy would never have stood up to the hammering Milly got when she told her father she was having a baby . . . it wasn't a hammering that ended there, either. No, by God."

Hunched motionless, his thoughts went back, to a blazing hot summer just before the War, when he and Milly Sykes, head-over-heels in love with each other, had spent every possible moment together in lonely out-of-the-way places, to which, as a precaution, they proceeded separately: he the son of a drunken, poverty-stricken scapegrace of a father, she the tantalizingly pretty daughter of a prosperous and bigoted man.

"Yes, she'd some spunk, had Milly," Sam mused. "She went through the mill, but she never wrote a letter out to France that wasn't as chatty and cheerful as you please, and she never allowed a whisper to escape that she wished I could be near her when Archie and then Nancy were born. Poor girl, she couldn't even write to me at all when Gilbert was on the way, and in her heart of hearts she must have thought I was dead. A telegram: 'Missing, presumed killed,' is pretty final, though she's always vowed since that she didn't believe it."

So Sam's reverie continued, a hotch-potch from the store-house of memory . . . a forty-eight hours' leave from a camp in the Midlands during which they were married; other leaves from the front, when he was summarily broken into the novel duties of a family man—and what fun they'd had out of that in their poky bed-sitting room at Garth End; and the ecstatic reunion on his return from Germany, when at one swoop he found himself with a wife, a talkative son and daughter, and a baby in arms.

"And now," he said to himself with renewed anger, "she's again going through the mill just at a time of life when she should expect something different. She's done her job, the children have got to an age when they should be a comfort rather than a liability—responsibility, anyhow. . . ."

Quite unconscious of his actions, he crumpled together the sheets of the *Ramsfield Reporter*, kneading them into a tight ball which he tossed towards the fireplace. This re-bounded from the marble mantelpiece, where Milly found it when she came back from her sister's.

The scar on the small table made by a slowly burning cigar was about five inches long, and so deep as to be evident at a glance that the combined efforts of cabinet-maker and French-polisher would not restore it properly. So it was with the utmost surprise and consternation that Sam examined the damage when it was pointed out to him.

"Oh, it's not as if you'd left your cigar on the piano, for instance," Milly remarked, smiling. "Now that would have been serious. You must have dozed off, that's all, so don't bother your head about it any more."

This seemed a quite feasible solution to her until she started to search for the *Ramsfield Reporter*, in which there was a woman's page on Friday nights. Eventually she located the small ball on the hearth.

"Why. . . ." She smoothed out the newspaper. "Yes, this is to-day's. Whatever. . . ." Swiftly she looked at her husband. "Sam, has something happened to annoy you?"

There had been sufficient warning. "Not a thing that matters, love," he replied. "But I have been champing about a mistake that was made at the office, and," he smiled ruefully at her, "it hasn't been the best of weeks here at home, has it? As a matter of fact I shall be real glad when you and I start off to-morrow for Hull. I'll go down to the office early and be back for you before eleven."

Milly had already gone to pick out a few wilted grape hyacinths from a bowl on the table between the two windows.

"Would you mind if I didn't go, Sam?" she said.

"You bet I should," he said. "Why in the name of heaven are you talking this way when you seemed pleased enough beforehand about the trip? You're not feeling poorly, are you?"

If she insisted she was perfectly well, he would insist on her accompanying him; if she feigned illness he would cancel an expedition part of which, to the horse-breeding establishment, he had been eagerly anticipating for weeks and, in truth, years. Torn by her dilemma, seeking a convincing middle path, she hesitated too long.

"I know what's holding you back," said Sam. "But we can't for ever continue putting the children first and ourselves second."

"You have to think of your children," she said.

Sam nodded. "Yes, and we'll start doing that when we get back on Monday afternoon. By to-morrow noon, when we're well clear of Ramsfield, you'll begin to be a new woman, so let's hear no more about it."

Hitherto he had had only a partial view of her, from the back. But now, her eyes troubled, she faced him.

"I . . . I can't go, Sam," she said.

"Now don't be silly, love."

She shook her head. "I can't."

"Oh, yes, you can, so we'll have no more of it," Sam said briskly. "Now come on and sit down and tell me the latest from Stonewood."

The remaining part of the evening was not enlivened for either of them, but at least Sam did sink into sleep within ten minutes of climbing into bed, and was so sound over that he did not hear the zooming arrival of Archie's Frazer-Nash-B.M.W. a quarter of an hour later.

Soon the house was completely silent, with Milly listening intently for her daughter, her anxiety taking a sharp course when midnight passed, for Alderman Joseph Hirst firmly upheld the adage: "Early to bed and early to rise . . ." and made sure that everyone beneath his roof conformed.

Her vigil ended a little before two o'clock. Then, taking infinite pains not to disturb her husband, she crept out of bed and, hardly daring to breathe, slipped into dressing-gown and feathered mules.

"Oh, Mummy darling, what are you doing?" Nancy said as soon as she entered the hall and saw her mother. "You look tired out."

Milly touched a finger to her lips and beckoned. Not until they were in the dining-room, with the door closed, did she consider it safe to speak.

"Nancy, I've been nearly out of my head worrying about you," she said. "Where have you been to this awful hour?"

Nancy slumped into a chair. "I got bored stiff at Bee's, and so I drove out to Outham to Major Bentinck's spot."

Shocked, her mother cried: "Oh, what will you do next? Going to a low place that exists for nothing better than to allow people to drink at any time they want. And he's not even a real major either, your father says."

Wearily tugging off her hat, Nancy dropped it on to the floor and, eyes partially closed, began to rub her finger-tips into her scalp.

"It could be cleaner I dare say, Mummy, but Major Bentinck takes jolly good care it isn't mouldy, whether or not he's a right to his military title," she murmured. "Anyway Archie and his crowd are often there, and so are lots of others I know."

Milly made no comment. Speechless with horror, she stared at the blood on her daughter's hand, and at a long rent in her camel coat.

"Nancy!" she gasped. "Your hand and——"

"It's nothing, Mummy." Nancy smiled faintly. "You see the police made a raid while I was there, but about four of us managed to escape through a back window, and I suffered some slight damage."

Her mother gulped. "You're sure you weren't seen? What about your car?"

Nancy laughed. "I parked where a few of the old hands do, hidden well away. No, I'm quite positive everything's all right, Mummy. Besides, even if it weren't, it would add to one's experience of life to appear in court, wouldn't it?"

"Oh, don't talk like that, Nancy," Milly said. "It sounds so clever . . . and it's so unbecoming."

Yawning, Nancy got up. "I won't talk any more at all, Mummy, because I'm just dying to roll into bed."

"I'll warm you some milk," her mother said.

Nancy screwed up her face. "No, really, Mummy. . . ."

"You're having some milk."

A few moments later Milly was in the kitchen. As she lifted a bottle from the refrigerator and poured half its contents into an aluminium pan, her thoughts were flowing along two very distinct channels—she was wondering if it would have been better if her husband had always been a man earning a weekly wage, a wage sufficient for comfortable, modest living and just adequate, with care, to launch the children into the world; and she was fervently wishing it was noon of the following day, when Sam would have left for Hull.

3

On the morning of the Hornets' match with Hull, the sun was shining brightly, with showers glistening frequently through it, the traditional April a little ahead of its due season.

In one of the dry intervals Milly hurried out of the back door towards the garage, from behind which she followed a winding path leading to the ravine, at the foot of which, in the kitchen garden, she had an important discussion with Johnson. When her talk in the greenhouse with the gardener ended she returned more slowly up the stony track in the bottom of the ravine, dallying still further to climb the bank rising to the wall of The Turrets, on which she gathered an armful of daffodils.

Some ten minutes later, when these were arranged in a large blue and white bowl, she placed them on a table in the hall, stood off to inspect her handiwork, and then, once again, gazed up at the grandfather clock.

"Twenty to eleven," she murmured. "Well. . . ."

Her next port of call was the conservatory, where she changed the position of a dozen pots of geraniums to a pattern which would ultimately assure that each benefited from the same amount of sunshine. This done, she went upstairs, opened her daughter's door carefully, nodded as she closed it just as silently, and collected a stool from the pink bathroom. Carrying this, she returned to the ground floor where she hunted for a tin of rose-coloured lacquer and a suitable brush. These various articles were taken to the cloak-room, the broad sill of which provided an excellent painting stand. The window also gave an angled view of the lower entrance in Moorheaton Drive, through which in due course she glimpsed the entry of a familiar cream and black car.

With a medium which dries very quickly work has to be kept in rapid motion, but despite this she was interrupted before the stool was finished.

"I thought you were upstairs but all I found was the bag you'd packed for me," Sam said furiously from the doorway. "If that wasn't enough evidence that you were bent on not going with me . . ." his nod embraced bathroom stool and paint, "well, that is. Now, for the last time, are you coming?"

Shaky and distressed, she appealed to him. "Sam, somehow I can't, but won't you just humour my silliness. Oh, I know you're terribly disappointed——"

"And you know I've looked forward to this outing for us both," Sam told her, his eyes hard. "But don't delude yourself that I'm not aware of where I stand with you. Aye, I'm second fiddle here."

Her breathing was uneven. "What do you mean, Sam?"

"Why, it's as plain as a pikestaff," he said harshly. "You think more about your children than about me."

"I don't," she wailed. "And it's cruel of you to say so."

Sam picked up his bag. "Prove it then," he said. "Hurry up and get ready and let's go."

"Oh, Sam," she begged. "There's nothing I'd enjoy better, but——"

"But . . . but," Sam shouted. "Three letters to make up a little word, just that, but it gives me my answer. And a right bitter pill it'll be for me to ponder over while I'm away."

"Sam!" she cried.

"Yes, Archie, Nancy and Gilbert," Sam seethed. "Every damned one of 'em worth more to you than I am. Me, I'm just a cipher compared with them. And now I'm off."

Blind with rage, he turned and bumped into Olga, which he would have considered very odd had he been in a more rational condition. And in that same rage he drove down to town.

On entering his own room he took off his overcoat, and savagely booted his hat when, after spinning it towards one of the antlers, it fell to the carpet. Next, he opened the cupboard at the bottom of the Sheraton bookcase, an unprecedented action so early in the day. Mixing an inordinately large whisky, in which the proportion of soda-water was of courtesy only, he drank generously before ringing for his secretary.

On entering, Hilda Schofield hid her surprise at what he was doing as well as she could.

"Good morning, Mr. Pilling," she said, smiling.

"Morning," Sam grunted. "Now let's take a look at what you've brought in."

While he skimmed through the letters, she completed her preparations for dictation, lifting a straight-backed chair closer to the side of the flat-topped desk. Then she sat down demurely, stenographer's note-book in readiness, pencil poised.

"Well, nothing much here," Sam muttered after draining his glass. "In fact I think there's nothing that Mr. Lumb can't deal with."

Watched by her with rising astonishment, he got up, walked down the room and re-opened the cupboard beneath the bookcase.

"Well, here's how, Hilda," he said in a little while, licking his lips after a protracted sip. "A toast to the day I've been anticipating, a trip off to watch the Hornets for one thing, and, beating even that into a cocked hat, to have a squint at a few fine gee-gees."

Nonplussed, she made the best of it. "I . . . I do hope you and Mrs. Pilling enjoy yourselves," she ventured uncertainly. "The weather forecast is good, too, and you couldn't be going on a more wonderful outing."

Sam growled. "My wife won't be with me . . . she doesn't find it convenient."

"Oh!" said Hilda Schofield. "Oh, what a pity."

Tugging hard with two fingers, Sam loosened a collar that had become a shade too tight.

"So you reckon it's a pity, do you?" he remarked ill-temperedly. "By that I suppose you mean it's an expedition you would have relished?"

His secretary coloured vividly and her mouth puckered.

"I . . . I wasn't bringing myself into it at all, Mr. Pilling . . . though I would have loved it," she confessed. "Just think, it will be a grand match . . . and then there's the horses—why it always gives me a terrible thrill just to stroke their satiny coats. And . . ." she gulped, "and it isn't nice of you to make out I meant something different."

She started to cry, quietly it is true, but enough to frighten her employer who, however, sank a little more whisky before attempting to soothe her.

"Now come, Hilda," he said, shaking her shoulder. "Good

gracious, you mustn't hold a bit of tactlessness against me."

"Well, it wasn't nice," she wailed.

Sam flew over his next fence without seriously considering it. It was a busy morning at the office, for backers of Reynoldstown were playing up their winnings by letters and telegraph, and thirty to forty telephones were in constant operation to cope with other clients' instructions. But despite the activity in all departments he was convinced there was a risk of her being overheard. In any event he felt resentful towards Milly, and if his secretary were so fond of football and horseflesh . . . well, she should have a treat.

"What about coming with me then, Hilda?" he said. "You'll be company for me there and back."

Motionless, lips parted, she stared at him. "You don't really mean it, Mr. Pilling."

Sam laughed. "Of course I do."

"No, you don't," she said, shaking her head.

"Certainly I do," Sam replied, ruffled. "When have you known me not know my own mind? Now if you're coming, look at my special list of addresses, ring up that Brid. hotel, and book a room for yourself. Then be off home to Scargate, get changed, pack what you need, and meet me . . ." he glanced out of the window at the Town Hall clock, "and meet me against the Mechanics' Institute in Sheepgate in an hour's time. Can you manage that?"

She was even more pale than usual, her dark eyes brilliant with excitement.

"Yes," she said, her breath catching.

Despite the considerable volume of spirits he had taken, Sam felt a cold trickle run down his spine. Overwhelmingly in the forefront of his thoughts was a belated recognition that he was acting foolishly.

"That's all right then, Hilda," he said, a trifle heavily. "Of course if your people don't like the idea of you going off with me—I'm not quite doddering yet, after all. . . ."

"*You* doddering!" The charge might have been to Hilda Schofield's detriment, and the strength of her feelings thrust out any nervousness. "Why, you're a young man in every sense, Mr. Pilling . . . in looks, physique, and everything," she protested hotly. "I always think so, always, and neither my mother nor my father will mind a little bit. Besides, I might be useful to take notes . . . you see I've already gathered you may be making various arrangements at Malton, and secretaries *do* go off with their employers for business reasons. I know several girls like that."

"Aye," Sam remarked, "and I know a few of the bosses that take 'em."

This comment, and his dubious tone, had an uncommon effect upon Hilda Schofield. Both outraged and shocked, she took a step backwards.

"You . . . you don't think I'm one of . . . of those flighty girls, do you, Mr. Pilling?" she gasped.

Sam recognized the warning signal. "Don't be so silly, Hilda," he said firmly.

Tears were welling freely. "Because . . . if you do," she said, gulping, "and if that's the sort you reckon I am——"

"No, I don't," said Sam in desperation. "And *sssh*, lass."

"Yes, you do," she cried.

Faced with rising hysteria, and just about beaten, Sam made a final effort. "It's because I'm sure you're not that I'm being so careful," he told her emphatically. "And if it's all right to them at home it'll be all right to me. But if either your mother or father has even the slightest objection we must call it off, Hilda, and I shall rely on you to tell me. I'll quite understand if they do, and if that's so . . . well, I'll make up for your disappointment in some way or other later on, with something far and away better than this."

Woebegone, but improving, she lifted her head. "You couldn't, Mr. Pilling," she said, smiling mistily. "Because there's nothing in the world could be so wonderful to me. And I'll promise to ring up from the telephone kiosk along the street if either my father or mother say anything."

Sam's voice was hollow. "Then we'll leave it at that, Hilda."

When she retired to her own room just afterwards, to touch up her face preparatory to scurrying off home, Sam sought further solace from a glass. Some fifty-five minutes after that, as he left the office for the rendezvous, he growled savagely to himself.

"It's all her bloody fault," he told himself. "Every damned bit."

This had no reference to the young woman he was shortly to meet.

When PILLING who ALWAYS PAYS picked up his secretary, he was slightly in an alcoholic daze. This daze never lifted from the moment when, sitting in the Bentley at his side, Hilda Schofield threw her hat on to the seat behind and tossed her hair back with a jerk of her head; on the contrary the daze grew thicker, encouraged by a call at a well-known public-house before lunch, and the drink taken with a meal subsequently, farther along the road.

Sam's grievance against his wife was nurtured again at a convenient pull-up in Selby, and still once more, considerably, at a road-house some miles short of Hull. But even at this stage he was capable of recognising the folly of appearing at the match with his companion, and so, forgoing the society of fellow-directors of the Hornets, they remained where they were. Joined by a stalwart of the fishing industry, a gentleman with a bottomless stomach and a cast-iron head, the afternoon and early evening were spent most congenially.

Later on, the road from Hull to Bridlington was covered erratically but safely, and then Sam visited the hotel bar before dinner.

That meal was the last event of the evening about which he had any recollection, and even this was hazy indeed. The rest was little short of a total blank, and for ever remained so.

*   *   *

His impressions were chaotic, but possessed a common factor: agonising pain. It was as though a vice were chokingly clamped about his neck, while elsewhere sadists were at work; one within his head, swinging a sledge-hammer regularly to ring a discordant bell; the other taking turn and turn about with his eyeballs, probing them relentlessly with a needle. There were other manifestations: a tongue too big for the mouth, tasting of decay and abomination; and a journey on the big dipper—up, up, over the top and then sheerly down, with the rolling of a ship in a beam sea as extra measure.

"This is it," Sam thought in his agony. "I'm done."

He came a few fathoms nearer the surface, and in the distance heard a voice and the tinkle of crockery. Then he groaned and, with extra care, raised his head. At that point he was shaken by a spasm which affected every nerve and sinew in his frame, when through blood-shot eyes he perceived his bed-mate. Next, before this shock had been absorbed, he was addressed from the doorway by a funereally clad individual.

"I have taken the liberty, sir, to leave *both* orders for morning tea," the waiter said, smirking unmistakably. "In the circumstances, sir."

Bowing more deeply than was necessary, insolently, he

closed the door. Before the latch clicked into position Sam twisted sideways on his elbow, to address his secretary.

"What the hell are you doing there?" he asked hoarsely.

Frantically Hilda Schofield pulled up the sheet, to hide a most revealing soft blue nightgown, a dull red tide of colour flooding from throat to cheeks.

"You . . . you were making such a noise last night that I thought I'd better come in to try to quieten you," she said timidly. "And . . . and afterwards you . . . you wouldn't let me go."

"I made you come to bed with me?" Sam said, horror-struck.

"Yes," she nodded.

For fully thirty seconds, more frightened than he had ever been before, Sam Pilling was silent. Then, gathering up his courage, he asked:

"What happened after that, Hilda? I didn't . . . you know what I mean, don't you?"

"Yes . . . you did," she said faintly, her eyes closed. "But please don't think I'm . . . I'm blaming you for any——"

"My God!" Sam muttered.

In one movement he swept the bed-clothes from him and swung out his legs. Sitting on the edge of the bed until the paralysing band around his forehead slackened off, he surveyed a room which he had not previously been in a condition to see. No bathroom was attached to it.

Barely suppressing a moan he stood up, staggered a couple of paces and started to collect suit, shoes, underwear and bag. Armed with this jumble he stumbled into the corridor outside, where a lady leaving her chamber naturally recoiled at the spectacle of a distraught-looking man lacking a dressing-gown.

At last, within the privacy of a bathroom, Sam could ventilate his thoughts.

"What a bloody mess," he murmured. "I've been canned more than once in my life, but never have I been pie-eyed to the extent I must have been this time. Well, I'll have to square things with her somehow whatever it costs me."

Not without difficulty he proceeded with his toilet, demonstrating without question that even the most superior of safety razors can inflict the severest cuts when wielded by a tremulous hand.

When he had done, he inspected himself closely in the mirror. "I still look like a three-day-old corpse," he groaned.

"Somehow I'll have to freshen myself up the hell of a lot before Milly sets eyes on me to-morrow."

From the bathroom, leaving his case with the porter, he went outside, and for nearly an hour and a half kept walking, drawing in deep draughts of sea air. At first the exercise taxed him immeasurably, but when he turned into the hotel again he was feeling fitter.

Hilda Schofield was lazing in the lounge and, while he had a cup of coffee with her, the idea of breakfast unthinkable, he acquainted her with the decision he had made: that she would not be going to the breeding establishment with him. He told her also that he would be staying away, returning the following morning.

Then he left, to drive off by himself in the bright Sunday morning sunshine, with a joyless prospect ahead—the sight of bloodstock he was too dispirited to appreciate, a lunch he was neither in heart nor condition to eat, and a lonely and anxious evening and night in a Malton hotel.

Sam Pilling of Ramsfield might be the card of the town, a man who had built himself up from nothing by his own exertions, thereby surely acquiring a fair knowledge of how to get round awkward corners. But never in his life had he been mixed up with a woman.

* * *

When a young woman has had the most grievous "wrong" done to her, which was how Sam Pilling put it to himself, and in addition has been summarily left to her own reflections afterwards, she is apt to cherish considerable resentment. And that was why, when driving from Malton to Bridlington on the Monday morning, he reached the conclusion that the situation had not been handled with all the guile desirable.

Thus, fully expecting the worst, he was greatly surprised right from the moment when Hilda Schofield, in her becoming but rather ladylike coat, came out of the hotel to climb into the car. There were recriminations neither then nor later, and though it was to some extent obvious that her cheerfulness was a little forced, this was far better than it might have been.

It was his own fault that her manner changed, through his grave suggestion that in view of what had taken place it would be advisable if she left the office.

"Of course it'll have to be just as good a job, Hilda," he explained. "And I haven't the least doubt that I can get you fixed up somewhere that will please you and——"

"Oh, but I don't want to leave," she blurted out. "Why should I?"

Sam shook his head. "Because you'll find it embarrassing after this, lass," he said. "Every time you set eyes on me it'll remind you."

She reacted sharply, with fierce anger. "I know what you're thinking about—you're thinking I shall take advantage at the office, because of what you've done. Like . . . like some secretaries do that I've heard about . . . who've had disgusting affairs with their bosses. But I'm not that sort, and I shan't be a little bit different. Besides . . ." abruptly the temper died out of her, and she whispered pitifully: "Besides, I'd . . . I'd be heartbroken if I left the office. You see—well, well, I like being there so much."

Surprised out of his gloom, Sam turned to her. She was, he noticed, not far from tears, though she was fighting hard to regain control of herself.

"All right, Hilda," he said gently. "If that's how you feel you must stop on, so we'll call it settled."

She smiled wanly. "Oh, I am glad you'll let me," she said.

Nevertheless Sam sighed inwardly, fully realizing the complications of a too personal association between them, and convinced that a clean and decent break would be in the best interests of both. But, without hurting her horribly, he discerned this was impossible for the moment.

In this despairing mood, too preoccupied to notice the timorous glances she kept stealing at him, he drove into the narrow high street of a red-tiled village, where he was slowed down to a crawl by a flock of sheep, with attendant shepherd and a brace of fussy working-dogs.

On the open road beyond, after several false starts, she managed to reveal her thoughts.

"You're very upset, aren't you?" she asked.

Sam nodded. "Yes, I'm upset, Hilda . . . upset both for you and for myself."

"You needn't be upset for me," she said softly. "And you needn't be upset for yourself either."

Curiously he looked sideways. "Why needn't I?"

"Because I'll never, never tell anyone—about what happened the night before last," she said. "So don't think I shall ever cause you any bother . . . because I won't."

Strangely moved and somehow impressed, he stared at her, noting hands tightly clasped together, her whole attitude that of imploring him to believe. The expression on her pointed face was sad but earnest, and her dark eyes seemed mirrors of truth and honesty.

"I'm sure you won't, Hilda," he muttered.

"I shan't," she said, trying to smile.

From then onwards, between there and York, Sam shed some of his depression, and long before the Minster came into view, far across the flat landscape, a small seed of optimism began to swell in him. Perhaps, after all, this disastrous episode would have no dire repercussions, would never become known to Milly. And if that were so, he thought with rising gratitude, it would be due to the decency of this young woman, whose attitude might have been so very different.

In one of the narrow streets of the old city he suddenly decided how, there and then, he might show his gratitude for that decency. And so, without a word of explanation, he swung into a parking-place.

"Hilda, you're being a brick about this business, and I'm going to buy you something that should please you," he told her. "A nice bit of jewellery, say."

Her cheeks flamed. "I don't want any jewellery . . . or anything," she blurted out. "It'd be as if I were one of those horrible creatures who——"

Sam checked her. "Well, you're not, and it's my suggestion, isn't it? And anyhow you should know by now that I'm not a chap who lets others take him for a ride," he said firmly. "So get it out of your head that I'm proposing giving you a present on the lines you're thinking."

"All the same . . ." she continued stubbornly.

They argued in the car for fully another five minutes, which, as opposition always did, made Sam all the more determined to have his way. But it was the quietest of remarks, uttered by him towards the conclusion of much forceful persuasion, which shattered her defences.

"Now, look here, Hilda," he said. "Let's leave it at this— that I really want to give you something nice, and let's forget everything else."

She swallowed. "All right then," she murmured.

There was to be still another argument, in the jeweller's, where she was frankly aghast at the price he proposed paying for a very lovely piece—a diamond pendant with a ruby drop, hung from a very thin platinum chain. Indeed, on leaving York, she hardly spoke for the first half-dozen miles, though every now and then she virtually betrayed the train of her thoughts, her fingers straying constantly to the jewellery round her neck.

"I . . . I shall be frightened to death of losing it," she said eventually, "or having it stolen."

Sam smiled. "There's plenty of attractive synthetic stuff about, and I don't suppose anybody will realize its value. And if anybody asks you questions at home you must say it came from Reynoldstown's win coupled with Overcoat's, which one of our clients staked a few of the girls to."

Her eyes were widely opened and serious as she looked at him. "Yes," she agreed, nodding, "I could make out it was that . . . and I shall have to."

His spirits just so slightly improved, Sam increased speed, anxious to reach Ramsfield as quickly as possible, where, after a week-end interlude which seemed nightmarish to him, he hoped to take up life again no worse than he had left it the previous Saturday morning. His mood varied enormously as the white milestones slipped by—occasionally, in a fleeting surge of cheerfulness, he assured himself that all would be well, but more often he sweated with apprehension and despair.

CHAPTER FIVE

On the second Monday in May, after an Easter which had been quiet, almost glum, at home, Milly took Kate Dyson down to Leeds to buy a summer outfit for her. Sam drove his wife and niece to the station and, as the guard was considering unfurling the green flag, expressed annoyance about Nancy who ought, he repeated sharply, to have taken her mother and cousin in the Riley.

"No, she really couldn't, Sam," said Milly. "But she's fetching us back this afternoon, so we shan't be bothered with the parcels."

"Well, that's something," he commented grudgingly.

Then he and Kate began to talk, and as they jollied each other Milly studied him carefully. In the past weeks she had been worried to death about him: he had changed so alarmingly, becoming a silent, preoccupied man whose face had gradually grown thinner But as she looked at him now she thought he seemed a shade better, though still far from his old self.

"Sam," she said impulsively, "I think you're improving a little, but I do wish you'd do what I've begged you to do times without number. Why don't you make an appointment with Dr. Lister Fox?"

"Because," Sam laughed, "as I keep telling you and telling you, there's never been anything wrong with me. It's just that I've been a bit overtired with the extra rush we're having at the office."

"Anyway," Milly persisted, "if you can't act sensibly why won't you at least start taking those white pills, the ones you boasted were making you as lively as a two-year-old? Sam, dear, I do wish. . . ."

The train began to move. Kate squeezed her head out of the window alongside her aunt's and shouted good-bye, while Sam stood waving his Homburg until the curve of the line took them out of sight.

Then, smiling a trifle ironically, he left the station.

"Those white pills," he muttered. "Well, that little joke never came to anything, and never will now. But doesn't it show how your own jokes can recoil on yourself?"

As he crossed the broad space outside towards Neptune Buildings, he chanced to notice the tall and slender figure of his secretary. She was walking past the Music Saloon on the low side of Market Square, her back to him, bound on a daily routine errand to the Post Office. Bookmakers of necessity work in close conjunction with the postal authorities, and her mission usually meant an absence of between thirty-five and forty minutes from the office.

"There's Hilda," he thought, his expression lightening. "And if ever a young woman has stood up to her bargain it's her. Neither by word nor inference has she been different in any way, and if ever a chap had reason to be thankful it's me, by Jove it is."

A few moments afterwards, still dwelling on the same matter, he shook his head.

"Yes, I've something to be thankful for, all right. If she'd been like some young women . . . if she'd been a gold-digger . . . why she could have given me hell. But she's nothing of the sort, and I reckon I've no need to be scared any more."

This conclusion cheered him enormously and, responding to the salute of the commissionaire standing against the tall, arched entrance to Neptune Buildings, he proceeded with energetic steps along the tiled vestibule, and then upstairs to his own suite of offices.

In the Dating Room two trusted members of the staff, each present as a check on the other, had shaken a sack of mail on to a trough-like table, and were now passing the contents through a machine which, by means of long needle-points that could be set as desired, pierced code figures on both envelopes and enclosures.

This correspondence was then transferred through a hatchway into the Letter Opening Room where, as Sam paused in the glass-panelled corridor outside, it was being dealt with by his son and another member of the staff with high credentials, a retired police sergeant. It was their duty to feed the letters through a guillotine which neatly cut off a sliver from one end of each envelope; the contents were then extracted, re-coded with date and hour of receipt, and handed forward to the next department, envelopes and clients' commisions being fastened together by an automatic stapler so that the entire documents of every investment were retained for subsequent recourse if necessary.

Archie Pilling was limping. Ostensibly he had been hurt during one of the matches of Ramsfield Rugger's Easter Tour, more generally known as the Easter Soak, from which he had returned much the worse for wear, but his father had reason to believe that the injury had been sustained otherwise than on the football field. For once the trio of Archie, Frank Thornton and Alec Murgatroyd had slipped badly—on separate occasions these young men had graphically described the incident to the victim's father; unhappily none of the accounts had even remotely coincided.

Sam moved on, entering the Telephone Room where a score of young ladies and a dozen men were busy at telephones placed either waist-high on narrow shelving at each side, or on tables in the middle. There he stood a moment, listening to a girl who was noting down a complicated commission on the afternoon's racing at Derby. The amounts named were small, in shillings, but the accumulators, doubles, and trebles desired were extensive. A percentage of clients preferred noms-de-plume—this one had chosen *Jehu*.

Nearby, Fred Lumb was reminding a trainee that she must always repeat customers' instructions, but he abandoned the young woman to the supervisor on glimpsing his employer.

"Morning, lad," said Sam, who suddenly had become in better form than for weeks past. "I say," he grinned, "who's Jehu?"

"The Vicar of Outham," Fred replied, remaining impassive.

Sam chuckled. "A rare sport, isn't he? Anyhow," he added, now poker-faced himself, "I've something else to speak to you about . . . you see I've just had a word with the Parks Superintendent on the station. I thought you were a dab hand on the Bowling Green up there. Now what about that licking you got on Saturday?"

Fred Lumb's eyes sparkled, but then his customary solemnity clothed him again.

"Even the best of champions can have a bad patch," he remarked loftily. "It's the same in most walks of life too—for example, I wouldn't mind prophesying you'll shortly find that the best secretary in the town is going to have an off day for once."

"Hilda!" Sam ejaculated. "Do you mean her?"

Fred drew him into the corridor. "Aye," he said. "As soon as she arrived this morning I knew she'd been weeping her eyes out."

"What about?" Sam licked dry lips. "Did you ask her?"

"I did," Fred Lumb replied, his expression kindly. "But all I got was that she'd been in a bit of trouble at home. She'll tell *you* all right, though."

Startled, Sam stared. "Why should she tell me?"

Fred Lumb's eyes wrinkled and he almost smiled. "Nay, can't you recognize devotion? Why, that lass would lie down in the street and let you walk over her. Oh, aye, she'll tell you, there's no two ways about that."

Sam made an heroic effort to pursue the subject on the same plane. "That's the difference between such as you, Fred, and a chap like me," he said, laughing loudly. "I'm a magnet for the ladies, while you—well, I don't want to hurt your feelings, lad."

"You'll not do that," Fred Lumb said imperturbably. "Anyhow, I thought I'd let you know."

"You did right," Sam said. "Yes, I'll try to find out what's wrong. Maybe it's just one of those days when she'd be better at home."

With practical knowledge of the vagaries of a large female staff, his manager nodded. "Shouldn't be surprised," he agreed.

Sam wandered off, his step very casual while under observation, but immediately on entering his own room he began to walk rapidly to and fro, between the windows overlooking

Market Square and the tape machine at the other end. Continually he glanced at his wrist-watch, impatient as always when wishing to get to the root of a matter.

More than once he muttered: "She ought to be here by now," but finally, prey to terrifying fears, he decided to meet her, unable to remain where he was.

On leaving the office he was compelled to loiter ignominiously in Market Square, until she returned from her mission. He sighted her coming round the corner of Church Street, and from that distance she looked as usual, without a sign of distress in her face; but when they met near the end of the Parish Church railings he noticed tell-tale indications: her eyes were still a little swollen and red.

"Good morning, Hilda," he greeted her, and then in the urgency of his need came directly to his purpose: "You've been crying, lass, haven't you? Mr. Lumb told me you seemed very upset earlier on, and it's made me wonder what it was about."

"Oh, he shouldn't have bothered you," she said.

"Is it anything I can help you with?" Sam asked.

Wanly she shook her head. "It's all over now, and it wasn't very serious either. But I'd an awful row with my mother and father last night, and I didn't sleep very well afterwards."

"What was it about?" Sam said, breathing more freely.

Hilda Schofield's glance travelled slowly along the Italianate façade of the station. Still avoiding his eyes, she began to speak, her tone quite flat.

"My mother and father found out I'd been to Bridlington with you . . . and not off for the week-end with a girl friend as they'd thought."

Sam felt as though he had received a modestly powered rabbit punch.

"What!" he exclaimed. "But. . . ."

"I know I've been awful, she confessed miserably, colouring with shame. "But you see I wanted so much to go with you . . . and I thought there might be just the odd chance that they'd stop me if I said you were taking me . . . and so. . . ."

"But how has it ended?" Sam demanded. "Ought I to try to smooth things over with them?"

She shook her head decidedly. "Oh, there's no need, honestly, because what they've been carrying on about is my telling lies. They wouldn't have objected if I'd been straightforward and not so silly."

"And there's going to be no more trouble about it?"

She smiled feebly. "No, they've scolded me, and they'll let it drop now."

There and then Sam decided he had had enough of the office for that day, and, sadly in need of easement from this new strain, determined to seek out Clem. A spell of purely masculine society was the most healthy corrective he could conceive at the moment.

Two or three minutes later they parted, Hilda Schofield turning into Neptune Buildings, Sam continuing along to Market Approach. Near Queen Victoria's statue another facet of this disturbing situation occurred to him, and, appalled by it, he came to an abrupt standstill.

"But why, if everything's blowing over at home . . . why has she been in such a state all this morning?" he mumbled. "Is there something else behind this?"

Taking out a handkerchief he wiped his brow. "Now come on, Sam, lad, less of this imagining of yours," he told himself. "All it'll be is that she's conscience stricken about telling a thumping untruth. There are still a few young women left who are like that, and I'll bet she's one of them. That'll be it."

Not in the least convinced by this explanation, he resumed his way towards Huddersfield Road, along which, an expensively dressed, well set-up man whose forehead was scored with lines of worry, he walked dejectedly as far as the town side of the broad, hump-backed bridge carrying the main road over the shining tracks of the railway. There he turned into a wide gateway.

Jim Roebuck and Vincent Uttley were outdoors, talking together as Sam went into the steeplejack's yard.

"Yes, I do agree it's queer, Vincent," Jim was saying. "On the face of it, anyway, though there may be a simple enough explanation."

"Aye, but what?" the foreman steeplejack demanded.

Both of them turned at the sound of footsteps on the setts, each greeting the newcomer. It was not long before Sam learned that they had been discussing Maggie Batten, whose sister had had several letters from her, all lacking an address.

"But what licks us, Mr. Pilling, is that every single one of 'em was posted in Ramsfield," Vincent Uttley said excitedly. "And I've been everywhere in the district and I can't get so much as a smell of her. It makes you wonder, doesn't it?"

Sam was hardly helpful. "Lots of things make you wonder," he said.

The Roebucks would shortly be repointing the enormous chimney of the Chemical Works, a monster over three hundred feet in height, and Clem Roebuck that morning had gone out to make preliminary arrangements.

"No, I didn't want to see your father particularly, Jim." Sam shook his head. "But will you tell him I shall be at the Golf Club this afternoon earlyish, and that it'd be grand if he'd have a round with me?"

Jim seemed rather struck with the older man's appearance. "I will," he promised. "I say," he continued, his hand still for once, "I say, Uncle Sam, are you a bit under the weather? You don't look A1 as you usually do."

Sam guffawed. "Hark at him, Vincent. He'll have room to talk about others when he's acquired a bit more flesh on that face of his. Anyhow, Jim lad, how are you crack Ramsfield batsmen going to fare against that demon fast bowler they say Spedding have got? Six foot three, only nineteen, as fast as Larwood they reckon, but not too accurate yet."

"It'll be interesting to sample him," Jim said, smiling.

For the next few minutes the talk was exclusively about the impending match between Ramsfield and Spedding, ancient and bitter rivals in the Pennine Cricket League, which was to take place the following Saturday.

Revived to some extent by a sporting debate, Sam started back to the town centre, and there, the idea of the office as distasteful as ever, headed for the George Hotel, halting for a brief chat with Mrs. Allan Oldfield on the way. While doing so, he was sighted from a window by several gentlemen, and as a result suffered their witticisms on going into the George bar. It was extraordinary how Phyllis Oldfield, a hot-looking customer always but who, according to the ripe verdict of Mr. Septimus Firth, "promised but never performed," powerfully exercised the minds of many.

Two gentlemen took no part in these deliberations: Mr. Law Watkinson, who was almost too self-important to speak to anyone, and Mr. Walter Murgatroyd, because he was reflecting how best to approach Sam, as his wife had instructed him, in regard to their son, Alec.

Five minutes later Sam, tickled to death by the theory that Archie and Frank Thornton were responsible for Alec's misdeeds, some of which had been enumerated, felt brighter than at any time of the day.

"Now it's all right you scoffing, Sam," Walter Murgatroyd said querulously, "but we're troubled about Alec. He just does as he pleases, and——"

"They all do," Sam grunted. "And I wouldn't be surprised if the Thorntons didn't think your Alec had a bad influence on Frank. It's always somebody else who's to blame in this town where the younger generation are concerned, but the fact is that *we're* to blame, us . . . us, their parents. . . ."

Sam was back again in his former mood of depression, nor did the cloud lighten at lunch with his son and daughter —Archie spoke to him when it was essential, Nancy not at all.

*   *   *

When Sam walked into the locker room at the Golf Club, Walter Crabtree, as ardent a soccer fan as Clem Roebuck, was regaling Simeon Calverley and Septimus Firth with an eye-witness's summary of the Cup Final.

"So you managed to get a ticket after all, Walter?" said Sam.

"Yes, Clem let me have his," the enthusiast replied.

Mr. Crabtree must have chided himself for a breach of confidence, for when Sam was practising short approaches while waiting for his friend, who had telephoned a message to the steward, he went out to him.

"Sam, don't mention to anybody else about my having had Clem's ticket," he said. "I'm afraid I let it slip out accidentally—he sort of gave me to understand he'd prefer I kept it dark."

In these circumstances it was hardly a striking coincidence that Sam received an almost similar request when, after losing four consecutive holes, he was tee-ing up for the fifth.

"Don't say anything about it at home, Sam," Clem Roebuck said awkwardly. "It'd land me into all manner of explanations with Laura, especially as I didn't get back until latish on the Sunday evening."

"Nay, lad, it's none of my business," said Sam. "I shouldn't have repeated it to you, but I was a bit dropped on by Walter Crabtree's remark."

"As a matter of fact," Clem confessed, flushing slightly, "I'd something else to do . . . business of a kind."

"Well, here goes," Sam muttered.

He then proceeded to lose that hole, a wickedly sliced drive settling it from the start. Seldom had he played so abominably, and an early tea in the Club House came as a welcome respite.

When he returned home, Sam's family was, to all outward appearances, a most happy one. On the far-extending lawn at the back, Archie was jubilantly demonstrating to his cousins, Lois and Cora Roebuck, the exceptional performance of the motor-mower, whose engine he had stripped down a couple of days before.

Indoors, Nancy was animatedly preparing to carry upstairs several boxes of summer dresses sent up on approval by Rafe Bottomley, of Madame Gladys Shires'. And Milly, though a little tired, was delighted by her purchases on behalf of Kate, the more so as Nancy, one of the younger generation and as such a stern arbiter, had expressed complete satisfaction.

"I got such a lovely coat for her, Sam," Milly told him. "And two of the sweetest dresses. Oh, I'm sure you'll think she looks nice when you see her in them."

"I'm sure I shall, dear," said Sam.

"And I've bought you that novel you were wanting, by Jean Richard Bloch," she continued, pleased with herself about that, too. "Hasn't it a queer title: '& Co.'?"

"My book advisers, Jim and Kate, both tell me I mustn't miss it—about a mill-owning family in Alsace, I think it is," said Sam. "Well, thanks very much, love."

Milly laughed. "I'm always thinking about you, aren't I?"

"I hope so," said Sam.

The click of the letter-box announced the delivery of the evening paper, and in due course he settled down with it, though with little interest. He glanced at the scores of Yorkshire's match with Essex, noted without comment the inquiry into the Budget leakage, and, for his wife's benefit, read out a gossipy article on Amy Mollison, who within a few days would attempt to add to her laurels with a record flight home from Cape Town.

It was a pleasant evening and, later, Milly took him into the garden to show him her display of jonquils, tulips and trollius, the first and last of which she was very proud. The tulips were not entirely to her liking and, while picking a few bird's-eye narcissi for vases, she listed possible causes of the decline.

She also referred with disgust to the state of The Turrets' long abandoned gardens, which, hardly the length of a cricket pitch distant, they could overlook across the ravine, through a narrow gap in the hedge.

"It's a horrible shame, Sam," she said.

From where they were, near the sundial on the Glenfield outer corner of the extensive lawn now shared by her own house and her sister's, they were quite high. On one side the ground fell steeply into the ravine, whose profusion of trees and shrubs hid the track in the bottom; while in front, beyond a thick thorn hedge, it dropped sheerly into their own kitchen garden.

"Yes," Sam nodded, "but I don't know who'd tackle a place like The Turrets nowadays."

"No, I must say that if I were going in for all those acres I think I'd rather have them out in the country properly," said Milly.

This most promising discussion was cut short by the arrival of Fred Lumb, whose attitude this evening seemed to be that of the privileged retainer whose loyalty had kept the family fortune intact.

"Now, Sam," he said. "And how are you, Milly lass?"

Though Milly was occasionally irritated by him, nevertheless he was quite a favourite with her. She was often amused by his mannerisms, and, possessing a most amazing knowledge of local families, he could reduce her to helpless laughter with his dry yarns. To-night, encouraged by her, his target was the wealthy but illiterate Mayor of Spedding, whose initial capital was attained by adroit manipulation of the cash-till when a shop-boy in his first two jobs.

Now and then Sam smiled feebly. All was peace as the shadows in the garden lengthened, but he felt with a cold certainty that he was standing on the crumbling edge of a bottomless pit.

2

When Mr. Ezra Sykes, the tripe-dresser, turned to point the finger of denunciation, he preferred his eloquence to be heard by a goodly audience. And so, when it came to his knowledge that his granddaughter Nancy was "carrying on," as he put it when telephoning to her father, with a suave gentleman of mid-European descent, by name of Josef Brozik, he endeavoured to arrange that, in addition to the culprit's parents, her Aunt Laura and Uncle Clement would also be present.

Sam nipped this project in the bud by saying he would call upon his father-in-law the following morning, Saturday, the day of Ramsfield's match with Spedding on the Swanroyd cricket ground.

Latterly there had been a spell of hot weather and it was already quite warm when he left home to fulfil this promise.

At the end of Penny Lane, Sam slowed down to stare up the valley, his glance resting on the Chemical Works' chimney, whose summit was level with the edge of the first terrace of wild moorland which hemmed Ramsfield in on the south. Ant-like figures were at work on the towering stack, one on the flimsy ladders, and three at the top, tiny dots outlined against a small, slowly-drifting, white cloud.

"I wouldn't go up there for a pension," he muttered, accelerating. "Anyhow, let's find out what the old devil's unearthed this time."

His father-in-law's house was in Barnsley Road, between the entrance to Knowlbank Road and the Hospital. It was a small-to-medium, semi-detached villa, with a grained and varnished front door, the remainder of the woodwork being painted a utilitarian shade of brown. Inside, the impression was one of cheerlessness: the furniture was just adequate, the curtains and carpets sombre, and in neither of the two front rooms was there a chair in which a man could stretch himself comfortably.

Mr. Sykes had hardly rounded off his preamble, admittedly lengthy, when the telephone rang. As the instrument was in the same room it was impossible for Sam not to overhear some of the conversation, and it was almost as impossible for him to hide his astonishment when his father-in-law's normally snappy voice slipped unmistakably into the maudlin.

"Now leave it to me and I'll see what can be done," Mr. Sykes adjured his caller. "You want to remember that it's noan a thing a young woman like you should be worrying her pretty head about."

Further exchanges continued in the same vein, but immediately they ended, Ezra Sykes's expression became as bleak as before with astounding swiftness.

"Now, about Nancy. As I was saying——"

"You needn't trouble yourself any more, because I've got the lot already," said Sam. "First . . . you spotted her as late as nine forty-five one evening passing through the town in a car with Brozik. Second . . . from the Methodist Chapel doorway you saw him leaning intimately into her car outside the George. Third, from an informant you won't name

. . . you know for a fact she's in the habit of supping gin and limes in his company——"

White beard bristling with annoyance, Mr. Sykes drew himself up. "I don't care for your attitude at all."

"I never cared for yours either," Sam retorted.

"All the same I shall expect——"

"What you expect and what you'll get are very different matters," Sam said. "Nancy's my daughter and you'll kindly leave her to me to handle. You're always making mischief by pushing your nose into——"

Mr. Sykes raised bushy eyebrows. "So I've offended by telling you that the daughter you're talking about, my own granddaughter, is consorting wi' a chap with a bad reputation," he said, a gleam of triumph in his eyes.

"You're a genius for putting folks in the wrong," Sam growled. "Course you haven't done anything wrong, but you're always trying to make a Roman holiday out of your righteousness. Anyway, now you've done your Christian duty I'm off. Good morning."

As always ruffled by contact with his father-in-law, he drove down to Market Square in a not very sunny mood, but a small item of innocent-seeming news, received at the office, so shocked him that anything else was forgotten.

This was nothing to do with Captain Gainsway-Sinkinson's last three accounts, all overdue, which were brought to his attention.

"Well, what are we going to do about him?" Fred inquired. "I haven't been able to get him on the telephone lately at Steeples Hall . . . and the last time I did so he as good as told me that a gentleman with an estate has more to do than bother himself about sending a cheque to a bookie. Course he'll pay up in the end, but sooner or later the same old how-do-you-do will start again."

Sam nodded. "We'll give him a bit more rope and then if he doesn't start playing fair we'll get rid of him. Now if you want to be off, Fred . . ." He flicked a switch on the intercom.

"Hilda isn't here this morning," said Fred Lumb. "She rang up to say she was having to go to the doctor."

Sam dropped his pipe and, bending, beat at the spilled ash with his handkerchief. "What's up with her?" he asked from this position.

"She didn't mention," replied Fred, staring down at him. "And for heaven's sake don't bother so much about that bit of 'bacca ash . . . don't you know they reckon it's good for a carpet? Aye, well, if you've nothing else I'll be on my way home."

His employer's smile was ghastly. "Have a good time at your bowling match, lad, and enjoy yourself."

"I'll do my best," Fred promised.

There are many very ordinary reasons why a young woman may be indisposed, but Sam, in those first few moments of fright, dismissed every one of them.

Racing that day was at Lingfield and Ayr, and, as Fred Lumb was taking the afternoon off, he went home a little earlier for lunch, so that he could return to the office in good time. Jim Roebuck, who was playing for Ramsfield that afternoon, was also home for an early lunch, and they chatted on leaving their cars.

"Tell your father I shan't come out to Swanroyd until the last race is over, Jim," Sam said.

"Father's off, on business," said Jim. "He'll be away quite regularly from now onwards, but I expect he'll be explaining to you."

Sam nodded. "I expect he will. Anyway, that's better than my first thought was—I wondered if he'd done it on me by sneaking off to Sheffield to watch Kent and Yorkshire."

"I don't think he'd do that, Uncle Sam," Jim said, smiling.

"Well, knock up a century, lad," said Sam. "Nothing less, mark you."

Then he started off despondently for home. Nancy was there, but this was not the hour to tackle her about Mr. Josef Brozik—nor had he the inclination, then.

*   *   *

The throng of spectators around the green circle of the cricket ground section of Swanroyd would not have disgraced in number many a county match. The scene was made very colourful by the dresses of the ladies, though less so by their menfolk, many of whom were in shirt sleeves. It was extremely hot, and four of Flassati's smart motor turn-outs were doing a roaring business in ice-cream.

As Sam was edging towards his favourite part of the stand, he noticed a couple of young ladies, one of them, his niece Kate, in a new and most becoming blue-and-white striped dress. Cautiously he seated himself next to her and slipped an arm round her waist.

"Oh!" she gasped, and then turned. "Uncle Sam!" she cried, delighted.

Her friend, Barbara Ramsden Lister, a tall, overgrown girl, the daughter of Mr. Geoffrey Ramsden Lister, junior partner in the firm of Ramsden Lister and Wainwright, shared in the ensuing fun. So did a gaunt-faced gentleman from behind.

"Can't you keep your hands off the women, Sam?" he inquired. "I reckon I'd better slip down a tier to keep you in order."

"Hallo, Jim," said Sam. "Yes, come alongside."

The umpires were sauntering out after the tea interval, and before play was resumed Sam was brought up to date by Jim Oldfield and the girls about the match, which so far had been dull, Spedding laboriously garnering 107 runs by tea-time, when their last wicket fell.

As the Spedding captain took the field, followed after a short interval by Ramsfield's opening pair, Mr. Oldfield began to talk to his bookmaker about long-priced gambles. The tin-canister manufacturer enjoyed fliers.

"Now let's consider doubles, Sam," he said.

Before much progress had been made in this, Ramsfield had made a disastrous start, losing two wickets with only six runs on the board, the captain of the side dropping too late on to a ball which beat him by sheer pace, his colleague caught in the gully fifteen yards from the boundary, from a ball snicked off the shoulder of his bat. The speed of Spedding's much-heralded young bowler was no false report.

"Jim's in next, Uncle," said Kate Dyson.

"And there he is, walking out." Sam nodded. "Well, now we shall see, eh?"

With that he resumed his conversation with Mr. Oldfield, pausing while Jim Roebuck scored a single off a left-arm medium-slow bowler, the first ball he received and the last of the over. He waited, too, while his nephew played three balls from the spearhead of Spedding's attack, two pushes out to cover and the third a rather hurried defensive stroke.

"Of course I'm glad enough to book doubles," he then continued, speaking to the other Jim, Mr. Oldfield, thereby missing an incident which caused a certain amount of controversy, both then and later in the town. "But I've never disguised my view that the man who thinks of doing business for the Autumn Double as early as April—and plenty of 'em do shortly after the Lincolnshire Handicap is run—well, he's the world's finest optimist."

"He's taking a sporting chance, Sam." Jim Oldfield laughed.

"He is that." Sam chuckled. "Why, the weights won't be published for another four months, and he hasn't the foggiest idea what horses will run. All I can say is that a punter like that is a gallant soul, for he's in a darkness blacker than——"

There was a shout, and a small babel of talk began as Jim Roebuck, even at that distance seeming to appear distressed, began to walk towards the pavilion, leaving behind him a leg stump canted at a dizzy angle.

"Well, I'm damned, he ran away from it," an individual to Sam's right cried in disgust.

"Not he!" scoffed a neighbour. "Can't you see there's a screen at yon end and children are larking about. He *drew* away, that's all, but didn't do it soon enough. Otherwise he wouldn't have been out."

"What happened, Kate?" Sam asked.

She was extraordinarily pale. "I don't really know, Uncle Sam. Jim just . . . well, sort of suddenly jumped away."

"Ah, well, even the best of batsmen do peculiar things now and then," said Sam. "Perhaps he mistakenly thought it was lifting dangerously or something."

As it happened he heard this incident being discussed that evening, when he was fetching his car to take his wife for a run.

Three young men, Archie Pilling, Frank Thornton and Alec Murgatroyd were squatting beneath the elms and ashes which screened the end of Glenfield's big garage, hiding it from the large garden shared with Stonewood. They had wound up their talk about Estelle Illingworth, who appeared to have disappeared from human ken, and were now speaking about a most displeasing encounter in the Vaults.

Archie flushed angrily. "If he'd uttered another damned syllable I'd have lammed him one," he said. "Jim's no funk and never has been."

"Wouldn't have lasted long at Ings Close if he were," Ramsfield Rugger's captain observed.

"Of course not," Frank Thornton supplemented this. "Mind you," he grinned, "I was taken aback myself when he explained he'd been in a daydream . . . a daydream, mark you, when you're batting. But he's always been an odd customer, hasn't he?"

"He's got worse these last three or four years," Archie said. "Come to think of it, it's since he left school."

"Perhaps he prefers the cloistered, scholastic life," Alec Murgatroyd laughed. "Evening, Mr. Pilling."

"Evening, Alec," said Sam. "Your father hunted me out the other day. He thinks Archie's a bad influence on you."

The three young men eyed him in silent amazement. But he left them to make the best they could of his remark.

From the heights of Barntat Moor, near Goblin Charlie's, where the Bentley had been parked at the side of the road for the past half-hour, the view of Ramsfield was very fine. As it was the week-end, chimneys were smoking only faintly, and the atmosphere was clear.

"Well, my dear," said Sam, "if you've had your fill we'll be off again."

Stuffing into the side-pocket a paper which in bold head-lines announced Mr. J. H. Thomas's resignation from the Cabinet, he pressed the starter. Fifteen or sixteen miles of twisting moorland roads were still before them, for, instead of returning straight home, they proposed dipping to the Ram far away below, and then climbing the opposite side of the valley. This would bring them back to Ramsfield by way of Outham.

Milly had been thinking of her father's strangely mellow manner on the telephone, a description of which she had heard from her husband.

"He's still far from being in his dotage," she said, laughing, "so it won't be one of the silly affairs elderly men get themselves into. I dare say she was one of the scholars at the Sunday School, or somebody like that."

"Maybe so," said Sam.

It was a heaven-sent opportunity to discuss domestic matters. There was the question of Cook, who *really* was getting married this year, and would be leaving in September. Then there was Olga, who had turned out very disappointingly.

"Somehow you can't ever rely on her obeying you, Sam," she said. "Otherwise she could be worse."

"I don't know why we don't have two maids as well as a cook," said Sam. "We used to."

"Oh, I don't know, we manage very nicely," Milly differed. "Besides, I like to do a bit of housework myself. It's good for the figure," she went on, preening slightly, "and if more women went in for it, we shouldn't see so many shapeless sights as we do."

"Is it?" Sam muttered.

Milly turned. "You don't seem to think so much of my figure."

After negotiating a rising and tricky hairpin bend, sufficient excuse for concentration, Sam improvised brilliantly.

"What I *am* thinking about is . . . Outham," he said.

She knew precisely what he meant. "No, you're not," she said, wagging her finger. "Emerald and Ruby will be sure to hear about it if you sneak through as you'd like to. We're calling in, Sam."

"Oh, all right," Sam murmured.

His sisters, the Misses Emerald and Ruby Pilling, were the principals of a most prosperous school in Outham. There were other private schools of good repute in Ramsfield for girls and small boys, but if you desired to be recognized as among the *élite* of the town your child, come what may, was a pupil of the Misses Pilling. The consequence was that fleets of cars travelled daily to and from Outham in term-time, mother-driven, father-driven, and chauffeur-driven.

To his relief his sisters were not at home.

Then past Law Watkinson's big house, in big grounds, then, farther along, Walter Murgatroyd's big house, in big grounds, and finally, at the other side on the left, the lodge and unicorn-surmounted pillars and wrought-iron gates of the entrance to the park of Steeples Hall, the residence of Captain Gainsway-Sinkinson and his wife, elder daughter of the late "Major and Bart."

From there the road was very quiet, until it joined Manchester Road at Ings Close, Ramsfield Rugger's ground at the back of the cemetery.

The weather on Sunday was as beautiful as Saturday's, and many of the Pillings and Roebucks spent much of the day in the joint garden. Before Sam went out after lunch, he read the *News of the World* and then had a short and not very promising talk with Nancy, who launched such a sustained attack upon her grandfather and his methods that her association with Mr. Josef Brozik was barely touched upon.

Meanwhile other Pillings and Roebucks were occupied as it pleased them. Lois Roebuck, accompanying herself at the piano, was singing in the drawing-room of Stonewood, and Kate and Scipio Dyson were talking to Cora and Jim—this quartette was sitting on a flight of steps descending to the lawn at the Glenfield end of the terrace.

"Oh, quite frankly, I haven't the least use for hiking," Cora was saying. "I mean . . . simply awful red knees and too, too *ghastly* perspiration."

The others, the tramping trio, eyed themselves, but found nothing more revealing than trousers, a skirt and stockings.

Scipio Dyson, Jim Roebuck's friend, took it upon himself to reply. In appearance he favoured his father, but had a much more kindly expression; he cultivated sarcasm extensively though not too successfully, but had an unerring eye for the weaknesses and foibles of others. In this case it was Mrs. Roebuck, who was occupying a deck-chair not far away.

"Cora, dear, dear child, isn't she?" he murmured. "My dear, we have one regret only, we hikers three, that at Goblin Charlie's our bliss will be incomplete in that you are not with us. But patience, my dear, we know your intense love of music. . . ."

"Oh, you beastly medicoes." Cora tittered.

". . . and we shall hasten homewards, so that you may join our expedition to the Park this evening," Scipio ended up.

Laura Roebuck turned. "I don't care for Cora being at the Park, Scipio. It used to be quite the thing in my young days to parade there when there was a good band, but times have changed. Only riff-raff go now."

Whatever daydream Jim Roebuck may have been in when dismissed so ignominiously at Swanroyd, his eyes suggested he had not slept well.

"Then me for the riff-raff, Mother," he said tartly. "Hang it, it's the Grenadiers' Band."

"You may please yourself, of course," Mrs. Roebuck said. "But Cora certainly not."

By then Sam had passed along the sloping path starting from the side of the garage and, beyond the end of the ravine, was entering the kitchen garden whose advantages were that it was a most pretty little world of its own, a place quite wrongly named.

True, vegetables were grown, and there was a potting shed, greenhouse and compost heap, but it was charming and secluded, with many fine trees. At the foot a shady orchard looked inviting, while along the side nearest the house a rock-face stretched vertically upwards to the level of the thorn-hedge margined lawn, with many plants and wild flowers in its crevices.

Hidden away from everyone, though not out of hearing, Sam sat on a small seat with his back to the cliff-like rise of rock. There he read "& Co." until the tinkling of crockery from over his head reminded him of other pleasures.

On this Sunday, tea was provided by the Roebucks and, when it was over and the elders were alone, it so happened that Laura introduced the subject of her husband's occasional absences of late. Clem, she said, had sound reason to believe that if he carried out a limited amount of pioneering there was every possibility of increasing the scope of the family business.

"To be perfectly candid," she summed up, more or less out-staring her sister and brother-in-law, as if defying them to state that the announcement she proposed making contained nothing new to them, "to be perfectly candid, we require a little more money than we have."

"Aye, I was going to tell you about my plans myself, Sam," said the master-steeplejack, and from then continued extremely talkative for him. "Anyway, I'm having a shot. Of course," he emphasized, "I can't expect results straight off, and I've made it clear to Laura she'll have to be patient."

"Where there's a will," said Milly. "Look what Sam's done."

Her sister, stiffening, embarked upon an insinuation which left little doubt about her opinion that a certain type of business, which appealed to the baser elements, could be advanced by crude and vulgar means.

"If you'll pardon me, Sam," she said.

"Granted," her brother-in-law said dryly.

Hastily Clem spoke of the annual holiday which for years the Roebucks and Pillings had taken together, at Scarborough, during the Cricket Festival.

"Well, I think it's much too late in the season," Laura said firmly. "Besides, you always meet the same people, and I think it would be better for the girls if we went elsewhere. Now take Bournemouth—it's decidedly more exclusive, and...."

She put up an amazing fight but for once was overruled, the final vote being three to one for the East Coast, although the result might quite easily have been a tie. But Sam's stony glare at a waverer who was torn between his wife's influence and his own desires, swung the balance in cricket's favour.

3

Sam felt that the sword of Damocles, ground to its finest edge, was hanging over his head. Monday morning, traditionally a difficult period in the mind of modern man, did nothing to dispel this belief; on the contrary, indeed, by cutting the suspending cord with one fierce blow, it brought speculation to an end.

He had his first shock when Hilda Schofield, with letters, notebook and pencil, walked slowly into his private room and listlessly arranged her chair. Invariably sparing with cosmetics, she was made-up much more than was her custom, but despite this she appeared dreadfully ill to him.

"Well, I . . . er . . . hope you are all right, Hilda, but you seem very peaked to me," he said apprehensively. "I heard you had to go to the doctor on Saturday morning."

Her smile was a travesty. "Yes, I did, but it was nothing really, and I ought to have come on to the office afterwards. Only I . . . I couldn't somehow."

Ceaselessly she twiddled with her pendant, the fine stones of which sparkled brilliantly. Otherwise she was perfectly motionless, staring fixedly out of the window towards the high roof of the County Club, her dark eyes tragic. As he waited for her to speak, Sam knew beyond doubt that she had more to say. And so it was.

"I've something else to tell you," she whispered eventually. "I'm . . . I'm having a baby."

As pale as she was, Sam looked at her. "The doctor told you so, did he?" he said.

Horrified, she turned to him. "Oh, I didn't visit him for anything like that."

"Then how can you be certain, lass?" Sam asked.

"How can I . . ." she began. Then she flushed painfully. "Well, a woman knows, that's why."

Already in a cold sweat, Sam leaned forward. "Come on, Hilda, this is terrifically important for both of us, so don't be quite so shy," he begged her. "When all's said and done I'm a married man, and——"

It was just about the most unfortunate remark he could have made, for she promptly burst into tears.

"That's the most awful thing about it," she sobbed. "Because . . . because you can't put it right for me, and——"

"Steady, lass," Sam coaxed her.

Leaving his chair at the big desk he tried to comfort her, his arm around her quivering shoulders. In a little while she was quieter.

"I am having a baby," she murmured brokenly. "I'm positive, and I . . . I couldn't have made a mistake."

Sam nodded. "Right, Hilda, and now I want you to listen to me carefully. Will you?"

She sniffed. "Yes, I will."

"Right!" Sam said again. "Now in the first place I don't think I need tell you how sorry I am about this, but it's no use crying over spilt milk, is it? All I'm after is to make you understand one simple thing very clearly—and it's that, financially and in every other sense possible to me, I shall take full care of you both beforehand and later on. It's much too early yet to discuss plans, but if you decide you'd prefer to leave Ramsfield in a few months, then you shall. It's all a disastrous affair, I know, but what I'm trying to drive into your head right now is that I shall shield you as much as I can, and you'll be my responsibility just as much as the baby will. Now has that sunk home, Hilda?"

Timidly she touched his hand. "It's no need to," she murmured. "Because it wouldn't be you if you let anybody down."

Sam straightened, some instinct telling him that if he were not extremely careful he would be involved in an emotional scene which would be to the advantage of neither of them.

"Now, next, Hilda, I'm going to be a bit heartless," he said, smiling to offset any fears this opening might cause. "It won't do you or me any good if gossip begins in these offices, so what I suggest is that you pop off rightaway to your own room and titivate your face up. When you've done that you must come back and we'll get on with things in the ordinary way. How's that appeal to you, eh?"

She brightened a little at this, responsive at once to him. "I'll go now," she said, nodding. "I . . . I don't feel half as bad as I did, now I've told you."

In due course she returned, looking appreciably better, though Sam decided it was inadvisable to comment about it. Instead, back to business and normality, he picked up a letter.

"Ready . . . to the Northern Bookmakers' Protection Association Limited. . . ."

When dictation ended and she left him again, he stayed where he was, huddled in his chair, staring into space.

In this attitude, nearly as motionless as Hilda Schofield had been previously, he remained until eleven o'clock, when his cheerless reverie was interrupted by the announcement of a caller. This was a willowy young woman whose appearance had already pleasantly fluttered a number of the male members of the staff; they all knew her by sight and repute, plucked eyebrows, provocative carriage and all, and many

146

heads were turned as, a welcome touch of colour to the morning, the former mannequin was ushered into the boss's room.

"Sit down, Mrs. Pickersgill," said Sam, pulling himself together. "And what can I do for you?"

Smiling, Mrs. Hildred Pickersgill crossed her legs. "I'd like a larger credit limit, Mr. Pilling," she said. "Say a hundred more."

"We'd better look into your affairs then," Sam said before speaking over the inter-departmental telephone to the chief clerk in the Ledger Room. "Cigarette while you're waiting, Mrs. Pickersgill?"

A glance through the account was enough and, just before his wife's arrival was announced, Sam had acceded to the request. Mrs. Pickersgill, the figures showed, was remarkably shrewd in her betting, and he suspected the same shrewdness would govern her whole life. Unless he was very much mistaken, his cousin James Wainwright was but the first of a line of increasingly wealthy men destined to provide for her desires.

Which is how Milly might have summed up Mrs. Hildred Pickersgill.

"Now then, love," said Sam, when his wife's observations about his client started to lose their force. "What is it you want?"

Milly's call concerned a trip she was making with Mrs. Crabtree that afternoon, to see the Crabtrees' first grandchild. She might be a little late home.

When she had gone, her husband resumed work. With the Derby only two days distant, the pressure on the office was heavy, and Sam was well in the fray. But, unusual for him, there was a tightness in the skin around his jaw which was reminiscent of early years of struggle, when he had a derelict business to build up and a wife and three children to support.

*   *   *

On an aerodrome between Bradford and Leeds a monoplane was standing, propeller revolving, pilot in the cockpit, with men in readiness to remove the wheel-chocks. Attached to the tail-skid were slender lines, which stretched forty or fifty yards behind, to a narrow banner on which, face downwards, was painted a sign whose wording would be recognized by anyone familiar with Market Square in Ramsfield. The upper side was blank as yet, but a can of black paint with a couple of broad-bristle brushes in it suggested the virgin white of the material might soon be altered. A 4-seater sports Bentley stood nearby, with aero windscreen, twin horns, and tonneau cover. The owner of the vehicle, Frank Thornton, and his companion, Archie Pilling, were steadfastly staring towards a small building on the perimeter.

"Here he is," Frank said quickly.

Archie was counting ". . . one . . . two . . . three . . . seven . . . *eight*."

Rapidly he scanned a list prepared beforehand. "Mahmoud," he yelped. "Come on, Frank . . . know how to spell it, you ignorant bastard?"

Painting alternate letters, they worked along the smooth, white canvas until the name of the Derby winner had been completed. Springing up, Archie signalled, and soon plane and trailing banner were vanishing in the distance, Ramsfield bound.

"Of course lots of folk will have heard on the radio, but it won't have passed round all the factories and what-not just yet," he said. "Anyway it isn't a bad stunt, putting it over Ramsfield within fifteen minutes of the winner passing the post, and that's the old man's main idea."

"Damned smart, too," Frank Thornton agreed. "Yes, he'll soon be above the Town Hall."

Archie laughed. "A great day this, Frank. Derby Day, the day the *Queen Mary* starts her maiden voyage to New York, and Pilling's Day."

At Ramsfield, the excitement had ended for the usual crowd of customers who collected at Sam Pilling's for important racing events, and Messrs. Simeon Calverley, Jim Oldfield, Walter Murgatroyd, and Mr. William Pobjoy, the stockbroker, were discussing the forthcoming Battle of the Roses at Leeds. With this particular group, but not of them, were Mr. Boothroyd Gee, a youngish man who was head of Jagger Gee & Sons and very much of a know-all, and Tony Flassati, a loud-mouthed, over-fat individual in the middle thirties.

The aeroplane and banner, as it shot across the skyline above Ben Buckley's and the Methodist and Baptist Chapels, naturally caused a stir.

"At it again, Sam," Clem Roebuck twitted his friend. "I shall seriously have to consider taking a leaf out of your book. Which reminds me, lad, I'll be all right for Headingley on Saturday, but not on Whit Monday."

"Oh," said Sam, for normally they saw together every ball

sent down in the Yorkshire and Lancashire match when it was at Leeds. "But you can't be doing any business on Whit Monday."

"I'm not," Clem agreed. "But I've an appointment away for early Tuesday morning, so I shall have to be off for a night."

Sam, while keeping a surreptitious eye on Hilda Schofield, expressed his regret but, with so much on his mind, was not as crestfallen as once he would have been.

In any event, he perceived a gentleman it would be advisable to coax elsewhere as soon as possible. Dale Watkinson had had a couple of hundred on Mahmoud and, despite his wealth, was toasting too frequently his win at 100/8.

4

From every point of the compass, by road and rail, bus and tram, thousands of people were converging on the cricket ground at Headingley, men, women and children joyfully anticipating every moment of the dour feast awaiting them, the great opening day of Yorkshire's battle with Lancashire, the War of the Roses again, white against red.

Moorheaton and Roydlea, as was to be expected of the best residential districts of a keenly sports-loving town, sent a considerable cavalcade of cars on that Saturday morning, and of these, three departed from Glenfield and Stonewood, with Sam's Bentley, Clem Roebuck as solitary passenger, the first off.

Milly saw the party away from the shallow step at the front door, Archie nudging her when his father started out.

"There goes Malcolm Campbell, Ma," he said. "And don't he look grim . . . who'd ever think he was pleasuring."

She slapped him for that. "You know what this is for . . . I'll teach you to call me Ma, I will," she declared amid cheers from the onlookers. "And your father's a very good driver, clever dick."

When the last car had swung through the gateway into Moorheaton Drive, Milly Pilling turned towards the front door, a suspicion of bright anticipation in her expression. Not for worlds would she have admitted that, just now and then, she rather enjoyed herself when all the members of her family were absent from home, and the charge would have been denied strenuously had anyone even hinted it was so. Nevertheless it was pleasant to be completely free for once, to be able to spend a few hours exactly as she liked—a view she somewhat guiltily consoled herself might be identical with that of other busy housewives who were eternally at the beck and call of husbands, sons and daughters.

She passed the day in her own fashion, occupying the time until noon, when the gardener left, in a comprehensive tour with him of her outdoor domain. Then in due course she had a light lunch, brought in on a tray, a rare treat for her. This permitted an unusually early start again, but despite this the afternoon was, of course, quite ridiculously too short for her work in the main flower borders, and before she had done half she intended Olga came out to remind her of the time —which meant that a few minutes later, after washing her hands, she was carrying a basket down the ravine, for a picnic tea in the shade of the trees in the orchard, on the grassy slope beyond the kitchen garden.

It was early evening before her round brought her into the house again, to the conservatory, where she had nearly three-quarters of an hour's purposeful straightening up before she heard, faint in the distance, the Town Hall clock striking.

"Why, it's never *so* late, is it?" she marvelled. "I'd never have believed it . . . and if I'm not quick Sam and Clem will be home before. . . ."

The conservatory at Glenfield was a projection of the front of the house, and her train of thought was interrupted when she saw a couple walking along the drive: an elderly man and woman, neatly but not expensively dressed, obviously of a respectable working-class background.

"They must be going to Laura's," she murmured, but was sufficiently curious to dally where she was for the moment. "*No!*" she added not long afterwards. "I wonder who they are and why they're coming here? Anyhow, I won't go through the hall until the door-bell has been answered."

Olga arrived in due course. "A Mr. and Mrs. Schofield have called, ma'am," she announced. "And they'd like a word with the master."

"Mr. Pilling hasn't got back yet," said Milly.

"I told them that, ma'am," the girl replied a little smugly. "But they said that in that case could they see you?"

"Oh, all right." Milly nodded as she inspected her hands, which were again grubby. "Tell them I'll be with them in a few minutes, and show them into the dining-room."

"Yes, ma'am," Olga replied before silently disappearing.

Milly followed her as far as the drawing-room, but remained there while the visitors were ushered through the hall. Then she went upstairs to her own bathroom.

Uneasy every moment, even the lure of first-class cricket, relentlessly waged, was insufficient to dispel Sam Pilling's dire forebodings, and so the day's play at Headingley was a complete fiasco for him; and when stumps were drawn he was glad to be at the wheel again, threading a course outwards through the busy streets of Leeds. It wasn't that the game had been dull, far from it; and, for all his private anxieties, he had from time to time been well entertained by a lantern-jawed Rochdale gentleman, who had imperturbably expressed the highest praise for the Yorkshire side, while deploring that the skill of individual members of the team could not be advanced sensationally with a few hints from Lancashire's stars. "And any of 'em would be glad and capable of doing it," he had warmly proclaimed. "Aye, even down to our twelfth ... or twentieth man." To which a rosy-cheeked nonagenarian from Pudsey, his opponent throughout, had made a dry and cutting rejoinder.

But Sam was continually on tenterhooks, and the sight of Ramsfield High School and the traffic lights at the foot of the hill beyond was a comfort to him, in a sense. At least he was now on the spot if trouble broke out.

"What do you say if we nip into the George for a drink, Clem?" he inquired.

"Suits me," the master-steeplejack nodded, smiling. "When haven't we done for that matter, when we've been homeward bound after a match?"

In the lounge of the George Hotel, Sam met Hilda Schofield, and, as she ran forward, his heart sank into his boots. She had been sitting tensely erect in a chair within sight of the door and jumped to her feet as soon as she saw Clem Roebuck and his friend, intercepting them near the bar entrance.

"I've been waiting for you," she said desperately to Sam. "Because I've got to tell you something, and because there's something you must do straight off." Ashen, with vivid circles beneath her eyes, tall figure swaying, she looked on the point of collapse.

Savagely Sam scowled at head porter, receptionist, and various people who seemed vastly interested. "And there's something you'd better have straight off, lass," he said grimly. "And that's a drop of brandy."

Violently she shook her head. "No, we haven't a minute,"

she gasped. "Because we must get up to Moorheaton as sharp as possible, or we'll be too late. Perhaps," she trembled, "we're too late as it is."

Shaken and bewildered, Sam nevertheless had himself sufficiently in hand to realize the folly of arguing with a distraught young woman.

"Right, Hilda, the car's outside, so pop into it and I'll join you in a jiffy," he said. "Then you can tell me what it's all about."

As she hurried towards the revolving doors, he turned to Clem Roebuck, upon whose face was the most complete stupefaction, nothing less.

"I'm in the hell of a mess, Clem," Sam said in a low voice, jerking his head in the direction his secretary had gone. "With her. And how it'll pan out I don't know, but I'm anticipating the worst. Aye, I've got myself into a bonny pickle, lad, and though I'm not making excuses . . . well, all I can say is that it behoves you to be discreet in anything to do with women—not that I've been any Romeo or Casanova either."

The master-steeplejack's expression was most peculiar. "Yes, I suppose a chap's wise to watch his step."

"He is," Sam muttered. "Well, I'll be off now. If I'm longer than you want to wait you'll have to go up by bus—or perhaps Archie or one of them will be calling in."

"Aye . . ." said Clem Roebuck, so softly as hardly to be heard.

For the next few moments, every now and then stroking his receding hair, he gazed into space.

Meanwhile, in the Bentley, Sam had turned to the young woman in the front seat.

"Now what is it, Hilda?" he asked.

"My mother guessed I was going to have a baby," she said rapidly, "and she and my father are on their way now to your house."

Sam took a deep breath. "So it's as bad as I expected, is it? Well, I suppose it was too much to hope it wouldn't leak out."

Imploringly she looked at him. "But I never let on it was you, will you please believe me about that . . . because I did mean, I did really, what I've said before, that I wouldn't *ever* cause you any bother. It was only with my having told a story about going away with a friend . . . and their finding out I hadn't, that they put two and two together. And I couldn't say outright that it wasn't you, could I?"

There was no mistaking her utter misery, and Sam shook his head consolingly.

"No, you couldn't, Hilda," he agreed, "and don't fret any more about that aspect. All we've got to do, both of us, is to take our medicine the best way we can."

Feverishly she came to the reason why she had rushed to the George. "But perhaps you needn't, if we can only catch up to my mother and father before they get to Moorheaton. You see I'm not going to have a baby, and if they knew that, though there'd be an awful row, it might make all the difference to them."

Half dazed, Sam gaped at her. "You're *not* having one, Hilda?"

Once again maidenly modesty made her red and confused. "No, I'm not . . . I . . . I knew I wasn't almost as soon as they had left the house. And . . ." she began to cry, "and I do feel poorly."

Sam was sympathetic, but firm. "I'm sure you do, Hilda, but tell me this—would they reach town much before you, and how long were you waiting for me in the George?"

The bus service from Scargate to Market Square was very frequent, and that to Moorheaton, a roundabout journey, much more widely spaced. Working it out, Sam came to the conclusion that, if the figures given him were correct, there might be an outsider's chance of intercepting the Schofields.

"We'll try," he muttered, thumb on the starter button.

That was the beginning of a frantic race—along Sheepgate, over Ramsfield Bridge, through Roydlea, and into Moorheaton—which failed by the widest of margins. At the end of Penny Lane they sighted their quarry, in Moorheaton Drive, but Mr. and Mrs. Schofield were walking towards them, leaving Glenfield behind.

Locking sharply, Sam swung the car towards Knowlbank Road, his heart sinking, for he knew Milly would be at home at that hour.

"Ah, well, Hilda, that's it," he said, his lips tightening. "All I can say is that you've done your very best, and I'm very grateful to you for it."

Bitterly disappointed by the failure of her scheme, she was slumped in her seat, and seemed quite unable to reply. But she recovered with surprising speed and, sitting upright again, touched his arm almost imperatively. Then, bracing herself to an undertaking dreadfully feared, she turned her luminous eyes on him and, a nervous catch in her voice, made a most unexpected suggestion.

"Will you let me go and see Mrs. Pilling?" she asked. "So that I can explain that you weren't really to blame . . . because you weren't."

"Nay, lass," Sam expostulated.

"You weren't," she insisted, with vehemence now. "Because on that night I . . . I went into your room deliberately . . . not because you were making a noise. I . . . I . . . anyhow, let me tell Mrs. Pilling. Because it does make it different, doesn't it? I mean you not really being to blame."

Utterly astounded, Sam stared at her, but as she pressed him again he waved his hand, the wash-out signal he and his friends had used in the war.

"It'd be useless, Hilda," he told her sadly. "As a get-out it sounds grand, but it's not the kind of excuse a woman will accept. No, I'm in for it, and nothing will save me. Aye," he sighed, "and now I think I'll run you home."

For her this was the end and, wretched, unhappy and ill, she sobbed feebly on the run back to town, and in Huddersfield Road also, as far as Scargate where, under her mumbled directions, he brought the car to rest against a small house, one of a long row. Then she told him, after shakily getting out, that her parents would not allow her to return to the office on Monday morning.

"No, I don't suppose they will, and I suppose that that makes this good-bye for us," said Sam. "But before you leave me, Hilda, I want you to promise me something—and it's that if you're ever in need or in trouble, whether it's shortly or a long time ahead, you'll come to me or let me know, so that I can give you whatever help you require. I'd really like you to make that promise, lass. Will you do it?"

"Yes, I promise," she said faintly, but somehow he knew this was a promise she would never keep.

"All right then, lass," said Sam. "Aye, I'll be off now. So good-bye, Hilda."

"Good-bye," she whispered, pointed chin quivering.

The cream-coloured Bentley moved away, and still she stood there, weeping unashamedly, careless of who might see her, whether neighbours or passers-by. When the tail-end of the car disappeared from view, she went very slowly indoors as though the effort were too much for her strength.

Milly Pilling had always secretly believed her own sex had

much too kindly a feeling for her husband: there was something about his hard masculinity, she thought, which greatly appealed to women. Her consolation, and pride, had been that he had never shown any sign of possessing a roving eye.

She was noticeably pale when, his own cheeks grey, Sam went into the drawing-room. For a few seconds, neither speaking, they looked desperately at each other, one begging for a denial and the other for understanding and forgiveness.

"Milly," he began at last, a pulse in his temple betraying his emotion, "I know the Schofields have been here, and I can tell by your face that you've been worse hurt than ever in your life."

A handkerchief was balled tightly in her hand. "Oh, how could you, Sam?" she asked, fighting hard not to break down. "How *could* you?"

"I didn't know much about it," Sam replied, his tone sombre. "And she isn't having a baby, by the way."

"Whether she is or she isn't doesn't matter," Milly retorted, not very reasonably. "The point is that you must have . . ." she hesitated. "Did you?"

The only recollection Sam had was a chaotic memory of soft limbs and potent perfume, and he wondered quite sincerely whether even this were imagination.

"It never occurred to me until now that I might not have, but with an inexperienced young woman like I now put her down as being, I may not have," he said. "But I can't remember a thing . . . I was blind drunk, that's why."

Her lips curled. "Inexperienced . . . I don't believe it. No one but a trollop would have gone away with you."

"She isn't that, Milly," Sam said. "No, you mustn't call her that, lass, because she's a very decent young woman."

Incredulously she stared at him. "A *decent* young woman. Have you gone out of your senses?"

"No, Milly," said Sam doggedly. "It's difficult to explain, but——"

"Rubbish!" she said, eyes sparkling dangerously.

"I dare say it sounds odd," Sam persisted. "But——"

"It does indeed," Milly said, and then switched from the particular to the general: "When I think of how you treated me to a rigmarole about why you were exercising on that rowing-machine," she continued, wholly outraged. "Of course it's plain your mind was on other women all the time. Any woman, I should imagine."

"Milly," Sam declared, "as God's my judge I did that

exercising, and concocted the yarn to go with it, for no other reason than to take your thoughts off Gilbert."

She had a rod in pickle for him and, as her arm jerked forward, a shining object flew across the room and struck his shoulder.

Sam looked down. At his feet was a small bottle, labelled, the large lettering of which read:

WONDER SHOTS—FOR GENTLEMEN

Restore Youthful Impulses

YOU CAN BE VITAL AGAIN

"They were in a suit of yours I sent to the cleaners," she said in a fury. "I suppose you took *them* regularly to take my thoughts off Gilbert. Beastly disgusting things that no person of any decency would buy. No, you'd better not make any more excuses."

If Sam had wished to do so, the opportunity was denied him. As she slammed the door behind her he sank heavily into a chair, alone with his thoughts.

The bustling to-and-fro taking place upstairs aroused Nancy's curiosity when she returned home, and so she went up to discover what was afoot. To her astonishment she found her mother carrying sheets from the linen cupboard and Olga placing hot-water bottles in one of the spare bedrooms.

"Whatever are you doing, Mummy?" she asked. "Is somebody coming to stay?"

Milly laughed gently. "No, it's my sleeping, dear. You know I'm getting worse and worse, and it's all because of your father. He's so restless lately that I thought I'd see how I was if I slept by myself."

"Oh," said Nancy, eyeing her closely.

"If it hadn't been for your father being so old-fashioned, I shouldn't need to do this."

"Why not, Mummy?" Nancy stared.

"Oh, if we'd had twin beds, I mean," said her mother. "But I really must have a full seven hours anyhow, or I just go to pieces."

That curiosity of hers far from satisfied, Nancy went downstairs again, and looked into the drawing-room, where her father was still sitting. She thought he seemed very tired. Impulsively she took a step towards him and then, her face suddenly mulish, she turned away.

CHAPTER SIX

If there has not been the semblance of a hint beforehand, it is impossible for any young woman, between Saturday noon and Monday afternoon, to relinquish a first-rate job without causing a great deal of surprised comment amongst the people with whom she has worked. This was certainly so in Hilda Schofield's case.

To begin with, the staff of PILLING ALWAYS PAYS speculated freely about why she had left without working out the usual week's notice, even if she had resigned, as they had been officially informed. From this point, however, interest might quickly have died had it not been revived by an item received from outside. This was a somewhat garbled account of a visit paid by Mr. and Mrs. Schofield to a young woman, their purpose being to inquire whether she had accompanied their daughter on a week-end jaunt.

The effect of this story was appreciable, but its most startling consequence was an argument about a very lovely-looking pendant worn recently by Miss Schofield. Were the stones real, it was asked. Was the chain platinum, that also was discussed. Hitherto it had been naturally assumed otherwise, but now a number of envious young women, who had wished to obtain for themselves such a wonderful piece, recalled that the owner of the pendant had been extremely evasive about where jewellery of this description could be cheaply bought.

Finally, bringing excited chatter to its peak, the ladies of the staff began to glance at one another. Shortly afterwards, mainly for the benefit of the men, various little incidents were more openly dwelt upon, each in the opinion of the respective contributor proving Hilda Schofield's devotion to, and passion for, Mr. Pilling. In due course heads were nodded most significantly indeed.

The conclusion reached, that of a not uncommon entanglement between secretary and employer, would have been unfortunate enough for any man previously regarded as exceedingly happy with his wife, but much worse was to follow when the tale spread outside Neptune Buildings. Misreported and zealously adorned, it was whirled hither and thither in the fierce eddies of local gossip, until it became quite unrecognizable, at least to those who knew the origin; within a matter of days, in many quarters, Sam Pilling's name was added to the list of the well-to-do womanizers of the town, and fully a dozen ladies were supposed to have associations with him. Their range was striking: from the nymphomaniac wife of a wealthy colliery owner to another equally known figure—an extravagantly attired, dazzlingly pretty eighteen-year-old, who was believed to live in a slum district on the Island.

In part, Sam Pilling was aware of these slanders but, during the succeeding weeks of late spring and summer, he was too much oppressed about his relationship with his wife greatly to care. More than once he told himself that the blood bath of the Ypres salient had been preferable to the present, for, though he had often sweated with fear, there had always been the spirit of comradeship along with the danger and the dirt.

Milly, too, had to face her sorrow alone, a sickness of heart which never left her. But it was not until the morning of the first Friday in June that she suffered the sharp jolt which made her realize what people might be expecting of her. Her father enlightened her during a call at Glenfield which did not last five minutes. To begin with she could hardly comprehend his purpose.

"What exactly that husband of yours has been up to I've not found out yet," he said. "But I'd better warn you I'm having no more scandal in the family. I had enough with Estelle, though I don't think that could have been avoided, but with you it's different. You, you've made your own bed and you must lie on it."

Milly sighed. "I don't understand what you're getting at, Father."

"It's plain enough," Ezra Sykes snapped. "I shall not allow you to divorce your husband even if I root up the evidence that would give you cause."

Shocked, she stared unbelievingly at him. "I've no intention," she said indignantly. "Besides, why should I?"

"Why should you?" scoffed Mr. Sykes. "All the same summat's suspected of him, isn't it? Which all bears out that I was right in being horrified when you had to wed an ungodly chap such as he is, making his living as he does."

Milly fired. "Sam's got a great deal more human kindness in him than lots of so-called Christians."

"You're blind, that's what you are," Ezra Sykes replied irritably.

He left then, with the intention of button-holing his son-in-law at the office. As it turned out he missed Sam by the width of Market Square.

Natures vary and some men, when under a cloud, shrink from their fellow creatures, while others more rationally pursue the middle path. Sam, however, tended to be aggressive, though he always regretted it when it was too late. And that morning, after a short visit to the County Club, he knew he had been bumptious to a foolish extent.

"I'm too damned pleased with myself, and I have been ever since I started to make real headway," he thought angrily as he nodded abruptly to the porter in the finely proportioned lobby. "Too damned fond of letting folk know what a success I am. Why the hell I couldn't keep my mouth shut in front of those chaps—they meant nothing, either, at least most of 'em didn't, though there's some delighted enough to take a rise out of me. But, of course, I had to begin bragging, saying Ben Buckley's business isn't an eighth the size of mine. Which it isn't, as a matter of fact—and there I go again. . . ."

Fulminating, he walked across the pillared front of the Town Hall.

"And to lose control *there,* at the County Club of all places," he growled to himself.

To become a member of the County Club set the seal upon a man's success in Ramsfield. It was eight years since Sam Pilling had been elected and he still remembered his joy on receiving the intimation, and the excitement with which he had shown the letter to his wife. Even now he often experienced a thrill as he went in.

In Church Street he met his sister-in-law who, pulling him up, attempted once more to discover what was the rift, if any, between her sister and himself. Thwarted in this, she might easily have been extremely annoyed, but, deeply gratified about an honour proposed for her, she had to tell him of it. She was to be Chairman the following year of the Ladies' Luncheon Club.

"And now I must hurry," she said, strangely enough not waiting for congratulations upon this social triumph.

Slightly puzzled by the sudden departure, Sam gazed after her. But he smiled faintly on appreciating Laura's reason: she was now chatting with the high and mighty Mrs. Law Watkinson.

Since the Hilda Schofield episode, he and Milly had discontinued their Friday night outings to the theatre, but at lunch that day Archie and Nancy began to talk with immense enthusiasm about the performances given by the Summer Repertory Company.

"Yes, they sound very good, lad," Sam agreed, when addressed by his son. "Er . . . Milly," he went on, "you wouldn't care to try 'em this week, would you?"

Milly refused quite nicely. "No . . . no, I don't think so really. You don't mind, do you?"

"Not at all," Sam said, over-heartily. "Well, I think I'll take a stroll round the garden."

As he went out, brother and sister eyed one another. Nancy's eyebrows were elevated, and Archie was cautiously shaking his head.

Meanwhile, scrutinizing his favourite rose bed and viewing a brilliant display of geraniums in another, their father was thinking about their mother.

"Well," he mused, "she may not want anything to do with me, but she's loyal as ever. It's as plain as a pikestaff that she's never so much as hinted a word to Laura about what's been going on—and she's her only sister."

At this point Cora came to complain about the Roebucks' jobbing gardener's omission to whiten the lines of the tennis court, and so he trundled out the marking-machine from the tool-place and, mixing whitening to a suitably consistent paste, spent the best part of an hour with her.

Estelle, who had now been back at home for a few days, sauntered out later on and as soon as her youngest sister had left them, she told him a story which she would certainly not have related at one time. Whether it was she considered this quite the thing to do, as a smart, sophisticated married woman, with the glamour about her some attach to divorce proceedings, Sam did not know; he wondered also if she felt it was safe with one whose moral standards, in her opinion, were less than they had been. Actually, it was nothing more than a snippet about the second son of Gustav Mallinson, Chairman of Mowat and Mackenzie, of Denecroft Mills, who had put three girls into the family way.

Estelle laughed. "What do you think of that, Uncle?"

"Nothing," said Sam curtly.

She waved a long cigarette holder. "Oh, come, Uncle. Surely you agree it shows *enterprise*?"

Thoroughly annoyed, Sam went indoors to wash his hands in the cloakroom. The telephone was ringing as he came out, and he answered it.

The message he received was highly alarming. Archie had been involved in a serious road accident, knocking down a pedestrian when driving at a speed variously estimated from fifty to seventy miles an hour. The mishap had taken place on the crest of the long, hump-backed railway cross-over on Huddersfield Road; the victim had been taken by ambulance to the Hospital and Archie to the Police Station, to undergo tests by the Police Surgeon for drunkenness.

The office buzzed with activity, as northern sportsmen supported their fancies for the Manchester Cup; to win this, crack horses from the South were making a powerful raid. But Sam's business was in the capable hands of Fred Lumb and a key man or two, while their employer did what he could for his son.

Margaret Berry, a pleasant-faced young woman promoted from the General Correspondence Department to succeed Hilda Schofield, had firm instructions, which were also given to the girl at the Inquiries counter—as soon as Mr. Archie arrived he was to go to his father's room.

He did so as Sam was signing a letter to Captain Gainsway-Sinkinson of Steeples Hall; the communication would be despatched by registered post, its purport to request payment of an overdue account.

Archie looked pale after an intense gruelling by the police, but his father at once hustled him outdoors again. An appointment had been arranged with Dr. Lister Fox who, to build up defence evidence as much as possible, even though the prosecution could rightly point out it was belated, made the necessary alcoholic tests.

On returning to the office they found a police inspector and a sergeant, further to supplement the statement already taken. Their line became apparent during a relentless interrogation, as again and again Archie was pressed about the amount of liquor he had had at lunch and afterwards.

When they had gone, Sam picked up his hat, but put it down again when Margaret Berry reported that the senior girl in the private exchange, by persistence, had at last penetrated the outer defences of the Hospital. The information gained was inconclusive: the injured man was still unconscious, and his precise injuries could not be ascertained until an X-ray examination had been made.

"Come on," Sam said grimly to his son.

Their next call was at the offices of Ramsden Lister and

Wainwright, facing the Parish Church. Mr. Wainwright was pessimistic from the start, and harped a great deal upon the changes brought about by the new Chief Constable.

"Now in the old days," he said, smiling, "we might have squared things very nicely."

"Dammit, James," Sam snapped, "we've got to deal with what's what to-day."

James Wainwright seemed pained. "You may be sure I shall do my utmost, Sam. But I must firmly impress on you the difficulties—and don't forget what I have said already: that the police intend to do their best to suppress drink and too fast driving by young people. There is, you know, far too much of that sort of thing in Ramsfield."

Archie groaned. "You haven't by any chance been retained by the police, have you, Mr. Wainwright? If so, you'll be aware I managed to walk the straight line, and did other tricks quite well."

James Wainwright took exception to this. Even in fun, he reminded them, it was a most inexcusable remark.

With little evidence of fun in them his callers returned to Neptune Buildings, where Sam summed up the position as he saw it.

"It's the drink they're after, Archie," he said. "If that chap dies, and if they can prove you'd had even half a glass more than you told them, the affair will have a very sorry outcome. Now you're absolutely certain that that's all you had?"

"I'll be able to repeat it in my sleep soon," Archie replied. "A glass of beer at lunch, which you can verify, and one double whisky at the George later. And another thing, the chap hesitated . . . if he'd gone on I'd have missed him."

"But what's all this about you flying round Queen Victoria's statue damned near on two wheels? Hang it, it's the busiest part of the town."

"The accident didn't happen there, so that doesn't count," said Archie.

"It all helps to build up a case. Anyhow, what was your hurry?"

"Oh, nothing much. Only that Alec swears he's driven to the bus terminus at Scargate in under four minutes, and I was out to try myself."

Sam's temper rose. "What about your job? You have one, haven't you?"

"Yes, but it doesn't pay enough," said his son.

"You weren't any better at timekeeping when it did."

"Oh, cripes," Archie said.

In that mood of antagonism and apprehension they went home in due course.

It had been very sultry that afternoon, and in the early evening, as grey clouds pressed down on the hills, a severe thunderstorm broke over the Ram Valley. While blue-bright lightning flashed overhead and the still air was riven by savage volleys, Milly continued to pack a parcel on the dining-room table at Glenfield.

Since her husband returned home she had been much more like her old self with him, both drawn closer through anxiety. And so, when he appeared in the doorway she smiled, though it was a wan smile.

"It's all right, I'm not frightened," she said. "And I've put away the scissors."

Sam's glance rested on the table, on which a dozen carefully-packed packages had been prepared for enclosure within a larger one. It was Gilbert's birthday at the end of July, when his ship would be in Rio de Janeiro, and adhesive labels were ready also, addressed to him there. Those gifts were emblems of a mother's love, but, sadly enough, on this day, when Milly was terrified for her elder son, she had once again been hurt horribly by her younger. The second post had brought another letter from Captain Crummock, but still no line of any kind from Gilbert, who had been five months away.

"Sam," she said, sorrow and fear in her eyes. "Sam, about Archie, if that poor man dies, do you think he'll go to prison for a long time?"

"I'm doing everything . . . *everything* I possibly can, Milly," he said.

Just about twenty-two hours later, at Bradford, he corrected that reply.

"Like the devil I am," he said savagely. "James Wainwright is nothing but a B.F., and I'm another for trusting anything to him."

This was when he was watching Yorkshire playing India. He left before the close of play.

To combine business and pleasure profitably is somewhat exceptional, but nobody has a greater opportunity than a bookmaker. Many of Sam's most valuable accounts had been obtained by contacts made on football and cricket grounds, and at other sporting events, so his frequent absences from the office could not be condemned.

Nevertheless he was condemning himself for a wasted day as he drove home from Bradford. Deciding that in solitude he would best ponder out what to do for Archie, he pulled up at a shop in Bradford Road, not far from Bankdam Mills, and bought a pork pie and a bottle of beer.

Not very long afterwards he was entering his own suite of offices, which were strangely silent, and soon after that he was munching away, drinking, thinking, and watching the passing scene in Market Approach.

From this vantage point he glimpsed Mrs. Allan Oldfield, who was strolling along with a gentleman whose face he could not see, talking to him very animatedly.

"Hallo, hallo," he muttered. "Who's Phyllis got in tow?" Then he stared unbelievingly. "Well, it's Alderman Joseph Hirst. I'll be damned. Bee's father."

The next person to interest him was his brother-in-law who, with long raking strides and black coat-tails flapping, disappeared into the Vaults.

Within a matter of seconds, cheek bulging with pie, Sam was locking up and descending two at a time the steps of Neptune Buildings, in pursuit of his aforetime solicitor.

When next sighted, the Rev. Alonso Dyson was chiding a couple who were leaning for support against the outside corner wall of the Vaults, near the old horse-trough. They were a tough-looking pair but, apparently obeying orders, linked arms and set an erratic course, glancing over their shoulders now and then, each rather scared.

"Alonso, you're just the chap I want to talk to," said Sam, puffing with exertion. "It's this bother Archie's in—you'll have heard. Well, I was fatheaded enough to discuss it with my cousin James, and dammit, he's worse than an old woman!"

"Huh! James Wainwright!" At this reference to his former partner, the Rev. Alonso Dyson threw his head back, emitting a bark-like laugh. "Very well, Sam," he resumed after this exhibition of contempt, "let me have the facts and tell me what was proposed as a defence by my ex-colleague, that pudgy-fingered fornicator."

The consultation which then began was continued while driving up to Roydlea. It was wound up in Mr. Dyson's back room in Highthwaite Road, overlooking an untidy garden in which his son and daughter were sitting with Jim Roebuck. Scipio Dyson was reading a medical text-book from which, every now and then raising his hand to command attention, he read out macabre extracts relating to the symptoms of tetanus, many of which he illustrated facially; Jim was sprawled against a tree-trunk, gazing into the sky, and Kate was busy with fountain pen completing her homework, occasionally appealing to him for help, which he gave with amused resignation.

"It's this drink business that bothers me, Alonso," Sam said after it had been arranged that his son should present himself to his uncle between tea and evening service the following day. "Give a dog a bad name, eh . . . and Archie's got one."

"I'll see what I can make of him," his brother-in-law promised.

"What I'd like you to do, Alonso——" Sam stopped, and for three or four seconds remained as if hypnotized. His nephew Scipio was responsible—mouth drawn back, eyes fixed, and features rigid in a ghastly grin. "If you'd . . . er . . . would sort of direct operations," he went on when the hideous demonstration ended, "I'd feel a lot happier. Of course, I know you can't act in court, but if you could guide James . . . he'll be on his high horse about it, naturally, but I think I can persuade him."

"Persuade nothing," Mr. Dyson snapped. "Scare the pants off him if he objects. Let him assume you are very well informed about a certain Mrs. Hildred Pickersgill. Ram it down his throat."

It was left at that.

Sam stayed to supper. The meal was simple, sufficient, and daintily set out, everything a credit to the young mistress of the house.

Six weeks were to pass before the dark shadow over the home of Sam and Milly Pilling really began to lighten. That period covered a spell of six days during which a man's life hung by a thread, to be followed by bulletins almost endlessly the same: "Still dangerously ill," and then: "Very poorly." The change for the better came suddenly, in the middle of July, and simultaneously the Rev. Alonso Dyson paid a call upon Sam at his office.

His news was nearly as good: the injured man had frankly conceded that had he not lost his head the accident would not have occurred, that he was entirely to blame.

"By God, Alonso," Sam said, with heartfelt relief, "but that's grand all the way round, for him and for Archie. Not that I mean we're wholly out of the wood, but surely we're much nearer to seeing a way out?"

Mr. Dyson may or may not have been troubled by his conscience, in that he had, under the guise of a friendly visitor to the sick, extracted a valuable admission towards a defence in which he was an interested party. But he promptly proved that he was aware his action was decidedly unethical, revealing also the broader view he took of matters such as this. He made clear his opinion that as a general rule more harm than good was done by sending a young man to prison; and that damages, as strictly interpreted by the law, from which iniquitous bills of costs must be deducted, seldom adequately compensated the victim either for pain suffered or material loss. Lastly he observed that Archie, through driving too quickly, was morally to blame.

"That's why this chap, who's an honest, decent fellow, must be reimbursed generously, and no advantage taken in the long run of his admission," Alonso continued, fiercely eyeing his brother-in-law. "He's lost wages, his family has been hard-pressed——"

"I'll treat him generously, make no mistake," Sam said, interrupting. "And as from now I'll have his family off short commons just as quickly as I can jump into that bus of mine."

The lawyer in the Rev. Alonso Dyson leapt sky-high.

"You'll not give them a stiver until the case is finally disposed off," he thundered.

Frustrated, Sam eventually smiled. "Well, I suppose you'll allow me to telephone Milly?"

Archie had still to face whatever charges the police proposed to bring against him, but nevertheless that evening at Glenfield was a more peaceful one than Sam had enjoyed for a long time, even though it was marred by an incident unknown to his wife and son.

Milly had cried happily, Nancy had been delighted for her brother's sake, and Archie, who had lost nearly a stone in weight, had behaved as a young man from whose broad shoulders a burden has been lifted.

Later on, an impromptu tennis party took place, in which Pillings, Roebucks and a crowd of friends participated.

Sam watched a few games and then, newspaper under arm, ambled off to his retreat at the foot of the rock-face in the kitchen garden, where, though he could not be seen by them, he could still distinctly hear the laughter and talk of the tennis players above.

He had begun to read with astonishment and concern about the attempt on King Edward's life in London, when his attention was distracted by the snapping of twigs, then almost soundless footsteps. Looking up, he saw his daughter approaching, in white tennis shoes, white shorts and shirt, and visored tennis cap.

"Daddy," she said evenly, neither coaxing nor otherwise, "I've promised to join a party flying out to Germany for the Olympic Games, which that funny little man Hitler will be opening at the beginning of August. Bee's one of them, and as Augustus Firth can't get off I'd particularly like to go myself, as Bee and I haven't been so much together since she became engaged. Of course, I'm thrilled to death about it, apart from that."

"Well?" Sam said.

She shrugged. "Only that I'm financially embarrassed."

"And this is only a fortnight and two or three days since I gave you your last quarter's allowance. You remember what I told you then?"

Nancy nodded. "It's engraven on the tablets of my memory."

Her father nodded also. "Then this will punch the lettering a bit deeper. I'm not giving you any more money, Nancy."

With an effort she resisted the desire to storm, which would not have been at all in keeping with the aloof, neutral attitude she had adopted as befitting her relations with him.

"But what shall I do? It's virtually arranged."

"I've no idea." Sam was unhelpful.

"But I've got to go," she insisted, almost losing the calmness she considered effective. "And I can't go without money."

"You've spent your money, and so that's your look-out," Sam remarked.

"I see," she said, turning away.

He watched her as she walked erectly off, until she passed from sight on turning up the ravine. Then he picked up the paper again.

2

On the morning of the last day of Ramsfield Thump, Archie Pilling appeared before the Magistrates and was fined ten pounds with costs.

On the same afternoon tens of thousands of sporting folk throughout the country, each an expert on sprint races until the next time, plunged to despair or cried victory after Solerina's win in the Stewards' Cup at Goodwood.

Shortly after the result came through on the Blower, Sam was in a specially partitioned-off section of the Making-up Room, where clerks, chosen for their mathematical skill, were working out gains and losses of clients who entrusted to the firm wagers based on their own pet systems.

Into this quiet, sound-proofed place his secretary hurried.

"Well, what's the matter?" he asked her genially. Lunch at home had been a very lively meal, its mood set by his wife, who had been relieved and delighted by the final outcome of the charge against Archie. "You look as if you've let somebody welsh us for half a million."

Margaret Berry smiled. "I don't think it's anything like that, sir. But Mrs. Pilling is so anxious to see you as quickly as possible. I've put her in your office, of course."

Feet sped by fear of the unknown responded to this wifely summons. He learnt that his daughter had, after all, gone to Germany, leaving a note behind for her mother, affectionate though airy.

"But why had she to do such a thing, Sam, without saying a word to us beforehand?" Milly puzzled. "And she'll be with such nice people, which makes her conduct all the more mystifying. We wouldn't have prevented her."

Of course it all had to come out: Nancy's appeal to her father and his refusal.

"No . . . no, I suppose you couldn't have done anything else after you'd warned her so plainly," said Milly. "But where has she got the money from? She hasn't asked me for any."

"One of her friends I should imagine," said Sam, scowling. "But it does just show that nothing will stop her once she makes up her mind."

"She's a very bad girl, and I shall tell her so when she gets back," his wife said with an emphasis which subsequently lost much of its force. "Though a few pounds aren't really anything, are they? I mean if she'd been anticipating it so much."

"Now, Milly," said Sam. "We've got to compel 'em to realize that they have to conform. And I'm making heavy enough weather of the job as it is without you aiding and abetting them—or at least sympathizing."

"I'm not," Milly declared, up-in-arms. "Surely I can tell you my thoughts."

"Aye, you can," said Sam, smiling.

Hardly once again during the remainder of the afternoon

did he recall his daughter's wilfulness. Glowing with hope, he continually assured himself that, if his relationship with his wife could be maintained on the level of to-day, everything else was possible.

The crazy-paved terrace behind Glenfield and Stonewood stood about four feet higher than the wide expanse of fine green turf below, and, sixty or seventy yards long, was a pleasant place along which to parade. Sauntering there that warm evening, Sam and Clem Roebuck saw Archie and Frank Thornton squeeze into the front seat of Alec Murgatroyd's Mercedes Benz. The three young men were bound for the fair, to test aim and strength at shies, rifle ranges, and anything else which took their eyes. The three set out with immense zest.

"A real lively lot," Clem commented, sighing just so slightly.

"Aye," Sam agreed.

It was still very warm when the two friends went into Glenfield for the game of billiards they had decided upon and, while Sam opened two of the windows in the billiards room for ventilation, and drew the curtains to discourage uneven lighting of the table, Clem was admiring a bowl of roses in the hall. At lunch-time the lovely blooms had been the cause of some family banter, when Sam identified them as filched from a bed he regarded as his special property.

When the score reached a hundred and seventy-three to one hundred and fifty, to his advantage, Sam proposed a rest. In shirt sleeves, appropriate refreshment on a table between them, he and Clem took their ease in the chairs on the broad dais, talking peacefully. It was only four days before the start of the Roses match, but as soon as this was mentioned Sam apologetically told his companion that this year he would not be going to Old Trafford.

"You see Gilbert isn't here, Nancy will be in Berlin, and Archie starts off on Friday for his motoring holiday in the South."

"Oh, you couldn't leave Milly," Clem said promptly. "As a matter of fact I'm not sure I shall be going myself. If I do it'll only be on Saturday."

For some time afterwards their conversation was that of men who knew each other well, but nothing was said about Hilda Schofield. Sam had confided in Clem, and with that it was tacitly understood that the chapter was closed. So they continued to chat, lazily, intimately, with lulls when neither was disposed to talk.

Alec Murgatroyd's return provided a new topic. Undeterred by the near-fate of his friend, he swung at high speed through the gateway and, with no less verve, roared between the two houses and on to the space between Glenfield and the garage. His passengers hailed this feat with a loud cheer.

"I sometimes wish Jim was livelier, instead of being so quiet, Sam," Clem murmured.

"He isn't bothering himself about that cricket match, is he?"

"I think he is . . . but that's nothing to do with what I mean, Sam . . . I mean generally," said Clem, picking his words. "He'd be better—and I reckon I would have been as well—if he wasn't . . . wasn't so bottled up. Maybe I'm wrong, of course, but I'd give a lot if he were more like those lads out there. Just listen to 'em kidding one another."

Every remark made outside was distinctly audible in the billiards room.

"You know," Frank Thornton was guffawing, "if right was right, Archie would be in jug to-night. Personally I think he should raid his old man's liquor and treat us to a bumper."

Alec Murgatroyd chuckled. "He *would* be in clink if he hadn't had a good head . . . and if our good friends at the Vaults hadn't kept their clappers still. God, and the coppers didn't half try to shake 'em."

Choking with rage, the colour of his face rapidly changing from fiery red to purple, Sam sprang up, mouthed incoherently as he tore into the hall, through the baize-covered door into the servants' passage, and then out by the back door.

"So you were damned well lying after all?" he bawled. "What did you have to drink at the Vaults that day, Archie?"

Three young men, holding a coconut, a spangled doll, and a woolly rabbit respectively, were glued to the spot.

"Two doubles," said Archie, pulling himself together.

His father's thumb jerked. "You go into my study and sharp . . . I'm going to tell you what this lying of yours is going to cost you."

Alec Murgatroyd glanced at Frank Thornton. "And this I fear is where we must trip away," he whispered.

"Like lit-tel fairies," Frank agreed, edging off.

Sam whipped round. "Get the hell out of here, you two," he roared.

The incident was already having consequences. Clem effaced himself homewards; Cook, concern on her plump features, was staring out of the kitchen window, and Olga, usually never too remote from the scene of family disturbances, was taking a duster to the dining-room when ordered back to the rear quarters by her mistress, who had run frantically downstairs.

The crisis in the study lasted for perhaps thirty seconds, and in those thirty seconds Milly experienced more acute distress than she had ever known in a similar period, with the exception of the time when she had opened a telegram informing her that her husband was probably dead.

"Why did you lie?" Sam demanded.

"Because the police damned well have a down on me," said Archie. "They'd have made out I'd had a skinful."

Father and son were standing on the hearth-rug, not more than four feet apart, the face of the former hard and unyielding, his son's pale.

"You'd had plenty for your age," said Sam.

Archie nodded. "Oh, I dare say."

"I wonder if you'll be as cocksure when it dawns on you that after all your smartness you're going to pay even a stiffer price for what you've done?" Sam growled as he glanced vaguely about for his coat. "Billiards room," he muttered.

"And how do you propose bringing that off?" Archie asked.

Sam turned towards the door. "I don't propose bringing anything off," he replied, his own colour now greatly diminished. "All I shall do will be to tell your Uncle Alonso the truth."

"Sam!" Milly gasped. "You mustn't."

"I've no alternative."

He had not taken two paces when, arms outstretched, she was pushing against his chest with all her might.

"You can't," she cried. "And I won't let you, Sam. You know what a fanatic Alonso can be . . . once he knows he's been deceived he'll move heaven and earth to start the inquiry all over again . . . you *know* he will."

"Yes, I reckon I do," said Sam, heavily. "And it doesn't make it any easier for me."

"Then why hurt yourself and me?" she said, trembling.

Sam sighed. "Because I must be on the level with Alonso."

Limply her hands dropped. Tears began to flow as her head lolled.

"You can't because . . . because you'd be sending Archie to prison," she whimpered. "You couldn't be so cruel to your own son, you *couldn't*. Please, Sam."

For those thirty seconds Sam stared pityingly at her, and then, sick within himself about his own weakness, he dropped wearily into a chair.

"No, I'm not much of a Spartan father when it comes to it," he said. "And there's no need for you to stay, Archie, but if this means anything to you, if you think of me and your mother at all, you'll cut out some of that senseless drinking . . . and bustle-to more at the office. Try to remember that some day you'll succeed me in the business, so act there as if you'd a stake in it, not as a perpetual playboy."

"*I've* some authority at the office, haven't I?" Archie said.

"You've never wanted any," said his father. "Would it make any difference if you had?"

"A change, if nothing else."

Steadily Sam looked at his son. "Still clever, aren't you? But all the same I'll arrange for things to be different in that direction. At least it will try out your mettle. Now off you go."

A few minutes later he went into the dining-room, where he poured out a small glass of brandy. This he carried back to the study, and coaxed his wife into drinking it.

"I'm so, so glad you were lenient in the end, Sam," Milly said, already stimulated by several sips. "I know it was awful of Archie to lie, but he's young yet, and there's many worse things he could have done."

"Such as?" Sam asked.

"Well, take that dreadful Mallinson boy, and all those girls who are having babies by him," Milly pointed out. "At least Archie's never shown any nastiness of that sort."

Irritation, fatigue and dejection may have been the cause of a remark made by Sam, which led to a climax he afterwards regretted.

"Like some we could name, eh?" he snapped.

Indignantly Milly rounded on him. "Gilbert wasn't as nice and respectful to girls as he should have been but he certainly never . . . excuse me," she said, after hiccoughing, "he certainly never misbehaved himself to *that* dreadful extent."

"Meaning I have?" Sam demanded.

She stared. "I wasn't thinking about you at all, Sam," she said. "Really I wasn't."

"But I can see you are now," said Sam.

"Perhaps I am," she said, flushing. "But it isn't my fault the subject's been brought up. So how can I help myself?"

Sam switched on to another track. "How long are you continuing to behave with me as you are doing? You're cold as ice with me if nothing's amiss with the dear children, but it doesn't take you long to wax warm if you've need of me."

She rose, spots of colour in her cheeks due to temper, brandy, or a combination of both.

"Whatever lies between us . . ." she began.

Some devil was in Sam. "Pure Theatre Royal," he commented.

"Anyway, whether that's so or not, we have still to do whatever's best for the children," she said furiously.

"Maybe so." Sam nodded. "But if a chap can't be forgiven a mistake, then what I say is that it's a hell of a pity for him. All the same you'd better get the idea out of your head that I've any intention of living the rest of my life in abject misery."

At the threat implied, she drew herself up. "There are certain things which can't be forgiven. No woman breathing would forget or forgive you for what you did . . . not one."

"Well, I've told you, that's all," said Sam. "So long as you understand."

She fired off a retaliatory shot. It was that, if he had not already done so, she expected him to increase their reservations at the hotel in Scarborough, by one bedroom, for herself.

Sam growled. "I'll attend to it . . . but remember . . . I shan't give you over long."

In a trice she shed matronly responsibilities. Eyes flashing, she became a spirited young woman in a tantrum.

"How dare you speak to me like that?" she said.

And then, skirts flying, she was gone.

Sam accurately summed up the latest situation after he had found a pipe in the rack and stretched for a tobacco jar at the back of the roll-top desk.

"Now I'm bloody well just as badly off as ever I've been," he murmured glumly. "Nay, dammit, I'm worse."

He pondered this aspect of his domestic troubles for nearly half an hour, before moving on to the problems posed by his son and daughter, when an expression of determination succeeded one of gloom.

"Somehow or other I've got to lick 'em," he soliloquized. "They're impertinent and wilful . . . untrustworthy . . . they put pleasure before everything . . . to them money is merely an article you use, not one you strive for. Yes," he sighed, "they must be mastered, by hook or by crook. But how—that's the question."

It was as far as ever from being solved when he went to bed that night, to the guest room of which he had sole enjoyment. But by then he was harrying himself with another disquieting thought: was there anything in his children which was worth redeeming, after all?

"Have they a ha'porth of backbone in them, that's the point?" he reflected. "How would they have made out in life . . . well, if they'd had the rotten start I had?"

Uneasily he shifted about, melancholy, exasperated, and as wide-awake as ever. "They'd have done damn all, and sunk lower and lower, that's what it would have been," he growled to himself. "And perhaps it isn't all our fault . . . maybe it's some throwback to real bad stock—there's their grandfather on my side, for instance. Then—anyway, what's the use? The fact is that they haven't any stiffening in their spines, and if ever they meet adversity of any serious kind—of any trivial sort for that matter—they'd howl their heads off."

Some two hours later he spoke aloud, to himself, savagely, bitterly, and self-condemnatorily.

"I wish to God they could really be up against it—but if they were their fathead of a father would see 'em through, whatever it cost. Yes, they'd gallop to me all right if they needed help—because they're bloody well gutless in the way I mean."

That was his last dismal thought before slipping into sleep.

3

Quarrels had again become the rule rather than the exception at Glenfield, and there was another fierce one on the day after Nancy's return from Germany. Asked by her father how she had obtained funds for the trip, she reminded him of his remark about lack of money being her own look-out. Beyond this she refused to explain, but otherwise was not at all silent in the ensuing row.

Milly, now day after day on the most distant terms with her husband, did not participate in the scene. This did not mean she failed to share in Sam's feelings, however, and later Nancy had to defend herself against the sharpest scolding her mother had ever given her.

"Home Sweet Home," Sam muttered on the morning before the Twelfth. "Yes," he went on, endeavouring to close his ears against the sound of the hot differences of his wife and daughter, "I think I'll take this gun along to that chap this afternoon for a little attention."

The grouse-shooting season opened the next day and, as for seven or eight years past, he was to be among the party of Septimus Firth, the wool merchant, who owned very considerable sporting rights on Barntat Moor. It was an event to which Sam looked forward with the keenest zest.

That morning, while walking to pay a call upon his stockbroker in Sheepgate, next door to the Cloth Hall, Sam chanced to glimpse his daughter talking to Rafe Bottomley in the comparative obscurity of the portico of the Town Hall. To his experienced eye there was little doubt that Nancy was seething with an anger she found extremely hard to suppress; it could be the anger, he thought, of an imperious young woman who had never before been in a cleft stick. Rafe Bottomley's manner, smiling but somehow insistent, strengthened that impression.

"Well, what shall I be imagining next?" Sam muttered as he resumed his way. "Anyhow," he grinned slightly, "there's one consolation . . . Bottomley's not the man to ruin my daughter . . . though I'll swear something damned funny was afoot between those two."

Still perplexed, he did not listen as carefully as he might have done to Mr. William Pobjoy's masterly exposition upon the prospects of a rapidly rising firm of radio manufacturers. A novel notion, feasible too, had struck him. Ladies who did not pay their own accounts were sometimes guilty, he had heard, of drawing a little supplementary cash in connivance with their suppliers.

"I wonder if that's how Nancy got the money?" He frowned when outside again. "Anyhow I'll have a shot at finding out."

Mrs. Allan Oldfield was shopping at Madame Gladys Shires' when he reached there. But the proprietor attended to him so promptly that he had not the time to speculate how she, on the meagre allowance her stepson made no secret about, could patronise such an expensive establishment.

"Morning, Bottomley," Sam said, his smile the ruefully amused one of a father aware that his pretty daughter twists him round her little finger. "I understand that girl of mine has nearly banked me with you, so I'd better settle while I'm able. Let me have the bill, will you?"

A statement: "To Goods supplied, £73 15s. od." was quickly produced, but there was quite an untoward delay subsequently when, still as jovial as ever, he guilelessly requested an invoice with details, "just to make sure you're not charging me twice. My joke, of course, Bottomley."

Not very long afterwards, Sam drove up to Moorheaton, an itemized and receipted account tucked away in his breast pocket.

It was a sunny day, but a touch of chill in the air gave notice that autumn was not far away, a hint accepted by Milly, who had worked a couple of hours after breakfast with Johnson, steadily potting cyclamen corms. This job done, the gardener wheeled the pots in relays through the ravine and then into the garden proper, where she picked out the most sheltered places in which to set them down.

While doing this, she noticed with surprise her husband's arrival. In small danger of being seen where she was, on the low side of the terrace, she stopped to watch him, but began to hurry indoors herself when she saw how very quickly he was doing so, though she slowed down to a negligent saunter nearer the house.

Eventually, after glancing into the various rooms on the ground floor, she located him through the sound made by clothes-hangers being pushed along a rail. Utterly astounded, she halted just inside the doorway of her daughter's bedroom, where one by one he was thrusting aside suits and dresses as he ploughed along the wearing apparel in a lengthy wardrobe fitment. Sam glanced over his shoulder before straightening. Then he turned to eye her.

"I'll meet you half-way," he encouraged her. "If you'll speak, I'll speak."

"What are you doing in here?" Milly inquired, brushing back a lock of hair with the back of an earth-filthied hand. "If you must examine Nancy's clothes for some peculiar reason I suppose you must, but you might remember the lighter fabrics soil very easily."

"Then *you'd* better keep your paws off them," Sam remarked. "I never dreamed I'd see you traipsing about the house in that mucky state. You'll soon be down to carpet slippers, holes in your stockings, and a cigarette dangling from your lip."

Invariably spotless save when gardening, the insult very

nearly caused a complete loss of her equilibrium. She remembered in time that a carefully built-up façade of dignity might be voided by bandying words with an outcast.

"Tongue-tied apparently," Sam observed. "Anyhow," he went on, holding out an invoice headed: "Madame Gladys Shires," "here's something you can check better than I can. Has Nancy had these clothes?"

Within forty-five seconds Milly's outraged aloofness succumbed to a womanly inquisitiveness.

"Why, she hasn't had any of them, not a stitch," she gasped. "What does it mean, Sam?"

"A hundred to six on Bottomley having advanced her the money to go to the Olympic Games," said Sam. "But I'll find out."

"Nancy's gone to Bradford with Bee," said her mother. "She won't be home to lunch."

Sam's face was grim. "I think I'll get to know without her assistance. In any event Bottomley's enough to answer for as it is."

"Will you be tackling him?" Milly asked.

"This afternoon, all being well," Sam replied.

"If it's true, I'll never buy another thing from him." Milly was furious. "And I'll take good care Nancy doesn't either."

"By God, but we're chatty," Sam said with aggravating relish as he examined his watch. "Anyway, I might as well dawdle at home until lunch time. Of course the business is going to the dogs while I'm dancing here and there striving to get my various encumbrances out of bother, but what does that matter?"

Milly nearly choked. "Are you calling me an encumbrance?" she demanded.

"You . . . *you* an encumbrance!" Her husband's eyebrows rose alarmingly. "You, my love, are the light of my soul."

That did it. Forgetful of the need always to be superbly poised when with him, she rushed from the room.

Before lunch, Sam wandered into the garden awhile, now glorious with phlox, dahlias, hollyhocks and heleniums. Then he went indoors and, in the study, read with pleasure a chapter of one of Sabatini's novels.

Shortly before half-past two, he was in the hall, speaking forcefully on the telephone. Ultimately all opposition at Madame Gladys Shires' was worn down, his final phrases being the most telling.

"I don't care a damn whether you were just leaving to buy

177

silks in Lyons . . . or loin-cloths in Manchester, Bottomley," he roared. "I shall be down at your place in ten minutes, and if you've gone the Lord help you when next I set eyes on you."

In his haste to be off he left the receiver lurched crookedly, and darted into the study, where he grasped a twelve-bore, double-barrelled, hammerless gun with a beautiful stock. Bearing this weapon, he cantered outdoors; springing into the Bentley, he set out for the town at a speed he had seldom equalled before.

In Teazle Street, his first call should have been at a work-shop behind Hoyle's fish shop, two doors away from Madame Gladys Shires', but, as he closed the car door, it so happened that he glanced along the street, towards the Market Approach end. Away in the distance, a man in a delicate shade of puce was walking, fat hams in rapid movement, carrying a pig-skin week-end bag and with a light overcoat thrown over his arm.

With a glint in his eyes and his gun at the trail, Sam started off in pursuit of Ramsfield's *couturier*.

He caught up to him in the palatial new premises of the Ramsfield Commercial Bank, where fully twenty customers were either being attended to by the cashiers, or gossiping while awaiting their turn.

But with the tempestuous entry of an enraged gentleman all business stopped; pound notes ceased to be counted, faces all turned in one direction, clerks rose from their stools, and Mr. Luther Whitehead Garside peeped out from the managerial office.

"So you were sneaking off, were you?" Sam bellowed. "What do you mean by cheating me out of over seventy pounds?"

Dark eyes fixed fearfully on one object only, Rafe Bottomley's accent lost its gentlemanly veneer and became at once Ram Valley. "You take heed of where you're pointing that there gun," he gasped. "There's a simple explanation, and——"

"Gun!" Sam exclaimed.

The tone of Ramsfield's *couturier* rose considerably as he misinterpreted a motion due to surprise.

"You be careful," he screeched as the twin barrels came round. "An' if you think you'll avoid serious trouble by making out it went off accidentally——"

Belatedly, Sam realized the reason for the younger man's

anxieties. "Oh, so this is what you're yelling about, is it?" he jeered, thrusting the gun into the hands of the nearest person, a sprightly person who was thoroughly enjoying herself. "Why, I don't need that . . . either to flatten your hooked nose or to thin out that scent you're swimming in . . . a *swim*, that's the ticket," he exclaimed, pouncing upon his victim.

It was Rafe Bottomley's misfortune to be the whipping boy for far more than his own sin—he suffered for the wrong-doings of the Pilling children, for the Hilda Schofield affair, for Milly's moods. Dragged out of the bank, he was forced along Market Approach and past Thorntons' showroom, where Frank Thornton most uncivilly abandoned a potential customer to elbow through the crowd growing about the horse-trough near the Vaults. Rafe Bottomley's ordeal ended there.

"That'll do for now," Sam said. "And if you want any redress, well . . ." he flourished Madame Gladys Shires' receipted invoice, "well, you might recall this before you rush into anything."

Water dripping from head to foot, his clothing limp from collar to sharply-pointed shoes, Bottomley was still gulping in air. But he was not incapable of speech, nor too addled to say the right thing when a police constable intervened in the proceedings.

"Aye, Mr. Pilling," the officer remarked with some regret on receiving an explanation not strikingly probable. "But . . . er . . . I'm afraid I'll have to put a question or two to him."

"By all means," Sam said heartily.

"The main point is whether or not he's willing to confirm what's been said," the constable continued, still most uncomfortable.

"I've nothing to say," Rafe Bottomley wailed.

An official-looking notebook was replaced. "That settles it," said the officer. "As far as I'm concerned he wanted to immerse himself and you lent a willing hand, sort of religious ceremony, like."

"Exactly," Sam agreed.

With that the bookmaker and the emissary of the law separated with a mutual regard personified in the exchange of two extremely sly winks, the constable immediately setting about the dispersal of the throng, Sam returning to collect his gun.

In the bank, the manager, Mr. Luther Whitehead Garside, and a lady were laughing uproariously.

"You're a one, Mr. Pilling," the manager said, chuckling. "But you haven't escaped quite scot-free."

"He hasn't," Mrs. Dale Watkinson concurred. "Just look at these gloves of mine, Sam. They were pale biscuit before you pushed that greasy gun on to me."

"Did I give it to *you*, Carrie?" Sam grinned.

"You did," nodded Mrs. Watkinson. "And now you're going to have the pleasure of buying me a new pair."

Sam laughed. "No time like the present, Carrie. Where do we get 'em?"

"At Iredale Mallinson's," Mrs. Watkinson giggled. "Now, come on. No shirking."

This, and the story of what preceded it, spread like wildfire. Nancy learnt of it as soon as she entered the George on her way home, and at once sped off to Moorheaton with the exciting news. However, her mother had heard everything already, down to the last detail, the information reaching her through five sources — the telephoned advices of four friends and a visit paid by her sister from next door.

When a man is warmly applauded by scores of acquaintances for a sensational action, he is in danger of becoming over-pleased with himself.

Sam was in that state of mind when he drove home rather late for supper, which he ate with his wife and daughter, who for the most part discussed the affair between themselves, both conspicuously omitting him from their talk.

"Oh, no, he wasn't dunning me for the money, Mummy," Nancy was saying. "But he wanted me to model for him at some wretched dress show and wouldn't accept my refusal. Positively he went on and on and on . . . you know, drooling away but always coming back to it."

"Did he mention the money then?"

"Sort of." Nancy nodded. "That's what made me so hellishly mad at the end."

Milly shook her head. "I dare say he got . . . and I won't have you swearing, Nancy . . . I dare say he got all he deserved, but I can't say that brawling in public appeals to me, Nancy."

"Oh, I don't know, Mummy."

"Not . . . *not* when we're so particular about Archie," Milly murmured. "It isn't setting a good example, is it?"

Gravely Sam helped himself to another generous slice of salmon.

"Lawks! But what wouldn't I have given to see that violet well and truly doused," Nancy said, surreptitiously eyeing her father. Finally, sheer curiosity overcame any qualms. "By the way, Daddy," she went on, much too casually for complete self-possession, "is it true that Mrs. Dale Watkinson helped you in the bank?"

Her father glanced up from the salad bowl, into which he was making extensive inroads.

"Certainly," he said.

Nancy's eyes opened wider. "But it isn't true, is it, that afterwards you took her along to Iredale Mallinson's and bought her a present?"

"Certainly," said Sam again, reaching for the dressing. "A chap's gun-moll merits a reward, doesn't she?"

Milly rose with careless ease. "If you'll excuse me," she said. "Cook wishes to see me before posting-time . . . she's arranging for her sister to stay with her while we're away."

As soon as she had gone, Sam put down his knife and fork with quiet deliberation.

"Now then, Nancy," he started off sternly, "I'm not asking for an explanation from you, because there isn't one that even your ingenuity could conjure up. But I want you to realize that what you've done is no different from stealing money out of my wallet."

That was the beginning of the fiercest quarrel there had ever been between father and daughter. It was also the beginning of a phase during which Nancy was out-of-hand as never before. If her parents had any consolation at all it was that her wildness was the wildness of the crowd with whom she spent her time, and, in so far as they could know, she never went out with Josef Brozik or anyone of his kidney. Indeed, if anything, it seemed almost certain that she avoided all excursions alone with a man.

4

The Saturday of Ramsfield Gala turned out sunny, with a fresh breeze. Sam was a leading patron of this old-established function in the Park, and as such it was a recognized thing that his wife and daughter would accompany him that afternoon. This led to a battle royal over the luncheon table at

181

Glenfield before Nancy would consent to go, and, afterwards, to take her mind off a bitter conflict, Milly slipped upstairs with a brush and a pot of quick-drying varnish, to carry out a small matter of renovation she had long planned for the first suitable occasion. Moreover, by hurrying over dressing, she was ready to start in time, with the comforting feeling of a job well done.

Towards the latter part of the afternoon, in the Flower Marquee in the Park, they met the Crabtrees, and while Walter Crabtree, a twinkle in his eye, drew Sam aside to discuss the Rafe Bottomley affair, the ladies rhapsodized over the blooms on show.

Before parting, however, Mrs. Crabtree mentioned an item of gossip she had noticed in the morning paper. On hearing it, Nancy turned away, to hide a total loss of colour and the warmer glow of anticipation which swiftly succeeded it.

"I see your niece's divorce has been made absolute, Mrs. Pilling," Mrs. Crabtree said.

"Has it?" said Milly. "I believe Laura said it would be about now, but that was a while ago and I'd forgotten."

"Oh, yes, it's through," said Mrs. Crabtree. "Isn't it a shame so many young couples seem to come a cropper nowadays? They didn't in my time, and I'm not inclined to believe that they *had* to stick it out then, as is often made out. They regarded marriage vows more seriously from the beginning, that's my conclusion."

As the family holiday started on the following Tuesday, Sam was putting in long hours at the office to clear everything up, and so as soon as reasonably possible they left the Park. Nancy was dropped in town, and then he ran Milly home, his intention being to return to the office again. However, as he was moving off slowly along the drive at Glenfield, he glimpsed frantic beckoning from the front door.

"Sam," Milly gulped. "Something queer's happening in my bathroom, and I think it must be Olga, because she isn't in the kitchen. And Cook's out."

"Let's see," said Sam.

They hurried upstairs and then through the bedroom once shared. At the far end, against a door, both halted and looked at one another, certainly one of them fearing a tragedy. Now and then they heard a light drumming noise, and moaning never ceased.

"I'll have to break it down," said Sam.

At the third attempt with his shoulder, the woodwork splintered, and he stumbled forward. After that, one glance was enough for him, and apparently for Milly.

"You'd better go downstairs, Sam," she said.

"You couldn't be more right," Sam agreed.

Ten minutes later, her face the picture of woe, she entered the drawing-room.

"Sam," she said, "I've tried a sponge and soapy hot water, but it doesn't make a bit of difference, she's as fast as fast on the seat. You'd better ring for the doctor."

Grimly he eyed her. "And you'd better let me have some details first. Is dynamite needed to blow her off it? What have you been up to?"

Distractedly she rubbed her forehead. "It was just quick-drying varnish, Sam. And it is perfectly dry where she isn't sitting. She's had a magazine with her—my new *Good Housekeeping*, mind you—and the warmth of her body. . . ."

"All right, you go back, and I'll get on with the telephoning," said Sam.

Fortunately Dr. Lister Fox was at home; he could afford to take things easily with two energetic young partners well capable of running the practice. On hearing the nature of the call for his services at Glenfield, he laughed his head off, and there was still more than a suspicion of a grin about him on arrival. But a more becoming professional gravity settled on his face while he was being ushered upstairs.

"Well, there you are, doctor," said Sam, halting sufficiently short of the open door, to keep himself out of sight of the occupant of the throne in the bathroom. "If there's anything you want me for I'll be downstairs."

About a quarter of an hour later Dr. Lister Fox appeared in the drawing-room doorway, sweating profusely.

"For God's sake, pour me a stiff whisky, Pilling," he said. "And then ring for the ambulance and fetch me a saw. She'll have to go to the Hospital with a portion of your sanitary equipment attached to her person. They'll soon part her from it there."

"She's still fast?" Sam ejaculated.

"Immovable . . . the Rock of Gibraltar in position," Dr. Lister Fox grunted.

When Sam returned from the garage, the doctor had finished his drink and had gone upstairs. Sam followed, coughing loudly in his wife's bedroom. Dr. Lister Fox appeared, took the saw, and turned back.

"Ah, Mrs. Pilling," he said, stepping forward breezily, "now we'll soon have her——"

At this point his left foot lost all contact with the highly-polished linoleum. With an almighty crash he tumbled, bringing down with him an array of glass-stoppered bottles and the glass shelving on which they had been standing.

Sam doubled back. When he peered into the bathroom, he saw his wife, with a look of sheer horror in her eyes and finger-tips against her lips; Olga had ceased to moan and, leaning forward, was gaping towards the floor on which, leg twisted strangely, Dr. Lister Fox was lying, beads of perspiration already forming on his forehead, and a greyness investing his cheeks.

"Fracture," he said between clenched teeth.

When the ambulance men arrived he coolly directed operations. Under his instructions Olga was released from her static position by cutting across the lavatory seat behind her. She was then placed face downwards on a stretcher, covered with a blanket, which then showed a queer projection in the middle, and carried downstairs and outside, where she was slid into the ambulance. Dr. Lister Fox, on another stretcher, followed shortly afterwards.

When the casualties, doctor and patient, had gone, Sam nodded at his wife.

"Well, I've tried to stop you painting and decorating, and I've warned you about over-polishing the floors," he said, abandoning the nodding to shake his head slowly, "but never in my natural could I have imagined a 'do' like this."

"It shouldn't have happened," Milly said crossly. "They've a perfectly nice bathroom of their own, and both Olga and Cook know they haven't to use mine. Perhaps I'm silly and faddy but I do like a bathroom to myself. The fact is that Olga is disobedient, and I'm not going to keep her any longer."

"I must say I'm damned well sickened myself of seeing her bob up somewhere or other when anything unusual happens in the house," Sam said.

Milly had finally decided. She would pay Olga a month's wages and send her home. This would leave them without a maid on returning from Scarborough, but that would not matter for a few days. And perhaps Cook's sister would stay over for a little while.

On both morning and afternoon of Sunday, Sam was at the office, drilling into Archie, who had returned from his holiday, the key principles of good bookmaking, upon which he must rely and from which he must never depart when using the extra authority now granted him. Father and son followed a procedure more or less in the same vein on Monday, Archie handling the morning's mail and dictating replies to Margaret Berry, while in the afternoon he sat at the big desk, finger on the pulse of the business as through the plate-glass panels in the wall he watched the blackboards in the Blower Room and the Telephone Room which reflected the course of market changes at Lewes.

Just before the "off" for the three-thirty, Captain Gainsway-Sinkinson leaned over the counter of "Inquiries" and asked for Mr. Pilling.

In view of his son's new duties, over which Fred Lumb would be keeping a watchful eye in his employer's absence, Sam interviewed his caller in the comfortably appointed waiting-room.

"Not at all, old man, deuced snug on this sofa." Captain Gainsway-Sinkinson was expansive, waving aside the explanation. "Preferable to a dug-out on the western front, what what?"

"Aye," Sam agreed.

Despite this friendly opening, differences arose immediately the Captain pushed his fingers into the flap of an envelope.

"This last letter of yours—this final letter as you call it," he observed reproachfully. "It won't do, old chappie . . . won't do as between sportsmen. Dammit, even if I have been a little dilatory at times I've always pottered up . . . unloosed the old purse-strings in the end?"

Sam remarked that the annual turnover of bookmakers, an occupation often considered vulgar, amounted altogether to tens of millions of pounds, with nothing more binding on either themselves or clients than their simple word of honour.

"And all the bookmakers I know would lose more sleep about failing in their engagements than many businessmen would do about breaking a written contract," he went on. "That's why paying up 'in the end' won't do for me, and that's why I'm closing your account."

Captain Gainsway-Sinkinson fiercely tugged his toothbrush moustache. "Why?" he demanded.

"Because you've caused us a great deal of trouble," Sam said. "Moreover, you seem to expect me to keep your account active even when you're behindhand with settlement, which means that eventually you hope to clear your debts at my expense when you've a bumper winning week. That game is no good to me, and in the long run it's no good to you."

White with chagrin, Captain Gainsway-Sinkinson rose with dignity.

"I suppose, old top, I was causing you a great deal of trouble when I recommended my friend Peter Entwistle to the firm," he said. "Or . . ." his lip curled, "is he one of your least desirable clients?"

Sam shook his head. "On the contrary, he's becoming one of my most valued ones," he said. "For that reason I'll be only too happy to pay you the usual commission on his business for the introduction . . . retrospectively."

Captain Gainsway-Sinkinson jumped as though he had been stung.

"What the devil do you take me for, sir?" he thundered. "A wretched tout?"

"Brass is always useful," Sam murmured.

"That, Pilling, depends on how it is acquired," Captain Gainsway-Sinkinson commented icily. "But I might have difficulty in convincing *you* about that . . . one of the problems a gentleman encounters when he is fool enough to consort with those not his equal."

"Isn't your wife a lady?" Sam asked.

"What the hell do you mean, sir?" his caller shouted.

"No need to get excited," Sam said mildly. "I was only going to remind you that old Simeon Crowther of Bankdam was great-grandfather to both her and me. Now hop it."

Captain Gainsway-Sinkinson withdrew, but hardly quietly. And then Sam, first muttering: "Of all the fatheads," glanced along the glass-panelled corridor. Deciding to leave Archie a little longer to his own devices, he crossed the Telephone Room to the private exchange in the corner, where one of the young ladies quickly obtained him a connection with Dr. Lister Fox's residence.

The news about the doctor was most satisfactory; his wife had an excellent sense of humour, and Sam was chuckling before their conversation ended.

*   *   *

With the exception of Gilbert Pilling, surely by now a deep-water sailor, and Bee Hirst, who had gone to Scotland with her fiancé's family, the Firths, the party for Scarborough was the same as that of the previous year: all the Roebucks, three Pillings, and Scipio and Kate Dyson, who, since their father had relinquished the law, had always been taken for holidays by their Uncle Sam and Aunt Milly.

Four cars were used, the Bentley being the last away, delayed unconscionably by the mistress of Glenfield's gardening conferences with Johnson. She was out of breath as she ran past the side of the house.

"Now there's no need to say you're sorry, Milly, and I'm not always harping, whatever that means," Sam said pleasantly enough as she climbed into the car. "All I asked was why you fixed nine thirty for leaving? We're on holiday, we've all day in front of us, and it'd have been just as easy for you to say ten o'clock, which by the way it nearly is. . . ."

"There he is, Kate, rubbing it in again," Milly was remarking when the Riley, driven by Nancy, flashed through the lower gateway on Moorheaton Drive. "Whatever has she come back for? I'd better see." She opened the door again, preparing to descend.

"Well," said Sam, in that philosophical tone which sends married women into berserk rages, "well, we'll be on the road some time. Not that I'm bothered."

"Be quiet, then," his wife turned back to hiss.

Actually Nancy's errand was completed before her mother came bustling into the hall. She had arranged already for any letters to be promptly readdressed and posted on to her, but the afterthought had been in connection with a telephone call.

"Cook, be a dear, won't you," she said, handing her a slip of paper on which a Scarborough number was written in pencil. "If anyone wants me specially, tell them where I am and give them the number, please."

"I will, Miss Nancy. And I hope you all have a right lovely holiday and——"

The arrival of Milly broke this up, though she was again guilty of holding up the departure for a minute or so more. She had had *her* afterthought.

"Oh, and, Cook," she said, smiling. "You know how Mr. Archie likes his rice pudding? Well, when you serve it will you make sure all the skin is off beforehand. I don't know why it is, but it seems to put him quite off it."

"I'll take good care of that, Mrs. Pilling." Cook nodded competently.

At last the Bentley began to glide silently along the drive, Sam's face wreathed in a smile.

Ahead was Scarborough . . . the M.C.C.'s match against

Yorkshire, and a three days' view, weather permitting, of the M.C.C. Australian team in action against a picked eleven . . . the orchestra on the Spa . . . games on the sands . . . golf on a grand course . . . a fishing trip or two . . . hobnobbing with famous cricketers, many of whom were friends met on similar holidays, some of them old friends of the Yorkshire team . . . Scarborough.

And, if he were lucky, this care-free interlude, respite not only for himself, might bring about something nearer the former relationship between himself and Milly. Sam felt very optimistic as, checked cap on his head and cigar between his teeth, he drove along that morning.

If Sam had been asked to outline outstanding recollections of that holiday it would not have been easy for him, but in the light of subsequent events he always remembered one late evening gathering in the bar of the hotel, when a score of people with renowned names pulled his leg and demanded a tip for the St. Leger.

"I'd tell you the winner if I knew it," he had said, and, this announcement greeted with a roar of friendly but ironical applause, he had gone on: "And, moreover, I'd accept all your bets, gentlemen. Mind you, I'm not making out I'm delirious with joy when favourites romp home one after the other, but if my job's done as it should be done . . . as I've instilled it into my own son it should be done . . . then I've nothing more to worry about than any other business-man. Of course there's an element of risk, but doesn't that apply to anything? No, I don't go after the fat kills you've been mentioning—all I'm interested in is a modest percent-age profit. That's how I run my business, and that's how every bookie worth his salt does."

More laughter, hearty claps on his shoulder, another small drink perhaps, and then a peep into the ballroom where, laughter wrinkles deepening about his eyes, he noticed that Estelle had still not captured her man, though this was not for want of effort.

On Sunday morning, golf at Ganton, he and Clem making up a congenial foursome with a famous Middlesex profes-sional and a revered former captain of England.

Then the return to the hotel, where Simeon Calverley and Jim Oldfield were staying, along with other Ramsfield people. But he had not known that his cousin James was there, until a smart and dazzlingly attractive young woman, wear-ing a model sports suit, swayed towards him in the lounge.

"Good morning, Mr. Pilling," Mrs. Hildred Pickersgill said, smiling. "I suppose you haven't seen my husband and Mr. Wainwright?"

"I haven't, Mrs. Pickersgill, but I dare say they're outdoors enjoying some fresh air before lunch, as I expect my wife is," Sam said. "And when did you arrive?"

"About an hour ago, Mr. Pilling," Mrs. Pickersgill replied. "Shall we try to find our missing partners?"

The next memory belongs more properly to Milly—who with narrowing eyes saw her husband advancing towards her, laughing and joking with a woman she quickly recognized as an ex-mannequin of considerable repute at home.

That afternoon Sam was frightened to death by the acrobatics of Kate. Feeling in disgrace for no reason he could think of, he had taken his niece out and, sitting on the warm side of a groyne, spent a peaceful hour or so. She was writing an immensely long letter to Barbara Ramsden Lister, and he was finding *Jew Suss* so absorbing that he read to the end of a chapter before filling his pipe, which he had been longing to do. When he put down his novel he discovered he was alone—one glance at the lofty sea wall not far away caused him to scramble anxiously to his feet. There Kate was, high above him, her sole foothold the interstices between great blocks of stone, none of which looked sufficient for anything larger than the claws of a tit.

"What's the matter, Uncle?" she cried, looking down.

"I'll tell you that when you're alongside me, and for God's sake be careful," Sam said, beginning to sweat when he noticed the jagged rocks below her. "And take it very slowly."

She laughed. "I'm as safe as houses, Uncle Sam."

Nevertheless, he stood beneath, hoping to check her fall if she slipped. But she descended safely enough, and did not joke again.

"I'm sorry, Uncle Sam," she said, her intelligent eyes full of concern. "I really did scare you, didn't I?"

Sam, mopping his brow, nodded. "I'd visions of all sorts of things, love. All nasty . . . why, you'd nothing worth speaking to cling on to. And at that height . . . weren't you a bit dizzy?"

"I'm like a monkey, Uncle," she said. "And heights never have bothered me. Perhaps it's because I never think of them."

"What I'm thinking of at present is a cup of tea," Sam groaned. "I need either that or something stronger to pull me round."

Kate giggled as she took his arm. "Tea will be much the best for you, Uncle. Let's hurry so that we get a table near the orchestra . . . I love watching them."

Laura Roebuck was already in the lounge of the hotel when they went in, talking to a lady from London with whom she had struck up a seaside holiday friendship. To the amusement of certain members of her party and to the dismay of others, her la-di-da accent had become much more pronounced. Within a few minutes of her introducing her brother-in-law to her companion, however, she fleetingly lost her composure when, in all innocence, he chanced to mention his profession.

Previous to this the Londoner had been speaking with admiration about the graceful lines of the Pillings' cream and black car.

"Oh, a bookmaker, Mr. Pilling," she said, as if this explained the possession of an expensive vehicle. "Oh, I *see.*"

Laura, dull red to the hair-roots, glared at her brother-in-law.

That was another of Sam's memories of Scarborough.

On the second Wednesday of their holiday, Pillings, Roebucks and Dysons went in a body to Doncaster for the St. Leger, Nancy alone remaining at the hotel, insisting she would really appreciate a quiet day for once. From Scarborough the drive was rather long, but Clem Roebuck was keen to see the race. The expedition suited Sam's purpose, too. He and Mo Barton, one of the largest operators in Tattersalls', had heavy dealings to their mutual advantage; they usually spoke to each other over the telephone three or four times a week during the flat-racing season, but seldom met. This would give them an opportunity for a brief talk in person.

After the usual soggy race-course lunch, Sam sought out Mr. Barton, with whom he had a pleasant conversation. Then he rejoined his party, the ladies of which were looking around for anyone they might know, either by acquaintance or as the result of a weekly perusal of a glossy-illustrated society magazine. Their total reward was two views of Tony Flassati of Ramsfield, once when screaming excitedly in the last furlong of a race, and once grasping a prodigiously thick wad of bank-notes in his large, fleshy hand.

"What a common creature," Laura exclaimed. She had gone down to the extent of four two-shilling place tickets, and one two-shilling win ticket. "And I do think it mean of you, Sam. You must know the best horses."

Sam shook his head. "I should be kicked out of my union if I lent a hand to such an ardent supporter of the tote as you, Laura."

The great event of the afternoon duly came. Boswell, the winner at 20/1, Pat Beasley up, came home to the never-to-be-forgotten roar of a Town Moor crowd on Leger Day.

As the frame went up with starters and jockeys for the last race of the day, a small man insinuated himself through the throng with the dexterity of his kind, his bright, sharp eyes alert. He carried in his head a message from Ramsfield, relayed by Blower to the course, then by tic-tac man to bookmaker; a minor miracle of communication to locate so speedily an individual among a crowd of a quarter of a million.

"They want me to telephone my office!" Sam remarked when he was found. "Right off?"

"That's what the governor told me." The runner's every syllable was pure Bow Bells. "Pronto, Mr. Pilling."

Sam felt in his pocket; two half-crowns changed hands. "Right," he said. "And give my compliments and thanks to Mr. Barton, will you?" After this he excused himself to those with him.

For an ordinary member of the public on the Town Moor of Doncaster on St. Leger afternoon it is a difficult matter to obtain quick use of a telephone, but, aided both by officials who knew him personally and those to whom his card was sufficient introduction, he was soon speaking to Ramsfield.

When he rang off, he stood for a few moments collecting his thoughts, his eyes angry, his face set in harsh lines.

"The god-damned fool," he murmured, his violence restrained but none the less apparent. "But how the hell did Fred come to let him do it?"

The story was tragically simple: late money had flowed in for the winner of the St. Leger, none of which had been laid off to balance the book. These additional investments amounted to approximately a thousand pounds, which, at a starting price of 20/1, meant that on these commissions alone the firm would pay out twenty thousand pounds on settling day, almost every penny unnecessarily.

"Twenty thousand pounds chucked down the drain," Sam muttered. "Well, the bloody young lunatic's finished with bookmaking after this."

The crowd was slowly dispersing, and knots of people could now more easily be distinguished where closely packed humanity had been before.

Milly saw her husband some distance away, and, knowing trouble when she saw it, went to meet him. As always in such circumstances she forgot Hilda Schofield and all her private and silly jealousies.

"Something's the matter, isn't it?" she asked.

Sam summoned up a smile. "Well, I'll have to go straight back home to square up a bit of a mistake at the office, that's all."

She bit her lip. "It's Archie, isn't it?"

He laughed. "Nay, Milly, that *would* be the conclusion you'd jump to. As a matter of fact I shan't know who's really to blame until I get back."

"Sam," she begged, touching his arm, "let me come with you."

"Not I," he scoffed. "You can't do any good. Besides, it's bad enough to think that the hotel won't have to provide me with roofing and food without you making it a double bean-feast for them. Our bill will be just the same, whether we're there or not, and you must know I'm stingy in these things."

She was not deceived by his levity, but she knew she was up against a stone wall.

"All right, Sam," she said, trying to smile. "But you'll telephone me to-night, won't you?"

"Of course I will." Sam nodded.

Laura Roebuck and Lois, Scipio Dyson and the others kept glancing curiously at them, and so, from then onwards, both Sam and Milly put their best faces forward. There was much joking about how Milly should return to Scarborough, and eventually she decided to squeeze with Kate and Jim Roebuck into the M.G., which had been loaned to him. The final leave-taking in the car-park was most cheerful.

It took Sam an hour and a half to get really free of Doncaster, but the enforced crawl, amid a seemingly endless stream of traffic fore and aft, enabled him to assess the situation much more judicially than he would have been capable of doing had it been possible for him to push down the accelerator and, in the heat of temper, rush home.

Before cooling off at all, he made a remark to himself which was ultimately responsible for an astonishing train of thought.

"Twenty thousand pounds or thereabouts," he growled.

"A damned fortune in itself . . . enough to smash plenty of bookies I could name, enough to cripple hundreds of others."

This line of thought was advanced during a lengthy hold-up, which motor-police, buzzing to and fro, were endeavouring to straighten out.

"Supposing just now I knew that the loss of twenty thousand would seriously embarrass me," he murmured, "what would be the effect upon Archie and Nancy when they were told I was in a tight corner, or at least that we'd have to cut down on spending all round? Would they whine, or would they show that somewhere or other in them they'd guts and common sense?"

Creeping along again at ten miles an hour he smiled unsmilingly.

"It'd be damned interesting to try 'em out," he thought. "And . . ." his eyes were intent, "it might be the best thing in the world for them to realize what short commons meant . . . or commons say a good deal shorter than they've been used to. But what about me—could I stick it?"

Sam was under no delusions about two things: the pride which he had always felt about his own success, which he had never been too successful in concealing; or the sly digs he would receive in abundance from many Ramsfield people if it were believed he had more or less come a cropper.

"Yes," he nodded, "I should be chafing to some tune, shouldn't I just. But it might be worth it, well worth it. I'm not really a bit forrarder in disciplining either Nancy or Archie, and unless I can pull something extraordinary out of the bag I don't reckon I ever shall be. This might be my chance. It needs carefully studying over though."

Previous to this his one desire had been to reach his office as quickly as possible, where Archie and the two senior members of the staff were awaiting him. But even when the road cleared he drove at a very modest rate, and, twelve miles from Ramsfield, pulled up for dinner at a road-house noted for its food.

Over the meal he gave the most scrupulous consideration to the most important factor of any, his wife.

"Yes, I should have to hoodwink her just as much as the others," he decided. "She's put aside a nice bit out of presents and what not, and if she'd even an inkling of what I was doing, she'd be slipping money to the children whenever they were tight . . . which," he added glumly, "would be often.

But if she thought I might have to use her savings some time, she'd hang on to every penny like grim death."

While cutting a piece of gorgonzola, he unerringly touched upon the ultimate truth concerning Milly.

"She might be shocked at the start, but it wouldn't last two minutes as soon as she realized here was something serious to face up to," he pondered. "And it's because she's always had something that's a matter of doubt in all of our children —guts. Of course she'd play steam with me when in due course I had to tell her it all had been pretence, but even at that she's gumption enough to understand just why I kept her out of the plot."

Not very long afterwards a gentleman washing his hands at a basin in the Gentlemen's was quite startled when his neighbour muttered unexpectedly: "And there'll be no half measures, I'm going the whole damned hog."

Doubts and reservations finally discarded, his future course of action clear, the part of a lifetime before him, Sam resumed the homeward journey.

CHAPTER SEVEN

THREE people were in the manager's room of PILLING ALWAYS PAYS—Fred Lumb, ploughing steadily through the evening paper as he smoked a hook-shaped pipe; Archie Pilling, pacing restlessly between tape-machine and window, through which he peered frequently at the Town Hall clock; and Harry Sutcliffe, Fred Lumb's chief assistant, an alert-looking man of about thirty, who that evening expected to experience his first set-back in a career which had begun as an office-boy in the same firm.

"The old man ought to have been here long ago," Archie fretted. "I hope to God he hasn't been indulging in some of his blasted continental road-hogging, as cheery as you please on the wrong side of the road."

Harry Sutcliffe shifted uncomfortably in his chair. "A head-on crash would just about put the tin lid on to-day."

"You've said it, brother," Archie grunted.

Their vigil was ended as Fred Lumb, who read a newspaper with precision and method, scanned the right-hand column of the back page.

"He's here," Archie cried. "Coming round the corner of Market Approach. No wings dented either."

They each braced up. The last speaker knuckled his square jaw; Harry Sutcliffe fingered his tie; and Fred Lumb knocked out his pipe with extreme deliberation.

A few minutes later they heard the outer door open, and then the sounds of rather slow, somewhat tired, footsteps proceeding along the glass-panelled corridor towards the big private office at the end, the door of which was quickly closed.

This entry, so different from what had been anticipated, was responsible for a brief silence.

"Well, I'd better be off to take my medicine," said Archie. "He'll want to see both of you, too, so you might lend me support until I get there."

His father was sitting at the desk when they went in, dictating into the mouthpiece of the dictaphone a memo. for his secretary, Margaret Berry, to transcribe the next morning. It merely concerned letters of apology to several eminent cricketers for breaking engagements with them.

"Sit down all of you," he said on finishing. "Now I've a fair idea of the figures of to-day's blundering, so we needn't bother about them. What I'd like to know is how it happened. Why did you allow Archie to do such a crazy thing, Fred?"

"I knew nothing about it until Harry sent a girl in a taxi with a note for me," Fred Lumb replied. "I was at home—I trod on a drawing-pin on Monday."

"You did what?" Sam asked.

Fred Lumb possessed a presence peculiarly his own, but he definitely appeared to feel his position after this trivial revelation.

"My boot soles were thin, and I stepped on it in the Adding Room," he said testily. "The thing festered and it's only just burst."

"I see," said Sam, swivelling his chair to gaze at Harry Sutcliffe. "And what happened to you? Did you post yourself in a letter-box or what?"

"I tell you I'd a real painful——" Fred Lumb started off, but was silenced by a firm: "That'll do, Fred," from his employer.

"Harry isn't to blame at all for what I did . . . or for what I didn't do," said Archie. "In fact we damned nearly had a stand-up fight about it."

"Why didn't you lay off?' his father continued. "Why did you violate the most important rule there is in this kind of business?"

"Because I felt certain Boswell hadn't a chance," Archie replied. "And nearly all the late money came from Scarborough, where several such as Mr. Wainwright, who's a numbskull where horses are concerned, must have followed Mr. Oldfield's lead. He's a rare kidder always, as you know. But he's a chap who's constantly dropping a packet through his preference for wild outsiders, and I reckoned we could safely nick nine hundred or a thousand extra."

"I reckon there'll be a few numbskulls celebrating at Scarborough to-night," Sam said dryly. "Anyhow, that'll be all for now, so you and Harry get off."

Surprise showed itself in three faces, and was to be increased considerably.

"Before you two go," Sam recalled them, "remember this, not a word is to be passed on to anyone—not even to your closest pals, Archie—as to who has caused our loss to-day. We shan't be able to keep it dark for long that we've taken a nasty knock, but I don't want the other to get out, ever."

Archie was gaping. "Why must it get out at all . . . about us dropping a fairish pile?" he asked.

Sam thoughtfully rolled a pencil on his desk before looking up.

"That's something I'm afraid I shall have to leave over until I've gone into things more carefully with Fred. That's why I want him to stay here with me for a while."

Nothing further was said just then. Archie's mouth opened, and Harry Sutcliffe risked a surreptitious rearward glance as he went out.

Meantime Fred Lumb was steadily eyeing his boss, but did not speak until the outer door closed. Then, clearing his throat, he went into action.

"And what's your little game, Sam?" he inquired, continuing with an impressive enumeration of Government stocks, industrial shares, and Building Society deposits. "Why, you could raise fifty thousand before noon to-morrow, and another forty or fifty thousand by Friday. And that's not reckoning the firm's credit balance at the Ramsfield Commercial Bank, which isn't to be sniffed at." He pointed his finger. "And I *know*, Sam."

Sam smiled faintly. "And you're the only one who does,

Fred, because Milly's never been money conscious, and that's why what I am contemplating is feasible. Now, listen, Fred . . . I'm going to talk to you not only about Archie, but about Nancy and Gilbert as well."

In due course, many emotions appeared on Fred Lumb's face: bewilderment, incredulity, the dawning of understanding, sympathy—and once he blinked as if upset.

"Yes, it could be done, Sam, and it might do 'em good," he commented very slowly at the end. "But have you thought what this may mean to you?"

"Yes, folk laughing at me up their sleeves. But my day will come, when they learn how I've fooled 'em. It needn't be long, either. Six months or so, just to prove that I had done the trick . . . or hadn't."

Fred Lumb had been deliberating. "There's another thing, Sam. Have you considered the effect of this on the business? Some of our clients might fight shy of us if queer rumours got about."

"Aye, I dare say," Sam agreed.

"No dare say about it," Fred affirmed, jerking his head in the direction of a small building at the opposite side of Market Square. "Why, Ben Buckley over yonder would get so many of our accounts he'd imagine the millennium had come."

"Ben Buckley." Sam almost whispered the name.

He stared so long at his companion that Fred, under that unseeing regard, began to wonder whether family cares could have caused some mental instability.

"What you lose on the swings you gain on the roundabouts," Sam started off again, his manner rapt. "That's it, Fred," he said, leaving his chair excitedly. "I know I can buy Ben out, and that's what I'll do. You and me will have a squabble—we can concoct what it's to be about—and then you'll take over Ben Buckley's business *as your own*."

Fred Lumb swallowed. "Hold on, lad, go a bit slower."

"Listen, Fred," Sam said once again.

When his voice died away at the conclusion of the explanation Fred whistled expressively. "I'll tell you what, Sam," he said, "the whole thing is just the kind of trick your great-grandfather, Simeon Crowther, would have revelled in, if all I've heard of him is true."

Sam beamed. "Do you really think so, Fred?"

"I do that, lad. Mind you," Fred Lumb seldom praised, and possibly repented being too free with it, "mind you, the

proof of the pudding's in the eating, isn't it? Not that it isn't
... well, a fairish idea."

The telephone was never left connected through to Sam's office, and the pair of them, marching to the private exchange, spent an exasperating period with a vast array of switches and vari-coloured plugs before contact with the Post Office Exchange was effected. Then Sam had a lengthy and most satisfactory talk with Ben Buckley, with whom he arranged an appointment, out of Ramsfield, for the following morning.

"That's that, Fred," he gloated. "And I'm willing to bet you that by a week to-night all the town knows you as the chap who's taken over Ben Buckley's concern. And, by jingo, aren't we going to be bitter rivals."

"But us and Ben have always been on the most friendly terms," Fred expostulated.

"Well, *we* shan't be." Sam grinned at his manager's stupefaction. "But I'll tell you the why and wherefore of that another time. And now, lad, I'm running you home as you've a gammy foot."

Fred Lumb lived on the north side of the town, opposite the Park Gates. On the way there an arrangement was made for a full-scale discussion of the project on the following Saturday night, at the office.

Desultorily playing snooker by himself, Archie thrust his cue so hastily into the rack on hearing his father's arrival that it tumbled to the floor.

Sam was in the study, selecting a key from his key-ring, to open a drawer inside the roll-top desk.

"Oh, you're in, are you, Archie?" he said, turning.

"I didn't feel overmuch like joining the gang," Archie admitted. "I say, Dad, maybe I'm off my rocker, but is this affair more serious than ... well, more serious than I might have thought?"

"How would you view it if you'd lost the amount I have?"

"Coldly ... but ... er ..." Archie hesitated, "it would depend, wouldn't it, on what I'd still left in the kitty?"

Sam, scrutinizing the figures in his private bank-book, clicked his tongue against his teeth.

"It would, and that's what I've to go into for the remainder of this week," he said. "Aye, I shall be dancing attendance on lawyers, bankers, stockbrokers and accountants right up to Saturday. It's the only way I can ascertain properly how my resources can be squeezed out."

"God, it's bad all right then," Archie muttered. "I . . . I suppose there's nothing I can do—no fetching and carrying?"

The reply Sam quietly made was designed to linger in the mind of the recipient. "If you and your brother and sister could pay me back what you've had in cars and other luxuries it would help. It amounts to a tidy sum, lad."

"I'll say it does," Archie murmured. "Though I'm afraid I haven't considered it very much before."

From then onwards Sam became brisk, beginning by telling him that the next morning he must leave for Scarborough to bring his mother home on Saturday.

"There's nothing you can do here, so you might as well have a couple of days' pleasuring there," he went on. "Go in your own car, and for heaven's sake don't alarm your mother."

"I'll do my best, but it's occurring to me that I'm pretty useless," Archie said gloomily. "Any idea when you'll really know how this muck-up of mine is going to affect us, Dad?"

Frowning with concentration, Sam drummed his fingers on the mantelpiece. "If all runs smoothly," he said, in a tone of cautious optimism, "I might be in that position by Saturday evening. Anyway, I want both you and Nancy to stop in then—tell her when your mother isn't about. And, by the way, remind me first thing in the morning to give you enough cash to clear the hotel bill. With a large settling day ahead of me next week it might be risky to issue cheques on my own account."

Horrified, Archie stared at his father. "Phew! It's bloody grim all right. And I knew in my bones something damned nasty had happened before leaving the office. Harry Sutcliffe hadn't a word for the cat, either, so you can bet he had the same idea."

"We shall see," Sam said, less hopefully. "Ah, well, now I'd better ring your mother up as I promised."

His conversation with Milly was a most difficult one, as he had to try to effect a compromise which was doomed from the start. But if he failed wholly to allay her fears, at least he succeeded in preventing her from rushing home at once. Anxious she certainly was, but that was the price she had to pay; and now, irrevocably committed to his scheme, Sam was paying it, too.

In explaining to his son how he would be engaged for the

next two or three days with sundry professional gentlemen, Sam had been strictly truthful; but what he omitted to confide was that these lawyers, accountants, bankers and stockbrokers would be strangers to him, not local men whom he had consulted for years. It was an obvious precaution if secrecy were to be maintained.

He chose Manchester as the most suitable base for operations, and by one o'clock on Saturday, after relentlessly driving everyone concerned into unflagging effort, the job was done. Ben Buckley's business had been acquired, the contract for sale containing a stiff penalty clause if the vendor should reveal the name of the purchaser. A substantial credit had been placed at Fred Lumb's disposal in a banking account opened in his name, and, subject to putting his signature to four or five documents, he could now take over Ben Buckley's business as the proprietor. An intricate web of nominees had served their purpose, and it would be next to impossible for anyone to link Sam Pilling with his manager's rise in life.

Tired, but entirely satisfied that all the ends were tied securely, Sam had no intention of returning home that afternoon. There was a moment which would be better than any other for him to make his entrance upon the stage at Glenfield, and he proposed to wait until then.

After lunch he went to the nearest Rugby League ground, Salford's, paying his entrance money at the clicking turnstiles in the ordinary way. The match was a fine exposition of football skill and he thoroughly enjoyed it, although not with the partisan vigour he would have shown if the Hornets had been involved.

Returning to Manchester, he had a mixed grill at the Midland Hotel, and then set out for Ramsfield.

The combination of a comparatively sedate occupation and a sedate appearance in keeping can often be deceptive. It was certainly a fact that Fred Lumb was thrilled to the marrow that evening, though he strove mightily to hide his excitement.

"Right, Sam, I'll give you my notice here at the office on Monday morning, and you and me will have a real ding-dong row," he said, nodding. "And in the afternoon I'll go by train to Manchester to sign the papers."

"That's it," said Sam. "And from then on you're on your own . . . we're at loggerheads, as would be natural . . . the old days of live-and-let-live between me and Ben Buckley's have finished . . . you're as hot a rival as can be . . . don't hesitate to let people know you're prospering at my expense . . . and gradually fit yourself out, suitable clothes and so on . . . you make a mock of me whenever you can, just as a chap might do who was taking good custom from his former boss, with whom he's quarrelled."

"Aye," mused Fred. "But how are you going to take it if I start ragging you? Oh, you'll not bother to begin with, but what when others follow my example? They will, make no mistake."

Sam laughed. "That's my pigeon, Fred. The point is that these are my instructions to you, and I shan't go back on 'em whatever happens."

Smiling just so slightly, Fred Lumb shook his head, a tiny glint in his eyes.

"I might nark you, lad," he said. "Once I set my hand to the plough . . . by, but I could easy be a real heller."

"That's the spirit, Fred," Sam chuckled. "No, I don't want you to pull your punches, and I shan't either squirm or do any rescinding. Yes, you do your damnedest . . . treat Ben Buckley's as if it were your own—you'll find out when you're at the lawyer's that I've given you all the scope you'll need. And hint if you like that you've got a wealthy backer if anybody questions the financial aspect."

A puzzled frown was growing on Fred's forehead. "Sam, you've told me already why you're faking up this affair," he said. "But isn't that enough? Why should you insist so much on us two differing, and me always having a shot at making you look small?"

Sam, taking great care, balanced his cigar on the broad edge of a large ash-tray. Then he leaned forward, elbows resting on the desk.

"What would you do if your well-to-do father had slithered off his pedestal, and you discovered that a lot of folk were enjoying themselves at his expense?" he asked. "I'll tell you what you'd do, Fred, if you'd nothing about you, you'd squeal because he'd let you down. But if you'd any spunk you'd grit your teeth, get as mad as blazes, and you'd draw together in your family, shoulder to shoulder, and you'd say: 'To hell with all of 'em'; and once you reached that stage, you'd be not so far off standing on your own feet. Isn't that so?"

Fully comprehending now, Fred Lumb just managed to check a few words of admiration.

"My word, Sam, lad, but you're a—you're right, I do believe," he said. "Aye, I reckon there's a reasonable possibility that you are."

Sam's eyes were twinkling. "There's another reason, too. The greater our feud, lad, the more we'll be in the public eye, and that will make it a bigger certainty that any clients I lose will pop across Market Square, to you—so that they're in touch with one of the principals."

"H'mm, yes," said Fred. "Aye, probably so."

"I must be off now," said Sam. "They'll all be waiting for me at home," he continued, his smile just a little grim. "It's a while since Archie wasn't pub-crawling on Saturday night, or Nancy not off to some dinner-dance or other affair."

On leaving the office they went together only as far as "Inquiries" and the outer door, where Fred explained the inadvisability of their being seen walking out of Neptune Buildings in each other's company.

"In view of next week's happening, somebody might think it funny afterwards," he said. "I mean, Sam, you and me bosom pals to-night...."

While glancing at a henchman, loyal for many years, Sam came to the conclusion that Fred was warming up to the play-acting he had envisaged for himself.

On a small, lacy cloth, laid at the end of the dining-room table, there was a pile of neatly cut sandwiches, pastries and cakes. Carrying the teapot, Milly hurried in from the kitchen, Nancy and Archie, appearing from the drawing-room, drifting along in her wake.

"Well, I'm very pleased you've had a nice run back," said Sam. "And I say, love," he expostulated, "I'd a very good meal in Manchester."

Even though he had arrived home only three or four minutes before, it was already obvious that at Scarborough many of Archie's fears had been wormed out of him by his mother. It was plain she had reacted admirably, and though it was not pleasant to see that she was greatly troubled there was also a briskness of movement about her that was most comforting.

"A few more sandwiches won't harm you," she said. "And a cup of tea is never to be refused."

"Well, before I start on anything I'd better relieve your minds by telling you that things are nothing near as bad as

I feared," Sam said, sitting down. "We'll have to retrench, of course——"

"You're not talking while you're eating," Milly broke in. "Its simply asking for indigestion, when it's about serious matters."

"All right." Sam nodded.

"But now you have brought up the subject, I will say just one thing," she continued. "And I'm not standing for any arguing, either. Now I mean it . . . is that clear?"

Sam had just taken an enjoyable bite. "As clear as a bell, that part," he said.

"I'm speaking about my own money," said Milly a little impatiently. "I want you to regard it as your very own . . . to bolster up the business—anything. It is really yours after all."

"I think—that's just what I should have expected of you, dear," Sam replied, not without emotion. "But nothing of the sort's necessary, Milly. Honestly."

Both Archie and Nancy were still silent. It was evident to them that their father's substance was more shadowy than they had ever dreamed, and both at heart felt bleak about the change. Archie was miserable on another count, cursing himself for over-cleverness which he now knew would lower their standard of living. Nancy, too, was immeasurably depressed for an additional reason, worried why she had not heard from Philip since he was legally free. And she could not help wondering what he would think on hearing that from being a wealthy bookmaker her father might well now be a shaky one. Up to the present their Crowther relationship and the Pillings' standing as an old Ramsfield family had offset the fact that her father's money came from an occupation not socially outstanding. In the eyes of others there might be a vast gulf between the daughter of a wealthy bookmaker and the daughter of a bookie who was shaky.

In the drawing-room, to which they went presently, Archie and Nancy were just as subdued while their parents thrashed out the position.

"Well, I don't reckon there's much else to be discussed for the moment," Sam remarked in due course. "I don't want to give up this house any more than you do, but if you can manage on the lines you've——"

"We can, can't we, Nancy?" said Milly. "If we've someone in for the rough we can do the cooking and housework between us, can't we?"

With a jerk Nancy brought herself to the present. "Yes, yes, Mummy," she said with a bright smile. "I used to be a dab-hand at joint and two veg., and a too, too marvellous cake-maker."

"You were doing very nicely." Her mother's tone condemned this flippancy. "And if you'd kept it up——"

The ear-splitting scream of a motor-horn, just outside the window, interrupted the conversation.

"It's Frank," Archie said, jumping to his feet. "I won't be a minute with him."

While he was absent the decision about cars was reviewed. With a load of debt he preferred not to disclose, Archie had insisted upon the disposal of his Frazer-Nash-B.M.W., but Nancy's Riley was to be retained, for essential shopping only. The Bentley again caused a great deal of controversy, however.

"After all, I don't think I'm justified in keeping it," Sam said. "I could exchange with cash adjustment in my favour for . . . oh, say a small Austin or something."

Milly coloured with vexation: everything about the Bentley had already been settled. "If you sell it, I shall buy it myself, or another like it," she declared. "It's the apple of your eye and I'm not having it going. If things were really desperate it would be a different matter, and we couldn't help ourselves."

"Aye, well there is that," Sam agreed.

"Of course there is." Milly nodded. "No, you're sticking to your car, just as I'm sticking to my garden here. As if I could let that go, after all I've put into it in one way or another—*and* the conservatory. But we'll be as economical as possible in other directions to make up for it, and I'm sure we'll be able to. Being without servants, apart from there being fewer mouths to fill, will cause an enormous difference —even the best of them are so needlessly wasteful."

Archie had returned and, as he sank into a chair, his father stood up to warm the backs of his legs at the fire.

"Well, that's about all, I reckon, except for this," Sam said. "It isn't an apology, either, because what's happened isn't because we've lived above our means, in one sense, anyhow. But we have spent more than we ought and that *is* my fault—for being too easy-going with money when any of us have had a fancy for something, however extravagant it might be. But . . ." he glanced at his son and daughter, "but I'm not intending to rake up any old matters, for as far as

I'm concerned they belong to a chapter that's closed. All I would like to say is that if we're more sensible in future, and if we pull together, we'll soon be glimpsing daylight through the wood.'

Milly sniffed. "Yes . . . yes, that's it, Sam."

Awkwardly, screwing himself up for the effort, Archie then rose to say his little piece.

"I suppose if I tell you I'm sorry for my fatheadedness you'll just think me a bl—a fool," he amended, catching his mother's eye, "because any crackpot would be. But that's what I am . . . damned sorry. It's done one thing, anyway, shown me I'll never shine as a bookmaker."

Milly's eyes were glistening. "You heard what your father said, Archie. That chapter's closed, so try not to fret."

"Yes, that's it." Sam nodded. "Why not," he laughed, "find your pals and bury sorrow in a pint. I said a pint, mind you."

Archie grinned, but he was still a shade white round the eyes. "Not a bad idea, Dad, and so I'll be off. The old bus isn't going to feel the master's sure hands much longer, and I'd better make a gentle start of breaking the news to her."

When he had gone, the others began to settle down, Sam with a lightheartedness he had never expected. The testing time for Archie and Nancy was far off yet, and would not be reached until both had seriously felt the pinch. But they had taken a surprisingly stiff hurdle without a whine, and that was a thought he hugged closely to himself.

Just before the front-door bell rang later the same evening, Milly was telling her daughter that they had two things to be thankful for: that Cook would soon be leaving and Olga had already gone.

"Providential!" she exclaimed from one end of the large sofa. "I mean it will save so many complications."

Nancy, on the sofa also, nodded assent. She was steadily hating herself more and more for ever imagining that money might influence Philip. Besides, she told herself drearily, her father's misfortune had occurred only that week, whereas Ramsfield Gala was ages before. Why, oh, why, hadn't he written, or telephoned, or seen her before now?

"Sam!" her mother cried imperatively. "What about Johnson? Wages, I mean. You know we practically keep the whole garden going. Laura's man only comes twice a week, for half-days."

In Germany there had been a great demonstration demanding the return of former colonies to the Fatherland.

The account was not absorbing, and Sam thought nothing of abandoning his paper.

"I've considered him," he said round the edge of the *Ramsfield Reporter*. "The lopsided choice is yours, dear—cook and maid; no gardener . . . or *vice-versa*."

Milly laughed. "As if I should hesitate . . ." she was saying when the bell tinkled. "I'll answer that," she said.

Next, Sam heard her invite Fred Lumb in. "Hallo, Fred," she said welcomingly. "It is nice to see you again."

Surprise was Sam's first reaction, but then he decided that though there might be an element of risk in his manager calling it was perhaps wiser if some point were not clear to him. Monday morning would hardly be the time for a confidential chat if a serious quarrel were to follow immediately.

"Evening, Fred," he said. "What's the matter. Been dropped from the committee of the Bowling Club?"

Even as he courteously declined his hostess's invitation to a seat, Fred looked ill at ease, and promptly admitted it when challenged.

"The fact is, Sam, I'm here to give you notice," he said. "And I'd be obliged if you'd release me before the full month. Mind you, I don't wish to inconvenience——"

Until he realized the curtain was up and that Fred had already assumed his rôle, Sam was speechless. Then he leaned forward in his chair.

"Give . . . give me notice!" he gasped most effectively. "What's all this nonsense about? And it is nonsense. Why, neither of us has ever thought you'd not be with me until the day you retire. What *are* you gabbling about?"

Fred Lumb shuffled his feet. "I reckon I'd better come out with it straight, Sam," he said. "I've bought Ben Buckley's business . . . with the help of a sleeping partner, mind you—very well-to-do chap he is an' all."

"But . . . but, Fred," Milly said. "You can't do an awful thing like this. You were with Sam's father, and you've been with Sam through all his business life."

"Nobody's sorrier than me, Milly," Fred observed with deep regret. "But a chap's got to consider himself, hasn't he? And . . ." he coughed, "the present situation isn't exactly propitious, is it?"

Slowly Sam rose, his expression stern. "When was this treachery arranged?"

"I can tell you, Daddy," Nancy intervened furiously. "Since St. Leger day, since he knew you'd been hard hit."

"I . . . I can't believe my ears," her mother murmured. "Fred, you must be aware that this sort of conduct isn't decent. You attend a place of worship—"

Sam snorted. "He goes to a different one every Sunday. Maybe he's weighing up the various prospects for a sure trip aloft. He seems to have been weighing up my prospects all right."

That roused their visitor. "Seemingly I'd better leave," he remarked austerely. "I knew you'd be upset, as I was myself, but I never suspected I'd land myself into this kind of nasty bickering. I'd hoped for a friendly understanding when us two were in competition as bookmakers, but I can see already that my hopes are in vain. Very well then, we'll soon learn who's the best man."

"Nancy!" Her father's voice rang out resonantly. "Show him out, will you? And as for you, Lumb, you'll be paid off on Monday morning. I'm not permitting you to snoop round the office a second longer than's needed."

Fred Lumb bowed. "That suits me, Pilling," he replied, tight-lipped. "But I trust you won't have cause to regret your manner to me to-night."

Nancy answered that at the front door. What she said carried quite clearly to Sam and Milly in the drawing-room.

"Rat! And if you don't know what I mean I may as well tell you that rats are supposed to leave sinking ships. But you've make a grave mistake if you think Daddy's ship is sinking. He'll save it all right, just as he saved your job before Grandfather Pilling died."

"And now I'll tell you something that's a sight nearer to date, miss," Fred Lumb snapped. "And it's that if your father hadn't ruined you and your brothers he wouldn't be as near the muck as he is to-day. It's the brass he's lavished on you lot that's left him higher and drier than ever he ought to have been. *Good night.*"

Nancy returned with head erect, scarlet cheeks and a determined set to her mouth.

"Daddy," she said, clenching her fist, "could I help at all at the office?"

Her father smiled. "You'll have enough on at home, love."

"Oh, I can guess what she really means . . . she wants to do something herself about it," Milly said, as angry as her daughter. "This has made my blood boil, too."

Another surprise was still in store for them, and they

learnt about that when Archie came in. Of course his mother had to tell him first about Fred Lumb's visit, with full details, and it spoke volumes for her mood that she did not rebuke him for the remark he made at the end.

"The bloody, dirty swine," he growled. "Anyway, we'll come to that again when you've heard my news . . . Fred Lumb's not the only one who's been doing a spot of visiting. Oh, no, no."

"And where have you been then?" his father asked.

"Up to Outham to interview Alec's old man," Archie replied, grinning, though not so freely. "And he's given me a job, accepted me with both hands nearly. I start Monday morning at Murgatroyd Conveyors, at the town end of the Island."

"Archie!" Milly cried.

Seldom had Sam been more taken aback. Often during the evening he had been cogitating about his elder son, pondering how best to fit him into the scheme of things for the future.

"And what's behind this, Archie?" he inquired, still nonplussed.

"Well," said Archie, "I'm no use as a bookie, so why shouldn't I try myself out at what I've always wanted to be . . . an engineer? Not . . ." he added ruefully, "that I shall be doing much engineering at the start, Mr. Murgatroyd made that very plain. As far as I can gather I shall be the general mug-about in a machine-shop, under the most brutal foreman he can plant me with."

"Why?" Milly demanded.

"Oh, I suppose it's the usual thing," said Archie. "And I've also a hunch he's looking forward to giving me hell at their place for another reason."

"I've never heard of such a thing," his mother remarked, very much up-in-arms. "How's that?"

"Alec?" Nancy suggested.

Her brother chuckled. "That's my idea, too. Straighten me out, and he'll be straightening out Alec's evil counsellor, the one who leads his cherubic son wrong. Gawd strewth!"

Sam was grinning. "What was your excuse for approaching Walter Murgatroyd? You didn't let on about your bloomer at the office, did you?"

Archie shook his head. "No, I just intimated I felt my qualities were suitable for a more *worthy* life's-work than bookmaking. That shook him."

"I don't wonder." Sam roared with laughter. "Well, I'm damned."

As yet he had not formed any final judgment on this fresh development, but at least he had concluded that Archie's decision to strike out for himself certainly showed enterprise, which was never to be sneered at.

Meantime the talk of mother and son ranged from the mending of a boiler suit, which Archie had, to a strident summons for early rising, which he had not.

As he listened, Sam could not help thinking that a family's dependence on an alarm clock frequently assigns them to a definite position in the social scale.

2

Two days later, on Monday morning, the staff of PILLING ALWAYS PAYS were electrified by a fierce quarrel between Fred Lumb and his boss. This rose to its peak in the glass-panelled corridor, when Mr. Pilling, arm outstretched and finger pointing, thundered at the retreating manager: "I'm having no spy working out his notice here, listing our clients to steal 'em from us afterwards. Get the hell off these premises, you."

This difference was pursued as far as the pavement against the main entrance to Neptune Buildings, where it was listened to wide-eyed by a small group: the commissionaire, a local accountant, an official of the County Court, and eight or nine passers-by.

After having "rid myself of the snake in my bosom," as Sam angrily put it to the gathering before leaving, he returned to his office and immediately sent for Harry Sutcliffe, who presented himself with some trepidation. To his relief, however, he was promptly appointed to succeed Fred Lumb, with a rise of fifty pounds per annum, to be increased "when conditions warrant it."

This done, Sam visited Mr. William Pobjoy, whom he instructed to sell on his behalf a considerable parcel of securities. "And I must have the money at the soonest possible, Bill," was his last but somehow ominous statement.

In his enthusiasm Sam certainly went a little too far, with next a call upon the manager of the Ramsfield Commercial Bank, who received him with extreme courtesy. In due course Mr. Luther Whitehead Garside nevertheless began tc wonder, when his client removed from the bank's safe-keeping a number of sealed packets which hitherto had always remained in its vaults. And Mr. Luther Whitehead Garside positively hedged when Mr. Pilling, after announcing with little conviction that his firm's credit balance was probably sufficient for all reasonable needs, fished about the prospects of financial accommodation. At that stage, very properly, Mr. Luther Whitehead Garside deftly insinuated into the conversation two words: "suitable security."

As might be expected, these activities had repercussions, and on the Wednesday afternoon, when directors of the Hornets met at Swanroyd to consider improvements in seating, both Mr. Dale Watkinson and Alderman Joseph Hirst fenced with Sam for a morsel of information, the former as a well-wisher, the latter out of sheer curiosity. And, in the early evening of the next day, on another football ground, that of Ramsfield Rugger at Ings Close, where a practice match was in progress, many people glanced at him as he climbed to the third row of the little stand.

Jim Roebuck, at right centre three-quarter for the Whites, was in scintillating form, a tall, very slender figure whose brilliance in attack promised that he would be a thorn in the flesh of opponents the coming season. Without doubt his uncle was delighted about this, but Sam's rather tight smile of satisfaction derived from quite another reason—Archie was *not* playing. Apparently neither Alec's bludgeoning of his father, Walter Murgatroyd, nor Archie's own appeal to his foreman had had the desired effect; officially speaking, Murgatroyd Conveyors had ignored the claims of Ramsfield Rugger for one of their best forwards to be released an hour earlier from work.

"Yes, this sort of thing's going to teach him some of the sterner facts of life," Sam muttered, less brightly. "But the question is, how will he stand up to it? He's been glum ever since the affair happened, and I don't think it's entirely because he's blaming himself."

He would have been greatly heartened could he have heard a conversation then taking place in the dining-room of Glenfield, between his son and daughter. Archie, washed and changed, had descended the staircase painfully, the effect of four days of manual labour upon muscles unaccustomed to it.

"My bloody back," he groaned on sighting Nancy, who was carrying a tray from the kitchen. "Talk about turning out at Ings Close for that special practice . . . wasn't I glad when that sergeant-major foreman of mine put his thumb down yesterday. If I'd had the strength I'd have slaughtered Alec when he came into the shop this afternoon to tell me he was having another shot at softening-up his father."

Nancy smiled. "And your finger-nails aren't clean yet, *dear*."

"God, and aren't they sore," her brother complained. "I've nearly scrubbed 'em off."

Glancing towards the door, Nancy lowered her voice. "Anything fresh?" she asked. "You know what about?"

"Well." Archie pondered. "One rumour has reached my shell-like ears that any morning we shall find the old man swinging at a rope's end. Funny, ha-ha! eh?"

His sister's eyes darkened. "People are horrible . . . beastly creatures."

Murmuring: "A bit sweeping, aren't you?" Archie eyed her speculatively. "And what have you to report? Did you have tea at the George to-day?"

Nancy grimaced. "Yes, with heaps of dear pussy-cats who positively oozed sympathy, gallons and buckets of it. I was simply soaked to the skin."

Slowly Archie nodded. "And if you'll forgive the expression, *dearest*," he inquired, "did you kick 'em in the slats?"

"Bang on," said his sister.

"Attagirl," said Archie.

Nancy laughed. "Us Pillings."

She was animated then, but as her colour receded Archie stared at her. "I say, old girl," he asked, "you as fit as you might be? You've all the appearance of a female who ought to lap up bathtubs of stout."

Nancy fluttered her eyes. "The women you consort with, my pet!"

She had to contend with a similar inquiry after supper, from her father, who had driven home from Ings Close in a despondent mood, more and more convinced that Archie's dejection arose from a sense of deprivation. Moreover, Sam decided, Nancy had not responded to the challenge as he had hoped: never before had he seen her so wretched.

Her bedroom door was open as he changed into slippers and, across the broad landing, he watched her for a few moments, noting with heartache the ethereal quality of her face. She was steadily losing ground before his eyes, he thought.

"Nancy love," he said, pausing on the way downstairs to look in on her, "are you very downcast?"

She turned quickly towards him, her breath catching. "Downcast, Daddy?" she exclaimed, as if prepared to deny it tooth and nail. "Why should I be?"

Sam shrugged comically. "Perhaps it has escaped you, lass, that it's on every tongue about us coming a cropper."

"Downcast about that!" Nancy exclaimed. "I should hope *not*. As a matter of fact, anything unusual you might have noticed on my peerless features is due to concentration, not dismay. To-morrow afternoon, at the silver and gilt emporium of Madame Gladys Shires, that stinker Rafe Bottomley is presenting a super-superlative dress show, and Mummy and I propose to attend—and boy, won't we knock the serried ranks of Ramsfield society when we sway elegantly into the *salon*. Any of Mummy's jewels she can't support the weight of I shall be portering at suitable points, and by the grace of God we both have resplendent dresses no one has seen before."

Sam chuckled. "Grand, love, give 'em an eyeful."

Nevertheless, though immeasurably relieved, he risked a little lecture. She was not eating enough, he told her, and no campaign could be successfully fought without the. . . .

"All right, Daddy, I'll do my utmost to stoke more away," she promised. "But . . ." she coughed delicately, "before you go there's a small matter I would like to mention . . . and honestly, cross my heart, it's the first and last demand before my wages as 'general' are settled . . . could you de-pouch an odd ten-bob note? Unhappily this lapse of Pilling who Always Pays has caught me most inopportunely."

"And when wouldn't it?" her father inquired.

Nancy sighed. "It's quite a time since I was more or less solvent, able to meet my creditors with nonchalance," she murmured. "Oh, *thanks*, Daddy, you are a darling. And it's a *quid*."

After this, Sam was so cheered that, on entering the drawing-room, he quite forgot the shadow which still clouded the relationship of himself and his wife, a barrier which seemed to diminish at moments of crisis, but stealthily and inevitably returned.

"Well, I hear that you and Nancy are parading yourselves at Madame Gladys Shires' to-morrow," he started off, grinning broadly.

Milly nodded vigorous assent. "Everybody's who's anybody will be there," she said. "I wouldn't stop away for worlds. Of course lots of people will be wondering if I shall turn up in the circumstances, but they'll jolly well soon see."

"That's the idea," Sam agreed. "Nothing like taking the offensive."

She very nearly giggled. "Nothing like taking two smart hats, either," she said. "That's what we shall be doing, on our heads. Do you know, Sam, I'd a little loose money from beforehand—so it'll be all right when the bill comes. . . ."

"Never mind about that . . . we're not down to a few pounds."

"Anyway, Nancy and I went down to Iredale Mallinson's this afternoon and we were over an hour in the millinery department before we were suited. Nancy was an absolute demon . . . oh! but we have got two really divine hats."

Sam said: "Splendid!" and though delighted was not too lost in delight to miss the change in her inflection when she remarked that they were not going to be patronized by anyone, whoever it might be.

Casually he asked: "Anybody in particular been patronizing you?"

Milly perceptibly hesitated. "No, but Laura rang me up this morning to say she and Clem were looking in to-night. It wasn't what she said exactly, but. . . ." She paused, at a loss for words.

"Anyhow, what conclusion did you come to?"

She made another attempt. "Well, she sounded sorry enough about our troubles, but somehow . . . it's awful even to think such a thing, but somehow it entered my head that she was just a tiny bit pleased also."

Sam nodded. "Human nature's funny, Milly, and it could be so. There's one good reason, anyhow."

Swiftly she glanced at him. "You mean because we've had so much more money in recent years than they have? But Sam, I've always tried so hard never to——"

A door knob rattled sharply, the front door closed, the handle of the inner door underwent its due punishment.

"That's Father," Milly said apprehensively.

Just then, Nancy and her brother were talking together at the foot of the stairs. The conversation began when Archie, with funds in his pocket reserved for three beers on Saturday, jerked his head in the direction of the billiards room.

"How about a hundred up?" he suggested. "Give you thirty-five start."

"Mmm," said Nancy. "Not a bad idea."

"Suppose we have five bob on it?" Archie murmured. "Always makes a game more interesting."

Nancy reconsidered. "Rather!" she said. "That's why it's such a pity about my right wrist . . . it's been awfully queer lately—neuritis, I think. But I'll take a wild risk with *fifty* start."

"What about my back?" her brother demanded unchivalrously. "It'll be agony to bend over the table. Dammit, you'll walk it even with thirty-five."

These negotiations were interrupted by their grandfather's bustling entry into the house. As usual, he tore across the spacious hall as though his life depended on speed.

"News from Ghent," Nancy remarked under her breath.

"Maybe he's bringing a pound of fresh, Ezra's best," Archie observed out of the corner of his mouth. "Anyhow, here's where I do my good deed."

Mr. Sykes halted in mid-stride on noticing his grandson's attitude: that of a policeman on point-duty, left arm rigidly extended towards the drawing-room door, right hand impatiently hurrying on a laggardly pedestrian.

"Are you being insolent, Archibald?" he snapped.

Archie sighed profoundly. "I merely assumed that your interest would not be in us, the common . . . er . . . fry. Judge not, that ye be not judged, Grandfather."

Leaving behind a half-veiled threat, Mr. Sykes swept onwards, into the drawing-room, where, confident that the influence of his wealth could no longer be ignored in that household, he inquired without finessing whatsoever into the affairs of Sam Pilling, Turf Accountant, about whom he had gleaned a crop of surmises of astonishing scope. When informed that the situation was not as grave as reported, he remarked that, even if it had been, not one penny of his money would have been loaned to sustain such an infamous business.

"And I wouldn't have done owt for another reason, either," he wound up, as tough as he had been when the Pillings were poor. "Not me, not likely, not when I was aware of how you'd brought your adversities on yourself—wasting your substance on women."

Sam growled. "Oh, and how many women——" he began, but stopped when Milly touched his arm. "Sam," she pleaded, "would you mind leaving me alone to talk with Father?"

Reddening with annoyance, Sam stared at her. "And what

214

do you want to say that can't be said in front of your own husband?"

"Please, Sam," she resumed. "It's . . . it's nothing that you couldn't hear, but it'd be better for—well, for everybody if you didn't."

"This is a nice look-out," Sam retorted in a huff. "All right, I'll be off, but you might let me know as soon as it pleases you when I can return to my own drawing-room."

Troubled but determined, she walked behind him towards the door, which she closed as he went along the hall to the study. Then, a resolute little figure, she turned to her father.

"Perhaps I'm all muddled up when I behave this way," she confessed, "but somehow . . . well, you'll be offended by what I'm going to say anyhow . . . and you'd be more so if some-one not of your own flesh and blood heard."

"Let's have no more of this tomfoolery," Ezra Sykes said irritably. "Come out with what you have to say without so much delay. What's the matter with you, acting this silly road?"

"The matter is this, that I won't have you making untrue charges against Sam under his own roof," Milly replied in a rush. "Have you an iota of proof that he's been carrying on with a lot of women?"

"He's been carrying on with one woman, hasn't he?" Mr. Sykes retorted. "And a chap who breaks his marriage vows once——"

"Do you know for certain he's done that?"

Exasperated by her persistence, Ezra Sykes's voice rose. "It's been all over the town for weeks, hasn't it? I can't tell you as yet who his partner in sin were, but I shall leave no stone unturned until I do find out. And where there's smoke there's fire."

Milly drew a deep breath. "And is that all you've to go on to make the statement you did?"

Her father adopted a different line. "I don't like your clever manner, Milly," he said thinly. "And if you don't look out I shall be telling you I'll never darken your doorstep again. You'd feel silly then, wouldn't you?"

"I don't know about silly, but I should feel sorry, Father," she replied.

Ezra Sykes laughed. "I think my meaning is dawning on you. All the same you've put me right out and I'm noan stopping here any longer to-night. To think that a daughter of mine . . ."

When he had gone, Milly's legs were a trifle shaky, but she was definitely unrepentant and quietly glorified in it.

Clem Roebuck and his wife, full of commiseration, arrived at Glenfield about nine o'clock, where they were speedily disabused of their strongest fears. Initial surprise over, both expressed their utmost pleasure and gratification, but the master-steeplejack pursued the matter a shade further in the study, where Sam had taken him for a drink.

"I *am* glad, Sam lad," he said, beaming with delight. "As a matter of fact, it's a load off my own mind."

A syphon ceased to squirt. "Why, Clem?" Sam inquired.

Ruefully Clem Roebuck smiled. "Well, I wondered if a thousand or so might help you to turn the corner—there's some pretty startling tales floating round, you know. And so I've been puzzling how I could raise the wherewithal somehow. I can't pretend I got much forrarder though, for I suspect we're spending more than we should. The truth is that you can't entertain fairly frequently without making it fly, and I suppose in a sense it's right to—for the girls' sake. But it does come hard when you find it difficult to lend a hand to a pal."

"Nay, Clem lad," Sam said, his tone warm.

The extraordinary thing was that, after this, he never even so much as contemplated revealing the secret to his old friend. Indeed he did not give a thought to this possibility until much later, when he was tugging off his socks at bedtime.

"Well, I'm damned!" he marvelled. "Anyhow, I suppose there's no point really. But it is rum when you think of how close Clem and me have always been."

Still a little perplexed about the omission, but never considering remedying it, which was just as extraordinary, Sam duly went off to sleep.

*　　　*　　　*

On Sunday afternoon Milly was cutting chrysanthemums in the garden when she was joined by a young visitor whose expression was extremely solemn. But Kate Dyson, advancing towards her objective by a series of lengthy, pre-arranged stages, did not conceal her purpose quite as dexterously as she imagined. The odds were against her anyway, though she could hardly be blamed for failing to realize that people widely reported to have lost a great deal of money often become very sensitive about references to money.

As soon as she perceived the drift, Milly straightened sharply.

"So that's what you've been leading up to, is it?" she said. "Well, it's very sweet and thoughtful of you, but it isn't at all necessary, dear. So I don't wish to hear any more nonsense about making-do with your last winter's coat and other things."

"But, Aunt Milly," Kate protested, "I simply can't let you buy me anything more . . . please do understand. I'd feel horrible . . . knowing about Uncle Sam's misfortunes at the office."

Milly brandished a pair of scissors. "You don't know anything about your uncle's misfortunes, my dear. And though he has certainly lost a great deal of money the situation has . . ." She reflected and then continued with quite an air: "The situation has been grossly exaggerated."

Distressed, Kate stared at her. "But, Aunt Milly, it can't be so good, can it? Oh, I don't like mentioning anything, but —well, you and Nancy are going to run everything at Glenfield with very little help, aren't you? And it is a big house . . . and that's really proof, isn't it?"

They had started to saunter together, past the elms screening the garage, along the back of the billiards room, towards the birches at the Moorheaton Drive end of the ravine.

"Kate," her aunt said gently, "we are much tighter for money than we used to be, and that's why we prefer to act sensibly. But the little that's needed for your clothes won't make any difference to us. And you'll hurt both me and your uncle if you persist in refusing."

For an appreciable while the girl looked at the older woman, and then, as if suddenly and full comprehending, she smiled.

"All right, Aunt Milly," she said.

Relieved, Milly smiled also. "That's a good girl," she said, adding in an amused, conspiratorial whisper: "Has Scipio come on the same mission?"

Kate's infectious laugh was ringing out when her aunt glimpsed two ladies entering by the lower gateway. They were her sisters-in-law, the Misses Emerald and Ruby Pilling, principals of the highly select and prosperous private school at Outham. She had not the least doubt about *their* mission —to ascertain beyond any question whether the change in their brother's circumstances might hold some disgrace which could imperil their affairs.

"Kate," she said hurriedly, "your aunts from Outham are just walking along the drive. Run as quickly as you can to prevent them reaching the front door. Say I'm in the garden and bring them here."

Meantime Sam was reaching the end of his talk with Scipio. No one can be more serious than a very young man who deems it his duty to sacrifice himself, and the interview throughout had been conducted on a very lofty plane by both parties.

"Yes, I think that that just about finishes everything," said Sam, gravely. "But before we apply the closure I do feel it incumbent to place on record my appreciation of your coming here with your scruples about accepting further money from me."

"It was the only thing to do, Uncle Sam," his nephew remarked, palpably stern of face. "You've been paying my fees, bills for books and so forth, and though I'll now admit I'd have been as sick as—I've been inordinately depressed at the prospect of summarily terminating my medical career——"

Sam held up his hand. "You can forget all that, as I explained. On the one proviso I've mentioned."

Scipio nodded. "Gladly, Uncle," he said. "I'll sign I.O.U.s for all advances in future, bearing interest at four per cent, repayment to begin two years after I start to practise on my own or take an appointment at a salary of six hundred a year or over, whichever may be the sooner."

Fingering his chin, Sam sauntered nearer the window-seat, towards which he might well have winked had there been a suitable occupant. As it was he yelped; "Your aunts Emerald and Ruby!"

"Christ!" exclaimed the embryo doctor.

"My God!" muttered his uncle. "Won't they just put me through the mangle about my concerns."

"Me as well," said Scipio, who had not attempted to be sarcastic all that afternoon.

"Kate's taking 'em round the side," Sam reported from his vantage point. "Your Aunt Milly's apparently stepping into the breach, as she usually does."

And that was exactly what Milly did, shielding husband, son, daughter, nephew and niece for as long as she could from those sharp-featured, vinegarish ladies, her sisters-in-law.

One of their habits infuriated Sam particularly, their

refusal to call him by his second Christian name, to which he had changed in early manhood, because it was his grandfather's, Sam Pilling's of Cutside, and thereby a reminder of better things. But, completely ignoring his desires, he was and always would be to them the "Hector" of boyhood and youth, a name he detested.

On the stroke of six, when these socially correct visitors departed, Archie threw himself into a chair. Both he and Nancy had suffered severe chastisement.

"If only those two could have a few weeks in that machine-shop I grace," he mourned.

"And pray what sparkling inference do we humble disciples draw from that?" Scipio inquired. "That it would break our dear aunts' hearts?"

Archie stirred. "Them be hanged," he said. "But it's a cert they'd break the heart of that fiendish foreman of mine. Lord, and it's Monday to-morrow, and all for thirty bob a week."

Released from influences which had stultified everyone at tea, the little party at Glenfield then became very lively, quite forgetful of the troubles which weighed upon the master of the house.

That evening many Ramsfield people were decrying Sam Pilling's vulgar methods of advancing his business interests, and in quarters here and there much satisfaction was being expressed about his financial setback.

CHAPTER EIGHT

WITHIN six weeks of Boswell's victory in the St. Leger, the Pillings had settled down into a routine sternly different from that of the days preceding it. The household had become one which rose early. Milly, despite her son's strident protests, insisted on getting up to make his breakfast before he left for work, and Nancy, too, was busy with her domestic duties from first thing in the morning, her avowed aim to ensure that she and her mother should, as before, regularly parade Teazle Street during the fashionable hour.

In many respects Sam was delighted with the outcome of his scheme. Archie, thanks to no one at home showing any indication of blaming him for their troubles, coupled with a growing keenness for his job, was becoming his old lively self; and Milly, anyhow as mistress of the house and devoted mother, seemed quite happy, and undoubtedly thrived on her labour.

But Sam had grievous qualms whenever he thought of his daughter, and there were many times when he seriously considered the advisability of calling off the whole hoax. Nancy was as full of fun as ever she had been, but steadily she grew more and more peaked, a wraith of the bright-eyed girl she had once been. Often he wondered whether the strain of her gaiety was proving too much for her. It worried him a great deal.

However, when calling in for a moment at the office on returning from the Ramsfield Commercial Bank on the Friday morning of the Second October Meeting at Newmarket, Sam was told by his secretary that Mr. Philip Illingworth had rung up requesting an appointment that afternoon to suit Mr. Pilling's convenience.

"He's telephoning again, sir," said Margaret Berry.

The previous day several clients had had very good wins in the Middle Park Stakes, which foreshadowed that gains might be played up.

"Better make it latish, Margaret," Sam said, after reflecting. "Say, a quarter to five."

Digesting this piece of information, he then left Neptune Building for the George, and in the crowded bar there joked with Dr. Lister Fox about the habits of maids, over-polished linoleum and broken legs before he pinned down the cause of many barely suppressed grins he had noticed on entering.

This was the presence of Fred Lumb who, a cigar nearly a foot long in his mouth, was sitting on a tall counter-stool, one leg negligently dangling.

Closely watched by the George's most gorgeous barmaid, and between forty and forty-five more pairs of eyes, the former master and man exchanged compliments.

"What'll you have, Pilling?" Fred Lumb called out hospitably. "Whisky and splash, B. and S. . . . name your poison and it's yours, old man."

This hail-fellow-well-met greeting delivered by an elderly gentleman of monklike appearance, had amused and astonished the habitués of the bar several weeks back. It completely staggered Sam and he was hard put not to laugh.

"I can buy my own drinks, Lumb," he retorted.

"Come, come, Pilling," Fred Lumb coaxed him, closing an eye towards those clustered near. "This won't do."

"I'll pay myself for anything I require," Sam snapped.

Shrugging extravagantly, Fred Lamb ceased to press, and at once began to speak loudly about the Autumn Double, his book on which, he remarked gravely, would be the largest in the town.

All of which was, of course, apple-pie to his hearers, who would have been struck dumb could they have seen Sam's broad smile when he left the George for home.

Lunch at Glenfield had always been to a set time, but nowadays it was served almost to the split second to accommodate Archie, who raced up in his filth from Murgatroyd Conveyors on the second-hand Norton motor-bicycle he had bought out of the proceeds of the sale of his car.

Throughout the meal, which was eaten in the kitchen, Sam kept a surreptitious eye on his daughter, but soon convinced himself she knew nothing whatever about the telephone message he had received from Philip Illingworth, whose visit, surely, must be concerned with her.

"But whether she's any interest to him now is another matter," he thought. "As far as I'm aware she's never so much as mentioned his name since the time I put my foot down. Of course," he half-mumbled his conclusion, " she might still be of the same mind about him, and if so that could explain a lot that's been worrying me lately."

"You were speaking?" Milly inquired coldly.

Startled, he excused himself, laughing heartily. "Jawing to myself, was I? I must be getting ancient."

She did not deign to reply. So far this was one of her more distant days with him.

The interview with Philip Illingworth, which took place after racing was over for the day, followed a course at variance with that Sam outlined beforehand. This was mainly due to the appearance of the young man, who looked very ill.

"Well, it's certainly fetched you down, Illingworth," he commented. "Appendicitis with complications, eh? And this is the first time you've really been out? When did you say all this started?"

Philip Illingworth smiled slightly. "I didn't," he said. "But actually I went down two days before my former wife obtained her final decree. Does that cover your point, sir?"

The impetus of Sam's sharp-toned response to this was lost before he had said a dozen words.

"I don't know that I had any special point to—all right,

I *was* angling after something, but we'll not trouble about that now. What is it you want?"

"Your permission to see Nancy, sir. If she still wishes to see me, that is."

Sam's keen eyes were on his caller, in whose favour he was already prejudiced on three very sound counts: Philip Illingworth had stuck to the undertaking he had given; the rumours of Pilling instability, of which he would be fully cognisant, had apparently left him unmoved; and he had an old-fashioned courtesy about him, or he would not be there. Against this was an unusual background: there was the strange charge made by Estelle, though this, in its vital essential, was quite unconfirmed; then divorce; and finally the folly of over-ardent love-making elsewhere while still bound to his wife.

But Sam, weighing up these matters, did not hesitate long.

"All right, if Nancy's willing I'll not stand in her way," he said. "But there's a condition—after this time, if you meet her again, it isn't to be more than once a week, and it must be either at my house or your own. And by yours I mean your mother's and father's."

The young man's rare smile, illuminating his face, changed it greatly. "Thank you, sir," he said. "I'll get into touch with Nancy—which means," he grinned, "as soon as I can dive into the telephone box at the George."

"Aye," murmured Sam, shaking hands.

When his visitor had gone he sat thinking a little before ringing for Margaret Berry. Then, with Harry Sutcliffe, who day by day was showing that Fred Lumb's tuition had not been in vain, the three of them worked through until a quarter to nine, with an interval for tea and sandwiches sent in on a tray. The flat-racing season was soon ending, and there was much to clear up.

When Sam returned home the stone-paved area between Stonewood and Glenfield, and the extensive court at the back, were more closely packed with expensive vehicles than even on the "gang's" Sunday mornings. Near the garage the headlamps of two appropriately-placed cars provided dazzling light for the auctioneer, Archie Pilling, who was standing precariously on a shaky box. His assistant, Frank Thornton, was near to hand.

"Ridiculous, ladies and gentlemen," Archie was bellowing as his father joined the rear ranks of a large crowd of young people. "Thirty bob *only* for this magnificent curly-headed

doll who blinks, winks, talks and walks. Now come, come . . .
I'll take half-crown rises, ladies and gentlemen, for this
pretty little creature won by my skill at the Fair."

"Thirty-two and six," a feminine voice squeaked.

"Thirty-five shillings," a profoundly bass-voiced gentleman
on the right boomed promptly.

"You, sir," the auctioneer shouted. "Thank you, sir.
Thirty-five shillings I am bid, ladies and gentlemen and
others, for this enchanting . . ."

The lot was eventually secured by the elder of the
Crowther girls for forty-four shillings.

Sam found himself much interested in the activities of
two bidders, one's voice squeaky and the other's deep as the
ocean, respectively his daughter and Alec Murgatroyd. The
pair, varying their tones occasionally, moved around the
fringe of the throng and, at sticky points in the proceedings,
usually succeeded in starting the bidding again.

Chuckling, Sam threaded a path towards the back door
of the house. Milly, flushed with cooking, was in the
kitchen, sticking a hat-pin into a fruit cake.

"Not quite done," she was murmuring as he entered. At
the sound of footsteps she turned, bright-eyed. "What do you
think of it?" she asked, laughing.

"Raising the wind, I suppose," Sam said. "But I should
have thought the surplus from Archie's car would have
done him nicely."

Milly nodded, as if very knowledgeable. "I imagine he's
cleared off some debts. And he vows he's having one binge
a week, on Saturday nights, and he can't do it out of that.
You know he will insist on me having most of it."

Following the direction of her glance, Sam saw a pay-
packet. "Mmmm," he said. "And where's Nancy come in?"

Nancy's mother giggled. "She swears she's going to knock
everybody flat with her evening clothes this winter, and
Archie's giving her a commission. The fact is, Sam," Milly
sobered, "that she's got a lot of pride."

"She doesn't exactly sit down under things, does she?"
Sam remarked wryly. "But it's better to be that way than
the other."

Now Milly seemed troubled. "Yes, I suppose so," she said,
and then added abruptly: "Philip Illingworth's coming here
on Sunday."

"I know what's bothering you most," said Sam. "It's not
that he's a divorced man, but that Laura and Estelle live

next door. It's awkward, I grant you, but short of forbidding them meeting there's nothing we can do about it."

Milly sighed. "I know, Sam, and we'd be out of our heads to try to stop Nancy seeing him. But, as you say, it *is* awkward, and I've been simply dreading this happening."

"Why?" Sam stared. "Had you any idea she was still so keen on him?"

Milly looked surprised. "Of course," she said.

"Had you, indeed? Anyhow, I can tell you one thing we can be proud about—the way these two have taken the change."

Milly's eyes became moist. "They've been wonderful, haven't they?" she said. "And I'm not sure if we can't be proud of all three. Is there time, Sam, for Gilbert to have received my letter—telling him everything, I mean—and for him to have replied?"

"Has he written?" Sam asked quickly.

She was quietly crying, tears of joy. "It's only a picture postcard from a place called Lagos, and he doesn't say much, but it has made me happy."

"Let's have a look at it," said Sam.

Perhaps ten minutes later Clem Roebuck came cheerfully into the kitchen, but at the signs of recent distress in his sister-in-law's face he was about to make an excuse for leaving when checked by Sam.

"We've had a few lines from Gilbert, Clem," he told him.

"In that case I can understand Milly giving way," Clem said sympathetically. "It's been a long time without a word from him."

"Ten months, Clem," said Milly. "But I don't care a bit now. It did hurt before, though—it does when you never hear."

"I'm sure, Milly," the master-steeplejack agreed.

After a little talk on this and a few jokes about the auction sale still continuing outside, the two men went to the billiards room. During the earlier part of their game Clem animatedly explained that, in going off the next morning to watch Ramsfield Town play Liverpool, he would be killing two birds with one stone, spending an enjoyable afternoon at the match and a profitable evening, he hoped, with the director of a company owning a chain of factories.

"That's why I'm so often away at week-ends now, Sam," he explained. "What I'm after doing is to extend my connection . . . build up a bigger business altogether."

"Why shouldn't you, lad?" Sam said. "What about advertising? Would that be of help in your line?"

There was an interlude when Nancy flew in. She threw her arms round her father's neck, hugged and kissed him, and whispered in his ear: "Oh, thanks, Daddy darling," before withdrawing as swiftly as she had come.

"Ah well, it's a long time since any of my girls did that to me, Sam," Clem said.

Sam chuckled. "And it's a fairish while, my lad, since *she* did anything of the sort to me."

Again they settled down to their game, the master-steeplejack in the highest of spirits; nor, all things considered, was Sam dissatisfied with the developments of the day. He had a grand football match in prospect, too, as the Hornets were entertaining Bradford Northern the next afternoon.

*　　　*　　　*

The slight and intermittent rain of the following day started much too late to affect the ground at Swanroyd, where the home side won a fine game by thirteen points to seven.

After the match the Hornets' directors held a special meeting, to fix up final details concerning the importation of two stars from overseas, a Maori three-quarter from New Zealand and a half-back from Australia, both with brilliant reputations.

As with many clubs in the League, the considerable sum needed for such a purpose was provided by the club's bankers on the guarantee of the directors, jointly and severally. On this occasion, however, the manager of the Ramsfield Commercial Bank, Mr. Luther Whitehead Garside, had intimated to Mr. Walter Murgatroyd, the Chairman of the Club, that the Bank would prefer the directors themselves to furnish the amount required, in cash.

Three of the directors, Messrs. Dale Watkinson, Simeon Calverley, and the Chairman, each annoyed by a reflection that his word was not as good as his bond, went into matters thoroughly; two more, the young Mr. Boothroyd Gee and the nearly elderly Alderman Joseph Hirst, dissented regularly from any suggestion put forward by the majority group; and Sam Pilling, his colour changing from red to the white of intense anger, remained quite silent.

Unfortunately for calm debate, various undercurrents existed. Alderman Joseph Hirst firmly believed he should have been Chairman of the Club, and was excessively jealous of Walter Murgatroyd; and Boothroyd Gee hated both Simeon Calverley and Dale Watkinson, the second and third husbands respectively of the woman who had been his wife.

Simeon Calverley, thumping his clenched fist on the table, was eventually responsible for creating a certain order out of chaos.

"Now I'm damned angry about this," he growled. "As any of us should be. But we shan't settle much if we go on squabbling. The whole thing's an insult to every man-jack of us."

Sam Pilling was waving his hand. "And the whole thing's aimed at me, Simeon, because of the talk there's been about me," he said. "But whether Luther Whitehead Garside has done it off his own bat, or whether he's been put up to it, by somebody present here, is more than I can say. But to begin with you've got my resignation, and I'm not giving it because I haven't the brass to potter out if needs be . . . whatever the wild rumours some of you might have swallowed."

Dale Watkinson laughed. "*I've* swallowed no wild rumours, Sam lad."

"As for you, Alderman," Sam continued, staring at Bee Hirst's father, "you've never forgiven me since I got up and declared that Walter had the most experience of any of us, and was most fitted to be Chairman when old Galloper Kaye died. And then there's you, Gee," he rapped out, switching targets, "I've given you hell more than once for introducing personalities into this board-room — you're always slyly opposing both Calverley and Watkinson, and we all know damned well why."

Boothroyd Gee and Alderman Hirst rose simultaneously, but Walter Murgatroyd, who could be severe when he wished, silenced them.

"Now, Sam," he said persuasively. "I'm not going to make out there isn't something in your contention, but——"

Much more quiet now, Sam interrupted him. "Let's leave matters where they are, Walter," he said. "You've got my resignation, and all I need add is . . . good afternoon, gentlemen."

That pair of good friends still, Dale Watkinson and Simeon Calverley, endeavoured to intercept him, but firmly he shook them off. Within two or three minutes he was driving through the gates of Swanroyd, on his way home.

After the evening meal, during which he was most uncommunicative, Sam withdrew behind the pages of the Saturday night sporting edition of the *Ramsfield Reporter*.

Nancy, who had been exchanging significant glances with her mother and brother, popped her head round the screen.

"What's the matter with you, grouchy?" she inquired, shaking his arm.

Her father stirred, dropped the paper across his knee, noticed that all eyes were on him, and grimly nodded.

"All right, then, I'll tell you something that'll be in the *Reporter* anyhow on Monday, that I've resigned my directorship of the Hornets. It won't say why, however, so you might as well learn at first hand the reason."

When he had finished, Milly said furiously: "I think it's dreadful. And you've worked so hard for the club and loved doing it. But I think you were right in resigning."

"It shows you, doesn't it, what can happen to a chap when a whispering campaign is in full blast," Sam said. "You for one, Nancy, have felt some of the draught, or you wouldn't be so hell-bent on retaliating with every weapon you've got. And what about your mother?"

"Oh, I don't know, Sam," said Milly. "You can so easily make much out of nothing in our position . . . when you suspect everybody's talking about you."

Sam turned a shade further in his chair, to eye her more squarely. "Now come on," he said. "All we're trying to discover is where we stand. Have you had a few nasty rubs or haven't you?'

"Yes . . . yes, I have," she replied after a little hesitation, tossing her head. "But I behaved just like a sphinx. No, nobody's taken a rise out of me so far, and I'll make sure they don't, either."

"And what about you, Archie?" his father asked.

A very real regret was in Archie Pilling's tone and expression. "A few digs have drifted down to me *indirectly*," he said. "The trouble is that I've a most undeserved reputation for whamming blokes on the beak at the drop of a hat."

"And not so undeserved," his mother said sharply.

"Ma!" said Archie. "Tch-tch!"

Sam got up. "Well, there it is. And now I think I'll run down to the club for an hour and read the paper later."

By the time he was passing his father-in-law's house in Barnsley Road, driving slowly, the salient factor of the situation was firmly in his mind. It was that for some months

227

yet, galling though it be, he must allow things to drift along unchecked; not until an appreciable period had elapsed would he be entirely convinced that his son and daughter had the character to meet adverse circumstances.

"But when I'm sure, I'll cut such a dash as Ramsfield has never seen before," he growled. "I'll buy Milly a brand new Rolls, and I'll engage a chauffeur just for her——"

This dream of the near future was suspended when he was compelled to deal with a traffic condition which was causing alarm in the breasts of oncoming drivers. It was due to a stream of fifteen or sixteen cars which, roaring down from Moorheaton, were playing high-speed follow-my-leader to an extent which sent pedestrians scurrying for safety. The last vehicle in the chase swung sharply across the bows of the Bentley preparatory to an all-out dash through the Cemetery.

"The god-damned silly young devils," Sam cursed, braking savagely. "What their parents are thinking of to——" Despite his annoyance, he had to laugh at himself. "That doesn't come well from me, after all."

The visit to the County Club he had mentioned at home was no part of his plan for the evening. After reaching the town he headed out along Leeds Road, turning off this at the High School, a quarter of a mile beyond which he parked in a dark and quiet street. A hundred yards' walk brought him to the Park Gates, where, avoiding as far as possible the bright lights of one of Flassati's Ice Cream and Soft Drinks Parlours, he sneaked across the road and was soon knocking at a door. This was opened by a good-tempered-looking woman of about sixty, his former manager's wife. She affected fright on peering out, hand on her heart.

"Oh, thank goodness, it's not the police," she said. "Come in, Sam."

"You're expecting him to be arrested, Mrs. Lumb?" Sam said, laughing.

"Well," she said, "what would you think? Here's Fred gone and sworn me to secrecy, and then there's his new pigskin cigar-case, and the suit of clothes he's having I don't know how many fittings for at the town's best tailor's."

"Part of the game of pulling wool over everybody's eyes, Mrs. Lumb," Sam remarked, smiling.

Fred Lumb appeared in a doorway. "Take no notice of her, Sam," he said. "As a matter of fact I'm beginning to suspect she won't be able to carry the big position I'm carving out for myself."

There was a great deal of jollying for the next ten minutes or so, but then the two bookmakers, behind tightly drawn curtains in the front room, got down to business with the ledgers and private books of the firm of Ben Buckley.

"Well, Fred," Sam observed dryly after a while, "at least I'm beginning to know who trusts me, and I'm having a few shocks in the process."

More than two hundred of his accounts had been strangely dormant during the past month. To a man, these clients had transferred their business to the rival house at the opposite side of Market Square.

Later on, Mrs. Lumb insisted upon making a light meal, during which she did her utmost to be very lively. But that she had some reservations about what was being done became clear subsequently, when she was alone with her husband. It was his part in the scheme, so it emerged, which was causing her a little anxiety.

"You know, Fred, it's a rum business is this, and only a very clever chap like Sam would have thought it up," she began. "You'll be careful, won't you?"

Fred Lumb was in high fettle. "Careful, lass. What do you mean?"

This was the crux of the matter, and she picked her words. "Well, of course, you'll help as he wants you to do, naturally, but if I were you, Fred—well, I'd be careful to keep my part within reasonable bounds. It's all right him giving you a free hand, but. . . ."

He was eyeing her a trifle suspiciously. "It's a job that I shall need to use my own judgment about from day to day," he remarked.

"I suppose so," Mrs. Lumb said dubiously.

Fred Lumb frowned first and then laughed heartily. "You're never thinking that I might go too far, are you?" he inquired.

"I am," she murmured. "Yes, that's what I am."

Mrs. Lumb had been a wife for many, many years, and although she was extremely fond of her husband she had sound reasons for knowing that, despite his air of dignity and omnipotence, Fred could be both over-impulsive and feather-brained at times.

*　　*　　*

Sunday morning service at the Wesleyan Chapel had ended. On the pavement outside, despite a chilling wind,

Ezra Sykes was talking to Mrs. Allan Oldfield; his hand was resting on her shoulder comfortingly. This mannerism of his, when forcing home a point, was well enough known to everyone in the congregation, men, women, girls and boys alike, who either avoided it, or suffered it, or were not troubled by it.

Whatever he might be doing, Mr. Sykes missed little that was taking place in his vicinity, hence his daughter Milly received a frosty acknowledgement, and his son-in-law, Sam Pilling, was ignored to a degree not to be mistaken.

"Clem didn't get back last night, it seems," said Sam, as he closed the car door. "He thought it might be to-day."

Milly was being a shade more forthcoming with her husband that morning, and at once told him that that was the reason her sister had missed chapel.

"Laura wasn't in a very good mood when I ran across to Stonewood before we left," she went on. "She as good as made out that whatever extra business Clem might be gaining the profit was more than being lost by his additional travelling expenses, entertaining and what not. It doesn't look as if he's done much so far, does it?"

"Takes time," said Sam.

"But afterwards she came round, and again referred to a terrific dinner party she's having next month," Milly went on. "Why it's so special I can't imagine, but she *is* making a fuss about it."

"Expecting Royalty, perhaps," Sam remarked.

Milly made no comment on this; to have done so, to have encouraged frivolous exchanges, would have been stepping too far beyond the barrier which separated them.

On reaching home, she got out at the front door and, after examining the chrysanthemums and michaelmas daisies in the hall, hastened into the kitchen before taking off her coat. Nancy was cooking lunch and reported: ". . . all's well . . . I darn well hope."

The meal turned out excellent, although the cook unduly deprecated it in certain aspects. Other conversation centred mainly on the weather, the effect of this being that the mistress of the house, fearful about possible frost, spent the earlier part of the afternoon in carrying from the garden into the conservatory her prized azaleas and cyclamens.

For his part, Sam seized the opportunity for a game of golf while conditions were favourable, but satisfied himself with ten holes in the company of an otherwise lively

nonagenarian to whom that was the limit. A nine-days
wonder had lessened, and he was no longer subjected to
surreptitious glances on the course and in the clubhouse.
But he did not fail to notice that he was saluted a trifle
differently from the days of progress and prosperity; smiles
were often not quite so free, hand-waves more cursory.

He was heartened immediately on returning to Glenfield,
where three large cars were standing in the driveway, two
Rolls-Royces and a Daimler, the property of Walter
Murgatroyd, Dale Watkinson—who never walked even the
length of Moorheaton Drive—and Simeon Calverley.

With these gentlemen he spent a most pleasant time in the
study, the only unharmonious note arising when he perceived
a hint to the effect that money might conceivably lie behind
his determination to sever his connection with the Hornets
. . . if that were just, just possible . . . then these friends
together would be delighted to assist in . . .

Nevertheless, although remaining adamant, Sam was
warmed by his visitors' kindly intentions. He saw them off,
and then went into the drawing-room, where the atmosphere
was a little stiff.

This feeling of restraint began to lessen shortly after tea,
when Archie left. This is not to say he and Philip Illingworth
had differed: on the contrary they had got on surprisingly
well at this their first real talk together, having regard to the
admission of Nancy's guest that he had no interest in rugger,
invariably a damning indictment in Archie's view.

Conversation during tea had ebbed and flowed, stilted on
occasion and too voluble at others. To begin with, Sam very
deliberately explained why his friends had called, which in
the presence of a wealthy outsider embarrassed his family,
for so long used themselves to the possession of considerable
means. And then Milly, strive as she would, could not adjust
herself to the idea that young Mr. Illingworth was any
ordinary, very pleasing young fellow; he had been through
the Divorce Court, and that made him different; then there
was that extraordinary tale which, for a few days only, her
niece Estelle had told about him.

The ice was finally broken when she and Nancy, who in
only a day or two had become the ravishingly pretty girl of
almost two years before, had each smoked a cigarette after
tea. It was time then, they agreed in silent conversation, to
deal with the tea things, but as they made a move towards
this the visitor firmly announced his intention of partici-

pating in various domestic tasks. In particular he alluded
to washing-up, proposing this for himself and Nancy.

"No, you're not, Mr. Illingworth," Milly declared. "As
if——"

"Oh, call him Philip, Mummy," Nancy broke in. "For a
minute I thought it was his father."

"This question of which of us shall dry, Mrs. Pilling . . ."
Philip Illingworth adjusted his spectacles carefully and then
pursued his theme with the utmost gravity. "If you fear for
your china, may I assure you . . ."

Inwardly shaken by his monumental seriousness, whether
assumed or natural she could not be sure, Milly had difficulty
in preventing herself from laughing outright. But her
laughter was merely delayed and, on her second return trip
from the kitchen, she had succumbed utterly. On passing
beyond the baize-covered door, however, the front door-bell
rang, and hastily she composed herself. A moment later she
was trying to conceal another emotion: nervousness.

"Laura!" she said. "And . . . and Lois and Cora . . . how
nice . . . do come in."

Just then, Philip and Nancy appeared, neither overburdened, free to join hands with each other in the privacy
of the hall. Linked together, one carrying a silver hot-water
jug and the other a teapot, both looked towards the front
door.

Eyes narrowed against the light, Laura Roebuck was
staring, the lines of her face becoming harsher.

"I see you've company . . . of a sort," she said. "No, we
won't stay, certainly not."

"Laura!" There was an unusual quality in her sister's
voice. "I want to speak to you alone, so will you please go
into Sam's study? And you two girls," she summoned up the
travesty of a welcoming smile, "your Uncle Sam is in the
drawing-room."

"Oh, I don't think we'll wait, Aunt Milly," said Lois.

Cora's lips curled. "Rather *not*," she said.

The insolence of Milly's youngest niece was not without
its effect. To her surprise Laura found herself ushered into
the study before she could assert herself. And there, with
the door closed, Milly spoke her mind.

"Why were you so rude, Laura?" she asked.

For so long the dominant one of the pair, her sister did
not relish this. "Because I'm disgusted with you," she said.
"Disgusted because you're harbouring such as him in the

house, after what he did to Estelle. You must have guessed Nancy was setting her cap at him, and it was your duty to have stopped it."

Trembling, Milly silently counted ten before speaking. "You're assuming a great deal too much. And you might remember that Nancy isn't a child."

"I dare say that the Illingworths' wealth and position help you nicely to forget your scruples," Laura remarked, her mouth sarcastic.

Really horrified, Milly blurted out: "What a nasty thing to say."

It seemed her sister was desirous only to wound. "I could say much nastier things about this shocking affair if I felt inclined to stay."

Scarlet with anger, Milly retorted: "Then you'd better go. Because while you're here there'll be no more talk of Nancy setting her cap at either him or anybody else. So far she's never lacked young men and I doubt if she will."

"Don't you adopt that tone with me," Laura shouted.

"And don't you speak to me as you have been doing," Milly replied, quite unyielding. "I won't have it, Laura, so there."

Laura Roebuck turned towards the door. As her fingers closed on the knob, she looked back.

"I don't even know if I want to speak to you again," she said icily.

Tears were not far from Milly's eyes. "All right, Laura," she said. "I can guess what you're thinking and expecting, because it's happened so often before when we've had a tiff. You're reckoning I shall come running after you in another day or two, to say I'm sorry as you've always made me do. By this time I shan't, Laura, no, I shan't."

Laura laughted lightly as she left. "To be truthful, my dear," she said, "it's quite immaterial to me."

When alone, Milly sat down shakily in the chair drawn up to her husband's roll-top desk, and began to dab her eyes.

"She's so hard and so unkind," she murmured. "And I think she's obsessed, too . . . obsessed about money and social climbing and the Luncheon Club and bridge parties, and going off to people's houses for dinner. It's what makes her contemptuous of me—because I'm wrapped up in my house and my plants and flowers, and my family. And because of them I'll never be lonely, even if Laura never again looks the side I'm on. At least . . ." her lips quivered, "I shouldn't be if Sam and I could be as we were before."

As the latch clicked she straightened hurriedly.

"Well?" Sam inquired.

She smiled. "Oh, we've had a real set-to, but I'm glad about it. It's cleared the air . . . they know he comes here . . . and I shan't have to be bothering myself how best to explain to her."

"Yes, there's that, certainly," said Sam. "And what now, eh? You're not remaining in here all the evening, are you?"

Milly laughed. "Of course not," she replied. "I'll go and do up my face properly, and then I'll come downstairs again."

The remainder of the evening was very different. Nancy played for a while, Philip turning over the music whenever she nodded, her father beating time with his finger from a comfortable chair, her mother always in the lead with requests.

Then Sam started a novel by Marjorie Bowen, Milly began to knit, and the young couple quietly talked, sitting closely together on the smaller sofa. Outside, the east wind was increasing, but the fire glowed all the more cosily inside.

2

The diminution of good feeling between the womenfolk of the Pillings and the Roebucks was apparent immediately after Philip Illingworth's visit to Glenfield, and demonstrated beyond dispute to a small circle of Ramsfield society on the night after Bonfire Day.

The same evening Sam reached home just as his son was leaving. Recently Archie had signed on for an engineering course at the Tec', and he was carrying four text-books strapped together. To a young man with the reputation of a roysterer, this, in the eyes of others, might seem to savour a little too much of the goody-goody. He made his position clear.

"Any reference to the industrious apprentice means a belt on the lughole for anyone," he remarked. "And that goes for you, too, Dad."

His father grinned. "You'd better conserve your energies for the match at Ings Close to-morrow, especially if Huddersfield Old Boys have included that big forward of theirs. You were both nearly sent off the field in the same game last year."

Archie's eyes gleamed pleasurably. "What a scragging party me and him had, a private scrap from beginning to end. Yes, the ref. did draw us to quiet parts once or twice for a fireside chat."

"Ar-chie," Nancy sang out, sugar-sweet, persuasive, "be a good boy, dear."

A coil of vacuum hose curved snake-like about the hall, at the far side of which, head swathed in a bright yellow scarf, she had been working.

"And now what's the matter with you?" her father asked.

"Archie might be late, Daddums," she exclaimed.

Her brother turned back. "The trouble with her is that ever since old gig-lamps and his Alfa Romeo staggered here she's been above herself." He closed his eyes and shuddered realistically. "And *how* that poor blind chap smells out the gateway at the speed he does without ramming a pillar is beyond me."

Nancy's head was roguishly to one side. "Ar-chie," she cooed, "the school-bell will soon be ting-a-linging, dear."

"Yes, by God, it will," Archie exclaimed on glancing at his wrist-watch. "Wotcher, pals," he shouted over his shoulder as he disappeared.

"And why are you doing this now?" Sam smilingly asked his daughter.

"It's me afternoon off to-morrow morning," Nancy answered patly. "Saturday morning's fashion parade in Teazle Street . . . oh, boy!"

Before her father could respond to this, the baize door at the rear of the hall opened. The mistress of the house clapped her hands.

"Supper's ready now, so take your coat off and come straight in, Sam," she called out. "And you hurry up with washing yourself, Nancy."

Eating in the bright kitchen was not without its advantages, for food when placed on the table was hotter than even that well-regulated household had ever known.

"I've had a talk with Simjoss Crowther to-day," Sam remarked during the meal. "He asked me how I was faring, and do you know I could see the working of his brain. Can you guess what he was going to say?"

Milly cogitated for the time it took a serrated bread knife to saw from top to bottom of a loaf.

"I can guess all sorts of things," she said finally. "But I've never been gifted enough to see a person's brain working."

"G'rrr," Nancy growled.

"Anyway," Sam said, "Simjoss was trying in a very pleasant manner to ferret out if I was short of capital. And I'd bet my boots that if I'd needed twenty or thirty thousand it wouldn't have taken him long to arrange it."

There was another rather special item of news. Milly, when in town, had met Fred Lumb face to face in Church Street. Vividly she described how she had cut him dead. When the last drop had been squeezed out of this dramatic encounter, less significant details followed.

"His overcoat was open, and Sam, I've *never* seen such a suit in my life . . . you couldn't believe that such huge checks were ever made!" she continued. "And there he was, with an enormous cigar in his mouth, flinging his arm out to salute people, flourishing his hat—and that's another thing, it was a *grey* bowler."

"H'mmm," Sam murmured. "It must be his notion of how a successful bookie should dress."

"I don't know about that," Milly said. "But I do know he was attracting some attention. My word he was."

Sam pushed back his chair. "Well, that's been very nice. And now I think I'll look at the furnace. Archie's made himself G.O.C. central-heating, but a little extra cleaning-out won't do any harm. It's very cold to-night."

The house was quite warm, but the Pillings had always believed that a room never feels really homely without a glow and flicker in the hearth. And so, after Sam had been into the cellars and washed his hands in the cloakroom on returning, he put a match to the drawing-room fire. It was blazing cheerfully when Milly joined him.

Nancy arrived just afterwards and, taking an arm of each, led them to the dining-room, the side window of which looked towards Stonewood.

"High life," she said.

"Well illuminated, anyhow," Sam remarked.

With his wife and daughter close to him he stared outside. It was snowing, but not sufficiently to obscure a line of cars standing on the drive in front of the neighbouring house, the majority of whose windows were bright rectangles of light.

"It *is* a big affair, isn't it?" Milly marvelled.

"Ah, dear," sighed Nancy. "Really I think I must make myself pretty on the off-chance we've hordes of distinguished callers—if Aunt Laura hasn't scooped the lot."

For no sound reason at all, Sam felt irritated. "Why aren't you off out with Bee more?" he demanded. "Dammit, she can't spend all her time with her young man."

"You'd be surprised." Nancy laughed.

In the drawing-room once again, while she was upstairs and after her mother had talked a little more about the dinner party, Sam was rebuked for his reference to Nancy's friend.

"Don't criticize Bee again, Sam," Milly said. "She's hurt Nancy badly enough I know, but she won't hear a word against her. There's jealousy behind it, too."

"Surely she doesn't think Nancy might capture Septimus Firth's lad from her?"

Milly nodded. "Far-fetched as it sounds, she might. It was one of those friendships when the boys were always hanging round one of them, and it wasn't Bee."

"Yes, it could be jealousy," said Sam. "And maybe also Bee's father has influenced her. From what I hear he'll do me all the mischief he can, in a careful, aldermanic way. Yes, this affair of mine soon weeds out those who aren't your friends."

That recalled to Milly a visitor who had slipped in for a brief stay about half an hour before her husband came home. Her brother-in-law had left a message for Sam—he would be away on business the next day, but expected to return early Sunday morning, reaching Moorheaton in time for them to drive down together in his car for the Armistice service in the Parish Church.

"Off again, is he?" Sam murmured. "Did he mention their dinner-party?"

Milly shook her head. "Not in any shape or form . . . and, of course, I didn't. But I did feel sorry for him—I've never seen him look so upset."

"It's not Clem's fault we weren't invited," Sam said, glancing steadily at her. "The truth is that the girls over there and their mother look down on him, and he hasn't much say in anything. No, there's very little give and take between him and Laura, as should be between man and wife."

Milly definitely flushed. "Generally speaking, yes," she declared.

Sam glared. "Generally speaking—bunkum," he snapped.

"There are certain things," Milly said with extreme dignity, "on which give and take are quite impossible."

Here it was again: you thought matters were improving and then a wet towel cracked and stung your cheek. Sam rose, to blunder out of the drawing-room—better to practise losing hazards by yourself than sit under this.

*　　　　*　　　　*

British Legion Headquarters in Ramsfield were at the former premises of the Ramsfield Commercial Bank in Sheepgate, beyond the Cloth Hall.

As members were forming up for the march in the slush of thaw outside, Sam encountered Captain Gainsway-Sinkinson, always a prominent personality on these occasions. That gentleman, obviously completely forgetting the brotherly significance of the day, scrutinized him with cool disdain, but the snub was deprived of any overwhelming effect because Sam remained unmoved.

As Captain Gainsway-Sinkinson reddened dully, Sam, smiling slightly, found his place, alongside Clem Roebuck.

In fours, medals on breasts, the company started off, striding out in martial step behind the Legion Band. From Sheepgate the route was along the low side of Market Square, crossing the front of the Town Hall, thence into Church Street as far as the Parish Church, which stood in the old graveyard on the corner of Teazle Street. At this point sections wheeled right in turn, to enter the broad, flagged court which led to the church porch, where ranks were broken.

Clem nodded up towards the spire. "I'm beginning a big repairing job on that before very long, Sam."

Head craned back, Sam stared at the slender, towering pinnacle.

"Is it so bad?" he asked.

The master-steeplejack shook his head in dismay. "You ought to examine it through powerful field-glasses, as I usually do before I make my first survey," he said. "It's crumbling so badly I daren't even wait for spring and finer weather."

As Chaplain to the Ramsfield Branch of the British Legion, the Rev. Alonso Dyson preached. His sermon was a scorching one, its fascination that, though culprits were not named, he left small doubt in the minds of his hearers as to their identity. In the main his theme was the danger inherent in any lack of discipline where considerable worldly riches are concerned. As tail-piece, he efficiently crucified two members of the Legion, the bachelor principal of a large engineering works and an equally wealthy cloth-finisher, for the sin of omission, not commission—he made no bones about declaring that the nephew of the one and the only son of the other, both these young men close friends and fairly recently married, indulged in the habit of exchanging partners when it so pleased them.

"Do you know, Sam," Clem muttered on the march back to Sheepgate, quite overcome, "I think I'd jump into the Ram if that brother-in-law of yours was after me."

Sam laughed. "He's mustard, isn't he?"

It had been arranged beforehand that their chaplain should ride up with them in the Chrysler, but no sooner had he inserted his lengthy person into a back seat than he opened the door again.

"Adultery!" he said as he climbed out. A second or so afterwards he thrust his head inside, so that his burning eyes were not far from those of his driver, Clem Roebuck. "You will wait," he announced.

Who his victim was on this occasion neither Sam nor Clem knew, although as the throng thinned they chanced to notice him talking to Alderman Joseph Hirst, present by reason of his wartime association with the Motor Volunteers, but the highly respectable Alderman could not be considered in such a connection.

In due course he returned, comporting himself as a man who has done his duty. The three of them were quite lively during the drive up to Roydlea, but after dropping Mr. Dyson in Highthwaite Road Clem fell silent. His friend was very jumpy, Sam thought, but this he attributed to worry about the sad state of their women-folk's relations. The dinner party was not mentioned.

It was mentioned, however, as soon as Sam entered Glenfield: by his wife, who rushed down the stairs.

"Well, Laura's pulled it off," she said.

Eyebrows raised, Sam inquired: "You were addressing me?"

Bursting with the news, Milly was not even checked by this. "Lois is engaged to Haigh Watkinson, the Law Watkinsons' boy. What do you think of that?"

"Only puts Laura where she was," Sam pointed out, but at his wife's surprised expression was explaining further when he heard Nancy's voice, not so far away. "I mean that Estelle's lost the Illingworths for her—oh, really, dear."

"Yes . . . yes, it was announced at the dinner party," Milly said hurriedly. "I believe there's talk of their wedding being in late spring or thereabouts, though I shouldn't think they've seriously discussed that yet."

"Neither should I," Sam agreed.

His daughter, passing through the hall, remarked to the vacant air: "Oh, so we're *on* again just now, are we?"

Nancy next contributed: "Falling in love again, more and more each day." She sang odd snatches of it for the next hour or so. It seemed to please her, but was less pleasing to her parents.

3

In the early days of December Sam and Milly had graver matters to speculate about than their own affairs. It was reported that the King had differed with his Cabinet and newspapers throughout the world openly referred to a constitutional crisis in England.

On the evening of the Friday when Mr. Baldwin made a statement in the Commons, while Nancy and her mother were avidly discussing the American lady involved, Archie announced that he was going out to leave a message for Jim. It had to do with a minor change in Ramsfield Rugger's First XV's departure the next morning.

Despite being enthralled by speculations concerning the royal love-match, Milly broke off to speak to him.

"Why not telephone, Archie?" she suggested. "After all, your Aunt Laura wasn't so nice to you when you went there last."

Archie grinned. "Not likely. A chap like me, with his nose to the grindstone, requires a bit of light relief now and then. Don't you try to deprive me of my simple pleasures, Ma."

It was a starlit night, bright enough for him to see two people in the drive as he turned at the back of Glenfield towards the front of Stonewood. Moreover he recognized his cousin Cora's voice: she sounded extremely exasperated.

"What ho!" he thought. "Don't say that that precocious child is having improper proposals made to her."

It was nothing of the sort, as he quickly discovered on joining the pair. Cora's companion was his Uncle Clem's senior steeple-jack, Vincent Uttley, who, he gathered, had met the youngest daughter of the house outdoors, after an abortive interview with Mrs. Roebuck.

"Nay, all I'm after is to pick up any morsel about Maggie,"

240

Vincent Uttley was insisting. "Anything that might give me a bit on a clue."

Cora, ruffled already by his use of her Christian name, turned to her cousin. "He's trying to find one of our old maids," she explained. "And I just haven't the *soupçon* of an idea where she could be."

"Keep it clean, woman," Archie murmured.

"Oh, *don't* be so immature," his cousin retorted.

"Sorry, ducks," said Archie.

Vincent Uttley made another despairing attempt. "You've noan any idea whether——"

"No, I haven't, whatever it is," Cora interrupted him impatiently. "All I know is that my mother dismissed Maggie because she found she was being familiar with my brother."

There was a brief silence. *"Familiar!"* the foreman steeplejack ejaculated. "Familiar with Jim?"

"Unfortunately, yes," Cora snapped.

Vincent Uttley licked his lips. "I see," he muttered. "Well . . . well, I'll be off now."

Turning sharply away, he set off with a raking stride towards the upper gateway; the two ill-assorted cousins proceeded more decorously towards the front door of Stonewood.

The combination of Fred Astaire and Ginger Rogers was always a potent lure to Sam, but, denied his wife's company, he was compelled to seek other companionship on excursions to the pictures. And so, a fortnight after Vincent Uttley had walked through Moorheaton as though the hounds of hell were at his heels, he arranged to escort his niece Kate to the big cinema at the junction of Church Street and Lowerhouse Street.

Kate left home early for her appointment, taking two books to be changed at the Public Library in Market Approach, where she met Jim Roebuck.

"Hallo, hallo," he said, smiling, "this is very late for you to be out in the town, isn't it?"

Kate laughed. "I am getting a little older, Jim, even if you don't notice it," she said. "Anyhow I'm meeting Uncle Sam at the Majestic."

"Come on then, Methuselah," Jim said. "I'll see you safely there."

On the way they talked a little about books but the abdication occupied them mainly, and in particular the

King's last broadcast to his people, before sailing from England in a destroyer, when, his voice so moving, he had said: "A few hours ago I discharged my last duty as King and Emperor...."

Kate was confessing that she still had a lump in her throat each time she remembered it, when, beyond the George Hotel, they met Barbara Ramsden Lister. The short conversation with Kate's friend was not outstandingly successful, primarily because she was stifling a tendency to giggle, a condition which had assailed her as soon as she sighted the pair.

"What's the matter with her?" Jim asked afterwards. "Is she missing on one cylinder or what?"

Kate's cheeks were red. "Oh, it's just shyness. She's lovely when you know her properly."

Sam Pilling was not at the picture house, but his niece had ample diversion in the foyer, where the Hildred Pickersgills were obviously waiting for someone, Mr. Pickersgill with a vague hint of resentment on his meek and mild face. Kate's interest was in his wife, however, and every now and then, until Mr. James Wainwright bustled in and bought three tickets, she stared wide-eyed at her.

When he arrived, Sam insisted upon Jim accompanying them. "Then you can take Kate home for me, lad," he continued. "I've got some important business to do afterwards ... it's cropped up since I fixed this with Kate."

So, the young lady enjoying herself between them, a box of chocolates on her knee, Jim and Sam revelled in the capers of Miss Rogers and Mr. Astaire.

As diffused lighting crept on at the conclusion of the picture, Sam looked at his watch, and then promptly excused himself. By then Fred Lumb would be sitting somewhere or other in a completely dark suite of offices in Neptune Buildings, the key to which he still retained.

When the Town Hall clock sonorously declared the half-hour after ten the collation of the more important accounts of the rival firms of Sam Pilling and Ben Buckley had been completed.

"Well, I reckon that's very satisfactory, Sam," Fred Lumb commented as he replaced his papers in a brand-new brief-case. "Taken together, we're only just slightly down, and that's after charging my extra salary and the expenses I've run you in for so far."

The work had been done in the large room of Sam Pilling, whose spirits did not seem very high.

"Course we can't really judge when it's only over the sticks," he remarked. "We'll have to wait until next year's Flat for that, and it's the hell of a way off yet, Fred."

"Don't wish time on, Sam," said Fred. "It passes quickly enough."

"Does it?" Sam grunted. "It all depends on——"

Fred Lumb's finger was jabbing. "Somebody's banging on the 'Inquiries' panel," he whispered.

Hitherto, whenever cloak and dagger business was needed he had played the leading rôle. He did so again, screening one side of his mouth while transferring certain instructions into Sam's ear.

"You go, but don't rush," he said. "I'll tiptoe into the Telephone Room, and stop there in the darkness. If it's somebody you feel you ought to bring in, bring 'em in, and leave with them, too, switching off all the lights and locking up. I'll find my own way out afterwards."

Sam eyed him. "Small wonder you don't want time to pass. All right, I'll go."

A few minutes later, on returning, he stowed a wallet away in his hip pocket.

"A bobby, Fred," he said tautly. "And if ever a chap withdrew knowingly it was him. Aye, he'll be telling his pals at the station that I've had a woman in my room, and you can't blame him really, can you? You'll have tumbled to it that I got myself into a mess with Hilda Schofield? It's common property, I gather, that I've been mixed up with someone, anyhow."

"I've got eyes," Fred said. "But one swallow doesn't make a summer."

"It can in time if you're cursed with a father-in-law of the same brand as mine," Sam retorted. "From the dark threats he's dropped about investigating me you'd imagine he expected hunting out a bunch of fancy tarts that I'd been keeping."

Fred Lumb reached for an overcoat hanging on the antlered stand.

"Tell him you'll investigate him," he said.

Sam laughed. "And a fat lot of good that would do. He's never stepped an inch off the godly path all his life."

"Don't you be too sure. We all have our failings and Ezra Sykes didn't succeed as quickly as he did by hard work only. Yes, I've an idea he took one or two short cuts to obtain the capital he needed to open out with."

"Nay, I'm not swallowing any yarn about a narrow-minded customer like him ever being otherwise than above board in all he did."

Fred Lumb dismissed the matter with a shrug. "Well, you stick to your opinion and I'll stick to mine," he said. "And now what about us getting off? I'll go first and wait for you in the car."

Overcoat collar up to his ears and hat-brim pulled down, he left the office and proceeded along the corridor and down the broad stairway of Neptune Buildings, unafraid of encountering either the caretaker or his wife, so familiar was he with their routine. When outside, he turned to the right down Market Square, but when nearly at the bottom paused to look into one of the windows of the Music Saloon, where a dance was in progress. While he was there he chanced to see Sam's daughter, gaily swinging round in the arms of an angelic-looking young man he knew well enough, Walter Murgatroyd's eldest son. Then, a smile lingering on his lips, he continued his way into a less well-illuminated part of the town, where the Bentley had been parked, deep in a dark alley between the offices of Ramsden Lister and Wainwright and the Spinners Hall. Its owner, who was running him home, arrived about five minutes later.

"I've been watching your Nancy dancing," Fred remarked on the first rise of the long climb to the Park. "She's a bonnie lass, Sam."

"She's a grand 'un, too, and has been ever since this set-back we engineered began," Sam said, a tinge of irritation in his voice. "It was her birthday yesterday, and I'd all on to prevent myself from giving her the whacking present she deserves."

"It wouldn't have done, wouldn't have done at all," Fred declared.

"I suppose not," Sam replied, more edgily.

As the zone of light from the next lamp-standard drew nearer Fred glanced at him. "You're not regretting this crackpot scheme, are you?"

Sam scoffed noisily. "Me . . . me regret it . . . when it's paying the dividends it is, both for Archie and Nancy! What will you imagine next, Fred lad?"

"Hey!" his companion barked out. "This'll do."

"Why, we're three or four hundred yards away yet," Sam expostulated. "Nobody will spot you even if we go nearer."

"You pull up under them overhanging trees ahead, against

the Park railings," Fred said firmly. "One touch of careless-ness could ruin this planning of ours. Now is there anything else before I step out?"

Amused despite his not very carefree mood, Sam referred to a new suit which had so startled Milly.

"I haven't been blinded yet, Fred, but I'm waiting for the moment."

"It'll come, lad," Fred Lumb said with confidence. "Aye, poor Milly, the lass was so upset when we bumped into each other. But I'm afraid both you and her have other surprises in store for you. Why, I haven't really started yet."

"Oh, you haven't?" Sam muttered.

"Not I," Fred declared. "You wait . . . just be patient."

For the whole of his short walk home he was grinning in a fashion none but his wife would have recognized. It would have alarmed her, too.

One surprise he certainly had in store, the expectation that very shortly he would be a member of the exclusive County Club. This was being brought about by Mr. Dale Watkinson and Mr. Simeon Calverley, neither of whom had remotely contemplated removing their betting accounts from Sam Pilling. But these gentlemen, and others at the Club, had a strong sense of humour.

Just as membership of the County Club was strictly con-fined, tickets for the Ramsfield Choral Society's Christmas performance of the *Messiah* were pearls of great price, and the number of applicants for them would have filled the Town Hall tenfold, with a substantial overflow.

Two of these prized pieces of pasteboard were in Archie Pilling's waistcoat pocket as he tidied up a pile of junk which had slithered to the floor of the capacious garage at Glenfield. His father, fresh from leaving Fred Lumb, drove in as he heaved up the last deck-chair. To him he explained a bitter disappointment.

"The devil of it is, I can't go to the *Messiah*," he grumbled. "Alec's invited me that night to a sort of rugger smoker at Bradford, captain and delegate representing Ramsfield kind of thing, and I couldn't back out. And I daren't refuse the tickets either, because that mad Harry of a foreman of mine unearthed them for me."

"What about Nancy?" his father suggested. "It's not a week since she was screaming to high heaven because she couldn't get any."

"Was she?" Archie murmured. "Then I'll approach her. Wonder if I can wangle a premium on 'em?"

The conference with his sister took place in the study, as their mother for the past couple of days had been "touching up" the drawing-room. Sam and Milly were present.

Regret and dismay grew visibly on Nancy's face. But before she burst into speech Archie tossed the ball to her.

"Well, there you are," he said, flipping up the tickets. "But what about a leetle, leetle bonus—say half a dollar to clinch the business?"

"Oh, why didn't you tell me sooner?" Nancy wailed.

"How could I?" her brother demanded. "Anyhow, am I to understand you don't want 'em? What's up?"

Exasperatedly Nancy referred to a party at the Hirsts'. "They *would* have it that night. Of course they haven't a note of music in them, and I don't suppose they ever considered what would be happening in the Town Hall. But I promised both Bee and Mrs. Hirst I'd go early—it's about games or something. They're always in a stew about arranging them."

Milly tossed her head. "And you're silly enough to do it for them. But they take good care not to give you any credit for what you've done."

Nancy had been glancing at her brother—they were nearer *the* moment. "Oh well, perhaps so, Mummy," she agreed, smiling. "But it doesn't hurt me."

The tickets were still uppermost in Archie's mind—that was plain to see on his face. "Of course I shan't be left with them on my hands," he remarked. "But it does seem a pity to let them out of the family. I say, Dad, what about a sale? You and mother have always been nuts on the Choral Society."

"Well," said Sam. "Well . . . er . . . it's all right to me, but it's entirely for your mother to decide."

Animation and chagrin, in that order, were artistically revealed on his wife's always expressive face.

"Oh, I'd have loved to," she said. "But what with Christmas baking and one thing or another I really don't see how I can. Bother it!"

"That settles that," Sam said.

"Ah, well," Archie muttered. "Seven more shopping days before we reach the season of good fellowship between men."

Sharply Nancy tapped her brother's arm. "I'm off to the kitchen to make tea for us all," she said. "You can help me for once in your life, my lad."

As eager as she to discuss a shot that had misfired, he followed her obediently.

Too angry to bother about either the poker or the niceties, Sam broke up a large lump of coal on the fire with a hefty kick. His feeling relieved to this extent, he turned round.

"Always a wise thing to keep up appearances," he said. "We'd have been doing that, if we'd gone to the *Messiah* together."

Milly, far too innocently, glanced inquiringly at him. "I don't quite know what you mean," she said.

"Skip it!" Sam snorted.

It was an Americanism he had acquired at the Majestic Picture House and similar resorts. To him it was perfect for the situation.

4

Both Christmas Day and Boxing Day were different from anything either Sam or his wife had known since the children were small. In the first place the Pillings ate Christmas dinner under their own roof. It was a delicious one, cooked in partnership by Milly and Nancy, but even a feeling of repletion could not drive out a sense of strangeness. Hitherto Milly's mother, and afterwards Laura Roebuck as the elder daughter, had always been hostess at a spread before which the whole family sat down.

Scipio Dyson and Kate called in the afternoon—that wasn't usual, either; nor was the visit, almost stealthy, of Clem Roebuck and Jim.

Of these two days Boxing Day was the more abnormal to Sam, who spent the afternoon sawing applewood logs in the kitchen garden. Milly, who had been fussing in the conservatory over a plant which was not wintering too well, walked down the ravine to tell him tea was ready, arriving at the foot just as the crowd at Swanroyd sent up a mighty cheer. It was the Hornets' annual match against neighbouring rivals.

"We've scored again," Sam said excitedly. "That's us all right. Now just let's listen, to see if we convert the try."

Low down, fiery red, the wintry sun shone through the haze as silently they stood, the tenseness of one communicated to the other. The seconds passed and then, from far away, a jubilant roar ascended once again.

"It's over," Sam exulted. "Another five points anyway."

Milly's eyes misted. "Oh, it's a shame, Sam."

He stared at her. "Good gracious, you don't think I've been

247

moping, do you? And, besides, what's a game? Why, I've been as happy as a laddie building up that pile of wood, and a rare good 'un it is. It'll open Johnson's eyes when he sees it."

She was wise enough not to say more.

Extra licence had been granted Nancy during the Christmas period, and about eight o'clock on New Year's Eve, just before Philip Illingworth was due to take her to a dance at Bradford, she ran downstairs to the drawing-room.

"There!" she cried.

"It looks *lovely*," her mother said. "What do you think of her Sam?"

With a critical eye Sam inspected his daughter, from sleek, wavy hair to smart gilt sandals. "Turn round," he said, judgment deferred until a delightful gold lamé frock had been examined from every angle. "Yes, you'll do very nicely, love. Yes. . . ." Pride in him he looked at her again, rejoicing that the hollows in her cheeks and the stains beneath her eyes had gone.

"And what about my . . . er . . . gown?" Nancy inquired. "Foundation, Rafe Bottomley's sweat shop, *chic* reconstruction by *Maison* Milly *et* Nancy, if I may borrow that brat Cora's devastating technique."

"Well, though I say it myself," her mother was resolutely affirming when Nancy, cocking her head, screamed: "He's here!" and then picked up her skirts and scampered upstairs.

Smilingly, Milly let in the caller, her husband greeting him from the doorway of the drawing-room. .

"Come in, Philip." Sam beckoned. "Nancy's all ready . . . all ready, bar shouting, that is, which means another ten minutes yet. Oh, yes."

"You'd better take your coat off then, Philip," Milly said, laughing. "And I think I'd better slip up to her room and hurry her up."

As she reached the spacious landing she saw Nancy in another bedroom. When her daughter skipped back to her own room she left a faint but tantalizing scent in her wake.

"My Chanel!" Milly exclaimed. "You've rooted out that bottle I'd hidden."

"Yes, Mummy," Nancy confessed, eyes sparkling. "I find it has a wonderful effect. . . . I mean, of course," she went on, simpering ridiculously, "on the wearer, Mamma dear."

For the next few seconds Milly shed her anxieties amazingly, to become an attractive young woman, an older sister of her daughter.

"And on more than the wearer," she giggled.

"Mother!" said Nancy, eyeing her. "Anyway," she added complacently, "speaking of *wearing* as distinct from wearing, if you grasp my meaning, it's just occurred to me that us Pilling women wear well."

Her mother bridled. "Go on with you, silly. And now be quick . . . and I'll straighten up everything after you've gone."

Nancy, who was busy at the dressing-table mirror, thanked her and then broke off operations to turn round.

"No woman worth her salt ever allows a man to get away from her," she said with the utmost seriousness. "Hence these delicate touches to the finished article. And that reminds me of something. Barbara Ramsden Lister's uncle and aunt are to be divorced, but for heaven's sake don't speak about it to Kate. She likes both of them and is terribly upset."

Milly was startled on three counts: the couple had been married for nearly twenty years and she had always thought them most united; she would never have dreamed of discussing such a topic with a young girl; and she was astonished about the subject being brought up—it was one, despite the usual crop of Ramsfield divorces, Nancy had never entered into since Philip and Estelle had parted.

"Some people joined me and Kate when we were downing cream cakes in Wood's Café," Nancy continued before her mother could reply. "That's how it came about. Of course, the whole thing's so stupid."

Her mother stared. "What do you know about it?"

Nancy had slipped into her fur coat, and was stooping to pick up a Chinese brocade bag which had fallen from the bed.

"Nothing really, Mummy, except that any woman, if she's really fond of her husband, is asking for trouble by continually sulking because he's strayed for once in pastures new," she said, flushed a little as she rose. "Wipe off the score for good and all with the whale of a row—that's my motto."

"Oh, you young ones can soon put the world to rights," her mother remarked with unmistakable tartness.

"I dare say, Mummy," Nancy smilingly agreed as she kissed her. "I must fly now . . . I haven't left anything, have I? Hankies, pennies, or other necessities?"

Instinctively Milly glanced back into the bedroom. As she

did so Nancy screwed up her nose towards her, a gesture as if to say: "Now chew that one over."

In the hall, Sam also received a kiss from his daughter, and remained there to watch the couple out, as did his wife from the top of the staircase.

Then Milly returned to Nancy's bedroom, where disorder had to be restored to order. The collection of scattered outer garments and flimsy underwear was not an absorbing task, but nevertheless as she hung up or folded or discarded, she looked exceedingly thoughtful.

Neither Sam nor his wife greeted the New Year. Both were in their respective beds by eleven o'clock. At midnight Milly heard the bells of the Parish Church ringing out, while Sam was awakened about two o'clock when the peace of the neighbourhood was intermittently destroyed by the slamming of car doors, the squeal of brakes, the roar of under-silenced vehicles, shouts and raucous laughter—this was maintained until half-past four, when the last reveller drove away from a house farther up Moorheaton Drive.

The next day, short of sleep, Sam was in a foul temper. To this he attributed the blame for a small scene which occurred during the late afternoon.

Sleet lashed incessantly across Market Square, but the large ground floor of the County Club was snug, and service prompt and cheerful. Various groups of members taking their ease were dotted here and there, but the largest party, of nearly a dozen, occupied the corner nearest Sheepgate, and they were discussing Lord Nuffield's magnificent gift of two million pounds to the unemployed.

"Yes," Mr. Ernest Illingworth was saying, "but personally I am afraid that the day is coming when many people, none of them conspicuous for brains or a capacity for hard work, will insist that no man should be in a position to give such an immense sum away."

An elderly gentleman, whose loud-patterned, individualistic-styled but superbly cut suit had been responsible for his causing still another sensation in Ramsfield, next stated his views.

"I agree with Mr. Illingworth. For myself I can't conceive the youngsters of to-day, when they reach my age, ever launching out as I am . . . on such an impressive scale, that is, if I might be pardoned the conceit."

"Oh, come, come, Lumb," Captain Gainsway-Sinkinson protested. "The spirit of Englishmen, what!"

Mr. Peter Entwistle was over from Manchester. For a very successful businessman he was extremely long-winded and, to prove any point he desired to make, appeared somewhat lacking in discretion.

"I think I can tell you a little story here which touches acutely upon these matters," he said. "It's to do with customers of mine, Barclay-Barrow of Birmingham. Now the youngest Barrow boy got himself involved—of course, this is *quite* confidential, gentlemen. . . ."

Mr. Simeon Calverley leaned towards his neighbour, Mr. Dale Watkinson. "Look who's come in," he whispered gleefully. "Then sit back and watch events."

From their side of the circle they had a direct view of the porter's annexe, where Sam Pilling was discarding overcoat, muffler and hat. Completely unconscious of what awaited him, he came round the screen. Fred Lumb's suit was a magnet for anyone, and so it was not extraordinary that his glance fell first on his former manager.

Lolling in a leather chair, legs crossed, whisky at elbow, Fred Lumb waved a cigar in greeting.

"Compliments of the season, Pilling," he called out. "What about sinking one with me on the first day of the new year?"

Almost everyone in the room had been agog for this moment, and not a soul among them failed to chuckle inwardly when Sam sourly remarked that the privilege of buying drinks belonged to members only.

"So I believe," Fred Lumb said, palpably unabashed.

Nettled, Sam retorted: "Well, then?"

Impassively, Dale Watkinson explained. "He's a fully-fledged member all right, Sam lad. You see with him being an up and coming representative of his profession we thought we ought to have him in the ranks."

Sam looked wholly stupefied. "Oh!" he muttered.

"Well, now that that's cleared up," Fred Lumb said breezily, "maybe after all you'll accept a——"

"Anything I want I'll buy for myself," Sam snapped.

Cursing himself already for ill-humour which had made him act so foolishly, Sam turned away from the grinning party, doing his utmost to cover his retreat decently by heading for the inglenook and Septimus Firth, as though his purpose throughout had been to join the wool merchant.

Of all the onlookers none had been more patently amused than Captain Gainsway-Sinkinson.

"Harking back to money for the needy," he remarked,

251

smiling broadly, "I don't think it would be difficult to name one chappie who wouldn't sniff at a charitable offering, eh? what! Apart from that, Lumb, I gather you're taking many of Pilling's clients from him."

Fred Lumb gazed into his whisky. "I'm not complaining, though of course the real turnover in our line won't begin until the start of the Flat."

"Ah, yes, the Flat," Captain Gainsway-Sinkinson said reminiscently. Then, smiling, bending to one side, he spoke as though conferring an immense boon. "And when that delectable time comes, Lumb, old man, I dare say Ben Buckley will be enjoying my patronage."

"Wouldn't touch your business with a barge-pole," said Fred Lumb.

Captain Gainsway-Sinkinson started up. "I . . . beg . . . your . . . pardon. . . ."

Jim Oldfield lent a helping hand. "He says he wouldn't touch your business with a barge-pole, Captain."

If the occupants of the room had been agog when Sam Pilling met Fred Lumb, they now had difficulty in concealing their hilarity.

"What the devil do you mean, sir?" thundered Captain Gainsway-Sinkinson. "You . . . Lumb . . . whatever your damn name is."

Raising an arm, Fred Lumb tapped his circular, bald patch. "I reckon I owe this to you," he remarked. "You seem to forget I'd the dubious pleasure of dealing with your account when I used to work in Neptune Buildings. Never again!"

Jim Oldfield held up a finger as though inspired. "I've gleaned what he's getting at now, Captain," he said confidentially. "He doesn't want your business, that's it."

Scarlet to the temples, deeply mortified by a scene that had taken place in the presence of his friend, Peter Entwistle, Captain Gainsway-Sinkinson failed to notice the departure of a bookmaker who earlier had refused to accommodate him further.

If Sam were amused by this late development, he did not show it when hurrying across Market Square or subsequently when he visited various departments at the office. But it was from sickness of heart rather than annoyance that he found fault in the Duplicating Room, where batteries of machines were churning out thousands of investment forms for clients' use—in preparation for the days from March until November when once again there would be the throb of strenuous activity.

In his own room he had it out with himself. "I'm fed up to the teeth, that's it," he mused. "Fed up about Milly . . . and . . . aye, I'm fed up with feeling myself a butt. The fact is that I wasn't acting a part when I was nasty with Fred—I *was* nasty."

Listlessly he went to the cigar cabinet, but did nothing more than open a drawer and close it.

"Well, I must stick it out a bit longer," he sighed. "Some way or other."

With scant zest in him he pulled forward a wire-tray and rang for his secretary.

CHAPTER NINE

CHURCH STREET was crowded with Saturday morning shoppers, many of whom were gazing upwards at the men working on the framework of scaffolding clothing the lofty spire of the Parish Church. Sam Pilling, heading for Hoyle's fish-shop at the corner of Teazle Street, was of these jaywalkers, and in consequence brushed shoulders with a lady to whom he had not spoken for some time, his sister-in-law.

"It's just as well," said Laura Roebuck darkly as she straightened her hat. "I've been wanting a word with you."

This "word" extended to references about Nancy and Philip Illingworth, and to the "women" who were breaking Milly's heart.

"If her heart is being broken by my carryings-on, *she* hasn't told you," Sam growled. "You haven't set eyes on each other since——"

"And another thing," Laura interrupted brusquely. "You ought to be ashamed of yourself for keeping on Glenfield instead of moving into a house more suitable to your means. What does it look like—having a gardener while Milly slaves herself to death . . . oh, yes, I'm aware you've a woman coming in, and I suppose that girl does something, but——"

"Morning," said her brother-in-law.

Leaving her to declaim to the air, Sam strode along to the fish-shop, where his curt salute was totally misinterpreted by Alec's mother, Mrs. Walter Murgatroyd, and Mrs. Septimus

Firth. As he carefully examined a few crabs, which were opened for his inspection, he glimpsed a smile which should not have been on the face of a white-coated assistant. Nowadays ever suspicious, he looked about and at once perceived that out of fifteen or sixteen shoppers the majority were not without an anticipatory expression. Then he saw the proprietor of Ben Buckley's, flourishing an immensely thick wad of pound notes from which he paid for his purchases, the notes without doubt borrowed from the office safe to provide the desired impression.

"Ah!" said Fred Lumb. "How's business, Pilling, my boy?"

"About the usual," Sam replied tersely.

"Well, it could be worse than that," said Fred, while listeners smiled. "But mine's up, well up I'm glad to say."

"Splendid!" said Sam.

Fred Lumb eyed him rather curiously, and then, bidding a general "good morning" and raising his grey hat, left the shop.

They met again within three minutes. Sam ordered two crabs to be dressed, which he arranged to pick up after a few calls, and next made for an old-fashioned tobacconist's near the Spinners' Hall.

Round the corner of Church Street, Fred Lumb was waiting for him. If anything, he appeared depressed.

"Hey!" he said, "I want a chat with you, Sam. Is this performance of ours getting you down?"

"Not it," Sam blustered. "Why should it?"

"I can't answer that," Fred commented. "But I know this, I'm not going on with it if it's causing bad blood. If we're both playing a game, well and good, but once or twice I've spotted an unpleasant gleam in your eyes, and that's something you couldn't assume."

"Stuff and nonsense," Sam declared. "If I've sounded gruff or looked out of temper it's because I'm bothered about something at home. I think that blasted affair with Hilda Schofield will dog me to my dying day."

Profoundly understanding, Fred Lumb nodded. "Oh, I see, lad," he said. "You know I was getting it into my head that you couldn't stand up to what I was dishing out to you, and as I've more rods in pickle for you I reckoned it was best to make sure."

Sam laughed. "What! Me not able to stand up to whatever you dish out! You go on and do your damnest, Fred, and for every squeak you get out of me, inwardly not out-wardly, of course, I'll present you with a hundred quid."

Visibly his companion brightened. "Well, if you're not countermanding my instructions, and if what you say is so, that's different. And the sky's still the limit, eh? Within what's been arranged between us naturally."

Again Sam laughed, this time boisterously. "Aye, do any-thing you like. As if I should worry."

Suddenly austere, Fred Lumb remarked sententiously: "It's no good you whining to me, Pilling. You've got to expect competition in this world."

"Eh!" Sam exclaimed.

The next second he was standing by himself on the pave-ment, while Fred Lumb strolled off with Mr. William Pobjoy, who must surely have heard his concluding observation.

Tickled despite himself by his henchman, Sam completed his shopping, and then went along Teazle Street to keep his appointment with Milly and Nancy outside Wood's Café. The Bentley was being checked over at Thorntons' and he was riding home in his daughter's car.

The Pillings spent the afternoon in their various ways. After lunch, as it was the last Saturday in the month, Nancy was ceremoniously paid four weeks' wages, the same amount as Olga's. She at once drew up a most meticulous and praise-worthy budget covering personal expenditure for a similar period ahead—later on she drove down to town and, in a wild outburst of extravagance at Ainley's the chemists in Teazle Street, blued in rather more than half her cash resources on cosmetics.

A knee injury sustained the previous Saturday, when a berserk Headingley forward booted first and apologized charmingly afterwards, prevented Archie from turning out with Ramsfield Rugger at Ings Close. He stayed at home, to take off the cylinder head of his motor-bicycle. Cora Roe-buck visited him in the garage, her purpose to discuss "*l'affaire*" of his sister Nancy and her ex-brother-in-law, Philip Illingworth, her verdict being that "one simply must be broad-minded in these affairs." She also commiserated with her Aunt Milly on the utterly appalling effect of house-work upon the hands.

During the afternoon Milly pottered about the house, washed a few pairs of stockings and a small pile of her own underclothing, and glued a section of beading which was loose on a lamp-shade. That was indoors.

Outside, high up the far bank of the ravine, she picked a nice bunch of snowdrops in a sheltered hollow close to the wall of The Turrets; and in the garden cut sprays of winter jasmine and daphne near the sundial, not far from the corner of the lawn from which there was a view, over the ravine, of the gone-to-seed grounds of that long unoccupied mansion.

Armed with these trophies she looked in on Archie, and examined her hands when Cora had gone.

As it was not worth while going to the office, Sam remained at home, closeted in the study, where he brooded in succession about Milly, Fred Lumb, his loss of prestige, and finally Clem Roebuck, who was away on another business-cum-pleasure trip, this time to Preston, where Ramsfield Town were playing the North End.

"Ah, well, he does right," Sam's glum soliloquy went. "But somehow or other, quite apart from him going off a lot, we seem to have grown away from one another, and I'm certain I felt the difference long before Philip started coming here. Why it is, I don't know, but Clem isn't the same person to me . . . or is it because I've changed? It could be, aye it could . . . because I have. Sad, but there it is."

At that moment, as if in sympathy with his mood, rain began to slash against the window.

Milly came into the study a few minutes afterwards, carrying a vase in which she had arranged the jasmine. She was striving gradually to bring about a better understanding between them but, stiltedly over-bright on occasion, was not advancing at all.

"I'm not disturbing you, am I, dear?" she inquired.

"Not at all," Sam replied in a die-away voice. "Are you wanting something?"

"No, not really." She flushed. "But I thought you might like to see this. It is lovely, isn't it?"

With lack-lustre eyes he stared. "Yes . . . very nice," he said.

With that she withdrew, closed the door behind her, and then stooped to pick up a second vase of daphne, which she had intended to parade before him if the reception of the first had been different.

It was perhaps as well Milly did not hear his comment when she had gone.

"The poor girl is just trying to make the best of things, that's all," he muttered. "But I've always been all or nothing, and somewhere in between won't do for me. Well. . . ."

He then glanced at the morning paper which, in heavy headlines, announced that thirteen Trotskyists had been executed in Moscow.

When the letter-box clicked after tea, Sam secured the sporting edition of the *Ramsfield Reporter,* and for the next few minutes devoured "our special reporter's" racy account of the Hornets' match with Oldham. A game of billiards with his daughter followed next. On their return to the drawing-room Nancy played a miscellaneous programme of records on the radiogram. Finally the three Pillings settled themselves with books.

As the last stroke of nine struck by the grandfather clock on the half landing died wheezily away, the readers were disturbed by unmistakable sounds: the rattling of a knob, the slamming of a door, the rattling of a second knob, and the closing of the inner door of the hall.

"Oh dear," said Milly despairingly.

Mr. Sykes, raindrops glistening on beard and bushy eyebrows, entered the drawing-room at a smart rate. He was very wet indeed.

"Nancy, I think you'd better make your grandfather something hot," Milly said. "Would you like cocoa or——"

"She can stay where she is," Ezra Sykes interposed. "It's her I want to see."

"Well, a few minutes won't make any difference," Milly protested. "And take some of those things off or you'll get your death of cold."

"And so will one of us if he sits down in that state," Sam pointed out. "Any chair he graces will be damp for weeks."

Discreetly Milly shook her head at him. Her "Ssss" was very faint. Then she nodded towards the door—obeying this hint, Nancy left for the kitchen.

The drawing-room of Glenfield was spacious and well furnished, but by the time Mr. Sykes had settled himself its elegance had been banished by the dispositions he made. A bowler hat hung over the upper corner of an oil-painting, and the gilt projection on a wall-bracket served as a hook for his overcoat; boots steamed within the hearth, and a pair of socks was spread out to dry on the pierced-steel fender. Rejecting an offer of slippers, he sat with bare feet, finishing off a cup of cocoa which he had been drinking from the saucer.

"Well, now you've made yourself reasonably at home, what is it you want with Nancy?" Sam asked.

"I'll speak about Archibald first," said his father-in-law. "I dropped on him to-night coming out of that low public-house close by the station, and he was so drunk that he had to be held up. It were my duty to remonstrate with him and I performed it. And what did he do? Well, I'll tell you what he did . . . he told me, his grandfather, to go to a warm place."

"Father, are you certain he was drunk?" Milly asked. "Because—well, both Sam and I are very pleased with him lately."

"And if he was drunk, didn't you realize the senselessness of doing anything then?" Sam said.

"He could talk plenty," Ezra Sykes snapped.

"Oh!" Sam murmured.

Very pale, the light of decision in her eyes, Milly took a deep breath.

"Father, you're staying here until Archie comes home," she said. "And don't bother to say you've never varied your bedtime for years. This is something which should be straightened up, and I'm going to have it straightened up to-night. It's not very long since I told you I will *not* have these disturbances brought into this house, and I won't."

With her dander up, she was to her husband the soft-hearted girl who had undauntedly faced an overbearing father as soon as she knew her condition: a girl whose immense reserve of spirit was so deeply hidden away as hardly to be suspected. Affectionately he applauded her in this fight for her children, and from then on he was content to remain more or less a spectator.

Mr. Sykes bleakly regarded her. "You'll do well to keep a closer guard on your tongue, Milly," he said. "I'm noan used to being addressed in terms like them."

"I'm sorry if I've annoyed you, Father," she replied. "But there are times when people have to speak their mind. And now what is it about Nancy?"

That fired him. "What about Nancy?" he said thinly. "And what about you and that husband of yours—for allowing her to go about with a man who in God's sight is still wed to her cousin Estelle . . . a man who's perverted, as you both know well . . . a chap whose pleasure is to scourge his wife when she's naked——"

Cheeks flaming, Nancy jumped forward in front of his chair. "Don't you dare say any more," she gasped. "And it's a beastly lie . . . you . . . you horrible thing."

Far from being annoyed, her grandfather was not without

an air of triumph. "So you and him talk about such matters, do you?" he said. "About men and women being naked, eh?"

"We don't smack our lips about it, which you're doing," Nancy retorted.

"I'm what?" Mr. Sykes shouted. "And don't think I didn't hear what you called me . . . me, your grandfather. The fact is you're associating with a man——"

Sam interrupted him, well remembering the acute fright Alonso Dyson had given his father-in-law on this same question. "Who is a pervert, so you've asserted," he snapped. "Well, I'm wondering what Ernest Illingworth will do about that if I tell him. He's a client of mine, you know."

In a trice, remembering also, Ezra Sykes abandoned his ground. "What I'm saying is being said in the bosom of my own family. It's noan a thing I should repeat elsewhere."

Sam's eyes were hard. "Maybe so and maybe not. But if you so much as mention it here again I'll be on the telephone to Illingworth's house in two jiffies."

"And while we're about it, before the subject's closed, Father," Milly said with quiet dignity, "it will be as well if you know also that Nancy has both Sam's and my permission to go out with Mr. Illingworth's son."

Her father swallowed, struggled with himself but choked back the answers he had. It was also significant that he allowed himself to be overruled about staying.

"No," Sam said. "We're either judging both cases or none, and if Archie's isn't considered to-night I'm re-opening the other, which means I shall pass it over to Ernest Illingworth . . . and *he'll* deal with it all right."

It was a quarter to twelve before Archie came home—nearly three hours of purgatory for three people in the drawing-room of Glenfield.

Well versed in such matters, Nancy identified the exhaust sound as that of Alec's Mercedes Benz. Immediately cheery farewells had been bawled outside, Sam went to the front door to meet his son.

"Hallo, Dad." Limping badly, Archie blinked surprise.

"You seem to have sobered quickly," his father remarked. "By the way, what have you been doing since you left home?"

One arm still in a sleeve of his overcoat, Archie paused to eye him. "What's all this? Any special reason?"

"It hardly matters now, lad," Sam said somewhat ambiguously.

"Anyway," Archie reflected, "we'd a drink or two at the

259

Vaults before driving in Alec's scooter for the second house at the Empire. Then me and Frank, clinging together like soul-mates, hobbled to park our fannies on the best plush seats. . . ." He chuckled. "Guess what? Frank's crocked his leg this afternoon, and he's a damn sight more lame than me."

"That'll do," said Sam. "Now go ahead to your mother and Nancy."

Archie's mouth opened slightly, but receiving a nod as signal he went into the drawing-room, where his mystified expression rapidly changed to comprehension on seeing his grandfather.

"I think I'm rumbling now," he muttered. "Mother, am I by any chance supposed to have been canned and incapable this evening?"

Milly had been inspecting him. "Yes," she said, smiling.

"He's getten over it by now," Ezra Sykes said.

In the four and a half months since Archie Pilling had gone into the workshops of Murgatroyd Conveyors Ltd., his face had changed perceptibly. It was leaner and more mature, sharper-etched and stronger. As he turned towards his grandfather, the line of his jaw was harsh.

"For years, Grandfather," he began, "when in your view I've misbehaved myself, you've always held a threat over me, that you'd not leave me any of your money if I didn't alter my ways. Well, now, as respectfully as I can, I'm going to tell you what your money means to me. The Lord knows I'm short enough of the ready, and I expect I shall be short for a mighty long time, but even if it spoils any chances of my ever touching a cent of yours there's something I've got to make plain to you—and it's that you'll never again speak to me like you did outside the Vaults, whether I'm alone or whether I'm with a bunch of pals, as I was. Oh, yes, I'm aware how the Vaults is regarded by people like yourself. All sorts and conditions go there . . . commercial travellers with their working-week floosies, prostitutes, porters from the station and grimy chaps from the loco. sheds, businessmen both poor and rich. And we all get on very nicely together, including the members of Ramsfield Rugger, who've just about adopted it as their unofficial headquarters. But you're not calling me a whoremonger just because——"

"Did he call you that?" His mother gasped.

Lips thinned, Mr. Sykes said: "You cannot touch pitch without being defiled."

Sam left the room. In the hall he picked up the telephone directory, the front cover of which advertised Thorntons' Taxi-Hire Service. By the time he had finished his conversation and arranged for a car to be sent up, Milly joined him. She was trembling.

"He's got another piece of my mind," she said, her eyes bright. "And it isn't as if I hadn't given him fair warning not long ago."

"Was that about me? When you ordered me out of my own drawing-room?"

Milly looked at him. "Yes," she said, only to continue hurriedly: "No, he won't forget in a hurry what I've told him just now."

Sam laughed. "If it was on the lines of what you came out with earlier it'll do. You were grand, love."

"Was I?"

"You couldn't have been better," Sam declared.

"Couldn't I, Sam?" she whispered.

The truth was that, thrown off balance by the row, Milly was on the brink of becoming coquettish. But the prospect of any further advance was utterly destroyed for the present when both became aware of the altercation in the drawing-room, which had risen to heights never before attained during their ownership of Glenfield. With one accord they hastened to the scene.

"And I'm going to say the same thing to you that Archie said," Nancy was storming. "You can go to hell. And the sooner the better."

"Nancy!" her mother shouted.

But neither she nor their father interfered after Archie's opening words. White with anger he confronted his grandfather.

"Well, if Nancy's the depraved creature you've just indicated, it won't soil her if I tell you where you can shove your money-bags as far as we two are concerned. And, boy, wouldn't I enjoy doing it for you."

Mr. Sykes spoke only once more before the taxi arrived. In the meantime he drew on his socks, laced up his boots, donned his bowler, and, declining assistance, struggled into a damp overcoat.

His parting words, addressed to grandson and granddaughter from the front door, were:

"Well, I hope you both know what you can expect from me."

During the ensuing family inquest, held in the drawing-room, Sam cheerily assessed this declaration at ten thousand pounds.

"Yes, I reckon you two have dropped five thousand apiece for your night's work."

"They don't care," Milly said recklessly. "And neither do I, if he cuts me off with a shilling. I'm just sickened to death of him causing bother, *damned* well sickened."

"Ma!" Archie grinned.

Nancy giggled. "Naughty, naughty," she said.

"Well, I am," their mother insisted.

Sam was chuckling. "There's only one thing to be done after that. With one dreadful word your mother's cast off respectability, and celebrate we must. What about it, eh? And . . . we've . . . got . . . the . . . stuff . . . in. . . ."

Confused, blushing, delighted, Milly nodded. "Champagne!" she said.

"Strewth!" said Nancy. "She'll be Ramsfield's vice queen in another week. Hide your drugs, Pa."

Milly shook her head. "I don't know why it is . . . I don't like quarrelling . . . but I feel as if a weight's been lifted off me. I've dreaded him coming, because it was always with some complaint. And now, when—if he comes again, I shall put my foot down right away if he's brought another tale."

"Aw, forget it," Archie said. "Let's start lapping it up. What about me fetching the doings, Dad?"

"And I'll comb through the left-overs in Mummy's special store cupboard," Nancy cried out. "Darned good job we once had lashings of oof." Murmuring: "caviare . . . anchovies . . . mushrooms," she disappeared after her brother.

"And there's some lovely cream cheese in the refrigerator," Milly called after her. "But don't touch anything we've got ready for to-morrow."

The party was a gay affair, although exclusively a family one. The revels ended at two o'clock on the morning of the Sabbath.

*   *   *

For many weeks the Pillings had been most irregular in chapel attendance, and their records were not improved on that Sunday morning. Breakfast, very much a dressing-gown affair, was eaten leisurely in the kitchen, but afterwards the two ladies began to scurry: preparing lunch, dusting, laying the dining-room table and, as important as anything

262

else, making themselves as presentable as possible before the visitor arrived. This was Philip Illingworth, who later on in the afternoon would drive Nancy to his parents' home in Wharfedale, where she would stay for tea and supper. It was a method recently devised by the couple, to ensure as much as possible of each other's society without infringing the arrangement of meeting only once each week.

Shortly after noon, when Sam, fancying himself as the driver of a small-powered but very lively sports car, was sitting behind the wheel of Gilbert's M.G., now raised on blocks, Clem Roebuck looked into the garage. The master-steeplejack, who sounded in excellent form, pulled his friend's leg and then proposed a brisk walk as an appetizer.

"Suits me," Sam beamed, hoisting a foot over the car's cut-away side. "When did you get home?"

"About an hour ago," Clem replied.

"Any luck?"

Clem was guarded. "Prospects, I'd go no further than that, Sam. But I have landed a nailing contract elsewhere, though it wasn't as the result of any of my excursions off. Ever passed the Sulpho-Aluminate Company's works — they're about twelve miles beyond Spedding, out on the Garthedge road?"

"Many a time," Sam nodded. "It'll be that chimney of theirs you're talking about, eh?"

Despite receding hair greying at the temples, Clem's smile of delight made him seem boyish.

"It is, Sam lad, and I'm as pleased as Punch about it," he replied in a voice ringing with sincerity, its tone lacking any of the affectation of his wife and daughters. "It'll be profitable for one thing, though there's more to it than that if I play my cards properly. Anyhow, I'll tell you my ideas as we go on, because in a sense I've a notion of copying you."

It was a bright day and they went as they were, bare-headed, their walk taking them to the upper end of Moorheaton Drive. From there, turning along a wooded, undulating cross-road, they were then in Top Moorheaton, where the residences at each side, though large, were not so considerable as those left behind. Among these was Alderman Joseph Hirst's, whose prim demeanour was in contrast to the scene at the next house farther along, where quite twenty-five cars, open sports models predominating, were assembled, another of the "gangs." A queasy-looking girl was leaning against a wall and a drunken youth hovered uncertainly near her.

"I'll tell you one thing, Clem," Sam commented on noticing this, a father without such cares on him, speaking as if from rarefied Olympian heights, "and it's that there's too much viciousness among the youngsters nowadays. I wonder how the majority of that lot in there would respond if the source of their money dried up?"

Affectionately amused by his friend's conceit, Clem smiled slightly. "Well, in your case, Sam, the ill wind's caused plenty of good," he said. "I reckon it's proved what Archie has in him. A machine-shop is no rest-cure for a beginner, especially a beginner who is six or seven years older than the average, and brought up as he's been."

Sam nodded judicially. "Of course it's early days yet, but so far I'm not ill-pleased. And Nancy hasn't lagged behind, either."

The master-steeplejack momentarily hesitated. "I haven't seen much of her lately, Sam," he said. "But she's never lacked character, even if in the last year or so she's been wilful to a degree. Anyhow, that's better than being milk and water."

Sam chuckled. "Sometimes, lad, only sometimes."

For the next couple of hundred yards Clem was strangely silent. Then, unburdening himself, he spoke of Nancy and Philip Illingworth, clearly revealing he did not share his wife's opinion about this. With a touching loyalty, however, he sought to find excuses for her, but throughout was obviously most uncomfortable.

As soon as possible Sam reintroduced the subject of the Sulpho-Aluminate Company's contract.

"I think you're on the right lines in considering advertising, Clem," he said. "Get long-distance shots of your men working aloft on the chimney, and have 'em reproduced in the most suitable trade papers, with arresting captions. Rub it in that it's one of the tallest chimneys in the country."

"It's just over four hundred feet." Clem laughed. "And that's higher than I've ever gone. Aye, it's a whopper all right."

Sam whistled. "*Four* hundred feet! I think I'll take a run over when you're doing it. When do you expect to start?"

"In March, all being well, and assuming there aren't any big gales. Yes, I'm very eager about it, Sam, because I think this can be the forerunner to much bigger things."

"I'm positive," Sam said stoutly. "If you use this as a lever, and don't hide your light under a bushel, you can easily give yourself a terrific fillip. What's Jim made of it, by the way?"

They had paused to charge and light their pipes on a brow of the road from which an extensive view of Ramsfield and the Ram Valley spread out before them: the grey town was below, with Scargate, a huddle of houses surrounding vast factories, farther away, seen along the course of river and canal; the village of Outham was more distant, higher up, backed by dun-coloured moors rising to a clear-cut skyline.

"Jim," said Clem, sucking away at his pipe. "Oh, Jim seems of the opinion I've stolen a march on a lot of competitors bigger than ourselves. Aye," he sighed slightly, "aye, he does."

Sam glanced at him. "Anything up, Clem?"

The master-steeplejack frowned. "No," he said, "at least, not about that. But I've got it into my head that Jim and Vincent Uttley are bearing a grudge against each other, and I don't care for it. I've tackled 'em, mind you, and they both flatly deny it."

"Hmm," Sam murmured. "When I've seen them on a job together they've always seemed to agree well enough. Jim hasn't been throwing his weight about, has he? I shouldn't have thought he was that sort, but if he's been tactless with an experienced man like Uttley it would soon cause bother. Uttley, outside his work, is pretty hot-headed I should say."

"It could be that, but I don't know," Clem said. "But I do know one thing—and it's that I'm having them both on the carpet before another week's out, and I'll give 'em hell till I root out what the trouble is."

Sam nodded understandingly, but kept his thoughts to himself; these were that his companion was much too gentle ever to inspire awe in anyone. As a craftsman of skill and repute, Clem Roebuck was respected by his men and, whether on the ground or far above the ground, his quietly-voiced orders were implicitly obeyed. Elsewhere it was different, however.

"Yes, I'll make 'em jump, even if I discover I'm only making a mountain out of a molehill," Clem continued with great earnestness. "In fact I must . . . it could so easily lead to disaster if there's bad blood between chaps who work at big heights."

"By jove, yes!" said Sam, suddenly impressed.

Nevertheless he was very happy to be receiving the confidences of a friend from whom so often, in gloomy spells, he believed he had grown apart. This was much more like old times and he rejoiced in their good-fellowship.

Pinpricks. imaginary or not, often play an overwhelmingly disproportionate part in man's life, and unhappily, in Penny Lane, Sam instantly reached the conclusion that he had been slighted. The reason for this was the manager of the Ramsfield Commercial Bank, who lived opposite the bus stop. Mr. Luther Whitehead Garside's "Good morning, Mr. Pilling," from the other side of a low wall, sounded quite courteous, but the recipient read into it other meanings.

"Thinks something of himself, that money-lending Mussolini," Sam growled. "But there was a time not so long ago when if he'd seen me he'd have bowed his forehead in the dust."

Surprised by this outburst, Clem said: "Nay, he was civil enough. What do you expect him to do—lay down a red carpet?"

"It's all right you talking, Clem," said Sam, pitying himself acutely. "You haven't suffered the sneers that I have. Oh, I dare say it's made me thinner-skinned than I might have been, but I've cause, and don't you forget it. If you'd been in my shoes sometimes, and listened to what I've had to put up with ..."

A little later, as they walked up Moorheaton Drive—with its mansions in miniature parks, belfries on stables, lodges at gates and pillars supporting griffins, lions and eagles— Clem Roebuck began to laugh.

"Come on, Sam lad, cheer up," he said.

Sam refused to cheer up. Every little bit of good had been undone by this encounter—and so it continued with him, for the remainder of the day, and more than that.

On Monday, Nancy made eight journeys in the Riley between Glenfield and Neptune Buildings, to take her father to the office and to fetch him home; progressively he became more ironical about her ability to handle a motor vehicle.

She discussed matters with her mother before supper—her news was nothing fresh to Archie, as after lunch similar complaints had been privately poured into his ear.

"Don't worry, old girl, I've given Frank an S O S," her brother said, grinning. "The Bentley will be ready for the old man at noon to-morrow, and if they leave anything undone they'll sneak it in later. All you've got to do is to gird your loins for one more trip in the morning."

"But fancy Daddy criticizing my driving, or anyone's," Nancy gasped. "Him!"

Her mother was in no better state. During various unpleasant phases of the day—breakfast, twice; lunch, three times; and, spread over the unendingly long hours of the evening, seven times all told—she had irrevocably resolved, so far as her husband was concerned, to withdraw into her former attitude of aloofness. It is true she softened on exactly a dozen occasions.

"Nobody can go on this way," she told herself at bedtime, dipping into a pot of face cream. "I mean he's worse than a bear with a sore head."

Working her finger-tips as directed on the label, in small circles, not exceeding the diameter of a penny, anti-clockwise, she pondered matters further.

"I can't help Dale Watkinson cancelling golf for Thursday afternoon, and why should it have been done deliberately?" she murmured. "And if Jim Oldfield missed him out of a round of drinks at the George it must have been because he hadn't seen him."

Duly forewarned, the foreman mechanic at Thorntons' Garage made sure that, on the dot of twelve the next day, Mr. Pilling's car awaited him.

The owner, on collecting it, was wise enough not to attempt to criticize any detail of the mechanical check-over. Instead he devoted himself to the condition of the leather upholstery, which he asserted was thick with grease.

"I thought a quality spot like this insisted on covers and clean overalls for interior work," he snapped. "The inside of this looks as if a pack of oily monkeys have been playing tag in it."

By ill-luck, for him, Frank Thornton joined the small group. "I don't think it's quite as bad as that, Mr. Pilling," he ventured to remark. "Perhaps there's just the lightest trace of a finger mark on the——"

Sam's arm shot out. "I've been wanting to speak to you. Is it true, as I have been told this morning, that about a fortnight after the Leger you and Alec Murgatroyd climbed on to the counter at the Vaults to make an announcement?"

"Well . . . er . . . we often do . . . er . . . peculiar things," Archie's friend said uneasily.

"And was this the announcement—that none of the company there, all Archie's trusted friends, ladies and gentlemen alike, should fear his home would be sold up . . . because your father and Walter Murgatroyd were determined to stave off the bailiffs? At *any* cost."

Frank Thornton tugged his collar and then coughed. "It was just a joke, sir, and everybody accepted it as——"

"It's not the sort of bloody joke I'm going to feature in," Sam bellowed, his eyes standing out, as Frank graphically described them to Archie later, "like a couple of bloodshot traffic lights."

In Barnsley Road, when Sam was driving to Moorheaton, Archie whizzed past him with an ear-splitting din, a working lad racing home for dinner. Sitting in a chair specially covered to protect it from machine-shop soiled dungarees, he was devouring a savoury stew when his father entered the kitchen.

The strictures upon his sister possibly occurring to him, Archie, between large mouthfuls of food, chanced to remark upon an aspect of driving; or more probably his engineer's soul had writhed when his father changed down on approaching the gates—the gearbox's agonizing screech must have jarred upon many sensitive ears in the neighbourhood.

"You ought to read the Bentley's specifications again, Dad," he said. "She's synchro-mesh on top and third only, and so when you drop from third to second you must remember your left foot's got to do an extra stint . . . if you don't rev. up a little and double-clutch——"

"Are you trying to teach me how to——" Sam roared.

Steaming pan in her hand, Milly advanced. "A bit more of you, and I shall be running away," she said.

Nancy's snort was most unladylike. "You won't be running, Mummy," she declared. "We'll be in the Riley, for as long as the petrol lasts out."

"If you're off this afternoon," said Archie, "will you leave my rugger boots at John Arthur Pilling's? Tell him I want them re-studded for Friday night certain — if my leg goes on as it is I think I might be able to turn out on Saturday."

Nancy nodded, but said: "We may have too much luggage to squeeze 'em in."

Quite astonished, Sam gazed at his family. "What in heaven's name is the matter with you all? Perhaps I have been a trifle impatient just occasionally, but surely you all realize I've a great deal of strain on me . . . surely you can make allowances for that. Of course if I can't hope for sympathy and understanding from my own—well, I'd better spend every minute of the day at the office."

That was a suggestion which, from Harry Sutcliffe downwards, his employees in Neptune Buildings would have regarded with horror, just then.

For nearly two days, chivied hither and thither, Sam Pilling's staff had passed through much tribulation. But when, at twenty minutes turned three in the afternoon, word sped round that Mr. Ernest Illingworth had called on the boss, a sigh of relief could be heard in every department. Mr. Illingworth was a valued customer, and had not been seen there for a considerable time; surely he should be good for a decent breathing spell.

"Well, what can I do for you, Ernest?" Sam asked, when his visitor had sunk into one of the deep club chairs.

It appeared that Mr. Illingworth favoured Go Canny, trained by Easterby at Malton, for the February Handicap Chase at Haydock the next day.

"Owen's riding, I understand, and I think I'll have a flutter to the extent of fifty each way."

Sam made a note. "You're on," he said.

Business completed, his caller became more conversational. "We've been seeing a good deal of that girl of yours," he remarked.

"We're not so pleased either," said Sam.

Ernest Illingworth sat up quickly. "What the devil do you mean?"

"Plain as a pikestaff," Sam replied. "Who'd want an innocent girl going about with a chap who's been through the divorce court?"

Mr. Illingworth's cheeks were rapidly becoming red. "Now hold on," he snapped. "That is, unless you're trying to pick a quarrel with me, which sounds damned likely."

"Of course I'm not," Sam snapped back, so emphatically as to ring true. "All I'm stating are the facts."

It was plain that Ernest Illingworth, for all his shrewdness, did not know what to make of this.

"There's something up with you anyhow," he said eventually. "Why, I don't think I've ever been in here before but you've offered me a drink and a cigar . . . not that I'm cadging for them . . . all I'm doing is—well, stating facts, like you."

Annoyed with himself about a lack of hospitality, Sam hurried across to the Sheraton bookcase.

"To tell you the truth, Ernest, I'm on edge somehow," he said. "But I meant nothing wrong about Philip, nothing at all."

"And I damned well meant nothing wrong about Nancy," Mr. Illingworth expostulated. "She's both a bonnie and a delightful girl."

"And so money isn't everything?" Sam flashed out sarcastically.

Ernest Illingworth barely acknowledged the glass of whisky handed to him.

"By God!" he grunted. "But you *have* got the black dog on your shoulders this afternoon."

"Nay, that's going to extremes——" Sam was saying, only to contradict himself when, without preliminary knock, his secretary's door opened. "What the devil are you coming in for, Margaret?" he demanded.

Margaret Berry, distress in her expression, stood her ground.

"Mr. Dyson's been on the telephone, but he couldn't wait to speak to you, sir," she said. "You're to go to the hospital as soon as ever you can, because Mr. Roebuck has asked for you. He's . . . he's fallen from the Parish Church spire."

Horrified, Sam stared. "Is he badly hurt?"

She gulped. "I believe so, Mr. Pilling . . . terribly."

Mr. Illingworth had risen. "You be off, Sam," he said, "as quickly as you can. I'm grieved about this. Roebuck is a very decent fellow."

Sam, hatless and without overcoat, began to run, through the glass-panelled corridor and into the "Inquiries" Room; on the main corridor outside, down the steps, and along the vestibule on the ground floor; then across Market Square to the parking-place.

Less than two minutes later, ignoring the red lights at the far end of Sheepgate, he swung into Folly Street, then round the corner occupied by his father-in-law's tripe works, and over Ramsfield Bridge. Racing up Barnsley Road he soon was compelled to slow down for the turn into the Hospital gateway.

For sixteen minutes by the clock on the wall Sam then paced a sterilized-looking hall, until he knew by heart every detail of the scrollwork on a bronze plaque, the wording below which declared that this annexe to the Hospital had been made possible by the munificent gift of Lancelot Handel

Crowther, Esq., J.P., in memory of his father, "Alderman Zebediah Crowther, five times Mayor of Ramsfield."

Before the seconds hand jerked thrice more a door on the left opened soundlessly, and the tall figure of the Rev. Alonso Dyson appeared, gaunt face sorrowful.

"Sam," he said gently, "you can go through now."

"It's hopeless, is it?" Sam asked.

Compassionately Mr. Dyson grasped his brother-in-law's arm. "Only a matter of time, Sam," he said. "A few minutes, maybe an hour or so . . . but not long."

Almost blindly Sam went forward, shortly to find himself within the narrow confines of a screened-off bed, staring down with aching heart at the prone figure of his friend, whose head from forehead upwards was swathed in turban-like bandaging.

"Clem," he said, bending nearer the pain-racked eyes, "I'm here . . . it's me . . . Sam."

The injured man's lips moved slightly. "Thank God . . . you've come, Sam," he whispered. "I've something . . . to . . . tell. . . ."

"Yes, and I'll be listening, Clem. Take it easy, lad."

Clem's eyes were closed. He moaned and then, as if to defeat pain and to summon up his sorry forces, he seemed to be gritting his teeth. And soon, very faintly, he began to speak again.

"I haven't done right . . . in not telling you . . . something . . . Sam, lad . . . my best friend . . . it's bothered me, lying to you . . . because you've always been open with me . . . about everything . . . of yours . . . do what you can . . . letter . . . letter for you. . . ." His eyes opened again, a dreadful urgency in them. "*Letter* . . . Sam . . . let——"

A doctor at the opposite side of the bed, hypodermic syringe in readiness, signalled dismissal to the visitor.

But Sam still had something to say himself, and he said it in a voice he desperately hoped would carry through the mist of pain enveloping the dying man. "Clem, there's a letter, I've got that absolutely clear. And I'll do whatever you want as soon as I know what it is, *everything*, and I'll start the very instant I read the letter. So worry no more, either about that or because you haven't told me something or other. Dammit, we're pals, lad, and I'll understand."

Clem Roebuck's eyes opened, affection for a brief interval conquering the agony in them.

"I know . . . you will . . . Sam, old lad," he murmured.

And then the more potent drug, which he had refused before, robbed him of consciousness and released him from the pains of his shattered body.

Vision blurred, incapable of speaking to anyone, Sam returned with halting steps to his car, in which he sat for a few minutes before driving off. From that position he saw his sister-in-law, with Estelle and Lois, walking quickly up the central avenue to the Hospital; and not long after that the breakneck arrival of the Chrysler, from which Jim jumped out, to sprint across the gravel.

Milly and Nancy had gone over to Huddersfield for the afternoon, so there was no point in returning home.

"Well," he muttered, "Laura won't thank me if I hang about, and I'd only be intruding, so I'll go back to town."

The telephone call he fully expected came about an hour later, when he was in his room at the office.

"Yes, put him through, Margaret," he said.

A few moments afterwards he nodded sadly to himself. "Thanks for letting me know, Jim lad," he said. "He's at rest now and . . . and we've both lost someone we'll never replace—you your father and me a friend, and he was grand as both. Yes, he'll always remain green in our memories."

Sam then went home, where Milly hurried to meet him as soon as he entered. Her eyes were reddened with tears.

"Oh, Sam, isn't it dreadful?" she said.

"It is," he replied wearily.

"Sam," she began again, "I'm going over to Laura's. Will you come with me?"

"Of course I will, dear," he said at once.

And so, on one of the most miserable errands of all, they walked slowly across to Stonewood, where Sam rang the bell at the side of a door recently painted cream: Ramsfield's latest craze.

The maid let them in, and soon the mistress of the house came.

"We're not stopping, Laura, because you'll wish to be by yourselves," Milly said shakily. "But we did want to tell you how . . . how terribly sorry we are, and how we're awfully cut up, too."

"And if there's anything I can do," said Sam, "just let me know, that's all. I'll be only too glad . . . any running about you might need, anything at all."

Traces of shock were evident in his Junoesque sister-in-law, but she was bearing up admirably.

"It's very kind of you both," she said with perfect composure. "But I don't think there will be anything, because I've got Father and Jim."

"Anyhow we're near, Laura, so don't forget," said Milly.

Then she and her husband returned home, where Archie was looking extremely upset and tear stains were visible on Nancy's cheeks.

It was a most unhappy evening for the Pillings. To Sam and Milly the gentle Clem Roebuck had always been a kind and devoted friend, and to the children he had been an adored uncle since they were toddlers.

*   *   *

The inquest on Clem Roebuck was held on the day but one following, when a verdict of "accidental death" was returned. It was attended by Sam Pilling, at the request of Mr. Geoffrey Ramsden Lister, junior partner in Ramsden Lister and Wainwright, who explained that the deceased had nominated Sam as his sole executor.

"Mrs. Roebuck wishes me to take the will to her home after the funeral," Mr. Ramsden Lister continued. "And so I suggest you should be present also, Mr. Pilling."

They had paused in Church Street before parting, and he went on to remark that the winding-up of the estate should be quite a simple affair. He proposed a meeting for Friday of next week, on his return from London, where, he confided somewhat consequentially, a series of appointments with counsel regarding a local lawsuit had been arranged.

"To-morrow week will do all right for me," Sam said. "By the way," he fingered his chin, "there's nothing else you want me for now, is there?"

"No, I think not, Mr. Pilling."

"H'mmm," Sam murmured. "I suppose Mr. Roebuck didn't leave any . . . er . . . documents for me—I don't mean anything to do with obtaining probate . . . more like just a personal letter? I rather expected something of that nature."

The lawyer shook his head. "But I'll certainly have our files thoroughly checked."

"Yes, if you will," Sam said.

Perplexed and uneasy, he then set out for Neptune Buildings.

The day of the funeral was raw, and mourners shivered both in the unheated Wesleyan Chapel during the service and at the graveside in the cemetery up Barnsley Road.

Indeed as soon as the widow and near relatives had gone, Clem Roebuck's men, steeplejacks, labourers and clerks, went off in a body to the nearest public-house, where with perfect reverence they drank a toast to their dead boss.

The warmth of Glenfield was very comforting to the Pillings when, sombrely clad, they returned home, but Sam, despite Milly's protests, insisting on leaving for next door immediately.

"Nancy's already put the kettle on," she persisted. "And we all need something to ward off a chill."

"A nip of whisky will be quicker," Sam suggested.

"No." Milly frowned. "They might smell you, and it wouldn't be nice."

"Oh, I'll be all right," Sam assured her. "In any case I don't suppose I shall be very long, so I'll get off straight away."

In any event he was not late in reaching Stonewood, for he met Mr. Ramsden Lister at the front door, and, after being relieved of their overcoats, the pair of them were ushered into the dining-room, where the three Roebuck girls and their brother already were. The gathering was completed by Ezra Sykes and his elder daughter, both of whom viewed Sam with little pleasure but did not comment on his presence.

Mr. Ramsden Lister unstrapped a brief-case, took out the papers in it, and then glanced at the widow. Receiving a nod, he began to read.

Clem Roebuck's dispositions were not complex. Estelle, Lois and Cora were each left five hundred pounds; his shares in the business, of which he and his wife and son were the sole shareholders, were bequeathed to Jim and Laura in the proportions respectively of two and one; everything else became the property of the widow, the more substantial items being: the house, now freed of its mortgage by the provisions of an insurance policy, and the contents of the same; the testator's private balance with his bankers; certain stocks and shares, and the benefits accrued from a number of insurance policies, including one covering the hazards of the deceased's occupation. One fact stood out: Clem Roebuck dead was worth much more than he had ever been when alive.

"When was this will drawn up, Mr. Ramsden Lister?" Laura Roebuck asked. "It's very strange my husband never discussed it with me."

At a gathering of this description Ezra Sykes was in his

element. "Nay, Laura, I don't think you've owt to complain of," he said. "What objection have you to the manner Clem's divided up what bit he had?"

"None at all, Father, except that now Jim will have control of the business by just a few shares, which I consider most extraordinary. And why wasn't I made the executor instead of bringing in an outsider. No wonder nothing was mentioned to me. And when was this will drawn up, Mr. Ramsden Lister?"

"Your husband instructed me in the middle of November," the lawyer replied, "and called in to sign just over a week later."

"*Only* three months ago?" Laura said.

Sam succeeded in catching his sister-in-law's eye. "I didn't seek the job of executor, Laura," he said. "And my first intimation——"

"Executors can't do anything, so let's get on with things," Ezra Sykes snapped. "Now what's my daughter more or less going to get in cash when all outstanding claims have been met, including my granddaughters' bequests?"

"About twelve thousand pounds, Mr. Sykes," Mr. Ramsden Lister replied. "Assuming your son-in-law's personal indebtedness is nominal, as I understand is the case."

"That much!" The old man's bushy eyebrows rose. "Aye, of course, I'd been forgetting all his insurances."

"It doesn't seem so very much," Laura said.

Exasperated, her father dealt with her. "It's more than you've ever had in your natural, so no more of your highfalutin talk. And on top of that there's the business, which has been keeping this big place going—although with the heck of a lot of pinching, it's true. And under James's management there's no reason at all for it not doing just as well."

At this point, Jim Roebuck dropped a bombshell.

"I shan't be managing the business, Grandfather," he said. "I've never been happy in it and I'm getting out. It'll have to be sold."

Enraged about the remarks her father had made in front of Mr. Ramsden Lister and her brother-in-law, Laura turned on her son in a fury.

"Don't be utterly absurd," she said. "As if I should allow the business to be sold."

Jim's thin face was stubborn. "We'll go into that later, Mother," he said quietly.

"There'll be no going into it later, James," his grandfather thundered. "Because I don't intend to listen to any such nonsense. You've a right good business and you're sticking to it. The very idea of bringing up such a daft notion . . . you must be out of your head, or talking for talking's sake."

"Not quite, Grandfather," Jim murmured. "You'll see."

Mr. Ramsden Lister began to buckle up his brief-case, and after suitable civilities bade the company good-bye, Sam leaving with him.

"To-day week then, Mr. Pilling," the lawyer said as he opened the door of his car. "We'll fix the exact time by telephone, shall we?"

Sam nodded. "That'll do for me," he said. "Ring me up."

Then, slowly, he sauntered homewards, oblivious of the cold wind as he pondered.

"There's real trouble in store if Jim's face is anything to go by," he reflected. "And this will of Clem's, made so recently. What's behind that? Something, and something queer, I'll be bound. And if that letter Clem spoke to me about isn't connected with it I shall be surprised. Clem wasn't rambling either—he knew what he was saying all right, and he stood up to nearly half an hour of intense agony for nothing else but to say it to me. Aye, it must have been damned important to him, that letter, but where the hell is it?"

A hundred and one wild surmises passed through his mind before reaching Glenfield, none of which gave him the least satisfaction.

CHAPTER TEN

THE DEATH of Clem Roebuck brought about a slightly better relationship between his widow and sister-in-law, though Laura was still reserved with Milly and there was little doubt she felt Philip Illingworth's courtship of Nancy constituted a form of family betrayal.

Milly was nevertheless glad about the improvement, and in all things, save the one to do with Nancy, met her sister more than half-way. Among these she resumed the custom, discontinued for four months, of slipping across to Stonewood now and then, a gesture never reciprocated.

On the third occasion she visited Laura in this informal

manner, which was on the Sunday evening following the funeral, between tea and supper, she walked into a quarrel between her sister and nephew. It was taking place in the drawing-room where Cora had rather carelessly told her to go, and flurriedly she tried to withdraw.

"There's no need for you to leave, Milly," Laura snapped. "I've wasted all the breath I intend doing."

"Evening, Aunt Milly," Jim said, smiling tautly. "Sit down while I have another shot to convince Mother that I mean exactly what I say."

His mother must have been baffled by a wall of resistance unusual in her experience, for she threatened him with his grandfather.

"Do just as you please, Mother," Jim retorted. "But it's my life and I've to live it, and it won't be anything of a life if I keep on with the business. That's why it must be disposed of, and that's what is going to be done. Any other suggestion —getting in a manager, for example—would be impractical."

Laura's cheeks were a dull red. "Do you realize that even if it were sold well the interest on the capital wouldn't be anything near as much as we've been drawing for years?"

"Yes, I agree about that." Jim nodded.

"Then don't talk so stupidly," his mother stormed.

She next pointed out that before long there would be the heavy expenses of Lois's wedding, which was not being postponed.

"But you're not contemplating a smart wedding so soon after father's death, are you?" Jim said.

"It won't be 'smart' in the wrong sense," his mother said. "But a hole-and-corner affair isn't to be thought of. You must remember your sister is marrying the Law Watkinsons' only son, and I owe something to their position when I make the arrangements.

"And then you appear to forget you have other sisters— Cora is still a young girl who has to be launched properly, and Estelle must be given suitable opportunity for making a second marriage . . . for all of which we must live at a decent rate, do plenty of entertaining and so on. It all costs money, and quite a lot of money."

Jim sighed. "The chap who ruined his sisters' prospects, that's me, because I shan't change my mind. We shall have to make do the best we can on what we have when the business is sold."

"Shall we?" Laura shouted.

On the following Wednesday another of the Pillings was present when the same subject was broached, a subject which kept the Roebuck household day after day in uproar.

Archie, shining with cleanliness, "clothed and in my right mind"as he put it, had just settled down in the drawing-room with his parents when the telephone rang. Nancy, who was coming downstairs, answered the call. The one-sided conversation, quite audible to her family, was not difficult to understand for the major part.

"Yes . . . yes, it was tragic, and we're *frightfully* upset . . . he was . . . oh, awfully nice . . . yes, I'll tell him, he's just barged into the drawing-room ahead of me . . . no, of course I haven't abandoned Ramsfield . . . but, Alec dear, don't you really think that Bradford men have just that little extra polish about them . . . *they* may be savages, but I'm not talking about rugger, idiot. . . . Oh! Alec, why didn't you declare yourself sooner? I never dreamed you felt that way. . . ."

Her mother laughed. "He's teasing her about Philip."

"In another ten minutes I'll stagger out and relieve her before she drops the receiver," said Archie, grinning.

"You don't know your sister, lad," Sam remarked. "She'll have hooked the leg of a chair to sit down cosily."

When Nancy came in smiling, after a chat quite as lengthy as her brother had anticipated, she gave him the captain of Ramsfield Rugger's message, which was a request for Archie to ascertain whether Jim would turn out on Saturday.

"I should think he will," said Sam. "Being in mourning doesn't stop you playing a game. Your Uncle Clem wouldn't wish him to do anyway."

"And we're having enough bother experimenting with the halves without having Jim out of the threequarter line," said Archie. "It's the cup-tie with Headford three weeks on Saturday, and we've damn well got to have a back division who've played together a couple of times before then."

"Headford, eh?" said Sam.

"Aye, and they'll be including about five county caps, two England trial blokes, and a thirteen-stone International flier at centre-three . . . capped the lord knows how often. Team of all the talents, collected from all over the shop."

"Think you can hold 'em?"

These were grave issues, and Archie applied the weightiest consideration to them. "We're reasonably optimistic at Ings Close," he said after deliberating. "The match is on our own midden, after all. One thing we can be sure of, if we pull it off it'll be a cake-walk to the final. Aye," he laughed, "hearts are high about the trophy travelling Ramsfield way. Anyhow, I'll totter off to Jim right off."

At Stonewood, the maid informed him that Mr. Jim was not in but was "about," which he interpreted as the garage. This was confirmed when, doubling back round the house, he perceived a lengthy strip of light beneath a door. Nearer the garage the conviction rapidly grew on him that his cousin was not alone—the indications of a heated argument carried too clearly for that.

"Hope I'm not interrupting anything," he remarked with absolute truth as he entered. "Or would it be that I might help?"

All his Roebuck cousins were there, Jim perched shooting-stick fashion on a wing of their smaller car. Clustered about him were his sisters: Estelle, blue eyes hard, angrily waving a long cigarette holder; Lois unsmiling, dark and determined; and Cora, a younger edition of her elder sister, a sulky-looking platinum blonde.

"You can rid me of these tyrants," Jim said wearily.

"Archie," said Lois, "Jim is still being obstinate about the business. What he doesn't realize is that if it were sold Mother couldn't possibly dip into the capital for what is required—it would have to be invested to make up her income, which wouldn't be very good even then."

"We'll let slide that two-thirds of that capital would be mine," Jim said. "But don't think I should hang on to——"

"Can you ram any sense into the silly fool's head, Archie?" Estelle demanded.

Archie's broad shoulders were shrugged impressively. "I'm not exactly a shining example of the cobbler who stuck to his last," he said. "Forgive the fancy lingo, Jim, but your learned reference to being rid of tyrants buzzed a bell hazily in my noddle."

"But it was different with you, because Uncle Sam couldn't afford to keep you on—oh, everybody knows that, Archie," said Cora. "But *we* have a good business, and Jim's being so crazy, so *inutile*."

"Not 'arf, sweetie-pie," Archie exclaimed.

The Ford creaked as Jim relieved it of his weight. The unshaded light immediately above accentuated the hollows in his cheeks.

"Now you can understand this, you three," he said quietly,

"I'm not having you nagging me any more. I've no desire to be a steeplejack for the remainder of my days and I'm not going to be. And that's final."

"What *do* you want to do?" Estelle asked.

"I haven't thought about it," he admitted.

Lois's voice rose. "And do you mean to say. . . ."

"Of all the unmitigated . . ." Cora started off simultaneously.

The girls made many more withering observations before leaving. And then Archie pulled out a packet of Woodbines.

"Thursday to-morrow, last gaspers to-night for us athletes, Jim," he said, stretching out his arm. "By the way, Alec's telephoned. . . ."

*   *   *

The mystery about Clem Roebuck's letter was solved in one of the partners' rooms of Messrs. Ramsden Lister and Wainwright when, at the conclusion of their business talk, Mr. Ramsden Lister pushed a bulky but light package towards Sam Pilling.

"Apparently this has been here all the time, Mr. Pilling," the lawyer said. "From what Mr. Wainwright tells me it contains a trifling gift which Mr. Roebuck left with him a few days after the will was signed—I wasn't at the office that day."

Sam had been busy with finger and thumb, tearing open the end of a stout Manila envelope. From it he took out a brightly painted Bavarian hand-carved figure, companion to one he had at home. There was a letter also, but he had read no more than a few lines before deciding the remainder must wait until he was alone.

"It's a sort of . . . Tweedledum to my Tweedledee, Mr. Ramsden Lister," he explained. "We bought 'em as souvenirs the first time we were allowed to hobble out of a war hospital in Germany, and Clem wanted me to have his, as a memento, if I outlived him. We've been friends ever since then and he says he preferred to hand it on to me this way, with a few lines, rather than bequeath it more formally."

The lawyer nodded. "I quite understand."

The first shock-wave diminishing, Sam became angry. "How is it I haven't had this sooner?" he demanded. "It's only a triviality, of course, but it might easily have been of importance. Why has it been hanging about here so long?"

Mr. Ramsden Lister skirted round his partner's deficiencies

as deftly as possible. Mr. Wainwright, it seemed, had stuffed the parcel into a drawer and forgotten it.

"No need to continue," Sam grunted. "Nature has made my cousin James a damned fool, and his good fortune is that his father, for one thing, wasn't a fool . . . the other is that as yet he's never been caught out properly. How the devil he ever scraped through his law exams beats me. Cramming, I should imagine. Anyhow, anything he acquired has leaked out since then."

Bidding the lawyer good day, he hurried into Church Street, intent on reaching Neptune Buildings, and the privacy of his office, as speedily as possible. Unluckily, however, he was sighted by Fred Lumb when crossing the road towards the Parish Church railings at a point where they curved into Market Square.

"Hey!" his former manager hailed him.

Although he knew he was being unfair, Sam nowadays acknowledged to himself how he detested meeting Fred, when Fred was in the guise of the owner of Ben Buckley's, as he was that morning, his latest acquisition being a magnificent four-in-hand tie.

"I haven't a moment," Sam called back, lengthening his stride, determined upon avoiding badinage at his own expense in the public eye, to which he was taking so badly latterly. "Not a second."

But he had misjudged both Fred Lumb's powers of acceleration and his motives. They met against the Music Saloon.

"All I'm after saying is this, Sam," Fred said sympathetically, "that I'd like to tell you how sorry I am about Clem Roebuck. I know how close you and him have been."

Quite off guard, Sam nodded, a lump suddenly in his throat.

"Aye, it's a sad job, Fred," he said.

"It is, lad," said Fred. "And that's all, so now I'll be on my way, too."

With that the "rising" bookmaker departed, leaving his employer standing on the pavement. But Sam did not dally either, and very soon afterwards was sitting at his big desk, opening out a quarto sheet of paper.

Clem Roebuck's letter began:

"Dear Sam, it's a thousand to one or more against you ever seeing these lines, but I must write them 'in case,' as

*you'll understand when you've read a bit further. I think
you'll understand, too, why I've had to use the little
wooden figure as an excuse, though this doesn't mean
there's anybody on this earth I'd sooner give it to than you.
You see I thought that if I just left a letter for you somebody might wonder what it was about, and that's the last
thing I want—so I've been trying to think up an excuse
that wouldn't excite a morsel of comment, and this is it.*

*The next thing is that I've left a letter for Jim, one that
anybody could look at. In it I've told him that if ever
anything happened to me during the next few years he
can always rely on you for advice, about business or
anything else, and that I expected you would be having a
talk with him in due course. And, Sam lad, I want you to
have that talk with him, and I want you to show him
this letter.*

*You know, Sam, it seems incredible that I am writing
as I am, because if ever a chap felt hale and hearty it's me.
And in a strange fashion I'm happier now than for a long
time, even if I am mixed up in a tissue of lies, which any
man must who is living a double life. Yes, that's it, Sam.*

*But before I go any further I must convince you beyond
doubt that the woman I'm sinning with is as good and
sweet a one as ever drew breath. She's . . ."*

So Sam read on, words penned by a decent man in duty
bound, words which sought to effect a provision which could
never, without scandal, be set down in a will. In moving
language, without excuses, Clem stated what he had done,
for which he must be responsible even after death—through
the friend whom he could trust to act as was most fitting.

"And if it comes to it I know you won't fail me, Sam,"
Clem Roebuck had continued. *"My one regret is that I
couldn't confide in you. But that would only have involved
you in my lies, and I am ashamed enough as it is about all
the lies I have told you, so ashamed that recently I've
avoided being with you as much as I might. Well, I'm sorry,
lad . . ."*

"Poor Clem," Sam muttered, moisture in his eyes. "I only
wish he could have known I wasn't so straightforward with
him myself. No, he needn't ask my pardon, not he."

Sorely affected, he remained there, his fingers now and then drumming the desk as he considered the next step. Once, still almost unbelievingly, he murmured the salient fact.

"Maggie . . . *Maggie Batten* . . . and with a baby . . . Clem's child . . . born in November, not yet four months old . . . yes, that would be why I thought him a bit odd on Armistice Sunday . . . poor old lad."

A few minutes afterwards, mind made up, he glanced at his watch and, flicking over a switch, spoke to his secretary. In due course Margaret Berry reported that Mr. Jim Roebuck was on the line.

There was a short conversation between uncle and nephew and then Sam went out into Market Square to the parking-place.

Not very long afterwards it so happened that, along Huddersfield Road, in the vicinity of the town side of the long-humped railway cross-over, quite a number of people were gazing at a white-bearded gentleman. Wearing a bowler hat and black overcoat, this individual was tearing along the pavement towards Queen Victoria's statue and Market Approach. There was reason for the onlookers' curiosity, for if ever a man's expression proclaimed wrath it was that of Mr. Ezra Sykes.

"H'mm," Sam Pilling murmured, watching the rapidly disappearing figure from the side of his car. "I wonder what has displeased his lordship? It looks as if he might have been here, but Jim didn't say anything."

As speculation on these lines was futile he approached the offices of Messrs. Matthew Roebuck & Son, Ltd., which were immediately inside the gateway. Before reaching the door, however, he was intercepted by his nephew, who appeared from the rope-storehouse on the other side.

"Hallo, Uncle Sam." Jim Roebuck was very pale and his face twitched ominously. "I think it'll be advisable if we go up the yard for our talk. It's very snug in the works office and we'll be quite alone."

"Anywhere you like, lad," said Sam. "By the way, has your grandfather been here?"

"Yes," Jim snapped. "I'll tell you about him."

The works office was a crudely furnished but nonetheless comfortable room, with a closed stove in the middle of the floor.

"Well, I'm now in the same boat as Archie," Jim started off explosively almost before he had closed the door. "My name's to be struck out of his Bible, and I'm not to expect a farthing

—all because I made it clear I wasn't having him interfering in my affairs."

"What was it about, lad?" Sam inquired. "The business?"

Jim nodded angrily. "And my damned well getting out of it, which I intend to do, however much they all clamour."

"You've really made up your mind?"

Speaking more slowly than hitherto, Jim replied: "Yes, I have, Uncle, though I want little or nothing from it myself. When it's sold Mother can have pretty well everything my shares fetch."

Sam frowned. "I've no doubt you mean that, lad, but if I've any influence you'll retain a fair share of what your father left you. For one thing I'm not a believer in people juggling with the terms of a man's will for quixotic reasons of their own, and for the other I'm afraid it's going to be necessary for you to be in a position to command money by one means or another. You'll have had a letter from your father, left with Ramsden Lister?"

The incisiveness of these remarks, and the hint contained in them, arrested the young man's attention.

"Yes, Mr. Ramsden Lister did give me a letter," he said. "And when I'd read it I was puzzled as to why Father bothered to write it, because it wasn't of any real importance—except that I could trust you if unexpected troubles cropped up, which I knew anyway. But . . . but I'm beginning to suspect now, from your manner, Uncle, that there's something serious at the back of it."

"There is, Jim," said Sam. "And it will be a nasty shock for you."

He unfolded and handed across the closely written sheet of paper he had taken from his pocket, and then sat silently waiting, watching for any play of emotion on the thin face. But all that happened was that the skin on Jim's jaw almost imperceptibly tightened; nor, in subsequent speech, did he reveal how he felt about his father's conduct.

"So there it is, Jim, and you and I have quietly to make the best of it for everybody's sake," Sam said, a little nonplussed. "What we've got to do is to provide discreetly for Maggie and the baby as your father wished."

A new light in his sunken eyes, Jim interrupted him. "Of course," he said, "this would be why Father asked for you first of anybody after he'd fallen."

"Yes, that would be it, lad," Sam agreed gently.

Jim had turned away and was glancing dim-eyed along the

yard. "For all his agony, Uncle," he murmured, "he stuck it out so that he could square matters by the surest means. Only . . . only, I just wish I could have spoken to him."

"Yes, I'm sure, Jim," Sam said.

Of one thing he was convinced just then, that his nephew would be better left alone. "Well, I must go now," he said. "But I think I ought to drop Maggie a line telling her about your father, which she may not know of. I've got her address, as you've seen, and I'll write myself from the office, asking her to reply there. And I think it would be a good idea, too, if we both visited her at Southport as soon as possible next week, and I'll mention that also. Now is that agreeable?"

"Yes, Uncle," said Jim.

"Then I'll be on my way," said Sam.

He was very much under the weather as he drove back to Market Square, dispirited by his own affairs, depressed about being bereft of a friend of many years under circumstances too harrowing to be easily forgotten. And now he must wrestle with the problem so unexpectedly forced on him, in which at all costs he had to hide Clem's lapse and at the same time ensure justice for a young woman and her child.

Inaction had never suited Sam Pilling, and it was a relief to him when the following Wednesday morning came.

2

A pot of cyclamen occupied the centre of the spotless tablecloth in the kitchen of Glenfield, where breakfast had just finished. Sam, who was reading the morning paper, which announced that fifteen hundred million pounds was to be devoted to defence over the next five years, murmured for the benefit of anyone who might be interested: "They must think there's some real danger of war," while Milly, either with herself, or with husband and daughter, explored the important question of whether the moment had arrived to take cuttings from the geraniums.

Nancy answered the back door when there was a knock. "Oh, come in, Jim," she said. "Daddy's ready except for his overcoat."

On this occasion staff-work had been faulty. "Hallo, lad," Sam shouted hastily from the kitchen. "Tell you what, if you like you can roll the garage door from in front of my bus. The key's——'

"Well!" Milly gasped. "That's a nice welcome for him I

must say. Surely he can put his nose inside for a minute or two. You're not late, are you?"

Outside, in the passage, Nancy was smiling at her cousin. "You'd better have a talk with Mummy or there'll be ructions," she whispered.

Jim saved a declining situation. "Good morning, Aunt Milly . . . morning, Uncle Sam."

Unfortunately, within the brief spell Sam was absent in the hall, Milly referred to the business which was taking her husband and nephew away for the day. She had been led to understand this concerned Jim's father's insurances.

"Don't you worry about it at all, Jim," she said. "Your uncle won't allow them to abate a penny. And why should they, when the premiums have been paid so consistently. It's scandalous for them to try anything on."

"Er . . . yes," Jim muttered, doing his best, quite in the dark. "Of course people do . . . er . . . try things on nowadays, Aunt Milly."

The collar of the jacket of his suit standing above his over-coat collar, Sam hastily appeared in the doorway to deliver a stream of scurrilities about the morals of three famous insurance companies whose integrity was unchallengeable. He likened them to sharks, however.

"I've been telling your Aunt Milly about them," he said, fixedly eyeing his nephew. "But we'll master 'em between us, even if it means spending a dozen days closeted in their main district offices."

"It's worth it, Uncle," said Jim.

"I should think so," his Aunt Milly agreed.

In due course, the ground prepared for further absences, Sam and Jim went out, and shortly afterwards the Bentley was sliding down Barnsley Road.

At the traffic lights on the near side of Ramsfield Bridge they turned into Manchester Road, and so past Ings Close and, farther along, the Chemical Works. Then the climb really began, over the eastern slopes of the Pennines into Lancashire, with Southport their objective by the western sea.

The house was small, its exterior undistinguishable from scores more in a lengthy street of working-class dwellings. In the kitchen, firelight danced on the well-polished surface of second-hand furniture, while overhead a line stretched, from which dangled a dozen or more napkins.

Although her visitors had been there for nearly half an hour, Maggie Batten was still embarrassed, wretchedly so, and more than once Sam glanced at his nephew, who so far had not spoken to her.

To Sam she looked very much the same; perhaps if anything a little more plump, but she was as comely as ever, and her brown eyes, now reddened with tears, were as soft and as kind as he remembered them.

"Now then, Maggie," he resumed, "the next thing I'd like to find out is why you settled here; the point being that if there was some special reason it might be helpful when we consider what's best for the future."

She was sitting in a low chair, alongside a cot. Before she spoke she darted another frightened glance at Clem Roebuck's only son.

"Well . . . when baby grew a bit older, Mr. Roebuck . . ." Her words tailed away, but she made another effort. "Somehow I . . . I never seem able to get used to calling him Clem, for all that. . . ." She looked down at her child, as though that explained everything she implied.

"Don't worry about that, Maggie," said Sam. "Call him Clem or Mr. Roebuck just as you please. We'll understand."

She swallowed. "Anyhow it were Mr. Roebuck's idea that eventually I'd move elsewhere, and with his help I was going to try to build up a connection in a boarding-house. You see I didn't want to be dependent on him . . . and he was nice about it . . . knowing, like, I wasn't being clever and silly."

Sam nodded. "Yes, of course, Maggie. It sounds a good notion, too, but you couldn't do anything like that just now, so let's get down to brass tacks. Now Mr. Roebuck paid your rent here and allowed you three pounds a week, didn't he?"

There was quite a scene when he offered her a number of banknotes she considered excessive, though she compromised, with touching dignity, about a smaller amount.

"I'll have to accept this lot, Mr. Pilling, but I shan't be wanting any more money, so thank you kindly," she said. "You see I feel sure that before long I'll be able to obtain some sort of work that'll allow me to keep myself and care for baby."

"I dare say, lass," said Sam, hoping for a word of support from his nephew. "But that isn't the kind of thing we're contemplating for you."

She may have sensed he was appealing to a young man known to her intimately since boyhood, for, quite suddenly, she turned in desperation to Jim.

"I want you to understand, Jim, that nothing wrong happened between me and your father while I lived under your roof, *nothing . . . ever.*"

As his nephew, after vaguely nodding, seemed to slip back into a melancholy daydream, Sam hastily intervened. "I'm sure not, Maggie," he said, "quite sure." Then, to tide over this awkward moment for her, he asked curtly: "How did it start, lass?"

Maggie shook her head. "I don't really know, Mr. Pilling. I can only remember how upset I was when Mrs. Roebuck turned me out . . . just because I'd been having a bit of fun with Jim, as we often did. And Mr. Roebuck was so concerned for me afterwards, and where I should go that night. And later he came to see me . . . and I thanked him . . . and. . . ."

"Yes, lass?" Sam encouraged her.

"Well . . ." she gulped. "He seemed so grateful about a little kindness . . . you see, I don't reckon he'd had much happiness."

With an unexpectedness startling to both of them, Jim spoke, his words tumbling out, a savageness about his mouth and eyes.

"He hadn't, Maggie, hardly any. If any brightness came his way it was only in odd snatches, at his football matches or with Uncle Sam, and at work, yes, at work. But outside that, in his own home, he'd a damned rotten miserable life —looked down on because he didn't make more money, worried to death about what was spent, and out of his element with the people we've entertained in recent years . . . the hell of a bloody life."

His voice sank. "Yes, and Father was the sort who craved affection, and if you gave him that and a few hours of peace and comfort now and then, I'll bet he was thankful—just as I'm thankful he had them, Maggie."

"You're . . . then you're not holding this against me, Jim?" Maggie faltered.

Jim Roebuck shook his head. "No, I'm not, Maggie . . . don't ever think that."

Tears of relief began to trickle down her cheeks, and as Jim seemed utterly spent Sam sent him out to the car, while he stayed behind with the weeping girl, until she was more calm.

"There, Maggie," he said then, "we'll have to be going now. But it won't be long before we're over again. Anyhow, you do realize that Jim hasn't any grudge—that was bothering you, wasn't it?"

She nodded. "I . . . I thought he'd turned against me . . . I suppose it might be natural if he did, but I never expected it somehow . . . you don't when you know anyone as well as I reckoned I knew him. And I do know him real well, Mr. Pilling, with all his nerviness, and his jumpiness, and his straightness, and his niceness—for he *is* a nice lad."

"He is, Maggie," Sam agreed. "And he's taking his father's death very hard. I never really learnt until the other day just how devoted to Clem he was."

"It's the quiet ones who feel most, and Jim worshipped Mr. Roebuck," Maggie said. "If it hadn't been for that I'm sure he would never have gone into the business, but his father wanted him to, and so he did."

"Oh," Sam murmured, "I never heard of that. So Jim hadn't much inclination for being a steeplejack, is that it?"

"Not at one time, not just before he left school," said Maggie. "And it took him a rare long while to settle down afterwards, but of course you can get used to anything, can't you?"

"Yes, maybe," Sam sighed, ruefully reflecting how badly he was reacting to his changed position in Ramsfield. "Anyhow, I must go now, and meantime if there's anything just write me at the office, marking the envelope 'private,' and I'll attend to it."

He stooped to the cot, lightly to poke the baby's cheek.

"She's a grand 'un, Maggie," he said.

Maggie's eyes were proud. "Oh, she's lovely, Mr. Pilling."

"That makes it all the more necessary that we scheme soundly for both of you," said Sam. "And we will."

His kindliness made her cry again, and as he waited until she was better the start of the homeward journey was delayed for another ten minutes or so.

In the middle of the same evening the telephone rang at Glenfield, about an hour after Nancy had gone to Bee Hirst's in Top Moorheaton and Archie had roared off on his Norton to the Murgatroyds' place in Outham.

Milly put down her knitting. "I'll see who it is."

Sam, too preoccupied with Maggie Batten, and other problems, to do more than fitfully read a book he had previously been thoroughly enjoying, turned *The Lacquer Lady* upside down on his lap. He watched Milly as she hurried out, noting shapely ankles and graceful figure enhanced by a beautifully-fitting dress. Far from livening him up, this depressed him further.

"A chap might just as well have a wife who's as ugly as sin," he mused dolefully. "There's nobody appreciates his home more than I do, but I do enjoy going out sometimes, and we used to have any amount of fun together. But now . . ."

Her return, her expression, and her tidings drove away this dismal trend of thought.

"Sam," she said, eyes startled, "I'm hurrying over to Laura, and I would like you to go with me."

"What's the matter?"

"I don't know, Sam. But she sounds almost out of her mind. She was nearly raving."

Jumping to conclusions may be dangerous, but nevertheless Sam could not be blamed for deciding that by some mischance Clem's secret had leaked out.

"Right, Milly," he said. "But put a coat on, it's nippy out."

By the time she came downstairs again he had mapped out the course to adopt when his sister-in-law burst out with her news.

Laura Roebuck, dark hair dishevelled, received them in the drawing-room of Stonewood, by herself.

"What is it?" Milly asked her.

"My father!" her sister gasped. "Had you any idea?"

Milly stared. "Any idea about what?"

Laura began to pace feverishly between the fireplace and the side window.

"That he was courting," she said shrilly.

"Courting!" Milly exclaimed. "And who on earth is he supposed to be courting?"

Her sister's lips curved viciously. "That baby-faced Mrs. Allan Oldfield. She's been trying to hook somebody for years."

"But how do you know? Who told you?"

For once Laura mentioned the name of Lois's future mother-in-law without mouthing it with relish.

"Mrs. Law Watkinson," she said. "She telephoned about a small detail to do with the wedding, and it was really an afterthought of hers."

"But, Laura," Milly protested, "you can't accept that as gospel."

"And Father, at his age," Laura said tragically. "I call it disgusting, I do really."

Losing patience, Milly said: "Oh, don't carry on so much, Laura. There may not be an atom of truth in it—surely by now you know what Ramsfield is."

"Where there's smoke there's fire," Laura declared. "I couldn't rest to-night until I'd satisfied myself about it, and that's why you must go down with me to Father's."

"But we can't ask him such a question flat out," Milly objected.

"We've no need," her sister replied, "because I've the best of reasons for calling. You see, Jim's dropped his silly ideas about the business, and he's going to keep on with it."

"Oh, is he?" Milly said.

Laura's expression hardened. "I should think so, too. He's caused enough anxiety for everybody as it is."

It had so happened that, as Sam walked with his wife from Glenfield to Stonewood, he noticed a lighted window on the east side of the latter, below the gable end. This belonged to a small box-room which Clem Roebuck had used as an office, and where he stored personal papers.

"Is Jim at home by any chance, Laura?" he inquired. "I'd like a word with him if he is, about one or two minor matters."

"He's upstairs, sorting through his father's things. You can go up if you want," Laura said ungraciously.

"Yes, I might as well," Sam murmured. "Er . . . thanks, Laura."

Puzzling about this latest development, he left the room and began to mount the stairs, sighting his nephew through an open doorway when a few steps from the top.

A clothes-basket at Jim Roebuck's feet was piled high with torn-up letters, old note-books, and valueless oddments. On the table near him was a small heap of papers and a few articles which either he thought wise to retain or desired to do so. As he was thrusting his hand into the dark recesses of a deep pigeon-hole, he heard footsteps.

"Hallo, Uncle Sam," he said, glancing over his shoulder. "I'll soon shift some of this rubbish out of your way, so come in and sit down."

"This'll do, lad," Sam said, perching himself on a rickety chair. "Nay, I've climbed up here because of something surprising your mother's just told me and your Aunt Milly. You're continuing being a steeplejack, I understand. Why the sudden change, lad?"

Jim laughed. "Oh, I've been making an infernal fuss about nothing, that's all."

"M'mmm," Sam rumbled. "And has this late decision anything to do with finding the wherewithal for the support of Maggie and her child?"

"Not a sausage, Uncle," Jim replied brightly. "No, the thing is," he went on with great frankness, "why chuck away a very good business just for a crackpot whim? After all, the substance is preferable to the shadow, isn't it? And, although the matter has hardly entered into my calculations at all, it will make everything easier so far as Maggie is concerned. I'll be able to allow her whatever's necessary, and keep everything to myself."

"M'mmm," Sam mumbled again. "You know, lad, this job of Maggie's could have been arranged quite satisfactorily in other ways."

Jim was sweet reasonableness itself about that. "Yes, I dare say, Uncle, but why worry about it any more?" he said. "The point is that I'm staying with the business, and that settles everything all round."

Far from satisfied, Sam said: "And how are you off for work at the once despised business? Plenty in hand?"

Jim had flushed. "Tons, Uncle," he said. "And don't forget that contract Father was so pleased about, for the Sulpho-Aluminate Company. We're scheduled to begin on that in about a fortnight's time."

"Oh, yes," said Sam.

As if by tacit consent no further references were made to business matters and, before parting, they were laughing uproariously about Mr. Sykes's supposed courtship and his mother's consequent alarm.

Nevertheless Sam's expression was sober as he went downstairs, and for reasons he could not fathom he felt troubled, though subsequently he attributed this to the effect of Jim's strained face.

For the moment, however, he had a more trivial question to consider. Lois had returned home in the Ford, but at her mother's wish had brought it round again to the front door.

Milly came out of the drawing-room as he reached the hall. "Sam," she whispered, shaking her head in despair,

292

"Laura's just putting her things on, and she is still insisting upon me going down to Father's with her. Would you mind?"

"How much difference would it make if I did?"

Milly drew herself up. "I think that's very rude."

"What is?" Sam asked. "I was only asking a simple question."

"It was your tone," Milly said haughtily. "I didn't care for it."

"I'm deeply sorry about that," Sam said with immense concern. "And what sort of a tone do you——"

The appearance of Lois and her mother cut short their differences, and within a matter of seconds the three ladies had departed for Mr. Ezra Sykes's house in Barnsley Road. The distance was not great, and it was not long before they were there.

A handful of fire, dark hangings, sober-hued carpet, and brown-patterned wallpaper, all inadequately lighted by a 40-watt bulb, made the living-room more gloomy than it need have been.

"And what are you lot wanting?" Mr. Sykes demanded as his housekeeper closed the door. "At this hour."

"We've a very good reason, Father," Laura said gravely. "*And* a duty . . . to let you know something as quickly as possible. You see, Jim has at last recognized the force of your arguments, and in deference to your wishes he has abandoned all his nonsensical ideas about leaving the business."

"So he's deferring to me now, is he?" Mr. Sykes commented. "He's realized what he's going to lose because of the way he spoke to me, has he? Only twice before in my life has anybody ever dared to say owt to me like that, and I've cast both of 'em out of my knowledge. However oft they come creeping back to my feet it'll noan make any difference, and . . ." he turned sharply to point a finger at his younger daughter. "you can tell your Archibald and your Nancy that."

Colour high, Milly retorted: "There's no necessity, because neither of them would dream of trying to crawl into your favour. They're not that kind."

Ezra Sykes eyed her. "If you continue to behave as you are doing I shall be compelled to do something about you," he said. "Aye," he shook his head several times, "aye, I shall . . . yes, I *shall* that."

Anxious about Jim's prospects, Laura began to talk about him. The degree of contriteness she attributed to her son would have considerably astonished him could he have heard.

In doing this she very nearly defeated her own object, for her father dwelt at such lengths upon the path of redemption Jim must follow that, for him, it was quite late when he had finished. Indeed Mr. Sykes looked closely at his watch and delivered himself of three words whose implication was well enough understood by his daughters.

As soon as her father mentioned "my hot milk" Laura Roebuck made a desperate attempt to prevent being forestalled. With scant artistry she referred to Ramsfield's proclivity to gossip.

"And guess what the latest is, Father?" she said.

"What are you blathering about?" Mr. Sykes demanded. "And when have I been one to guess about silly tales? Anyroad, what is it?"

Laura's laugh was equally inartistic. "Oh, it's going round that you're courting someone."

"Well, it'll be a lady, I suppose," Mr. Sykes said testily. "Who is she?"

"Mrs. Allan Oldfield."

Bedtime though it was, Ezra Sykes deemed it worth while to give her a stern lecture.

"Rumour can do much grievous harm and them as passes it on are as sinful as them who starts it," he intoned. "You'll do well to remember that, Laura, and if you're a true servant of the Almighty as I've striven to bring you up to be you'll remember also it's our duty to be charitable. Not that I am casting any aspersions on the person you've named, for in my opinion she's a greatly wronged woman to whom the sympathy of all Christians should be extended."

Laura swallowed. "I can't say I know much about her, Father."

Frostily Mr. Sykes stared at her. "You know well enough she belongs to a very wealthy family, don't you? And it'll noan have escaped a picker-up of gossip like you that her stepson won't even provide the poor thing with decent clothing for her back. Now I'm wondering if by some miracle it may have occurred to you that James Oldfield has something on his conscience, for my words, he has."

"I only thought I'd just mention it," Laura said nervously. "As the tale was going about."

"What you ought to have done was to deny it," Ezra Sykes said.

"Oh, I didn't even discuss it with anyone, Father," Laura asserted righteously.

That availed her little. "You should have known better than to ask such a question, Laura," he snapped. "If I were courting there'd be nothing hole and corner about it."

"Oh, of course——"

"It's over four minutes past my hot milk," Mr. Sykes said with asperity. "Now you ring that bell for me, Lois."

"Good-night, Father," said Laura.

"Good-night, Grandfather." Lois smiled at him.

Of all his grandchildren Lois had always been Mr. Sykes's favourite. "Good-night, lass," he said. "God be with you."

"And with you, Grandfather dear."

The mission then retired, two in quite good order—the third, the shattered member, began to recover in Penny Lane.

"Well, there's no truth in that anyhow," she said.

"I never thought there was, Mother," Lois said from the driver's seat. "Did you, Aunt Milly?"

"I didn't care," said Milly, still seething. "But let your grandfather say anything nasty again about Archie and Nancy in my presence . . ."

"And Jim's as big a fool," Laura said angrily. "Just recklessly throwing his chances away."

For the remainder of the journey she brooded about her son. The outcome was a row within a few minutes of reaching home.

3

For at least seven years it had been Sam Pilling's pleasure, in the early days of March, to take a party to the pantomime at Leeds, and usually he booked seats in January. Despite a presumed financial tightness he had done the same thing about a fortnight before the tragic accident on the spire of the Parish Church, and though none of the Roebucks would occupy the reservations made for them, he saw no reason why the others should be denied an enjoyable evening's entertainment.

It proved far from enjoyable. To begin with, Clem Roebuck's absence was a sad reminder to each of the Pillings. But what started the excursion off badly was a heading in the *Ramsfield Reporter* which caught Sam's eye shortly after Archie had gone to bring the Bentley to the front door. After reading a short account of the final day of the Test Match at Melbourne, won by Australia, he glimpsed a few arresting words:

THE COMING FLAT-RACING SEASON
An Interview With
FRED LUMB (OF BEN BUCKLEY'S)

In all, the appreciation ran to two half-columns, contained in a neat panel.

"Look at this, Milly," Sam stormed as he leapt out of a chair. "The *Reporter's* turned me down every single time I've tried to have something written up on those lines, by one of their own sports reporters, mark you, but apparently they'll be more lenient with Fred—with Lumb. It's bias and nothing else, and I'm damned well asking the editor for an explanation right off."

"It isn't fair," Milly agreed warmly. "But don't you think it might be best to treat it with silent contempt? I mean . . . you haven't been on good terms with the *Reporter* for ages, and you know why."

Indirectly she was alluding to an advertisement he had once sent out in thousands, a costly and very successful project made up in the form of a remarkably faithful copy of the paper, including a heading in Gothic script: the *Ramsfield Snorter*. Now newspapers, from *The Times* downwards, are not infallible, as is shown by extracts from them naughtily printed by *Punch*. And so, far more to arouse mirth than to denigrate the *Ramsfield Reporter*, Sam had drawn extensively upon his ingenuity when preparing the material surrounding racing affairs: small ads, purporting to be *bona fide*, ran into one another with ludicrous consequences, grammar was shaky, and there was a fantastic leader packed with *clichés*, composed of them indeed. Since then, probably wrongly, Pilling who Always Pays had assumed that the proprietors and editor of the *Ramsfield Reporter* regarded him with disfavour.

His conversation on the telephone was not satisfactory. "Well, all I can say is that you must be a damned funny sort of editor," he shouted. "I thought editors decided what went into their papers, but we live and learn, don't we?"

Milly, Nancy, Archie and Philip Illingworth, who had just arrived, watched him leaf through the pages of the telephone directory, in search of the private number of a gentleman named Quaid Mackintosh.

"Isn't fit to hold his job, yon fellow," Sam snarled, referring to the editor. "All I can assume is that this chap he's mentioned, Mackintosh, must run the show."

His talk with Mr. Mackintosh, the *Reporter's* advertising manager, began on a high note, but ended with a most deflated: "Oh!" Had it started a minute later much embarrassment might have been saved, for Archie, glancing at the offending matter, came across a word in very small type at the foot. It was: "Advt."

Sam, fiery red, slammed down the receiver. "I've made a bloomer," he confessed, but added, temper getting the better of him: "They ought damn well to make it plainer that it's an advertisement. But they'll stoop to anything for revenue, I reckon. Nothing's too low for 'em. And now let's be off—good God, look at the time! Why didn't you tell me?"

Three miles beyond Spedding, on a level stretch, the journey to the theatre was ruined for Milly when, to the accompaniment of a high-pitched whine, Philip Illingworth flashed past in his streamlined Alfa Romeo.

Joyously Archie rammed down the accelerator of the Bentley, which was cruising amiably around fifty-five, fully prepared to chase the fast-disappearing tail-lamp ahead.

"No, don't, Archie," his mother screamed. "And wait until I see Philip—won't I give him it for such fool-hardiness."

Archie chuckled. "He's a heller, all right. Doesn't look it, but he is."

"He can be as reckless as he wishes by himself," Milly said crossly. "But I shall speak to him, make no mistake."

Immediately on arrival at the theatre, she was as good as her word. Philip received a stinging rebuke in which Nancy shared, as she was rash enough to point out his superb qualities as a driver.

"I don't care about that and it's nothing for you to smile about, Nancy," Milly declared, really worked up. "If Philip doesn't promise me. . . ."

Scipio Dyson had stayed on in Leeds after leaving the Medical School and was waiting for the Ramsfield party at the theatre. When the argument ended in the only way Milly intended it to end, a move was made towards the stalls, where in due course they all settled down. On Nancy's insistance, Kate sat next to her—she always vowed that, even if a show were poor, a close-up of her cousin's expressive face during the performance more than compensated for the price of the ticket.

Unhappily Kate's display fell far below expectation, and frequently her Uncle Sam, missing her laughter, which usually led the remainder of the audience by a split second, glanced at her.

Much later that night, when the two Dysons had been dropped in Highthwaite Road and the Pillings were at home, Sam spoke about his niece.

"Yes, she was quiet," Milly agreed. "And I thought she was very pale, too. But I'll be on to it, and before long."

"I should." Sam nodded. "Alonso won't notice if she's poorly. Either of his own could be gasping for the final absolution before he spotted anything amiss. Aye . . ." he yawned, eyeing Philip Illingworth, "I think it's about time we went to bed now."

"Daddy," said Nancy, just a shade wheedlingly, "could Philip and I talk to you . . . just for a moment?"

"I don't know about Philip," her father remarked, "but if anybody has ever succeeded in stopping you talking he's a better man than me."

Nancy laughed appreciatively about what she hoped was fatherly humour, though she had qualms as to that. As a result she was not altogether skilful in submitting a request, which was that she be permitted to meet Philip more often.

"We wondered, sir," said Philip, stepping into the breach, "if you would allow three or four times a week."

"Twice," said Sam. "And that's the limit. It's plenty, too."

"Oh, Daddy, but it isn't," Nancy asserted. "No, really, darling, be more gen——"

Philip Illingworth was eyeing her unwaveringly, the lenses of his spectacles inducing a magnetic effect.

"I think we must accept your father's decision," he said, adding: "gratefully" when she seemed rebellious. In a decidedly lower tone, while Sam glanced vaguely about the drawing-room as if searching for something, he continued: "We Illingworths, my sweet, have an accurate ear for that point in negotiations when a little too much pressure will lose everything previously gained."

"Oh," said Nancy. "Oh, I *see*. Oh, you *are* clever, dear."

"I have my points," Philip conceded. "Even if I am occasionally referred to as 'giglamps' or likened to a pair of P.100 headlamps."

Archie, who had missed nothing, chuckled, but then, becoming aware of his parent's perambulations, achieved a tactical move of some merit. He dropped with deceptive leisureliness into a chair, where his large person effectively concealed the whole of the *Ramsfield Reporter*. He had a sound idea of what would happen if his father picked up the paper again.

Fred Lumb's article on the coming flat-racing season was destined to have repercussions far outside Glenfield. From every part of the district covered by the *Ramsfield Reporter*, bitter letters of protest poured upon the editor. A more immediate consequence was the meeting, two days later, of the author of the article and one of the stalwarts of the non-conformist conscience.

Ben Buckley's open invitation for those whom it might please to open an account for the Spring Double had more than irked Mr. Ezra Sykes, who considered his encounter with the perpetrator as an act of divine providence. This was about a quarter to twelve on Saturday morning, when Teazle Street was especially busy, for a large proportion of shoppers, with Ramsfield Rugger's cup-tie engagement with Headford in mind, wished to reach home for lunch a little earlier than usual.

Fred Lumb, by now a personality in the town, delighted to be saluted by policemen and nodded to by all with sporting instincts, was passing Iredale Mallinson's series of windows when peremptorily addressed.

"You're Lumb, Fred Lumb," Ezra Sykes opened. "I'm wanting a word with you."

"And you're Sykes, Ezra Sykes," Fred Lumb retorted. "And if that word has anything to do with starting doing business with me I'd better acquaint you right away that I shall require satisfactory references."

"Me . . . bet!" gasped Mr. Sykes.

"Not until I'm sure of your financial stability," Fred Lumb remarked, winking at an onlooker.

Quite nonplussed, Ezra Sykes passed what was possibly the briefest stricture in his life.

"Parasite!" he snapped.

"Hypo*crite*!" Fred Lumb observed blandly.

A growing crowd soon was of the opinion that a sketchy midday meal was preferable to missing any of this; nor were they disappointed by the dispute, which reached its climax and conclusion on a note poles apart from that on which it had begun.

"Ah, well, there's all sorts of swindling," Fred Lumb remarked comfortably. "For instance, I've rather got the idea that there was once a contractor's bill, for repair work to that Methodist Chapel of yours in Market Square, which turned out a sight bigger than anticipated."

"I wasn't the contractor," Ezra Sykes shouted.

"You don't say," said Fred Lumb, with deep admiration.

Thereupon, grey hat held aloft, he made a superb withdrawal, leaving behind a pillar of Bethel whose anguished cries were lost in the laughter of the throng.

That crowd then disappeared as if by magic, hastening to bus stops or hurrying to cars. For days there had been talk of the match at Ings Close, and, in the indefinable manner of such things, word of mouth had gone round that Ramsfield Rugger believed they might just pull it off against their redoubtable opponents. A record gate, for Ings Close, was expected.

It was Sam Pilling's firm conviction that Ramsfield Rugger's prospects depended entirely on the defensive ability of their backs and the powers of the forwards to make the game a battle between the packs. This appraisal he developed at Glenfield during lunch, at which Archie confined himself to a bowl of soup and a small dish of stewed fruit.

"Anyway, lad," he said as Archie got up, "we shall be there in force to cheer you on."

"And wear that elastic band on your knee," said Milly. "And no fighting, remember."

"If anyone annoys you, turn the other cheek, dear," said Nancy. "I'm authoritatively informed that it's perfectly devastating on the rugger field."

"I'll pass the tidings along." Archie grinned.

Sam saw that his two ladies started to prepare themselves in ample time, and to the dot, in their second-best fur coats, they came downstairs; nor was there any delay in Highthwaite Road, where Kate dashed out from home as soon as she glimpsed the car.

Lower down Barnsley Road, it soon became apparent that an outstanding event was afoot; pedestrians from town-wards were streaming over Ramsfield Bridge, past the traffic lights and into Manchester Road, additional buses had certainly been put on; and cars in regular procession were converging on Ings Close, situated behind the cemetery and the waterworks' distributing dam.

Sam swung away from the main road at the tall-towered Regal Cinema, and from there, as far as the field used for parking, followed the car of the President of the Ramsfield R.U. Football Club, Simjoss Crowther, who greeted him when they both got out. But just then everyone was single-purposed, to reach the ground as quickly as possible.

The little stand was nearly full, but the Pillings and Kate squeezed up a couple of tiers, where they found themselves near some of the directors of Ramsfield Hornets. There had always been the friendliest feeling between the two local rugby-football playing sides, and as the Hornets were away that afternoon many of their supporters had come along to encourage the amateur club, and right royally did they do it, even to the introduction of noisy rattles seldom heard at Ings Close.

At the head of the white-painted flagstaff, newly washed as were the corner flags, Ramsfield Rugger's own flag flew proudly in the light breeze, and the playing area, a rectangular patch of green hemmed in by deep ranks of spectators, looked in first-rate condition—ideal for Headford, as someone dourly remarked.

Be that as it might, the large local assembly was cheerful enough, and gave of their vocal best when the teams came out, the stars from Headford receiving a fine ovation, tribute to visitors and to their quality, though this was as nothing compared with the Ram Valley roar which went up when Alec Murgatroyd and his men trotted out in their purple and gold striped jerseys. Both sides indulged in a little loosening-up, running and punting, and then the captains tossed and the new ball appeared.

The crowd had barely settled down when the home spectators were disheartened by a sensationally early setback, after being elated by a mighty rush which took their forwards well into the enemy's twenty-five. Headford's crack backs, perhaps contemptuous of their opposite numbers, began a passing movement within a dozen yards of their own posts. The ball whipped along the three-quarter line to the wing, who cut inside. Finally, when the bulk of the Ramsfield team were still streaming up from far behind, the touch-down was made in an easy position, by the same deceptively jinking half-back whose opportunism had initiated this brilliant piece of work. The goal kick was successful.

This reverse fired the home side to heroics, but nearly twenty minutes elapsed before they were able to pierce Headford's defence. This followed a scrum-down close to the line, when, encouraged by a berserk roar, the home pack shoved mightily to take the ball over for a try. Unhappily the attempt to convert failed.

"Anyhow, it's five-three now," Nancy exclaimed. "And if only Alec would drop one of the goals he often talks about——"

Ramsfield's opponents were retaliating swiftly and her father, swaying with the throng to watch a raid by Headford's backs, cried a word of warning.

"It looks as if it might take more than one dropped goal. If this isn't real dangerous for us—by God, but they'll score."

As so it was. And, a minute later, an English Trials goal-kicker carefully saw to the placing of the ball, retreated a few paces, wiped his boot on his stocking and then ran forward, to send the ball sweetly sailing between the posts.

Kate's expression was tragic. "Ten-three," she groaned.

From nearby, Mr. Simeon Calverley smiled at her. "Cheer up, lass," he said before speaking to her uncle. "Of course, Sam, we know that you can only play as well as the other side allows you. But . . ." he shook his head, "our lads are acting as though they're too conscious of what they've got on their plates. That's what I think anyway."

Sam nodded, for it did seem as if, in particular, the home team's backs were overawed by the metal opposing them; they fumbled lamentably when favourably placed, and passes were all too often wild, seldom coming nicely to hand. Of them, Jim Roebuck was especially out of form, although as worthy compensation he was tackling beautifully, and again and again, notwithstanding a disadvantage in weight of more than two stone, he cleanly brought down Headford's International centre, once slightly injuring himself in the process.

"Oh, we haven't lost yet, Mr. Calverley," Milly declared. "You just wait."

Better things certainly were in store, for Ramsfield quickly scored twice, the result of play notable more for bustle, vigour and tearaway following-up than for science. Unluckily they did not receive the maximum award for these efforts: one of the consequent shots at goal bounced back from the crossbar, while the next was yards short.

Kate tried to make the best of it. "Can't be helped," she said. "What's a point down, which is all we are now?"

Stimulated by recent successes, every member of Ramsfield Rugger's XV was putting up a terrific performance, and the last seven or eight minutes of the first half, when Headford, defending desperately, were penned in their own twenty-five, were as palpitating as anything ever seen at Ings Close; and when, in its dying seconds, one of Ramsfield's forwards, a powerful, sandy-haired young man, went over in the corner, a couple of opponents on his shoulders and nothing but the blue of Headford on either side, the crowd rose to him, though as yet uncertain whether he had been able to touch down.

Milly Pilling was jumping up, to see better. "It's Archie," she gasped, eyes blazing with excitement. "Is it a try, Sam?"

Sam, no less thrilled, stared into the distance, diagonally across the field, towards the referee, down on one knee viewing at close quarters a heap of bodies.

"I don't know," he said, as limbs were disentangled. "But it's a damned near——"

"Yes, he has, Daddy," Nancy yelped, fractionally in front of a great roar. "That makes us——"

"Two points up," Kate shouted. "And if for once we can convert——"

The home side's goal-kicker had had an unhappy afternoon, and so Alec Murgatroyd summoned up Frank Thornton, who all too often missed sitters but not infrequently steered over lengthy, narrow-angled shots. On this occasion, however, he sliced dreadfully.

"Still, we're leading," Milly said as the whistle went. "It's twelve points to ten now, and a bird in the hand is worth two in the bush."

Lemons were being taken on the field, where the cherubic-faced captain of Ramsfield Rugger made such comments as he considered essential to various of his backs, one of whom, crimson to the ears, remarked subsequently that his sole desire there and then had been "to scamper home for a good cry with Mother."

Meantime Sam had nodded distantly to Mr. Boothroyd Gee, and was now chatting with another gentleman to whom he was more favourably disposed.

"By God, lad, but we might do it yet," Simeon Calverley gloated. "And if we do . . . phew! . . . but that'll be a feather in our caps. They carry some guns, you know, this Headford lot."

Sam clapped his gloved hands. "We're doing very nicely, touch wood. Aye, I've visions of the cup coming Ramsfield way with any luck, and if it does—they're starting again, Simeon . . . we'll discuss ancient history on another occasion."

If the first half had been electrifying the second was uncompromising, neither side making any impression on the other, no quarter given or asked for. Fifteen . . . twenty . . .

and then twenty-five minutes elapsed, and still no further score, Ramsfield Rugger ahead by that slight but precious margin of two points.

Tension increased and the home throng grew quieter, willing their men to succeed, praying that the wearers of purple and gold would hold the fort.

Jim Roebuck lost the match for Ramsfield Rugger. That, and very much worse, was said in the short spell between the referee's glancing at his watch for the second time and the final whistle. Within that brief space Headford's famous left centre-threequarter, a flying mass of bone and sinew, changed direction towards Jim—who palpably, unquestionably, hesitated. It was more than enough rope to give a great player, and the Ramsfield crowd was stunned into silence, which lasted until the players had called three cheers and were walking off the field, the visitors victors by the slender margin of thirteen points to twelve.

"Well," said Boothroyd Gee, whose manner was as if his utterances could not be contested, "I've never in my life seen anything a tenth as disgraceful on a football field."

"Let it drop," said Mr. Calverley.

For some time Milly had been worrying about her husband's temper, which, she thought, was more and more uncertain. But before she could draw him away he flared into speech.

"Whatever you've seen of football, Gee," Sam said, his voice rasping, "it's been from outside the touch-line. In fact I've never heard of you playing any game, so keep your opinions to yourself."

"Oh, Daddy, I know quite positively he plays one game anyhow, at the Knowlbank Club, a sort of variation of tennis," Nancy protested warmly. "I've often heard some of the members describe what a demon he is at pat-ball . . . me to you, and now you to me, sort of thing."

Since his divorce, Boothroyd Gee's glance had strayed towards a number of young ladies, among them Nancy Pilling, who had sublimely ignored his attentions, which must have been galling; irrespective of that, most men writhe under the cool, off-hand manner of a pretty girl who has already shown she has not the slightest use for them.

Boothroyd Gee's mouth was ugly. "I'm beginning to see daylight now," he said. "Blood's thicker than water, isn't it? And of course young Roebuck is related to you lot, isn't he?"

"Thank heavens you're not," said Milly.

"Perhaps so, perhaps so," said Mr. Gee. "Then in that case I'm not connected with a chap who funked a tackle, which is what——"

"Shut up," Kate Dyson shouted.

She seemed all eyes, large and agonized eyes in a deathly white face.

"Kate dear, don't," Milly said as Nancy took her cousin's arm. "It really isn't worth it."

"No, I don't know why we're wasting our time with him," said Sam. "And why the devil he's a director of the Hornets is beyond me, and always was. Dammit, Gee, can't you recognize a touch of concussion? Didn't you notice that hell of a crack he got on the head a few minutes before?"

Boothroyd Gee laughed ironically, and there might have been an unpleasant scene. "You're performing nearly as well as you do in business, Pilling," he said. "But you're not kidding me—young Roebuck showed himself yellow, and your fairy tales won't change either my view or that of a few thousand others."

Fortunately Milly and Nancy, Kate between them, had moved away, and Simeon Calverley was quick to nip in the bud any fisticuffs.

As he and Sam were walking slowly to the parking-place, Mr. Calverley again referred to the incident which everyone in the crush about them was discussing avidly.

"Do you really think Clem Roebuck's lad was dazed?" he inquired.

"I don't think," Sam said stoutly. "I'm as sure as you and me are here. Hang it I saw, and I *heard*, the bump he got beforehand . . . bang under our noses it was, just in front of where we were. Surely you spotted it yourself, Simeon?"

"Aye," Mr. Calverley murmured. "Well, all I hope is that plenty of other people did, because that young fellow is in danger of being smeared in the kind of way that'll stick—he'd never be rid of it, not in Ramsfield. If it isn't the main topic of the town to-night, among rugger addicts of all ages and both sexes, I shall be surprised, Sam. I'm very sorry indeed about the affair."

Mr. Calverley's judgment was sound.

In the County Club, where Sam called during the evening, tongues were wagging about Jim Roebuck's lapse, and it was the same in the bar of the George Hotel and at the Vaults. Here and there voices were raised in his defence, but even these were silenced when someone or other, somewhere or other, recalled how he had once lost his wicket in an important cricket match by running away from fast bowling. This confirmatory account sped round like wildfire, relentlessly stripping a fine athlete of all he held dear.

At the Dance Club, held in Wood's Café, Nancy Pilling was so upset and infuriated by what she had heard that, before ten o'clock, she asked her escort to take her home.

"Would you mind, Philip darling?" she said. "I'll make us something nice to eat there."

Philip Illingworth shook his head. "Not at all, sweetness," he said. "I'm more than bored already with this infernal Headford match . . . with apologies, dearest, to an ardent Ramsfield Rugger fan."

"Granted." Nancy inclined her head majestically. "Look, darling," she squeezed his hand, "I'll dash off for my doings . . . back in a flash, meteoric."

This withdrawal was arranged on the top floor, the dance floor. A few minutes afterwards, on their way down, the pair had a trying encounter in the supper room below. Already Estelle Illingworth, just arrived, had caused two minor sensations: by appearing at all, so soon after her father's death; and because of the company she was keeping—well-to-do but vulgar Tony Flassati was not the type with whom Moorheaton girls associated.

Mrs. Estelle Illingworth, smart in black, which suited her, and heavily made-up, was responsible for a third stirring of interest when, two score pairs of eyes on her, she advanced towards her former husband.

"Hel-lo, Philip darling," she greeted him, completely ignoring her cousin, his companion, "would it ravish you too, too utterly if your ex-wifie chin-chinned with you?"

This meeting was to have its outcome, for shortly after noon on the next day, on returning from chapel, Laura Roebuck rang up her sister to inform her that neither she, Lois nor Cora would present herself at Glenfield for Sunday afternoon tea.

Long before Milly answered this call, Sam had gone outdoors where, attracted by the sound of dispute, he had wandered to the garage.

Five people were there: Nancy, Archie, Alec Murgatroyd and Frank Thornton, all flushed, with Philip Illingworth the exception.

"Admittedly he took a hammering beforehand," Frank was declaring. "But you have to grin and bear it . . . he didn't, and that's why we lost. And . . ." he ended angrily, "by a single blasted point."

"He'll never again turn out for a team I skipper," Alec growled. "So you two Pilling orators might as well pipe down."

Archie rose from the collier-like position in which he had been squatting at the rear end of the Bentley, greasing a hub.

"Now, listen," he began. "I've larked about with Jim since we were youngsters——"

"So have I," Nancy burst out. "And if he'd been one of the white-feathered brigade . . ."

Shaking his head slowly, Sam turned away. Tragically difficult days awaited Jim Roebuck, there could be no mistake about that.

There had been heated exchanges elsewhere, in the house, and as soon as Sam went inside he recognized the symptoms on his wife's face.

"Laura flares up again every time she hears of Nancy being with Philip, and Estelle saw them together last night," Milly told him, more annoyed than she had been for many days. "Well, they needn't come to tea—as if," she continued indignantly, "I should dream of asking them if Philip were going to be here. Yes, *that* was Laura's first sarcastic inquiry."

Sam, in the mood to put his foot down about anything, was interrupted before he had really started.

"You needn't carry on about Laura, because I've just about had as much of her as I can stand," Milly declared, determination in every line. "In future if she wants me she knows where to find me, and I don't intend to budge from that. I'm sick and tired of her rampaging about Nancy going out with Philip . . . *we* can't help it . . . and even if I could stop it, I don't think I would. Philip's a very nice young man and I'm quite liking him now."

"H'mm," Sam murmured. "And did you tell Laura that?"

Milly nodded, very emphatically. "I did, with a bonus, too. I said I'd never set eyes on a bridegroom more miserable-looking than Philip was on his wedding-day. And it was true."

That roused him in spite of himself. "By jove, love, but that's carrying war to the foe, isn't it? There won't be much popping over from Stonewood now—not that there has been for a considerable while."

"Well, I'm very sorry it's occurred," Milly said quietly. "But both Father and Laura interfere too much, and they ought to be taught a lesson. I will *not* have either of them dictating what I have to do."

"No, you don't," Sam agreed.

They had drifted from the hall into the kitchen, and in that homely atmosphere Milly shed the mantle of an autocrat.

"Sam, dear," she said, coaxing him, "why don't you have a round of golf this afternoon? Oh, I know very well how you're feeling Clem's loss, but it would do you good."

Sam sighed. "The funny thing is that Clem and I didn't spend much of our leisure together latterly, and yet I'm missing him the devil of a lot. Of course for years, as you know, we were inseparable, and I suppose you don't throw off that sort of thing easily."

Milly wrinkled her nose. "You go, Sam."

Eventually she persuaded him and was very happy about it.

It so happened that when Sam went out for his car after lunch he walked into a trio round the Alfa Romeo, in which Philip and Nancy were sitting. The others were Scipio Dyson, Archie and Jim Roebuck, who looked very ill.

The two friends, Scipio and Jim, were also on the point of starting out, to catch a trolley-bus to Garth End and from there to tramp over Garthedge and Barntat Moor to a favourite resort for a ham-and-egg tea. Archie had decided to join them.

It was a very lively little gathering, the fun revolving round Nancy's capabilities as a driver—she was behind the wheel of her young man's car—and many were the dire warnings received by the owner. But Sam, smiling as he listened, could not help thinking that everything was a shade over-hearty: it was as if the others' jollity were designed to reassure Jim.

"What about saving the bus fare one way?" he suggested. "If you foot-sloggers ride with me as far as the Golf Club all you've to do is to drop down the hill to Holmluff Bridge."

"It's a deal." Archie grinned. "That two-way ticket was bothering me."

"Hear that, Jim, but what's he propose doing about anteing up at Goblin Charlie's?" Scipio demanded. "Of course the charm of his society is well worth our dipping down for the grub he'll so delicately consume, isn't it?"

"Everything's settled then," Nancy gurgled, crouching low. "Five seconds to go before the flag drops. One . . . two . . . by the way, a trifling afterthought, is there any wind in our tyres, mechanic? Three ... four...."

At "five," under her joyous pilotage, the Alfa moved off smartly, followed in due course by the Bentley, which headed to Roydlea, thence more or less alongside the river as far as the Golf Club gates, where passengers descended.

In the Club's premises the first member met by Sam was Captain Gainsway-Sinkinson, who merely gazed glassily at an invisible point about a yard above his former bookmaker's head. Next, a foursome preparing to go out, consisting of Dale Watkinson, Jim Oldfield, Walter Murgatroyd and Walter Crabtree, with whom he chatted.

Mrs. Dale Watkinson was there also, and as Sam was without engagement and as she, as always, preferred male company, they fixed up a game on the spot.

"But nine holes will do for me, Sam," she said.

"That suits me, Carrie," Sam nodded.

The much-married Mrs. Dale Watkinson was an entertaining woman and, up to a point, Sam enjoyed himself. Nevertheless, too fidgety to be at ease anywhere, he was pleased to be able to buy her a drink after the round, delighted to get into his car afterwards, and glad of the change when driving home.

As he was in this frame of mind it was not remarkable that, after tea, when Milly suggested their attending evening service he agreed with alacrity, to her surprise. She had noticed when glancing over the front page of the *Ramsfield Weekly Reporter*, that the Rev. Alonso Dyson was advertised to preach at the Wesleyan Chapel in Market Square. This was an innovation which had had twofold consequences: the Vicar of Ramsfield's quarrel with his saturnine curate, and the division of the chapel's elders into opposing camps.

"Yes, it'll be better than any turn at the Empire if Alonso is in good fettle," Sam said, a remark quite out of keeping having regard to the circumstances. "Aye, we'll go, love."

Milly looked at the clock. "We've nice time," she said. "And he always grips you, which is more than most of them with their drooling."

As it turned out, Mr. Dyson's address was not sensational, although in the strength and conviction of his fervent appeal for a simple approach to God he certainly offended every dogmatist who heard him. Once, seeking the appropriate word, he caught and held his brother-in-law's eye, an incident of no significance in itself. But unfortunately, from the moment of sitting down, Sam had been aware of how much interest he was arousing in his own vicinity: continually heads turned his way, and never before had he been more surreptitiously scrutinized, not even in the early days when a fantastic report of his paralysing losses flew round the district. Uneasily he wondered if his brother-in-law intended to utilize him as a peg upon which to hang some embarrassing homily, and that this was generally known. The notion was quite crazy, of course, as he knew well.

A little later, when the service had ended quite normally, the congregation began to file slowly out.

"Alonso's a rattling good speaker," Sam murmured as they approached the door. "Whether it's his sincerity, or . . ."

Milly's mouth opened and then closed, as with a superb effort of will she drew herself up, disdainfully to acknowledge with a slight movement of her head a lady who had rubbed shoulders with her. The recipient of this snub, a very pleasant-looking elderly woman, seemed extremely uncomfortable.

Then a voice familiar to Sam, carrying the length and breadth of the Chapel, boomed out: "Good evening!" thereby attracting the attention of the few who were not already watching the proceedings.

"A very good evening," Fred Lumb continued affably, ignoring his wife's attempts to restrain him, "a very good evening to you."

Sam had learned his lesson and stuck to his vow, which was that never again would he let Fred catch him out in public.

"Evening," he replied.

The crocodile of worshippers advanced at a crawl, those ahead craning round, those behind gaping forward.

"Amazing open weather for March," Fred went on sunnily. "After all it's only the seventh to-day."

The door was still a couple of yards away and Sam was perfectly certain that Fred's opening remarks were leading to one diabolical end only, a reference to the start of the flat-racing season the week but one following; and that this, with suitable embroidery concerning the impact of Ben Buckley's upon a rival concern, would be broached as soon as the House of God was left.

Milly's fingers were digging painfully into his arm, presumably as a warning to him not to be goaded into rash speech. But she need not have worried; tightening his elbow against his side, thereby imprisoning her arm more securely, Sam hooked her along with him. The pair of them trod on a few toes and bumped several persons, but even if the retreat were humiliating it served its purpose.

"Oh, it *does* make you wild," Milly said as the car entered Sheepgate. "To think what Fred Lumb was once—and he does it deliberately, because I could see the glint of delight in his eyes. But he always was a silly thing at the bottom, I do believe. Right enough he used to be trustworthy and hard-working, but I've often noticed in the old days when I helped at the office how he could be pleased with himself—in a pompous sort of way—pleased about some little thing or other he'd done, out of all proportion. The fact is, Sam, that for all his appearance he's really a bit of a shallow-pate, in some respects anyway . . . silly respects."

Brick-red, Sam was in a queer state; seething with annoyance while more squarely recognizing that Fred had done nothing that was not in their compact. In so far as he was able he tried to make light of the episode.

"Well, I suppose not," Milly agreed in Folly Street. "Yes, it really is too trivial for us to get heated about."

She did not conform to this sane principle, however, and chattered away on the same subject until they reached the junction of Barnsley Road and Manchester Road.

The proximity of Ings Close caused them to talk about the match and Jim's blunder.

"The worst of it is that even level-headed people are putting the beastliest construction on it . . . everybody . . . women included," Sam mused. "Take Carrie Watkinson, for instance, who isn't bigoted and who's knocked about, and is intelligent into the bargain. Well, it's thumbs down for Jim as far as she's concerned."

Milly turned. "When have you been talking to her?"

"We'd a round together this afternoon."

"Who were the others?" Milly inquired.

From behind the gentlemen's lavatory in the middle of the main road, pedestrians were crossing towards the entrance to Knowlbank Road.

"Just the two of us, for nine holes," Sam replied, checking speed.

"Oh!" said Milly.

That was just about her last observation before reaching home, where she went immediately upstairs and was an inordinately long time in coming down again.

Meanwhile, Sam wandered uneasily about the house, a patrol between drawing-room and kitchen, during which he thought exclusively about his own ignominious position.

The effort was fruitful and, after passing through the hall for perhaps the eighth occasion, he made a decision.

"I'll carry on like I am until the end of May, just over two months," he muttered, banging his fist on the lid of the grand piano. "And then . . whacko! Between now and then I'll have to take care Fred doesn't get my goat . . . he'll do his best, the play-acting old devil."

After weeks of unrest and perplexity it seemed a priceless boon, to appoint the date for the termination of an affair which he knew was too much for him, and, filled with contentment, he went out to the foot of the stairs.

"Ahoy there!" he shouted, reflecting that just as important an item was to bring himself and his wife to terms somehow. "How much longer are you going to be, love?"

Milly's tone was distant. "Can't you stir a hand, instead of prowling about like a lion in a cage? You'll want some supper, won't you?"

"I shall, love," Sam called back.

"Then please put the coffee on, if that isn't too much for you to do."

Sam scratched his head, glanced upwards again, wondered whether to reply, and finally started off towards the green baize door and the kitchen quarters of the house.

CHAPTER ELEVEN

KATE DYSON could stand no more and, avoiding her friend, Barbara Ramsden Lister, during the first break in the afternoon, she hurried off to her form mistress. Pleading violent toothache, which her pallor did nothing to deny, she received permission to leave school.

Then, walking and running, the combination of long-vented coat and abbreviated gym tunic revealing shapely legs, she flew down to town, her objective Neptune Buildings.

The many departments of PILLING ALWAYS PAYS were keying up for a vast increase of activity, and, the Lincolnshire Handicap and the Grand National being so near, a spate of commissions for the Spring Double was pouring in by letter and telephone.

When the private exchange call tinkled in Sam's own room, Margaret Berry answered it, meantime her employer and Harry Sutcliffe continued to check the larger figures for some of the doubles: Edgehill coupled with Royal Mail, Lauriat II/Golden Miller, Liscloon/Don Bradman, and so on.

"A Miss Dyson has called to see you, sir," Miss Berry said.

Sam waved his hand irately. "I haven't time for—what Miss Dyson? Why don't you find out properly, Margaret?"

Three or four seconds later, his secretary reported: "Miss Kate Dyson . . . your niece, Mr. Pilling."

"Kate!" Sam ejaculated. "Well, tell them to send her through and make her comfortable in your place, Margaret. I'll have her in here when I've finished these with Harry."

Ten minutes sufficed for this, and then Kate was ushered in.

Sam eyed her. "Well, you're troubled about something, aren't you? So sit down and tell me what it is."

"I had to see you, Uncle," she faltered. "I just had. But will you promise never, *never* to breathe a word to anybody? I can't tell you if you don't."

Sam nodded. "Now go on, love."

Kate took a deep breath. "It's about Jim keeping on with the business, and he mustn't, Uncle . . . because he's frightened of heights."

"Frightened of heights!" Sam exclaimed.

"Yes, Uncle," she went on, hands clasped tightly together. "And I don't know whether it could be so or not, but I think that might be why he hesitated in the match last Saturday. Oh, I've thought and thought about it, and I always come back to the work they're doing now, on the Sulpho—Sulpho-something company's chimney, and it's over four hundred feet high. And that even isn't the worst of it, because there's terribly bad feeling between him and that wild-looking foreman, Vincent Uttley, and Jim has often to go up to check the work. . . ."

"Steady," said Sam.

She swallowed and tried to smile. "I'm all right, Uncle, only . . ." Her brave attempt failed, and she continued brokenly: "Only I can't bear any longer to think of Jim climbing to big heights . . . because I'm sure it's killing him."

"Has he told you he's scared?"

Alarm flickered in her eyes. "No, he hasn't, Uncle. He wouldn't, because he's too proud, and if ever you let on——"

"I shan't, Kate," Sam reassured her. "All I'm trying to ferret out is why you've got this idea."

Slowly, tears in her eyes, she shook her head. "It isn't an idea, Uncle, because I'm sure, and I've been sure since I was a small girl, as sure as sure. If you'd ever seen Jim's face when he was starting on the ladders, if he didn't know anybody was watching him, you'd be sure yourself. It made me horribly sick when I realized he was forcing himself, and that's why for a long time I've never gone when Uncle Clem said they were doing something interesting."

Sam began to pace across the room. Whether she were correct in her assumptions he could not be certain, but one factor necessitated immediate action—it would not do to have two men who were at loggerheads at a great height together. And Clem, too, had worried about that.

"Kate, love," he said, turning impulsively, "don't fret any more. Leave everything to me and one way or another I'll make things right. Is it a bargain—my tackling the job and you handing in your cards?"

Her lips quivered, but before she put her head down on folded arms, to cry on his desk, she smiled mistily at him.

"Oh Uncle Sam, will you?" she said.

When she was calmer he patted her hand consolingly, and then pointed to a door in the corner.

"Inside there you'll find a wash-basin, love. You freshen yourself up and then when your eyes aren't so red I'm taking you over to the George for tea."

And that is what they did.

The lounge of the George was quite full and, after passing a word with Mr. Peter Entwistle, now frequently in Ramsfield—Entwistle & Partners, of Manchester, had secured the contract for a vast new reservoir on Barntat Moor—Sam joined his niece in a pleasant lamp-lit corner.

During tea both of them were entertained by a party of ladies nearby, the central figure being Mrs. Law Watkinson, who was not always treated as deferentially as by Laura Roebuck. Skilfully handled by Mrs. Septimus Firth, the majestic Mrs. Watkinson allowed it to be known that her son's marriage, which might have been postponed owing to the recent death of Lois's father, was taking place as originally arranged, at the Watkinsons' desire . . . a case, as it were, of the purple issuing its Ukase to the commoners. Mrs. Walter Murgatroyd scored a point next, if her tiny smile towards the corner were any criterion. She elicited from Mrs.

Watkinson the following observation, which was made with a hint of reserve: "Oh, yes, quite a nice girl, Lois. And so talented a singer."

To Sam's delight, Kate ate a really healthy schoolgirl's tea, announcing herself "fit to burst" when he rose to leave. This synchronized with the appearance of Rafe Bottomley in the lounge—the *couturier* may or may not have mistaken the movement as implying a threat to himself . . . in any event he waved furiously to his lady admirers and faced about.

After calling at the office to sign his letters, Sam drove his niece home, where she persuaded him to go indoors with her. Her father, she said, had for several days wished to see him.

The Rev. Alonso Dyson had had tea, and so, when his daughter plugged in an iron to finish off a small pile of linen, he led his brother-in-law into the chilly breakfast-room, now used as a clearing house for his parish affairs. From a drawer he pulled out a number of sheets of foolscap, the first one headed "Sports Ground and Pavilion—Non-denominational." On each line there was a name, with a sum of money written against it, some of these being marked with a tick.

"You might care to glance at the contributors, Sam," he suggested genially. "The majority were my clients when I was practising law—know too much about 'em for 'em to refuse."

"Blackmail, by Jove!" Sam grinned even more when he noticed his own name, two hundred and fifty pounds against it. "You must have made these assessments a while back, before my misfortune, anyhow."

Mr. Dyson was enjoying himself hugely. "I made them less than a fortnight ago, my boy."

Sam stared. "Nay, Alonso, how the devil can you expect that amount off me?" he expostulated. "And another thing, even though you were my solicitor, you haven't anything on me, so you might as well stop looking so cryptic."

With outstretched arm the Rev. Alonso Dyson plucked a straight-backed chair from its position against the wall; he placed it in front of his brother-in-law's and sat down, so that their faces were not more than four feet apart.

"Two hundred and fifty . . . or else," he said, and then shook his visitor to the core by pointing out that whatever the firm of Pilling might have lost on the St. Leger he was perfectly certain that this was a mere fleabite compared with resources. "Don't imagine, my dear Sam, that I'm swallowing this pantomime you and Fred Lumb are putting up."

"Nay . . . nay, Alonso," Sam replied feebly. "Wherever have you got this mad idea from?"

Mr. Dyson hooted. "Of course, if you deny it, Sam, I can investigate the matter *really* thoroughly . . . for instance, there is the intriguing question of how Fred Lumb acquired Ben Buckley's business."

One inadvisable word, as Sam knew, would put this hound relentlessly on the trail. "I give in, Alonso," he groaned, "but you'll have to make it anonymous."

His brother-in-law was accommodating enough. "Just as you wish, my dear chap."

Sam was recovering, indignation effacing stupefaction. "And you call yourself a minister of Christ, eh?"

The Rev. Alonso Dyson's long frame was quivering with laughter. "At the moment, Sam," he said, tears streaming, "at the moment . . . excuse me, ha! ha! At the moment I'm calling for two hundred and fifty of the best from you."

"Grr . . ." growled Sam.

But, despite this, he settled down for an amiable smoke with his brother-in-law, and afterwards, driving home from Highthwaite Road, he never gave another thought to the expensive nature of the last half-hour. All the way he pondered about Jim Roebuck.

"It's a pretty kettle of fish if what Kate says is accurate, and I must bottom it somehow. Well," he sighed dismally, "it's only just a bit more for me, on top of everything else, that's all."

In the same doleful state he sat down to supper, only pricking up his ears on learning that, on the next afternoon, Nancy and her mother would be leaving early for a Sale of Work. At the end of the meal he asked Archie to go to Stonewood.

"I'm not keen on telephoning," he explained. "Get hold of Jim and tell him I must have a talk with him to-morrow. Now, let's see . . . yes, it might as well be here before I go back to the office. Say, about two-thirty."

"Right you are." Archie nodded.

Sam glanced at Milly. "I'm Clem's executor as I suppose you may remember, and it's necessary for me to discuss things with Jim occasionally."

Milly slammed the refrigerator door. "I dare say, but I'm not being curious, which is what you're certainly making out."

"Are you not?" Sam observed with great surprise.

Out of sight of their parents, Archie and Nancy mimed the most abysmal despair.

*   *   *

Mrs. Sam Pilling and her daughter Nancy, a very smart pair, had left in the Riley some time before, and the house was very silent when Sam led his nephew into the study.

"Jim," he started off, "a thought occurred to me yesterday, about a matter which perturbed your father, and that's what I really wished to see you for. It's to do with you and Vincent Uttley—how are you getting on together now? And what's up?"

Jim's hollow cheeks flushed with anger. "He's under the impression I'd been having . . . well, relations with Maggie Batten, and of course I couldn't tell him the truth. But I've settled his hash only this morning, and I don't think he'll bother me again."

"Well, that's a good thing," said Sam, relieved. Jokingly he added: "And where did you have it out, on top of a chimney?"

"You've hit it, Uncle," Jim said laconically.

"What!"

Jim nodded. "The Sulpho-Aluminate Company's."

Horrified, Sam stared at him. "God, the very idea of it makes me sweat, for I'd be scared stiff even to be up there. But I suppose chaps like you think nothing of it."

His nephew's reply was quick. "Why should we, Uncle? It's what we've been trained to, isn't it?"

Sam considered. "Yes, but supposing a man hasn't a head for heights, what then?"

Jim's eyes narrowed. "What's all this leading up to, Uncle?"

Sam had certainly inherited a quality from his great-grand-father, Simeon Crowther: he could look extremely innocent when needs be. And, with immense thankfulness, he had realized that here was an opening which, if competently exploited, might allay any suspicions.

"Nothing, lad," he said with surprise, "at least not until now, and that's due to your own queerness of manner. Yes, and when I come to think of it you didn't want to continue being a master steeplejack, did you?"

Jim took two or three steps to the window, out of which he gazed.

"I wasn't exactly dead set on it, Uncle, but that's neither here nor there," he said.

Sympathetically Sam glanced towards him. "Jim lad," he said, very quietly, "I want you to answer a question squarely and honestly. Are you queasy about heights?"

There was a long silence. Then, slowly, Jim turned about, and saw the kindly concern in his uncle's eyes. Perhaps that was what broke him down, for at last he began to unburden himself, the scarlet of embarrassment in his face fading away to the white of shame.

"I've . . . I've always been scared, Uncle Sam, always. I've tried to conquer it and I can't, until it's become a nightmare that never leaves me. Sometimes, when I think of where I might be working the next day, my feet seem rooted to the ground and . . . and I'm just paralysed. That's what occurred last Saturday against Headford . . . I think it was because I happened to notice the Chemical Work's chimney, and that brought everything back to me. It's not the first time, either."

Sam was very matter-of-fact in his treatment of this confession. "In that case you're going to be out of steeplejacking before long," he said. "How, I don't know, but we'll discuss that in due course."

"But, just a minute, Uncle——"

"Hold on, lad," Sam interrupted him. "You're all ready to list the difficulties, aren't you? Your mother's objections, and how to take care of Maggie and your baby half-sister. And last but not least, you're wondering whether I'm intending shouting from the house-tops about this phobia of yours . . . which, by the way, is nothing to be ashamed of. It's something you can't help."

Jim licked his lips. "I dare say, Uncle. Common sense tells me that's the way to regard it, but . . . but I've got eyes and ears, and when a lot of people are calling you a coward as it is, you don't want to give 'em another handle to crack you with."

"Of course you don't, Jim, and I'll take every damned precaution so they won't have," said Sam. "Now listen."

Quietly and persuasively he began to talk, endeavouring to bring a measure of calm to the tortured soul of a young man who for the few years of his working life had been living on his nerves; a young man, too, who had been thrust so much nearer the abyss of total collapse by an incident on a football ground not so many days before.

"So just leave me to put my studying cap on, Jim," he

wound up. "But somehow I'll get you out of an occupation you aren't suited to, just as Archie wasn't suited to being a bookie. And I'll do it, lad, without hurting you in any way, remember that."

Desperately Jim tried to retain a grip on himself, but he could not keep his hands still nor remain stationary.

"It'd be a weight off my shoulders if you could, Uncle," he confessed with tragic inadequacy, and then, the sands of control running out swiftly, he added: "I'll have to be off, Uncle . . . some of the men are waiting for me at the yard and . . ."

Sam nodded. "Yes, you shove off. You can find your own way out, can't you?" He laughed. "You should be able to by now."

"I think so." Jim smiled. "And . . . and thanks, Uncle Sam. I . . . I . . ."

When he had gone, Sam, his expression grave, sauntered out of the study into the dining-room, where he waited in the window until he saw the Roebucks' Chrysler, his nephew at the wheel, swing out of the upper gateway into Moor-heaton Drive.

Already he had decided what was the most direct method of dealing with Jim's problem, and so, putting on his hat, he started out on an undertaking he disliked, walking across to the front door of Stonewood, where he inquired if Mrs. Roebuck could spare him a few moments. The maid, definitely embarrassed, returned shortly with a message that her mistress was very busy.

Sam's mouth tightened. "Will you go back and tell her I'm sorry to be a nuisance, but that it's most important for me to see her. And if it's inconvenient just now will she let me know when it will be more suitable."

This achieved its purpose, though he was left to cool his heels for some time before his sister-in-law appeared. She began with quite a wrong assumption.

"If it's about Nancy's disgusting affair with Philip Illing-worth you can save your breath," she snapped.

"No, it's not that, Laura," Sam replied with wonderful restraint. "It's something that has struck me, to do with the business, which I'm becoming more familiar with because of being Clem's executor. Don't you think you'd be wise to consider whether Jim ought to remain there—in my view he hasn't his heart in it."

"Oh, we had enough of that nonsense when his father

died," she said impatiently. "And I won't allow it to be brought up again."

"H'mm," Sam murmured. "There's another thing that's troubling me, Laura. Wasn't there once a question, even before he started work with Clem, of Jim having slight attacks of vertigo when climbing?"

This leap in the dark paid dividends. "That was ages ago, and Clem took every care with Jim until he said himself he'd got over it," Laura answered. "Good gracious, Jim has generations of steeplejacks' blood in him, so why should he be an exception?"

Though he was not conscious of it, her brother-in-law's voice deepened with appeal.

"Some things aren't necessarily handed down, Laura," he pointed out. "And if you've even a shadow of doubt——"

Laura scoffed. "You ought to join the Thespians, for I'm sure you'll say next that if he has an accident it'll be on my conscience. Well, I haven't any doubts at all, as you're asking me that. The truth is that Jim fancies doing something else, some wild scheme or other he doesn't care to tell his family about. I suppose what's happened is that he's put you up to——"

"He's put me up to nothing," Sam grunted. "And if you've a grain of sense, Laura, you won't mention this conversation to him."

She laughed. "Not I. I've better things to do than to pass on rubbish. Besides it would only stir up a matter that's already fully and finally settled."

Before then, Sam had realized the hopelessness of his quest, that he was dealing with a woman who was a monument of stupidity and folly.

"All right, I'll say no more about that, but I will refer once more to what I began with, the business," he said. "No business, Laura, will prosper if the boss isn't wholehearted about it, and if you'll take my advice you'll examine the question from that standpoint."

Laura pressed the bell-push at the side of the fireplace. "If I required advice," she remarked, "I shouldn't seek it from someone who's made the mess of his affairs that you have."

The maid came in, concealing as best she could hands that were dirtier than those that a parlourmaid in a more completely staffed house would have had.

"Show Mr. Pilling out," said her mistress.

Summarily dismissed by his sister-in-law, Sam did not

repine, for he had never expected a satisfactory outcome to the call. Indeed, he had no sooner got into his car to drive to the office than his mind was on another tack, to do with Vincent Uttley.

"Jim may believe he's shut him up, but that won't prevent Uttley still thinking that Jim's been in bed with Maggie, or something of the sort," he mused. "And if Uttley's a fancy for Maggie—and as I look back I'm sure he has—and bears a grudge . . . well, I'm not at all happy about the situation. Jealousy of that kind could lead to anything."

Lowering clouds, from which sleet was beginning to fall, promised that the cheeriest place for anyone that evening would be in front of the fire. But Sam, before reaching Market Square, decided he must see the foreman steeplejack before the day was out.

For thirty-five minutes that evening three Pillings had periodically eyed the master of the house, who, remaining in the same position throughout, stared steadfastly into the drawing-room fire. Their ordeal ended when, rising abruptly, he announced he was driving down to town.

"If ever that bloke Epstein requires a male model," Archie remarked just after the howl of the gale rose higher when his father opened the back door, "I can introduce him to the ideal. Anyhow, Nancy old girl, what about another session of our marathon pills game?"

"How are you getting on with it?" Milly smiled wanly. "And why . . ." She waited as a volley of hail-stones rattled deafeningly against the window ". . . and why ever your father needs to go out on a night like this is beyond me."

Archie snorted. "A young and attractive piece of skirt, mark my words. No chap ever ventures abroad for any other reason in appalling weather like this—except, of course, to attend at that infernal Tec'."

For this remark he was severely castigated by his sister, in the privacy of the billiards room.

"But why did you say such a horrible thing?" Nancy persisted. "Poor Mummy went all colours."

Archie grinned. "She gave me hell afterwards, whatever else. But we've tried finesse and we've failed all along the line, haven't we? And so crudeness is my motto now."

"I'm perfectly certain there isn't another Hilda Schofield, even if Daddy's behaving like he did at that time," Nancy said. "You know, I can't help feeling sorry for that female.

I'm quite sure Daddy never saw her as a woman at all, but she had such a frantic fix on him."

"Which is more than she had for me," said Archie, chuckling. "Gawd's truth, didn't she hand me the glassy eye if I did anything to disturb the old man. Anyhow, a few broad hints won't do Mother any harm."

Unaware that his most personal affairs were being discussed by his son and daughter, Sam drove to town. At the end of Teazle Street he swung past Queen Victoria's statue into Huddersfield Road, along which he continued nearly as far as Bankdam Mills. At a fish-and-chip shop on the left, on the steamed window of which there was a declaration that 'Ezra's Tripe' was sold there, he turned left down Cuddling Lane. He had been there before, on men-collecting missions with Clem Roebuck, usually on windy Sundays when the services of steeplejacks are often required for first-aid security work on newly discovered, dangerous pieces of masonry high up.

Vincent Uttley, in decent clothes, clean shirt, but collarless, was sitting in front of the fire, a stout black cat on the hearth-rug near his feet. He glanced in astonishment at his visitor.

"I want to have a talk with you, Vincent," said Sam. "Is there anywhere we can have a private word?"

The steeplejack's landlady, who had answered Sam's knock, picked up a shawl which she put over her head and shoulders.

"I'm just nipping in next door, Mr. Pilling," she said. "So you and Vincent can be comfortable here with nobody to bother you. No," she laughed, "you're not pushing me out . . . I was going anyway."

When she had gone, Sam began. "It's about you and Jim Roebuck."

A memory of that morning must have been very close to Vincent Uttley, for as he spoke beads of sweat formed on his forehead.

"That damned lunatic," he spluttered. "Do you know he tried to force a fight on me to-day, at the top of that bloody great chimney we're on with. He was demented, nowt less."

"It's your own fault, Vincent," Sam said sternly. "You shouldn't have suspected him of something he hasn't done."

A pair of dark and passionate eyes were fixed on him. "And what are you meaning by that, Mr. Pilling?" the steeplejack asked.

Sam left no room for misunderstanding. "I'm alluding to Maggie Batten, and I'm telling you here and now that she was sacked by Mrs. Roebuck for nothing worse than a bit of innocent play with Jim. And I might add also that Mrs. Roebuck's got a bigger idea of herself than her position warrants."

"Everybody's aware of that," the steeplejack murmured. "And there was nowt . . . familiar . . . between her and Jim?"

His tone had changed and Sam stared. "There was nothing of any sort, on my word of honour, Vincent, so rid yourself of any suspicion you might still have. And another thing, you've been convinced for some reason that Jim knew where she was —well, he'd no more idea where she was than I had."

Absentmindedly the steeplejack stroked the cat, which had jumped on to his knee. It was obvious he accepted everything told to him.

"I seem to have made a muck of it, Mr. Pilling," he said. "Well, it were just the same when I had my one and only go at walking a lass out—like a bull in a china-shop, me."

"Maggie?" asked Sam.

"Aye." Vincent Uttley nodded, and then sighed. "I wish I could see her again, I do that. And it's so queer, Mr. Pilling. Why has she hid herself away from everybody, including her sister?"

"Human beings behave strangely," Sam said as he got out of his chair. "Well, I must be off now, Vincent. And all I can end up with is that I sincerely hope the old relations between you and Jim will be restored."

The cat over his shoulder, Vincent Uttley saw his caller to the door. "Aye, I'm sorry about that and I'll have a word with him to-morrow. He's a decent lad is Jim, and unless he's in the mood he was on that chimney, I reckon I shall be able to make it all right."

"I think you should," Sam agreed. "Good night, lad."

"Good night, Mr. Pilling."

If no worse, conditions were no better and, wipers clogged by sleet, which also sprayed outwards from the wheels of the car, Sam was compelled to drive slowly, through streets quite deserted. It gave him time for reflection, and his first thought was of a narrow escape.

"Phew!" he whistled. "If Uttley had asked me if I'd any notion where Maggie was *now*. By George, I was skating on thin ice, but it came off, thank the Lord."

For the remainder of the journey he considered the more important problem: how to withdraw Jim from an occupation which might destroy him in more senses than one.

As the Bentley ploughed up Barnsley Road, the germ of an idea came to him.

"Yes," he mused. "I might force a sale of the business in that way. Laura won't consent as things are, but she would under her father's pressure. And, assuming I can persuade Maggie to turn herself into a vindictive little shrew, I might easily bring about a condition in which old Ezra would put the screws on Laura."

Still testing the many aspects of the proposition, he continued along in a world peculiarly its own, the steamy-windowed interior of a car on a bad night.

On reaching home Sam at once went into the study, where, seated at his roll-top desk, he took a sheet of writing-paper from the rack. Picking up his pen he struck out the embossed lettering on the heading, writing beneath this the office address in Neptune Buildings.

His letter to Maggie Batten was brief, merely informing her that he would be over in Southport to see her the day but one following, Friday.

Not very long afterwards he was in the hall, thrusting an arm into the sleeve of his overcoat, when Milly came out of the drawing-room. Hastily, with his disengaged hand, he picked up an envelope from an antique blanket chest, and stuffed it into a side pocket, an action certainly not missed by his wife.

"Just going to the pillar-box at the top of the road," he announced. "Shan't be long."

"It sounds awful outside," said Milly. "But Archie wouldn't mind running up with it for you."

Sam showed himself full of consideration for his son's welfare. "No, let him enjoy himself pursuing Nancy's two thousand start. He works hard enough at Walter Murgatroyd's place, not to mention the mathematics and slide-rule stuff he digs into most evenings."

"Well, he could drive down later to the G.P.O.," she suggested. "You can post there up to ten-thirty, and he'd enjoy going."

"And so shall I." Sam laughed heartily. "Do you know, there are times when a chap likes to feel rain and what-not stinging his cheeks. Harking back to primitive man, I suppose."

With a cheerfulness which was not echoed in Milly's
bosom, he went out into the filthy night.

2

Three items, and exactly twenty-four hour's reflection
upon them, were sufficient for Milly. There was Archie's
impudent remark about his father; her own belief that
women were naturally drawn to her husband; and Sam's
present mood.

In the drawing-room, while busily knitting, she scourged
herself and simultaneously considered tactics for the future.
Both the children were out, but Sam was sitting opposite,
reading a novel over the top of which he occasionally
frowned, as if his thoughts were elsewhere, far away.

"I've moped and been stand-offish, so it's small wonder
he's got sickened," her reflections ran. "But it's not too late
to bring about a better understanding, and that's what I'm
determined to do. Women of the world just don't allow their
happiness to be taken away from them. They fight for it, and
I'm going to fight, too."

When Sam was mixing a whisky and soda, he was somewhat startled when she began to talk about the theatre.

"And I've heard . . ." this burst into speech after a long
silence was causing her to sound a shade throaty, "that it's a
really good play this week."

"Why . . ." He was gaping. "What of it?"

"Well," she smiled gaily, "it's Friday to-morrow and . . .
and we used to enjoy our theatre outings. Why can't we start
them again?"

As soon as he fully comprehended, Sam beamed . . . then
his jaw dropped. "Damn it, I don't think I can get home early
enough, Milly. I've to meet Mo Barton in Leeds in the afternoon—you remember, he's the course bookmaker I always
see at Doncaster . . . we do a lot of business together."

Milly remained bright. "You can't help it, Sam. It's a pity,
but there it is."

"There's other Fridays," Sam said eagerly. "What about
to-morrow week?"

"We'll see," she promised.

Again she settled down to knit, but now her heart was
thumping; nor was Sam unaffected, and whenever he
deemed it safe he shot a quick glance at her.

That was how the evening went.

The following afternoon Mrs. Crabtree called at Glenfield. She had been staying a few days in Lancashire with her married daughter, and had returned only an hour or so before.

"I knew you weren't satisfied with your Christmas roses, and so I brought some very nice ones back from Marguerite's," she explained. "I thought we might divide them, one lot for you and one for me."

"Oh, I'd love some," Milly said gratefully. "It is kind of you to walk up from Roydlea with them."

When two ladies get together to whom the approach of spring is the best period of the year they are seldom at a loss for conversation. In fact it was only an afterthought when Mrs. Crabtree, just as she was leaving, laughingly described how they had met the Pillings' very distinctive big car about fourteen miles out from Ramsfield. According to her humorous estimate, its driver would soon be compelled to brake, otherwise he would be in danger of running off one of the piers at Blackpool.

This was in quite the opposite direction from Leeds. "Are you sure it was Sam?" Milly inquired, gallantly bearing up. " I mean if he was driving so quickly."

"It was Mr. Pilling, all right, we recognized both him and the car," Mrs. Crabtree said. "Walter said he was doing every bit of seventy."

"Was he really?" Milly said. "I'll give him what-for about this. No . . ." she laughed, "I'll improve on that . . . I'll scare him about a police trap."

Mrs. Crabtree was amused. "You do," she said.

"I'll concoct something." Milly grimaced darkly.

But she had little heart to listen when her caller began to discuss, another afterthought, the most recent scandal, a Bohemian party given by a local accountant, pyjamas and the rest of it, at which Septimus Firth's niece had been taken ill, mysteriously so.

After about an hour's confused thought, Milly reached a final conclusion while coaxing the drawing-room fire, whose under-framework of kindling had collapsed so that half-smouldering sticks pointed uselessly up the chimney; it had been laid by Nancy, who had never learned by the hard way how to make a twopenny bundle of firewood spin out.

"Of course Sam needn't have been lying to me, and perhaps his plans were changed for some proper reason," she murmured to herself as she rearranged and blew. "But if it's

another Hilda Schofield . . . and I'm not saying that yet
. . . but if it is, I'll do what I decided last night, I'll oppose
her with all the weapons I've got. Yes, I will."

Meanwhile, a cream and black Bentley was standing in a
street on the west coast, its proud owner totally unconscious
of all this.

Maggie Batten was less shy than on the previous occasion
and soon was talking with reasonable freedom. To Sam's
amazement he learnt she was perfectly aware of Jim Roebuck's horror of heights.

"Oh yes, I've often known him vomit after he'd been working high up, and just after he left boarding school and started
with his father I've made him many a cup of tea in the night.
But I thought he'd got over it, the poor lad. It must be awful
for him."

"Yes, it is," Sam agreed. "And that's where you can help."

Her foot stopped and the cradle stilled. "Me!" she ejaculated.

To begin with, he told her how and why Jim's mother was
the stumbling block. Maggie was a good-natured girl but at
this reference to Mrs. Roebuck's lavish ideas her expression
changed signally. A further remark about money, however,
turned her thoughts in another direction.

She leaned forward in her earnestness. "Mr. Pilling," she
said, "Jim needn't think about starting to send me money
some time, because I just couldn't bear to accept anything
now I know how he's suffering to make it."

Sam would have none of that. "It's only right that you
should be looked after," he said. "What I'm bothering about
is how to bring things about so that the business is sold, and
I've the glimmering of an idea that it might be worked
through Mrs. Roebuck's father. Now, Maggie, if I asked you
what struck you most about old Ezra Sykes, what would
you say?"

She snorted. "His hatred of parting with brass for one
thing. And the way he carries respectability to extremes, and
his anxiety about what other folks might say."

A crack rang out as Sam slapped his knee. "And now let's
suppose you act like a young woman who's bent either on
getting a packet of money out of the Roebucks or showing
them up by any means there are."

Her eyes widened. "You don't mean that, Mr. Pilling . . .
because I couldn't, I couldn't really. Besides I haven't any real
claim and they'd know it."

"What I'm pondering about wouldn't be done by going to law," Sam said, his mouth grim. "But," he relaxed and winked, "it doesn't follow that Mr. Sykes wouldn't think so."

She was so bewildered that she let the matter drop for the time being, and began to talk of Ramsfield and of Ramsfield people, among these mentioning Vincent Uttley.

"He thinks a rare lot of you, Maggie," he said.

She had insisted upon his having a snack and a cup of tea before leaving. Now, the bread knife stationary, her cheeks suddenly pale, she stared at him.

"There was a time, Mr. Pilling," she confessed, "when I thought I might be thinking a lot of him."

Wisely Sam left it at that. He did not hurry away, but stayed on and smoked a full pipeful while the baby was bathed. Eventually, when the gurgling little creature had been generously dusted with violet powder and freshly robed, he took her on to his lap.

"No, I haven't forgotten how I used to deal with my own," he said later, surrendering the sweet-smelling bundle. "Anyhow, I must be off now, but before I go there's a question you've left unanswered. Will you help me, as I've asked you, to get Jim out of what he's in?"

Maggie Batten's kind and homely face became very solemn. "I've been thinking about that, too," she said, gently swaying the child cradled in her arms. "About Jim being so terrified, I mean. And I'll do it, Mr. Pilling, because it's cruel for him to go on."

Sam clinched the matter. "Champion, Maggie," he said, lightly clapping her shoulder. "Now let's see, to-day's Friday, isn't it? Right, I'll be over here again a week to-morrow, Saturday, and by then I'll have studied out the details. But remember this, lass—you won't be dragged into any kind of unpleasantness, and you mustn't lose any sleep wondering what I'm letting you in for. Promise me that."

She smiled. "I promise, Mr. Pilling."

Sam poked the baby's soft cheek before saying good-bye. When he left the house more than one curtain in the windows nearby was twitched a little aside; no doubt there had been speculation upon a car of a quality seldom seen in the neighbourhood, just as there must have been for much longer about the young woman who lived in the house.

Lost in thoughts about practical plans and less practical schemes, Sam's homeward journey passed quickly enough, and surprisingly soon, to him, he was turning to the right at the far end of the flagged expanse between Stonewood and Glenfield. As he swung round, the powerful headlamps of the Bentley brought into sharp relief the boles of the elms and the ashes at the side of the garage, and the birches in the ravine beyond. The Riley stood immediately in his path; Nancy sitting in the front in the passenger's seat, while Archie, the door open on the driver's side, prepared to slide behind the wheel.

"What are you two doing?" Sam inquired, on getting out.

"Philip's rung up to say he's wrapped the Alfa round the top of a gas-lamp," Archie grinned.

Nancy giggled. "It isn't quite as bad as that, Daddy, as I'm sure you'll be immensely relieved to hear. But we're flying off on a salvage errand anyhow."

Archie closed one eye towards his father. "She knows already what I think about his mad jarveying," he observed "As a matter of fact I've just informed her that she's every prospect of being an attractive young widow in due course. And wealthy, too, thank God."

Sam hid his good humour. In days gone by laxity of every kind, and allowing too much to be taken for granted, had done infinite damage to his children. There would be no more of that.

"To be a widow a woman has to be married first," he said. "And at the moment there s no question whatever of Nancy acquiring a husband, so let's have no more jokes of that sort, Archie. They're not in the best of taste for one thing, and for another I'm not allowing them."

It is almost certain that brother and sister commented suitably about the rebuke, but Sam had at least the satisfaction of stamping across to the house without hearing a whisper from either of the dumbfounded pair.

Milly, sweetly welcoming, came out of the drawing-room as he was hanging up his overcoat. Immediately her overwhelming impulse was either to burst into tears or to slap his face, but she mastered it.

"Had a good day, Sam?" she asked. "I hope you gave my kind regards to Mr. Barton."

That very nearly trapped him. "Well . . . well, as a matter of fact I didn't," Sam said lamely. "But you know how it is."

"Yes." She nodded understandingly. "Yes, I know how it is, dear."

This ambiguous sally comforted her until she had passed beyond the green baize door, when anger gripped her. In the kitchen she eyed with utter loathing the tray she had prepared beforehand: on it was a pile of neatly cut sandwiches and his favourite *café noir* biscuits.

"And to think I've been wanting to make up with him . . . to think I was near to forgiving him about that Hilda Schofield," she said, fanning herself into fury. "A man who'll let himself be snared by any cheap creature who drowns herself in nasty, violet scent. I could smell it straight away."

As she waited for the kettle to boil, she had second thoughts, however. After all, she told herself judicially, what had happened merely confirmed her suspicions and the remedy remained the same.

And so with the air of a handmaiden serving a loved one she carried the tray to her husband, placing it on a small table drawn conveniently near his big chair.

"How will that do?" she inquired. "Of course you'll be having something else later when the children get back."

Unhappily Sam had not noticed the stagy entrance. "Grand," he said, rubbing his hands. "Yes, this little lot will keep me going nicely."

She expressed wifely gratification. "I think I'll pop upstairs and change now, Sam," she said. "When you've finished just put the tray to one side. . . . Nancy can wash them up with the rest afterwards."

"Yes, of course." Sam, chewing with relish, spoke rather indistinctly. When his mouth was empty he mentioned a point which had just occurred to him. "Milly," he went on, "just a word of advice if you don't mind. Drop calling 'em children in future. They're getting on now, but we're still in the habit of speaking about them as if they were youngsters, and I'm sure it's not wise."

She immediately recognized the value of the suggestion, and Sam, thus warmly approved, was in danger of becoming a trifle oracular when he remarked: "We want them to be responsible citizens, men and women who'll face up to life . . . and play the game in every way."

This observation might have undone all her good work, but she somehow succeeded in biting off the sizzling reply which leapt to her tongue. After that she withdrew in quite good order, but vented her feelings upstairs.

"And *he* talks about 'playing the game,' the hypocrite!" she gasped, while selecting a most becoming dress from a long line on hangers. "Him, who's got a cloud of scent about him. And I'm positive he's not even set eyes on Mr. Barton

— caught him very cleverly there, and he never suspected a thing."

In due course she changed. As final preparation she inspected herself very carefully in the pier-glass, pushed her hair here and there, and then extracted a bottle of Coty's Chypre from one of her Glastonburys, a hiding-place as yet undiscovered by Nancy. Removing the stopper she dabbed her wrists and behind each ear.

Then she crossed the thickly carpeted landing towards the head of the stairs. Accompanied by the tantalizing frou-frou of her skirt, she began to descend.

*　　　*　　　*

Sam did not see Jim again until after tea on Sunday, when, as soon as was possible without attracting attention, he took him off to the study. There he told him about his visit to Maggie and the tentative scheme he had evolved.

"But it all depends on this, lad," he went on. "Would you be willing to pay her a capital sum out of the money your shares would fetch if the business were sold?"

Jim looked ill and even more pathetically fine-drawn, and Sam could not doubt the reason for the decline—his nephew could not fail to be aware of the slurs still being passed about him, and it was significant that he had resigned his membership of Ramsfield Rugger; and although the prospect of leaving his present occupation might hearten him, he had also the humiliating knowledge that this desire arose from fear.

"I'd be only too glad to, Uncle, because she'd *have* it, and I shouldn't be wondering if I could keep the payments up."

Sam chuckled. "You see this question will come up later, as the result of a hint I shall drop to your grandfather. When, that is," he smiled tightly, "I've forced him to realize it's the only alternative to him providing a biggish amount to save a nasty scandal."

The younger man, more sensitive than ever, had grown tense.

"But what else will you say to my grandfather?" he asked. "I mean about my willingness for the business to be offered for sale."

Leisurely Sam clipped a cigar. "Only what you've told him already, Jim, nothing more: that you'd never been keen to be a master-steeplejack and that you'd rather think of some other line for yourself."

"Oh!" Jim nodded.

"And there's just another thing, Jim," said Sam. "You know nothing about your father and Maggie. I shall reveal that to you in my own good time, if you understand."

Jim was looking a little more relaxed. "I don't, Uncle. But I'll leave everything in your hands," he said.

"That's it, lad." Sam laughed.

Next he mentioned his call upon Vincent Uttley, and in return Jim told him how the steeplejack had apologized the next morning.

"Well, I'm glad all's well between you two again," Sam said. "Jim, just what kind of a chap is Uttley? He's fiery-tempered, that stands out a mile, but is he the sort to be trusted? Could he keep his own counsel, do you reckon?"

Jim stared. "In my opinion, yes, definitely so, and I'm not basing that entirely on my own judgment. For example, there are quite a few secrets in our type of business, especially when you're tendering, and my father was never frightened of letting Vincent into them. Any special reason for your asking about him, Uncle?"

In turn Sam stared. "Not exactly, lad," he said, with surprise. "I was only looking ahead. You never know, when it comes to selling the business we might have to take him into our confidence to some extent."

To his relief this not very satisfactory excuse was accepted at its face value; in fact, Jim at once responded to a mild joke made about Archie, who latterly had been under a severe mental strain.

It is not easy for a young man to begin schooling after a long interval, and still less so when in his formative years games have taken precedence over a sound educational grounding.

On the same evening, Archie, who had been dilatory with his homework from the previous Thursday night, was being coached by two of his cousins, Jim at his left elbow and Scipio at his right. Exercise books and text books were strewn over the dining-room table, and periodically, throughout the earliest part of the second hour's intensive tuition, the harassed student begged to be excused.

The scene in the drawing-room was much calmer. Milly was reading; Nancy and Philip, sitting on the small sofa, their heads suspiciously close together, were hidden behind the *Tatler*, the pages of which were not very frequently turned; and Kate, who had come up with her brother after evening service at the Parish Church, was sitting on the arm of her uncle's chair, talking to him most confidentially.

"Yes, I've started moving in that little matter," Sam was saying.

Kate glanced about cautiously. "Do you think, Uncle," she whispered, after having taken this precaution, "that you'll be able to manage it?"

Sam winked. "I'm not downhearted, love."

Her eyes glowed. "Oh, Uncle Sam," she said.

Milly smiled at them over her book. "Secrets, Kate?" she inquired.

"Oh, it's something really terrific Uncle Sam and I have in hand, Aunt Milly," Kate said, laughing. "We couldn't possibly tell you, could we, Uncle?"

"I don't care for that, Kate," said Milly. "It isn't decent under my nose."

"Well," Sam remarked, "it's been awkward for us ever since the High School headmistress had me on the carpet for giving her a lift twice in one day. She said she would not allow the girls to have followers, and I was a bit too old anyway."

Milly rocked so much with mirth that even the devoted pair on the sofa emerged from their shelter.

"Oh, Sam dear," she cried, "you *are* a perfect scream."

Strangely enough Sam did not appear hopelessly overcome by the compliment. "Aren't I?" he said, feeling his chin thoughtfully. "M'mm."

The attention of everyone, with a solitary exception, was almost immediately diverted to Archie, who entered with his mentors.

"I don't give a hang about that, Scipio," he groaned. "If $2\pi r$ isn't the same as πd. . . ."

Jim Roebuck grinned. "It is, fathead. What——"

"Our brilliant colleague may now be suffering some confusion relative to πr^2," Scipio Dyson suggested.

Philip Illingworth chuckled. "Explain by a practical example," he said. "Show him a car wheel and he'll pick it up quickly enough then."

For some reason this roused the would-be mathematician. "And what have you picked up, my lad?" Archie demanded. "Been in Mother's paint store to snaffle some of her art-red?"

Nancy's hand, flapping quickly low down at her side, shooed her brother's nonplussed target to the door. The cloakroom was down the hall and there she intended to remove several daubs of lipstick from his cheek.

"Nancy!" Milly said severely.

"Yes, Mummy," Nancy replied, humbly accepting the re-proof before turning more spiritedly to her brother. "And it's *Exotic Flame*, oaf."

"Alluring . . . irresistible . . . it invites HIM," Kate quoted accurately.

Lost in an odd reverie about his wife, Sam had heard little of what was taking place. Never had she puzzled him so much, and he could make neither head nor tail of her arch behaviour. A roar of laughter broke up this bewildering chain of thought, and, putting aside unprofitable speculation, he gave himself up to a more solvable problem—how he might cover up his absence when at Southport the following Satur-day. His son and nephew, between them, furnished him with a clue.

This came about through a piece of tactlessness for which Archie could have kicked himself, when he spoke about Ramsfield Hornets' match with Wigan the next week.

"Two of the finest sides in the Rugby League in opposi-tion," he said, fervently wishing that Jim, to whom any reference to football must be painful, were not there. "It'll be a wonderful game . . . grand backs . . . open play."

Jim faced up to this by giving a workmanlike discourse on the two Rugby codes. In common with many amateur rugby players of the industrial regions of Lancashire and Yorkshire, he had a first-hand knowledge of the professional game, admired its great stars, and had none of the snobbery about it so prevalent in Rugby Union circles in the South.

"Hear, hear," said Sam. "And what about war-time? The Rugby Union allows pros. to play in their sides then, but as soon as peace comes along they behave as if they were bearers of the Holy Grail. The whole thing's illogical."

The Medicals had a blank the following Saturday. "Where's it to be played?" Scipio inquired. "At home or away?"

Sam sighed deeply. "At Wigan," he said, and, not quite sure whether his wife had heard the wistful note, he sighed again. "Yes, at Wigan, and wouldn't I like to be there."

It was time for supper-making and, as Milly went off to the kitchen with the two girls, she squeezed his shoulder con-solingly, knowing so well how much he felt the severance of his connection with the Hornets.

Sam was moved by her understanding though perplexed by these very recent manifestations of tenderness. He was also a little vainglorious, with a tendency to liken himself to several of the more subtle characters portrayed so admirably by Mr. Raphael Sabatini. There was, he modestly decided, a resemblance to a fine Italianate hand in the manner in which he was dealing with obstacles as they loomed into view.

*   *   *

The Lincolnshire Handicap was won by Marmaduke Jinks at 33/1, and, as not one of Sam's more substantial clients was able to celebrate this victory, the party in his office broke up earlier than usual.

Sam himself left Neptune Buildings a few minutes after his last visitor had gone, and then drove out to the Sulpho-Aluminate Company Works, a run which took him less than half an hour. He made this trip for two reasons, to watch the cream of steeplejacks operating on such a project, and to have another look at Vincent Uttley, whom he was now seriously thinking about in connection with Maggie Batten.

From a mile away the chimney was impressive, a slender, tapering pencil stretching into the sky; but at the base its dimensions were even more breathtaking. Neck craned back, Sam stared upwards, his glance following the ladders which gradually, as they rose, merged into one thin line. Far distant above his head the outbulging top of the stack was surrounded by a skeleton-work of spidery planks, on which now and then he glimpsed a tiny, fore-shortened figure.

"No, not for all the tea in China," he remarked afterwards to the ground crew, who were busy with a petrol-driven winch, sending up supplies of special bricks and mortar. "And you can throw in the Mint as well."

Smiling at their response, he climbed into his car, and drove off, very well pleased with his trip, and the talk he had had.

"I reckon Jim's right about Uttley," he told himself, on joining the main road to Ramsfield. "But I shall have to take great care because it's Clem's secret, after all . . . though of course it could get out in scores of ways: if Maggie herself ever opened up, for example, and there's no reason why she shouldn't—she doesn't need to seal her lips, after all."

He chuckled farther along. "Fancy me as Cupid! But all the same, *if* those two are really attracted to one another, it would be a damned good solution, assuming Uttley can swallow a bitter pill about Maggie's baby. Ah, well, I'll tread lightly and we'll see what we do see."

That evening, on his mid-week engagement with Nancy, Philip Illingworth arrived at Glenfield sooner than was customary, and Sam, in the role of one admirably fitted to toy with the destinies of others, took him off to the billiards room. It was time, he felt, to evaluate much more searchingly a young man with whom his daughter was so passionately in love. The investigations did not proceed far, for he quickly discovered that his opponent was a first-rate snooker player; another discovery was about golf, in which he learned Philip's handicap was four, and before Nancy came in, a game for the week following, at the Ramsfield Golf Club, had been arranged.

Leaving the young people to their own devices, Sam went off to join his wife in the drawing-room. At his entrance she looked up smilingly.

"You know, love," he remarked after sinking into his chair, "Philip's not a bad young fellow at all."

"I'm quite certain he thinks the world of Nancy," Milly said. "And to tell you the truth I'm not always remembering he's divorced, which I did when he first started coming."

"Naturally." Lured by the sporting page of the *Ramsfield Reporter,* Sam was a trifle inattentive as he read that there was every hope of the Hornets being at full strength for Saturday's match, as the injuries of several prominent players were responding satisfactorily to treatment.

"For two pins," he muttered, loudly enough to carry, "I'd run over to Wigan on Saturday."

"Well, why not?" said Milly.

The newspaper was abandoned for the moment. "After all, just because I felt I ought to resign my directorship is no reason why I should debar myself from something I've always enjoyed."

"And how many times have *I* told you that? Yes, do go."

Sam shook his head. "Eh, I don't know," he said cunningly.

They argued the matter for a while, with inconclusive result. More positive was the outcome of Milly's suggestion that they should visit the Theatre Royal during the week.

That outing, their first real one together for so long, was an immense success, not in the least spoilt by a slight dispute at the end of the performance as to whether Mr. and Mrs. Luther Whitehead Garside, whose car was out of action, should be offered a ride to their home in Penny Lane: since the St. Leger, for purposes of his own, Sam had sedulously decried the banking profession.

On arriving at the theatre they were singled out for special attention: faithful patrons of old returning to the fold; the play was enjoyable, and afterwards the society of the manager of the Ramsfield Commercial Bank and his wife was not unpleasant. And finally, after companionably garaging the car, they walked arm-in-arm to the house, where Nancy, businesslike in an apron, greeted them with the news that some supper would be ready in seven or eight minutes. She had been delighted by their expedition.

"So don't go upstairs, Mummy. Just take off your coat and put it down somewhere. And wait in the drawing-room until you're called."

Archie's face appeared, narrowly framed by the slightly open baize door. "What about some fizz to celebrate, Dad?"

Milly giggled. "You don't celebrate because we've been to the theatre, silly."

"Who suggested we did?" her son inquired. "I have to inform you that the exam results were out at the Tec' to-night, and I have performed with quite reasonable distinction in Elem. Engineering, Class A."

"Right ho, lad," Sam chuckled, adding: "This is just like old times, Milly."

Milly smiled as she carefully drew off her best gloves. "It's been lovely, Sam dear, every minute of it."

Sam hugged her round the shoulders, confessing that it had put him in the mood to taste other pleasures far too long forgotten.

"Yes," he grinned, "to-morrow I'll do something else that will be a bare reminder of what I used to do. Yes, love, I'll watch the Hornets at Wigan after all. Harry's doing champion, and he can manage at the office all right."

Milly's eyes were as mischievous as those of a girl who proposes playing truant.

"And I'll tell you what will make it even more like old times," she said.

Sam's expression was indulgent. "What, love?"

"I'll go with you, of course," she said, laughing.

For two or three seconds there was silence, during which Sam's dismay was quite evident. Up to then Milly had had no suspicion that he might have ulterior motives, but it was very different afterwards.

"Just as you please," he said, on recovering, overwhelmingly genial. "It'll be grand to have you with me, but the weather isn't so very promising. It can be extremely cold in a grand-stand when the wind whistles through it, and I don't want you laid up."

She laughed heartily at this absurdity. "I'm not so very fragile, and I should wrap up well."

From the day he had first known her Milly had always been a very lively creature; but never in Sam's experience had she behaved as she did now, giving the impression of a fluffy, feather-brained idiot. That, and her peculiar conduct recently, caused him to smell a rat, smell it very strongly.

"Very well then," he said, after a swift thought.

"Oh, goody, goody!" she exclaimed. "I'll put up something nice for us to eat, and we'll take a Thermos. Oh, I *am* looking forward to it, Sam dear."

Complaining of a touch of grease on his hands, from the Bentley's wheel, Sam retired to the cloakroom, where he proposed to sort out his thoughts. By then he had decided that his wife, as more than once before, was motivated by some ill-founded jealousy.

"All right, Milly *dear*," he muttered.

Grimly he determined that, if it could be contrived, she should have the shock of her life to-morrow.

3

It was a fine day, and as the car swept along, Milly chatted vivaciously. So far they had certainly kept to roads which headed towards Wigan, and the same held good after their picnic lunch. And then, at last, the name of their supposed destination appeared on a signpost, Sam meticulously following the course of the pointing finger.

In Wigan, however, quite expressionless, he drove through the town and into the country beyond, Milly still talkative though perhaps a little constrained. On the familiar South-port road, past Ormskirk, she achieved a gay comment.

"So you're taking me to the sea, are you?"

Sam's gaze never moved from the road in front. "Maybe you'll see the sea, but I'm taking you for something very different."

His demeanour was so strange that her flow of incon-sequences dried up. As a matter of fact neither spoke for another twenty minutes, when Sam gently braked in a street of very small dwelling-houses.

"Well, here we are," he said. "You'd better come along

338

just behind me, so that I can first break the news that I've got my wife with me."

He slid back his seat and slipped out of the car, leaving Milly more agitated than ever.

The atmosphere in Maggie Batten's kitchen shortly after her visitors' entry could hardly have been improved on from one person's point of view. Both women were silent, Maggie's shamed blush more expressive than words; while Milly's pallor, already noticeable, increased immediately she perceived the cot and the sleeping child.

Before either could speak Sam asked for writing paper, and Maggie was so flustered that she ran as far as the door of the shop opposite before remembering that a few sheets were still in her pad. In her brief absence only one remark was made, accompanied by a significant nod towards the baby.

"Who do you think she favours?" Sam inquired dourly. "Her mother or her father?"

Given time, Milly would probably have replied, but just then she was too overcome, and when Maggie hurried in it was too late.

From his breast pocket Sam took a letter he had drafted out the previous day.

"Now then, Maggie, I want you to copy this out," he said. "It's only for Mr. Sykes's benefit and there's nothing for you to worry about."

Maggie's lips began to move as she read. "Oh . . . oh! I couldn't be so cheeky, Mr. Pilling. It's awful."

He nodded. "And deliberately so, lass. But it's the only way to bring off what we have in mind, and it won't ever go out of my possession.

Eventually he soothed away her fears and, sitting up to the deal table, she began her task, brow furrowed and her tongue appearing now and then as she wrote. Meantime Sam devoted himself to the baby, whose blue eyes were now open, while his wife watched him, her colour ebbing and flowing.

When the letter was finished, Sam read it through and then slapped it with the back of his hand.

"Right, Maggie," he said, "I'm starting operations with this as soon as we're home, so we can't stop. No," he laughed as she glanced at the kettle on the hob, "no, not even for the cup of tea I think you're contemplating. But before we leave I want to tell you how things are going generally."

And so, as a result of their conversation, Milly learnt what had happened; that the child was her brother-in-law's, and how the present manoeuvre was designed to remove her nephew Jim from an occupation which was remorselessly destroying him. Soon her eyes were welling and, partly to hide this and partly because she was aching to do so, she bent down to the cot. Shortly after that, crooning softly, she was walking to and fro with the baby in her arms.

This was too much for the child's mother. "Oh, Mrs. Pilling," she gulped, "you're not mad at me then . . . with Mrs. Roebuck being——"

"No, of course I'm not, Maggie," Milly said fiercely. "It's only because I'm very upset, and you mustn't take any notice of me . . . and then there's your being left alone . . . it's hard for you——"

"Don't you fret about me, Mrs. Pilling, because I'm all right, and I've got baby. And Mr. Pilling has been ever so kind . . . and Jim was real understanding."

"Well . . . well, they should be," said Milly, avoiding her husband's ironic glance. "And, Maggie, you *do* keep her nice, and she *is* lovely."

As their talk seemed destined to become an orgy of baby-worship, Sam changed the subject by mentioning he had spoken to Vincent Uttley again.

"It'd put me in a difficult position, in more ways than one, if he asked me if I'd any idea where you are, Maggie," he said.

Maggie Batten shook her head. "Anyhow, he wouldn't want anything to do with me now, Mr. Pilling, not when he knew I'd been bad."

"That'd be for him to decide, wouldn't it, not you," Sam suggested.

She looked quite surprised. "I hadn't thought of it that road," she said.

"Ah, well, it hasn't happened, lass," Sam murmured.

This small seed dropped, he said nothing more about the foreman steeplejack.

The visitors remained there for a little longer. Milly was determined to efface any wrong impression Maggie might have had at the beginning, and Maggie, responding to the warmth and kindliness of her former mistress's sister, quickly became herself. Their chatter, of course, centred round the baby, about whose charm and intelligence there was complete unanimity.

Sam's hand was on the door latch. "Well, Maggie, apparently I've to go," Milly said, smiling. "But I'll be

340

coming over to see you again soon. And don't worry about anything; just leave things to my husband and everything will be all right." Her expression became solemn. "I know him better than anybody else does, Maggie, and I'll tell you this, you can trust him up to the hilt."

The door was noisily opened, Sam bawled: "Good-bye, lass," and, after that, little time was lost by the Pillings in departing. Milly was unceremoniously thrust into the car, and her husband's first attempt to get into gear, during which he inadvertently forgot the clutch, raised a din shocking to hear. And when they did move off, the seats seemed to project the occupants forward; grit was scattered by the rear wheels, while farther behind the smell of rubber lingered, from the tyre-scrub of over-rapid acceleration.

As Milly apprehensively glanced sideways she had an alarming close-up of her choleric-eyed driver, who, with the dash of a racing motorist but none of the expert's skill, flung the Bentley round a blind corner.

The journey home was as unreal as the outward trip had been, though differently. Milly was crying quietly; in Ormskirk she touched Sam's arm and said miserably: "I'm sorry, Sam," just after he had flamboyantly raised his checked cap to a vividly-attired female who was leaving a garish public-house. It was still early, and at Wigan, where the streets were filled by throngs hurrying to the match, Sam remarked loudly: "To hell with the Hornets." In Bolton, when held up by traffic lights, he started an intimate conversation with a most attractive young woman, to her patent astonishment; while in Bury his glance darted here and there, until he had to confess regretfully: "Of course she won't be about now, this isn't the day she expects me."

"Oh, don't, Sam," Milly wailed.

Sam snarled. "Don't nothing. I've women all over the place, and why shouldn't I? Everybody believes it, including my own wife."

"Please!" Milly begged.

"And you oughtn't to be surprised either, not when you come from Ramsfield," he growled, "where morals nowadays are based on the cat world. And me, why I'm a regular Tom."

Speeding furiously, Glenfield was reached before tea-time.

Some twenty minutes later, after aimlessly wandering about the ground floor of a house which seemed extraordinarily silent, Sam went to the telephone in the hall. His talk with Ezra Sykes was brief.

"I can't refer to it on this thing, but I'm coming to see you immediately," he wound up. "If we don't take the utmost care there's going to be a scandal of the greatest magnitude."

A startled exclamation brought a smile of sharp satisfaction to Sam's face as he replaced the receiver. Then he put his overcoat on again, but hesitated when reaching for his cap. Next, he walked to the foot of the staircase and listened intently before beginning the ascent.

From the landing he could see into his wife's bedroom. Cheeks streaked with tears, she was sitting in a low chair, a very woebegone figure. But at the faint sound of footsteps she hastily dabbed her eyes and switched round so that her back was towards the light.

"Don't go on so, Milly," Sam said gently.

She sniffed. "I . . . I can't help it. I'll never forgive myself for what I thought when I first saw Maggie's baby."

"Well, you'd a bit of an excuse, love, after that business with Hilda Schofield," Sam admitted.

"Yes. . . ." She seemed to consider. " . . . there was that. It was enough to make any woman suspicious after that, wasn't it?"

"Yes, I suppose so," Sam agreed.

Plainly she was now inclined to believe herself less at fault. "And anybody could be excused for wondering if Carrie Watkinson was thinking of still another husband if they saw you and her laughing together," she murmured. "Then there's that glamour queen, Mrs. Hildred Pickersgill —I've actually seen her making eyes at you."

Sam looked exactly like a man who, overbrimming with rectitude, nevertheless is conscious that the tables will be turned on him unless he acts with firmness.

"Hey!" he said. "If we're going into all the entanglements you suspect I'm capable of we shall be a long time before we get down to brass tacks. And they are that you've either got to forgive me properly about Hilda Schofield, or you must divorce me."

She became quite rigid. "Divorce you!"

"It's that or the other," Sam said grimly. "And if it's the other, I mean *properly*. No more of this damned nonsense of separate rooms, and no more waxing hot and cold, dependent on whether or not you need me."

"That isn't true. And I shouldn't dream of the other . . . divorce I mean."

"Why not?" Sam persisted. "Anyway, you can tell me this: is it that you don't want it for the chil—for the sake of Archie and the other two, or because you're still fond of me?"

Indignantly she turned. "Because I'm still fond of you."

Sam sighed. "Is that all, love? I could do better for you than that."

For an appreciable period, while tell-tale signals flew, they looked at one another, and then Milly, springing to her feet, came tumbling into his arms. She was almost incoherent.

"Oh, Sam, I love you as much as ever I did," she said, face pressed against his chest. "That's why it's been awful, because we weren't as we used to be."

"Let's start to be then," Sam said, stroking her hair and lifting her chin to kiss her. "From now on, love."

Milly nodded violently. "From this minute, Sam darling," she said. "Oh, it's lovely, *lovely*."

"I think we ought to celebrate," Sam remarked.

No sooner were the words out of his mouth than the idea came to him, and he went on to remind her of the crazy things they had once done, when the "children" were really children, and Laura, more human then, had been willing enough to take care of them during their parents' absence for a few days.

"Remember that little holiday we had when I'd made a profit of ten pounds for six weeks running?" Sam chuckled. "Well, what about an outing to London, and off *to-night*? We can't catch the five-thirty from here, but we could drive to the Junction and get a train from there."

After the first startled reaction of a housewife, Milly's lovely eyes began to sparkle.

"I'll telephone the station . . . and pack," she said eagerly.

"And I'll be off to your father's, but I'll tell you about that later," said Sam. "And ring up to London and book a room— say we won't be there until midnight or so. Try the Ritz first——"

Flushed with pleasure, Milly was already opening drawers.

"You silly, have you forgotten?" she giggled. "We're not like we were, and we can't afford——"

"Aye—aye, of course," Sam said. "I think the excitement's gone to my head."

"It's gone to mine," Milly admitted.

She was as animated as a girl, and Sam as lively as a boy as he leapt down the stairs two at a time to the hall, where he snatched up his cap and then sprinted to the garage.

Each room in Ezra Sykes's house was provided with a Bible, and Sam, immediately on entering the sitting-room, used one of them with dramatic effect, by thrusting it into his father-in-law's hand and then demanding Mr. Sykes's solemn promise, on the Book, never to reveal to a soul certain information now being brought to him. Sam knew perfectly well that without efficient muzzling Laura would quickly be informed about her husband and Maggie—to do so would be in line with her father's conception of his Christian duty.

Fearing a catch, Mr. Sykes temporized, but further treatment proved efficacious.

"Right, now that you've sworn as God's your judge, I'll tell you what I've learned in my capacity of Clem's executor," Sam said. "Maggie Batten, their old maid, was his mistress and there's a child only a few months old."

Mr. Sykes found speech difficult. His first croak, however, was a very nasty backhander.

"Seemingly I've had two bonny sons-in-law."

Sam controlled his temper. "Us two quarrelling won't help, so I'd better let you know I've interviewed this girl, and you can take it from me she's out for real money. And she'll get it, too—either from us or from the Sunday papers."

"The Sunday papers!"

"Yes, and can't you picture the headlines?" said Sam. "'Was it suicide?' 'Why did an experienced steeplejack fall to his death?' 'Seduction under mistress's nose!' . . . . with photos of Ramsfield spire and Maggie . . maybe they'd even snap you: 'The betrayed wife's father.'"

Horrified, Mr. Sykes stared at him. "She'll have to be stopped. I should never hold my head up again."

Succinctly Sam disclosed his plan, to ensure absolute secrecy by consulting solicitors in London, which was why he was taking Milly—he explained that, as Laura's sister, she should be there—to London that night.

"Our only hope is to prove blackmail, but I doubt if we can," he ended lugubriously. "You'd better read a letter I had from the Batten girl this morning."

Through steel-rimmed spectacles Mr. Sykes began to scan lines framed in terms their creator considered appropriate to a young woman of little education, save the postscript. A sum was demanded which the writer had "been told would bring in five pounds a week."

"*Five* thousand pounds!" Ezra Sykes gasped.

"It's the few lines extra at the end that bother me," Sam remarked. "How does their tone strike you?"

The ultimatum was couched very differently. It ran: "If, within fourteen days of this date I have not received the above-named amount I shall without further notice take such steps as I may be advised."

Mr. Sykes groaned. "They strike me as if some whipper-snapper of a lawyer's clerk is behind her."

"Anyway, thank goodness, there's still brass in the family," Sam said. "And now I must get back home as we haven't very much time for the train."

"What's that about brass?" Mr. Sykes inquired. "Whose brass?"

"Why, yours," said Sam. "Laura couldn't spare that sort of money even if she could be told, and you know how *I'm* placed."

"Me fork all that out!" Ezra Sykes whispered.

In due course, with a sense of having performed not at all ill, Sam left a house in which fear of *"Maggie Batten's Own Story,"* with a rocketing local circulation of the paper featuring it, hung ominously in the air.

A couple of hundred yards along Barnsley Road he pulled up at a telephone kiosk where he rang up Ben Buckley's, as usual tendering any name which suited his fancy. This sort of conspiratorial effort was more and more meat and drink to Fred Lumb, and he took elaborate pains to confirm his caller's true identity. This established, they discussed a new date for their next fortnightly secret meeting, originally scheduled for the following Thursday.

Sam was grinning as he came out of the box. "He's a grand chap is old Fred," he told himself. "And why I've ever got my hair off about him is beyond me."

In this broadminded spirit he drove home.

Arrangements for Sam's absence from the office had been completed, and the more personal activities at Glenfield were drawing to a close. The suitcases were in the boot of the Bentley, and Archie, who had stowed them, raced into the hall with the warning that if his passengers were not aboard in forty-five seconds he would not guarantee to catch the train.

Nancy, who had thrown her arms round her father's neck, now turned to hug her mother, and to whisper: "Oh, I'm so glad, Mummy . . . that you and Daddy have made it up. And have a wonderful time in London."

Her father caught the tail-end of this remark. "Aye, we will, Nancy love," he said, grinning. "But . . ." sobering, he wagged a finger at his son and daughter, "but remember to keep that to yourselves. Don't let on to anybody at all that we're off on a pleasure jaunt—just put them off if they inquire."

Then, when Archie and his father had gone out of the front door, Milly was guilty of still another warning. Over-excitement had made her forget that Nancy was not seeing them off at the Junction, as Philip was coming.

"And give our love to Philip," she said, thinking the pair would have Glenfield to themselves. "And mind what you're doing."

Nancy eyed her. "Mind what I'm doing?"

"Take care of yourself, I mean," Milly replied in a flurry. "Both of you—you and Archie."

"Of course I *could* run you through to London," Archie bawled from outside.

He and his parents had a near shave on emerging from the gateway, and his "God damn 'em," was excusable when three cars, packed with young men and women, one of whom waved a bottle in salute, raced three abreast down Moorheaton Drive.

But the delay was slight and the connection was just made, after a twelve-mile drive which was fairly fast in the town, faster still as the lamp-posts thinned out, and at racing speed on the moorland roads beyond. At their destination, Archie darted to the rear for their luggage, and overtook his mother and father as they were climbing into a first-class compartment. Already the guard had his lamp in readiness, and farewells were brief.

"Well, we've done it, love," Sam said, tugging at the window-strap when his son's figure, eerily illuminated by inadequate lighting on the platform, became indistinguishable. "Yes, we're off now."

The corridor door slid open and a cheery-faced individual put his head in.

"Second dinner in a quarter of an hour, sir."

"Two, if you please," said Sam, adding when they were alone again: "And no chiding by you, either about travelling first or a bottle or so of wine."

Milly laughed. "I'm not grumbling," she said blissfully. "Oh, Sam, isn't it wonderful?"

They looked at each other with immense satisfaction, she seeing a man most certainly pleased with life; what he saw was a radiant, bright-eyed woman who seemed to him as desirable as she had been as a girl.

Which of them made the opening move is neither here nor there, but a passenger passing along the corridor a few seconds later would have been rewarded by the spectacle of a couple in close embrace: a gentleman slightly over forty involved in a lengthy kiss with a lady who might have been in the early thirties.

"Mmm," Sam murmured thoughtfully as he relaxed his grip. "You know, Milly love, you always were a hot little devil."

His wife's smooth cheeks flooded with scarlet.

"*Sam Pilling*," she said indignantly.

But they were both laughing on the next stage of their holiday, the walk along the swaying train to the dining-car.

In London they enjoyed themselves marvellously: theatres, restaurants, and the thrill of the Boat Race, won by Oxford for the first time in the last fourteen years. And if there were regrets they were Sam's alone—he dare not suggest buying any of the expensive articles his wife admired while they were out window-shopping.

Originally they had intended to make it a long week-end, but a letter forwarded to them changed that. It was the first letter Gilbert had written them since he went away, and its tone was such as to rejoice their hearts.

So they remained in London a full week, journeying north again on Easter Saturday.

4

The George bar was very crowded, and many toasts were being drunk to the Hornets' fine victory over Leeds, fourteen points to three, at Swanroyd that afternoon; other sections were animatedly discussing the police raid on Major Bentinck's the previous night, when sixty of Ramsfield's socialites had been hauled off to the police station.

Archie Pilling, in a strategic corner with Alec and his mother, Mrs. Walter Murgatroyd, a lady full of fun, was listening intently for the grinding squeal of the London train as it negotiated the sharp curve just outside the station.

"There she is," he shouted. "Cheers, Alec, see you to-morrow. 'Bye, Mrs. Murgatroyd, and thanks for the tankard of wallop."

It spoke well for his fleetness that when his parents appeared at the barrier, a porter carrying their bags, he was in position to greet them.

On the drive up to Moorheaton he responded to their desire for news.

"Oh, nothing very unusual. Nancy's been into the office regularly and says everything seems to be going smoothly. And Grandfather's been burning up the wires lately asking when you'd be back—three times to-day so far."

Milly was fully informed about her husband's activities. "It'll be something and nothing," she said. "You know what he is."

In Moorheaton Drive the travellers at once noticed that Stonewood was well lighted.

"Tremendous preparations afoot day after day for Lois's wedding," said Archie. "So my private eye, cuzzin Cora, informs me. The function takes place, by the way, the week before Whitsuntide."

The front door of Glenfield was opened by Philip Illingworth as the car drew up.

"Has he taken up permanent residence?" Sam inquired.

"Sssh, they'll hear," said Milly.

Nancy was not far behind her young man. "Mummy!" she exclaimed. "Why, you look like a bride." She sought confirmation. "Doesn't she, Philip?"

Milly blushed. "Silly! And less of your nonsense."

About ten minutes after they had sat down at the dining-room table, the strident telephone bell brought the lively talk to an end.

"I'll bet that's yon old—the old gentleman again," Archie grunted.

Sam pointed towards the hall. "You answer it, lad, and if it's your grandfather let him know we've arrived. And you might tell him also that your mother and I are very tired indeed, but I'll be ringing him up later on, when I've rested."

Three young people stared at him, and then their glances switched to the vivacious lady who was presumed to share his exhaustion.

CHAPTER TWELVE

On the second Saturday in April, in the middle of the afternoon, Laura Roebuck was in an excellent humour as she settled down in the drawing-room of Stonewood for a cosy chat with Lois and her *fiancé*, Haigh Watkinson.

The arrangements for the wedding were dropping into place splendidly, and she was inclined to congratulate herself upon the skilful manner in which, using the Watkinsons' prestige as a lever, she had persuaded her father that a quite considerable outlay was unavoidable, at her own expense, of course. In quite another matter, too, she felt lighthearted: really she had made an unconscionable fuss on hearing Mrs. Law Watkinson's silly piece of gossip about Mrs. Allan Oldfield.

Mrs. Roebuck's beatific mood was completely dispelled when Cora came in with a hatless youth employed, she gathered, in the laboratories of the Chemical Works. Clad in soiled flannels and a disreputable jacket, he monopolized the conversation from the moment of arrival, incomprehensibly so.

Worse was to follow when a sky-blue Cadillac, dazzling with chromium-plated gadgets, pulled up in the driveway. Estelle descended from this over-ornate vehicle, showing plenty of leg in the process, to the satisfaction of the driver who passed some jocular remark, thereby earning a slight slap from his passenger. Laura's gorge rose when she recognized this over-fat, swarthy man as Tony Flassati, and furiously she wondered when Estelle's folly would cease.

Kate Dyson, who was walking up to the house with her brother, served some twenty minutes later as a scapegoat for Mrs. Roebuck.

"Good heavens, that girl's here again," she snapped.

"It'll be about a play at that wretched High School," Cora drawled. "Or something else too, too *incroyable*."

Her swain's prominent Adam's apple bobbed fantastically. "My delicious poppet, if you love me," he declared, circling a Turkish cigarette in the air, "*surely* you wouldn't deny our great Bard . . . or could it be the so-worthy Mr. Galsworthy? Or Strindberg?"

Tony Flassati had been sadly ruffled in recent exchanges with the stripling. "If you keep jawing long enough, somebody's bound sooner or later to understand something," he said with profound sarcasm.

Before Laura could intervene she was tackled peremptorily by her son, who had been quietly enjoying himself. The expression on Jim's face was one with which his mother was not familiar.

"Why shouldn't Kate come?" he demanded. "What's wrong with the kid?"

"Oh, nothing, I suppose," his mother replied irritably. "But you really ought to be more careful. The way you take her about is apt to give her the silliest ideas."

Jim gaped. "Why . . . why, she's only fifteen, or is it sixteen. It's plumb idiotic."

Laura was further distracted by seeing her father talking to their jobbing gardener. Hitherto Mr. Sykes had not met Haigh Watkinson and, embarrassed by the old man's broad speech, she wished to keep them apart as long as she could.

"Why has Cora brought that queer creature?" she fumed. "And as for Estelle . . ."

Thoroughly annoyed with his mother, Jim went out to meet Scipio, who suggested that, as summer would be along soon, it might not be a bad idea if they visited the Baths that evening.

"A grand idea, but let's clear out of here and have tea somewhere beforehand, my treat," Jim said. And then, on the heels of that, he proposed a variation, possibly to show his mother how he dealt with interference, possibly because there flashed into his mind the memory of Kate's pretty little figure when swimming at Scarborough the previous year.

"Instead of that, what about running over to Spedding Baths, and then Kate can come along with us? How about it, Kate, my delicious poppet?"

Kate blushed to the roots of her bright hair. "Oh, I'd love to, Jim," she said. "Can I, Scipio?"

Her brother rolled his eyes. "Your presence, dear, will add that perfect touch. Can I say more?"

Jim dashed upstairs, to hunt out bathing trunks and to escape his grandfather, now briskly walking up to the front door; and Kate hurried off to Glenfield, her errand to do with a recipe for seed-cake for which her Aunt Milly had a notable reputation.

It was that dead season when rugger is dying out and groundsmen contemplate setting up nets for cricket. In the garage, Archie was stripping down a nine-year-old Lea-Francis he had bought for its break-up value. He was examining a gasket when Kate called in carrying a bulging bag of queen cakes and an enormous bunch of daffodils.

"The trouble is, lass," he explained, waving to indicate his acquisition, "that I seem to collect women who aren't well enough upholstered to squat on the back of the Norton. And that raises an extraordinarily interesting biological problem —how is it that men of my type, handsome, deeply tanned, magnificently built and so forth, have always to be on the defensive against pocket-sized females?"

"I'll bet you're faking it up to make a profit," Kate remarked.

"I take strong exception to that," said Archie. "It conveys some doubt about my commercial . . . er. . . ."

"Ethics? . . . probity?" suggested Kate.

"Morals is the superior word," Archie corrected her coldly. "Moreover I find in it a hint that women don't tumble over themselves for me to date 'em when I'm in the toying mood."

This promising by-play was suspended when they heard the crash of gears in Moorheaton Drive, a cacophony sufficient to identify the car and its driver.

Sam Pilling, who had stayed at the office until the result of the Newbury Spring Cup had come through, chatted with his son and niece a little while, but on leaving the garage made an excuse to draw Kate along with him, to tell her that Jim's matter was moving slowly along. But although she was delighted he sensed some reservation, and he had to bludgeon her to extract an admission, that she had another cross to bear.

"You see, Uncle Sam, people will always think he's a coward," she said forlornly.

"Good gracious, child," Sam scoffed, "all that will be forgotten in no time. Are you *trying* to find something to worry about?"

Nevertheless, on leaving her, he felt gloomily certain she was as little convinced as he himself was, and he knew his sporting Ramsfield.

"Yes, she's hit it," he mused. "Those slips of Jim's won't be forgiven him quickly, and that's the one thing I can't put right for him."

The risk of frost had passed and Milly was busily employed carrying pots of azaleas from the conservatory. While he helped her with this important operation she told him her father had telephoned.

"Well, Nancy's off hill-climbing with Philip, and Archie's

out there, so this afternoon couldn't be more convenient, love," he said. "And this job of Jim's has been hanging fire long enough now."

"I'm frightened every day about him," Milly confessed.

"It's not pleasant," Sam agreed. "But they've finished at the Sulpho-Aluminate's place, and that's a load off my mind."

Mr. Sykes arrived when they were both indoors. The rattling of the front door knob gave them due warning.

On two occasions skilful negotiations had reduced the figure Maggie Batten was demanding, and twice extensions of time had been wrung out of her. That was the fabrication, the full drama of which had, of course, been reported by Sam to his father-in-law.

And now Mr. Sykes and his son-in-law conferred again, in Sam's study.

"Well?" asked Ezra Sykes, who looked both apprehensive and watchful as he perched on the edge of a chair. "How did you get on this time?"

Sam's demeanour was that of one meriting approbation for the acumen which has resolved a most delicate situation.

"Judge for yourself," he said, leaning forward. "Yes, I've got her to agree to what I consider is a very low sum having regard to the circumstances . . . a thousand pounds."

Mr. Sykes groaned. "It's a terrible state of affairs when a man of my years, who's led the unblemished life that I have, has to be shamed in the sight of the world."

Sam frowned. "I don't follow you."

"There's nobbut one thing for it," his father-in-law said dismally. "Laura'll have to be prepared. She'll have to be told about her husband's wickedness."

"You mean you won't find the money?" Sam spoke as if he could hardly believe his ears. "A man of your wealth, to save your daughter from humiliation."

This outcome was precisely what he had gambled on, nevertheless it was a nasty jolt to realize to what extent insensate greed could affect any man.

"Of course, we could try with five hundred if you gave me an open cheque," he resumed, with an effort, determined to test his father-in-law to the limit. "A thick wad of bank-notes might be much more likely to impress a young woman like Maggie Batten."

Ezra Syke's expression was pained. "I haven't that amount in the bank, and only a chap like yourself, easy come, easy go,

352

could talk about such a sum so lightly. The market's low just now, and to get it I'd have to sell securities at a loss——"

"You heartless old skinflint," Sam interrupted violently.

Mr. Sykes recoiled. "You'll withdraw that or I'll——"

"I know what you'll do, but to hell with you and your brass," Sam roared. "Money's your god and always has been, or otherwise this job of Clem's would have been settled without anybody being any the wiser, but naturally you supported Laura against Jim . . . never considering that Jim might be happier doing something else."

"I'll never again darken the door of this house . . ." Ezra Sykes shouted.

It was not surprising that Milly decided to intervene. When she hurried in her father was bringing the morals of the other party under review, as he usually did when acute differences arose.

"As a sinner on this earth I'm fully aware of my failings," he was bawling. "But I don't bedeck fancy women wi' jewels worth a king's ransom like you did that so-called secretary of yours. Oh aye, I've found out at last what you've been up to."

"Go on," Sam growled. "Cause more mischief if you can."

Pale but determined, Milly confronted her father. "I've warned you before," she said. "You've no right to speak to Sam in that way, and I won't have it."

Ezra Sykes jeered. "So you're a woman without any pride, are you?"

Sharply she told him that at least she had understanding. But her tone changed when, a quality of ripe wisdom in it, she added: "Men sometimes behave foolishly at a certain age, Father. But it passes, it's only a phase."

Sam glared at her. "How old do you reckon I am?" he demanded. "But if you've got the idea I'm at the stage when I pinch young women's behinds you can damn well lose it."

Tempestuously she turned on him. "There's no need to be vulgar. I was only explaining. . . ."

Completely engrossed in their dispute, husband and wife failed to notice that Mr. Sykes had snatched up his bowler hat; but it sobered both of them when they heard the double slams of the front doors.

"Well," Sam muttered, "I've made a muck of things. But I'll get Jim out some other way."

Milly nodded approval but made a remark which had

nothing whatever to do with the problems of her nephew.

"I didn't know you'd given Hilda Schofield some expensive jewellery," she said.

"Oh hell, is all that starting up again?" Sam said. "Yes, I did."

Smilingly she shook her head. "No, it isn't, dear, and do you know why? Because we're so happy together now, and I wouldn't let anything spoil it."

Apprehension changing swiftly to relief, Sam beamed as he took her into his arms.

"Well, love," he said, kissing her, "that's grand news."

"No, I shan't say a word," Milly promised. "In fact I shan't mention the subject again as long as I live."

"Milly!" Sam said very lovingly.

This pleasant interlude would have lasted longer had not Mr. Sykes faced about on reaching the gates. He returned in as much haste as he had left.

"You leave him for me to deal with," Milly instructed her husband. "However beastly he is."

Despite this order, Sam found it highly desirable to answer the question put to him by his father-in-law on re-entering the study: why would the sale of the business clear up the matter?

"Because Jim was very fond of his father, and out of the money he'd have received I think he would have paid off this Batten woman, assuming she'd wait, which I think could have been arranged," said Sam. "Anyway, that's my opinion. But there's always Laura to remember, and though Jim is in a position to force a sale of the business I don't think he would unless his mother stopped opposing it."

Ezra Sykes, defending his elder daughter, was definitely austere. "Laura would want her lad to be happy, the same as me," he said. "And now I'm fully aware as James is so dead-set on doing something else I reckon it's in everybody's interests to make the change without delay. I've no doubt that Laura would see the sense of what I was saying if I tackled her."

"Still remembering your oath?" Sam reminded him.

Mr. Sykes took exception to the suggestion that he might forget his pledged word never to reveal to anyone his knowledge of Clem Roebuck's mistress and child, but was not offensive. Before he left there was a short, business-like conversation during which it was agreed that Sam, after breaking the news to Jim about Maggie Batten, should sound-out his nephew in financial directions. It was agreed also that Sam, Jim and Ezra Sykes should meet as soon as possible.

Milly danced excitedly as her father disappeared down Moorheaton Drive. "You've done it, Sam," she said. "I've known him too long not to be sure he'll make Laura do what he wishes."

"It looks like it," Sam agreed, very pleased. "Yes . . ." he was already pondering about the next hurdle, "yes, Laura is always at pains never to go contrary to anything he says."

Delighted, Milly chattered away, but soon realized the meagre responses she was receiving. Taxed about this, Sam admitted he had been wool-gathering, wondering how Clem's business could be disposed of to the best advantage.

Milly was confident. "You'll manage that," she said, and, this wifely tribute paid, then announced there was work to be done. "So I'll start."

"Right." Sam smiled.

At the doorway she turned round, however, all at once very serious.

"Sam, you didn't . . . didn't . . ." she faltered.

"Whatever is it?" Sam asked.

Suddenly she blurted out her anxieties. "You . . . you didn't care a lot about Hilda Schofield, did you?"

This return to a subject banned for ever by herself was not without its consequences. To be accurate, Sam's mouth twitched slightly.

"You're laughing," she accused him stormily.

"I'm not."

"Yes, you are," she said in a fury. "And why shouldn't you? It's only because I haven't the right sense of humour that I'm not convulsed like you are."

"Now hold on . . ." Sam said desperately.

"No doubt such as Hilda Schofield are tickled to death by your jokes. Or . . ." her lips curled incredibly, "or *pretend* to be."

She ended quite abruptly, eyes swimming, but before he could reach her she had spun on her heels in frantic retreat, sobbing broken-heartedly.

"Of all the B.F.s," Sam muttered, disgusted with himself.

Experience had taught him that as a stone thrown into a pool starts up countless ripples, so can a brooding woman widen the range of her grievances.

Suppressing an affectionate but unmistakable smile, he

355

hastened off to make his peace in the bedroom they now shared as of old.

*   *   *

As soon as the ring prices for the last race of the first day of the Newmarket Craven Meeting began to come through on the blower, Sam Pilling left the office. When crossing to the parking-place in the middle of Market Square he nodded to his cousin, James Wainwright, who, preoccupied and worried-looking, did not respond.

"He's probably mislaid all the property deeds of a Building Society," thought Sam uncharitably.

His destination was the yard of Messrs. Roebuck & Son, Ltd., in Huddersfield Road. On arriving there he was told by a clerk that Jim was expected shortly, and so he went into the private office to wait, whiling away the time by glancing through a glossy-paged technical journal. A double-spread advertisement in the centre captured his attention, setting out as it did the manifold activities of Entwistle and Partners, the Manchester contractors; among these were mammoth sports arenas, airfields, and towering steel and cement erections. One of the pictures was of men at work on a lofty Admiralty mast, the caption above which riveted Sam's attention.

"Well, I'm hanged!" he ejaculated. "I never knew they did steeplejack stuff. I wonder if I could interest Peter Entwistle in this show here?"

He was considering the possibility when the clerk came in to inform him that Jim was staying at Doblea Mills, where Roebucks had been entrusted with straightening the chimney, which had gradually leaned over until it was now nearly three feet from the vertical.

On hearing this, Sam left the office, but paused in the yard, where he surveyed rope store, electric motors, cradles, bosun's-chairs and so on—as though already he was gathering together the salient features for a sales talk.

Doblea Mills was farther up Huddersfield Road, and as he reached there Jim was on the point of leaving for St. Paul's Church in Scargate, where he had another gang working.

"No, don't let me detain you," Sam said. "All I've to tell you is that we're meeting your grandfather at eight o'clock to-night at my office."

"I'll be there, Uncle," his nephew said. "Anything else?

Though I think you made my part clear when we discussed it on Sunday."

"Yes, a very negative one," Sam remarked grimly. "There's been so many lies told that if two of us are at it we might very easily contradict one another."

After this they separated, Sam wandering to the foot of the chimney, from which a line of brickwork had been cut out half-way round the circumference. In the gap, jacks had been placed, on which the full weight of the chimney rested. When preparations were completed these jacks were powerful enough to raise one side of the chimney, until they brought it back to a plumb-line position.

Vincent Uttley was in charge of this ticklish operation, and Sam had a talk with him. The nature of that talk would have surprised Milly, just as she would have been surprised could she have eavesdropped on a conversation or two her husband had had with Maggie Batten.

As he passed Bankdam Mills when returning to town, Sam chuckled. "Well, I may be that little fellow Cupid before I've done," he said to himself.

In a very mellow mood he looked in at the County Club, where he joined a group very knowledgeably arguing about Yorkshire's prospects in the coming cricket season.

Early that evening Bee Hirst called for Nancy, which at once meant extra liveliness in the house, to none of which Archie contributed. Collecting text-books and foolscap, he proceeded glumly to the solitude of the dining-room, from which he emerged twice, the first time to speak to Alec Murgatroyd, who was suggesting a binge in Bradford.

The second call, from Frank Thornton, merely implemented the first, and sought to persuade him to change his mind.

"No bloody cash, lad," he growled out in the hall. "What brass I have I earn by the sweat of my brow, and it's damn-all, you fancy-pants motor salesman. Of course it's good for the morale, *they* say, and if you want to have a final despairing shot at making a man of yourself you could try it out. But if ever I find out who *they* are who do the saying, I'll slaughter 'em on the spot."

With that he returned to his studies.

When the two girls were leaving they peeped round the dining-room door to congratulate him teasingly on his industry, to which he failed to respond. Not long afterwards, when his father and mother were in the hall, he started to slam his books together very much in the style of an angry housewife clattering the pots; and, as he brushed by his parents, he passed a few pungent comments on the coefficient of friction and centrifugal force.

"When I compare our palmy days and these," he said, grabbing overcoat and cap. "I say, Dad, do you think Fred Lumb would give me a decent job if I pleaded hard enough?"

Luckily he did not stay after making this suggestion, one likely to be of little appeal to his father, a man who, as a parched traveller thirsts for water, yearned for the day when, with every flourish possible, the town should learn of the trick played on everyone.

Sam dourly inquired how often Archie had showed similar signs of ill-humour about the change in their fortunes, and Nancy, too.

"What on earth are you going on about?" Milly said.

"They've been whining, haven't they?" Sam said, utterly crestfallen.

Milly had always shielded her children but, intuitively realizing the folly of evasion, she admitted that both Archie and Nancy had occasionally been irritable.

"I thought as much," Sam said hollowly.

Energetically she handled that. "And could you expect anything else? Take Archie, who's always had a carefree time, working hard all day and often at his books at night. And Nancy—she's a very pretty girl but she hasn't bought any new clothes for ages, and her pocket-money is now in shillings where it used to be in pounds."

Sam sighed. "The fact is that neither of them has been able to stick it out."

Milly lost patience. "They've behaved splendidly. What do you expect them to be—angels?"

"You're treating it very lightly." Sam shook his head.

She took a deep breath, preparatory to declaring that she had had quite, *quite* enough of his nonsense. And then, reminding him of his appointment, she hustled him along the hall; this degenerated into a struggle exhilarating to both parties.

So Sam left for the office in a much better mood.

The extremely private conference in Neptune Buildings started badly. Although Ezra Sykes had already cast out his grandson Jim Roebuck, along with Archie and Nancy, he apparently deemed it fitting to speak to him about the underlying reason for the gathering there.

"What your mother's sister's husband had to tell you must have been a sad shock, James," he began. "And though it's noan incumbent on me to do so, I cannot help grieving for any young fellow who's just learnt his father was a whited sepulchre."

Passionately Jim rose. "Father was all right, and we'll have less of that, if you please."

Mr. Sykes eyed him. "Oh, and so a chap isn't evil who's dishonoured both himself and——"

Sam banged the desk. "Clem Roebuck was no whited sepulchre. But . . ." he delved into his pocket for a letter, which he threw across to his father-in-law, "but Ramsfield will have the opportunity of judging that question if we don't do something quickly in the shape of a definite undertaking, even if it can't be implemented straight off. Go on, read what she says . . . or what the chap behind her says."

The second letter was a scorcher, and breath whistled through Mr. Sykes's false teeth as he noted the Sunday newspapers which were keenly interested in the story of Maggie Batten and her steeplejack lover.

"You'd be willing to buy off this fallen woman in due course, James?" he asked without further parley.

After that he revealed some of the qualities which had enabled him to amass a considerable fortune, and inside five minutes he had remarked sententiously that it was a son's duty to safeguard his father's good name, if possible. And within ten minutes he had virtually promised on his daughter's behalf to agree to the disposal of the business.

"I shall see her to-morrow night, James," he said, as he pulled himself out of a deep chair. "And I shall tell him . . ." his head jerked in Sam's direction, "the day after, that is Thursday."

"Then I can meet the zero hour she mentions in her letter," said Sam with relief. "First post on Friday morning."

Mr. Sykes desired to call at the Wesleyan minister's house before supper, adding also that he wished as quickly as possible to shake off his feet the dust of evil surroundings, his last sally. When he had gone both his son-in-law and grandson expressed themselves about him very freely. Then Jim accepted a cigar but refused a whisky and soda, and they settled down to a comfortable talk, their deliberations resting on the assumption that the next step would be to find a buyer for the business.

Sam referred at once to Messrs. Entwistle and Partners' advertisement.

"If all goes as we imagine it will, I don't think it would be a bad notion for me to ring up Mr. Entwistle on Thursday or Friday," he said. "I could tell him I was in a position to put him in the way of acquiring a sound connection in this district for your line. No harm in trying him out, is there?"

"Not a bit," said Jim.

Later on, his future was discussed, and Sam was quite dumbfounded by the very contrary nature of the occupations his nephew seemed to be considering, these being the purchase of a bookshop elsewhere or joining the R.A.F.

"I gather by that, Jim," Sam remarked as he savoured the fine tobacco of his cigar, "that you're meaning to leave Ramsfield?"

Gravely, Jim nodded. "Maybe it looks like running away, but the fact is that I can't forget certain things, whether or not other people do."

"Aye, lad," Sam said sympathetically. "That's all right, but you've got to shake it off somehow—you can't live your life repining."

The Town Hall clock was booming ten when they were passing through the vestibule on the ground floor, and Jim Roebuck was probably brighter than he had been for a very long time. At all events, in Barnsley Road, he raced the Chrysler past his uncle's car in fine style, grinning and waving as he shot by.

2

Laura Roebuck's consent to the business being offered for sale was the prelude to a period of intense activity for Sam Pilling, who was particularly heartened at the onset when he found that his original hunch promised to be fruitful. It soon appeared that Messrs. Entwistle and Partners definitely wished to obtain a stronger foothold in the Ramsfield area, and with a willing buyer and a willing seller the negotiations went apace—subject, of course, to the thrust and parry naturally expected when men of Yorkshire and Lancashire are in conflict.

The price of ten thousand pounds for the property and goodwill raised no serious objection, but several boisterous interviews were needed before the Manchester firm would consider taking over the plant, machinery and stores at a valuation, as it had been their intention to start with everything new.

By the third week in April the final figure for purchase had been agreed upon, and, on a lovely spring day, Sam Pilling, Jim Roebuck, and Mr. Geoffrey Ramsden Lister travelled to Manchester for the signing of the contract. Within half an hour of entering Messrs. Entwistle and Partners' fine offices in Piccadilly, the matter had been entirely completed, and Mr. Ramsden Lister, who was returning home by train later, excused himself and, with the purchaser's solicitor, took himself off.

Strange to relate the fiercest battle of all then began, as soon as Jim, informed that his uncle desired a private word with Mr. Entwistle, closed the door of the office behind him. Despite the modern construction of the building, the roar of that battle was heard by executives, clerks, secretaries and typists alike; it certainly carried to the waiting-room, although Jim could not catch the sense of what was being said.

When alone with Mr. Entwistle, Sam mildly inquired how soon he might expect to receive his cheque for commission.

"Ten per cent is reasonable, I think," he continued. "That'll be fourteen hundred for me. Then there's my out-of-pocket expenses, though they'll not amount to much."

"Neither will your commission," Mr. Entwistle snapped. "Why should we pay you anything?"

Sam's eyebrows went up. "Because I introduced the deal to you. And if you remember, when I first telephoned you, I asked if I should go forward with obtaining further particulars for you."

Peter Entwistle scoffed. "I remember nothing of the kind."

"A chap like you, handling so much, can't expect to recall everything," Sam remarked. "But I dare say your files will prove me right. You see I wrote you at once confirming what had been said . . . and you acknowledged my letter."

"You haven't a damned leg to stand on."

"I've two damned good ones," Sam retorted.

"You Yorkshiremen." Deeply grieved, Mr. Entwistle shook his head. "You've no more scruples in business than you have on the cricket field."

"Let's keep off scruples," Sam begged gravely. "I don't

want to have to mention Old Trafford, a couple of years ago."

"And what happened there?" bellowed Mr. Entwistle. "I saw every ball sent down."

All of which made it most extraordinary for Jim Roebuck when, a considerable period afterwards, the waiting-room door opened to disclose two gentlemen on the happiest of terms. His Uncle Sam looked quietly pleased while listening; and Mr. Entwistle was squeezing every scrap of fun out of a lengthy and involved tale—it was a comical story of how Captain Gainsway-Sinkinson had tried to borrow five hundred pounds.

Messrs. Entwistle and Partners were not to take over the Roebucks' business until all outstanding engagements had been finished, the main items among these being a repair job on the cooling tower at the Electricity Works, and pointing up the coping of Hirst & Calverley's stack at Dodthong Mills, on the Island.

"And how high is that chimney at Dodthong?" Sam inquired, once again nipping in the bud his nephew's thanks. "Not big, I hope."

In bright afternoon sunshine they were speeding along a road on the hump separating Lancashire and Yorkshire.

Jim, an intolerable burden shaken off, looked a new man already. "Merely a baby, Uncle," he said, laughing. "About a hundred and twenty feet."

Other affairs were then gone into, Jim proclaiming the intention of giving his mother a reasonable proportion of the money received from the shares left to him, after he had made matters right for Maggie Batten—this, of course, when his family's company had been wound up.

"I don't actually require so very much," he explained.

Far ahead and below, as the road started to dip and bend, industrial Ramsfield began to reveal itself, beneath a slowly drifting canopy of smoke. Nearer, breasting a steep, curving brow, a line of heavily-laden vehicles was approaching, carrying pieces of grey cloth for finishing in Lancashire and goods of various description to Liverpool for export.

Sam, ignoring a situation demanding care, wrestled for his wallet, steering single-handed.

"Wait until I've shown you what I've got here," he chortled.

At the last moment Jim grabbed the wheel. The car

lurched towards the verge, and rolled dangerously before straightening. "Near thing that, Uncle," he gasped.

"They want all the damned road," Sam remarked, smiling about the impending disclosure. "Incompetent devils, some of 'em, not fit to be trusted with anything more powerful than a donkey and cart."

"Aye," his nephew said dryly.

An elastic band twanged as it was tugged from around a wallet. Delving, Sam produced Messrs. Entwistle and Partners' cheque for a thousand pounds.

"That's for Maggie, lad, and never mind your money," he said, grinning. "We'll take it to Southport to-morrow and make her have it, which may not be all that easy."

"And that's what the commotion was about?" Jim marvelled. "Well, I don't know what to say, Uncle . . . how best I can express my gratitude for. . . ."

"Never mind about that," said Sam. "But all the same I'm not quite the numbskull your mother thinks me, am I? Yes, I could make her eat her words if I wished and cause a lot of other Ramsfield folk to look damned silly at the same time. Aye, if I opened my mouth properly. . . ."

"You what, Uncle?" Jim asked.

A brand-new Rolls-Royce was ahead, tooling along sedately with Frank Thornton at the wheel. Sam saluted him jauntily, and then eased down, immensely considerate for a group of cows grazing at the roadside. By then he had taken a vow to keep a closer guard on his tongue.

Uncle and nephew went their different ways in Ramsfield, Jim with long, hopeful strides towards Market Approach and Huddersfield Road, a new light in his eyes except when he met anyone connected with Ramsfield Rugger; and Sam to the office, where he signed his letters, attended to various matters Margaret Berry had noted for him, and with Harry Sutcliffe inspected the credentials of a client in modest circumstances, a bookkeeper and cashier at Ainleys' the Chemists, who for many weeks past had consistently met fairly heavy losing accounts.

On leaving business he walked round the block to Teazle Street, along which he saw Lois Roebuck coming out of Madame Gladys Shires'—Rafe Bottomley was designing her wedding dress.

At Hoyle's he bought a generous piece of fresh salmon, repeating the order when he noticed his brother-in-law, at the front of the shop, examining the fish on the slab. The Rev.

Alonso Dyson was shaking forward and counting the coins in the leather till of his purse when a soft, cold package was pushed into his free hand.

"A bit of salmon, Alonso," Sam said. "Give it to Kate with my love . . . and you might tell her also that that little affair we've sometimes talked about has been completed most satisfactorily."

Mr. Dyson's gaunt face lit up. "I shall be delighted to execute both commissions, my dear fellow." He nodded and then gloatingly added: "And as for this salmon . . . perfection, Sam, my boy. Indeed am I blessed that the rich man, in his charity——"

"Shurrup, you damned fool," Sam hissed. "Everybody will hear you."

By now his brother-in-law had other interests. The Rev. Alonso Dyson's bony grip seized upon the shoulder of a podgy, middle-aged gentleman who was passing by, spinning him round.

"Ah, well met, Wainwright," he said. "My underground channels advise me that shortly you are to be involved in litigation of a personal character."

"You . . . you've nearly tugged my coat off," Sam's cousin stuttered. "What do you mean by grasping me like that, Dyson?"

Mr. Dyson's tone was reproving. "Merely to inform you, my dear Wainwright, that I shall be only too glad, *ex officio*, to place my services at the disposal—of the other side."

Mr. Wainwright broke free and, an uncomplimentary observation escaping him, continued along the street, Alonso Dyson's dark eyes twinkling as he watched him.

There were many people about, and those near were certainly startled by the Rev. Dyson's pleased roar of: "James Wainwright: Ha! Ha!" Then, waving his parcel of salmon aloft, he took up an earlier subject, his voice almost as loud. "This, my dear Sam, this rich emblem of the crumbs which fall——"

Sam did not hesitate . . . he fled.

On the run up to Moorheaton, to which he went by way of Highthwaite Road, he had three not very well-assorted passengers: Kate Dyson, Barbara Ramsden Lister—Mr. Geoffrey Ramden Lister's daughter—and the youngest Roebuck. Throughout, Cora talked as though she were six or seven years older than the other girls, her exclusive theme the splendour of Lois's *trousseau*, with notable details about the underclothing content.

Beyond the homes of Kate and Barbara, Cora still continued to prattle, but her uncle's thoughts were elsewhere as Glenfield drew nearer.

Sam was boyishly agog to tell his wife about the magnificent outcome of the visit to Manchester, but wondered just how his story would be received.

Milly, for quite a fortnight, had been a little strange in her manner: not peevish, not ill-tempered—but somehow different.

When Sam went in home Nancy met him in the broad back passage. He gave her the salmon and a message for her mother, and then withdrew to the study.

Milly soon appeared, in business-like apron, and when he recounted the day's doings she was as pleased as he could have wished, and by no means niggardly in her congratulations.

"And now I've another surprise for you," he said. "I want you to go with me and Jim to Southport to-morrow . . . for a very special sort of ceremony, handing over the cheque to Maggie."

It was very short notice, but Milly never blinked. "All right," she replied immediately. "I haven't anything really fixed, except to go round the orchard with Johnson. Yes, I'd love to, Sam."

Nothing wrong there. However, within two minutes—during which the letter-box clicked and she went out and returned with a large envelope delivered by her sister's maid —Sam guessed why her manner had been strange of late: they had not until now received an invitation to Lois's wedding.

Never before had Sam seen her in such a rage. "Look at this," she said, holding up a rectangle of pasteboard with shaky hands. "It's for you and me and Archie only—and it's nothing more than a nasty slap about Nancy and Philip. Good heavens! If Laura had a ha'porth of sense she'd have realized she was perfectly safe in being polite, by inviting all four of us, because wild horses wouldn't have dragged Nancy, not after the way her aunt's raved about her. And she's safe with me, now, nothing would persuade me to go."

"Nor me either," said Sam. "Not likely."

"The insolence," Milly cried. "For two pins. . . ."

After his first onrush of anger, Sam's next thought was

that if relations with next door continued to deteriorate he would have to replace the dividing wall in the main garden, which Clem and himself had with such pleasure seen demolished and carted away.

"Yes, I'm going staight over to Laura about this cheap insult to Nancy," Milly declared, fumbling with her apron-strings. "I couldn't eat a thing until——"

Sam shook his head. "I shouldn't. You'll only stir up dirty water."

Milly differed. "I want to stir up all the dirty water I can."

"Far better to make her feel small," said Sam. "Why not send her a very courteous note saying how sorry we are we shan't be there . . . treat it airily. Anyway, let's talk it over after supper—or better still after I've been down to the George—there's a chap there I'd like to see."

Despite this appointment Sam did not leave the house as soon as the meal was over. While Nancy and her mother were washing up he sneaked to the wine-cellar.

"No," he muttered when down below. "Port's more suitable for her than champagne. I'll take a bottle of whisky as well, and some cigars."

Armed with the bottles, he reconnoitred carefully, and then stealthily left the house by the front door and a round-about route to the garage, where he inspected the junk which disfigured it.

"Enough for anybody to start up housekeeping," he remarked to himself. "Well, if there's a box, and I can find some straw, that will do nicely."

Ten minutes later he set out in the Bentley for Cuddling Lane, where he had a lively talk with Vincent Uttley. When he left there, the foreman steeplejack travelled as his passenger, but was dropped off at the bus stop in Penny Lane.

Whether or not Milly had been awaiting his return Sam did not know, but she came out in the twilight to meet him.

"I've been thinking it over, Sam, and I'm sure you're right, even if it is absurd for sisters living next to each other to be exchanging formal notes," she said. "But would you help me with it? You're such a dab-hand at concocting things. And I *would* like to make her bite her lip."

Sam shrugged deprecatingly. "Nay, I'm not so wonderful, love."

"Yes, you are, dear," she said, supremely sure.

Together they rolled the garage door into position and

then, arm-in-arm, walked homeward to construct a few lines for Laura's discomfiture.

*　　　*　　　*

Both Milly Pilling and Jim Roebuck had a great surprise when Sam, at the door of a small house in Southport, stood aside to let them precede him. Maggie was in the kitchen, but they hardly expected to see her blushing and radiant, and they were even more unprepared for Vincent Uttley, spick and span in clean linen and Sunday suit.

"And now I'd better inform you," Sam chuckled, "that this little party is to celebrate an engagement."

"Oh, I am pleased, Maggie," said Milly, smiling with delight.

"And *this* is why you came up last night to ask for to-day off, Vincent," said Jim, grinning. "And what a tale you told ... family matters, eh?"

There were handshakes all round and a kiss or two, and then the mistress of the house busied herself with the meal, for which the table was laid. The men began to yarn together, and Milly took the baby into her lap.

"Eh, Mrs. Pilling," Maggie said with a giggle, "who'd ever believe you'd a grown-up son and daughter."

Jim was laughing. "She looks exactly as if she'd presented me with a new cousin."

Milly turned to him. "Don't be *so* silly," she said.

Meantime Vincent Uttley was expressing his thanks to Sam for bringing Maggie and himself together. This he proposed to mark by removing his racing account from Ben Buckley's, provided he was granted the same credit, twenty pounds.

"With pleasure," said Sam. "And I appreciate it, Vincent."

"No limit on winnings, I suppose?"

Sam made an entry in his pocket-book. "A book of my rules will be posted to you tomorrow. If the facilities I offer aren't as good as Ben Buckley's I shall be astonished."

"Aye," the foreman steeplejack nodded, "I've oft heard you're very liberal in your interpretations of moot points."

"Well, I don't wish to blow my own trumpet, Vincent," Sam said expansively. "But . . ." At that stage he glimpsed his wife and Maggie, who were smiling and nodding to one another.

"You must be patient, Maggie," Milly remarked. "They haven't as yet got on to next Wednesday's Chester Cup, or the Grand Jubilee at Kempton to-morrow week."

"Are we holding anything up?" Sam asked sheepishly.

"Oh, just something to eat, that's all, dear," said Milly.

"See what you're in for, Vincent," Sam said.

It was the jolliest of meals, with toasts drunk in tea, beer, whisky or port, according to taste. But this congenial atmosphere changed subsequently when Vincent Uttley, who was joggling the baby on his knee, made his views felt about Maggie accepting money for the child.

"I'm a steeplejack not without a bit of a name, and I can always addle enough," he said with quiet pride. "Besides I'm real fond of the little lass, and she'll have everything she requires."

"Yes, that's all right, Vincent, but——" Jim began, nearly blundering by pointing out that the baby was, after all, his half-sister. But his Uncle Sam's: "Now listen, Vincent," and his Aunt Milly's fortunate touch: "Anybody can see she's the apple of your eye, Mr. Uttley," forestalled the introduction of a false note.

Then Sam played his trump card, by exhibiting Entwistle and Partners' cheque in support of his contention that the money would come neither from him nor the Roebucks, making out the best case he could for this. That turned the tide and shortly afterwards he seated himself at the table and, watched by all, wrote out his own cheque for a thousand pounds.

"Keeps it darker this way," he explained, presenting it to Maggie. "If I gave the other cheque to you, you'd have to write your name on the back, and someone in Manchester might wonder. But if it goes through my own account . . . well, so far as the curious are concerned I've had the money and that's all. Nothing like tying all the loose ends up."

Maggie was overcome. "You have been good to me, Mr. Pilling," she gulped. "To both of us for that matter, hasn't he, Vincent . . . *hasn't he, Vincent*? Been *good* to us?"

The foreman steeplejack, to prove his independence to Milly and Jim, was remarking knowledgeably: "Mind you, this brass will be banked away, and not a penny piece used until she's twenty-one, when it will be hers." Then Maggie's voice reached him.

"He has that, love," he switched hurriedly, "and I've been trying to tell him so."

"Then you can try a bit more, Vincent," Sam said. "Because I've put in a good word for you with Mr. Entwistle and . . . well, you'll see, and a lot will depend on yourself."

Before the engaged couple's thanks became embarrassing, Sam spoke about their wedding, which was to take place as soon as possible.

Vincent Uttley was returning to Ramsfield by the last train, and so he and Maggie, who held the baby in her arms, saw the visitors off from the door of the little house.

"Well, I think it's a splendid solution," Milly said as they were driving through the streets of Southport. "But Sam, you *are* a dark horse. Isn't he, Jim?"

Sam, very grave, turned his head. "Jim," he began, "I want you to understand thoroughly that before I told Uttley about your father and Maggie I made sure of my man. He's all right, and he'll never breathe a word. And if I couldn't be a hundred per cent positive beforehand, I was as soon as I'd done it. When I'd said it was your father—'the boss' as he called him —well, I hadn't a vestige of doubt. You know, lad, your father was very quiet and unassuming, but somehow . . ." Sam's voice broke just so slightly, "but somehow folks were very fond of him."

"Yes . . . they were," Clem Roebuck's son said softly.

They arrived in Ramsfield in the early evening, Jim as a precaution leaving the car at the bus terminus in Manchester Road.

Between the Chemical Works and the traffic lights at the junction with Barnsley Road, Sam sneezed five times.

"You've got cold," Milly accused him. "You should never have worn that white shirt."

Sam sniffed. "Why, was it a damp 'un?"

Milly enunciated clearly. "None of your shirts are ever damp. But you could have put a thicker one on, couldn't you? This is the last day of April, not the last in May."

"Cup Final tomorrow," said Sam. "Sunderland and Preston North End. Well, there won't be an illuminated bus here this year, carrying the Cup and the Town team on a tour of the district."

"You men," Milly remarked with asperity.

This trifling clash did nothing to affect an opinion they both shared, that it had been a most satisfactory day.

*　　　*　　　*

According to his carefree declarations, Sam's cold was fast clearing when Philip Illingworth, in plus-fours, arrived at Glenfield on Sunday afternoon; but on returning home after eighteen holes with his daughter's young man he cast all pretence aside. Groaning audibly, he sank into his chair in the drawing-room where, old remedies best, he disposed of a stiff whisky.

"Just flying in the face of providence, you playing today," Milly chided him.

"Yes, dear," Sam agreed, quite die-away.

In a little while, however, he began to take an invalid's interest in a group of young people, particularly Kate, who was bragging about the good head she had for heights, a topic he thought she would have avoided in Jim's presence. To counter this, Archie was asserting that he felt perfectly safe, notwithstanding attenuated resources, in promising her a pair of silk stockings if ever she reached the top of a three-storey ladder without screaming her head off.

"Pooh!" Kate grimaced. "It wouldn't be worth the effort."

Archie laughed. "All right then, I'll increase the spoils and I'll increase the height at the same time. If ever you climb anything that's a hundred feet high, a cliff or anything else, and get down under your own steam, I'll make the stockings half a dozen and throw a pair of gloves in as well."

"Fair enough," Scipio commented. "What say, Kate?"

His sister shrugged elaborately. "Only that the loot is as good as mine one day or other."

Archie grinned. "Trustworthy witnesses, remember."

About this time the front-door bell rang, and Philip Illingworth, who much to Sam's and Milly's amusement was making himself more and more a member of the family, went off to answer the summons. For a young man whose emotions were usually well concealed he returned decidedly out of countenance, with the news that Mrs. Roebuck was the caller.

"Laura!" said Milly, sitting bolt upright. "Er . . . thank you, Philip," she managed to say graciously, but, impressions instilled into her in youth of what was due to the Sabbath prevailing, thrust her knitting with such abandon under a cushion as to ensure for herself later a homeric struggle picking up dropped stitches. "I'll . . . I'll go to her," she ended, glancing swiftly towards her husband.

Groaning, Sam hoisted himself out of his chair, to follow her into the hall, where, to his surprise, Laura seemed more apprehensive than aggressive, and certainly the wind had been taken out of her sails.

"But . . . but, Milly, people will talk if none of you come," she was saying. "And then there's Father—he could easily suspect there's more in it than I've made out, and there isn't. Not," she added hastily, "that I intend referring to Nancy again."

"I'm very glad to hear it, Laura," Milly remarked with dignity. "But I'm afraid it is quite impossible for us to attend the wedding."

"Well, you know how my father is about family affairs, and he's not going to like it, and you're all enough in his bad books as it is," Laura solemnly warned her. "And if he takes strong objection to your attitude—well, you won't talk so clever if when he's passed away there was nothing left to you. And you couldn't expect me to—how shall I put it——"

"Do any private sharing afterwards," Sam said thickly. "And if you think I'm standing here arguing about dead men's shoes and catching more cold into the bargain you're mistaken."

Laura drew herself up. "I realize now my call is a mistake, but I made it from a sense of duty and I shall tell Father so, because I'm not going to be blamed," she said, turning to stalk majestically away. On reaching the inner door of the hall, she paused for a last cutting word. "People in your position would do better with your feet on the ground, but you'll regret your folly one day."

When she had gone, Sam, forgetful of the germs he carried, put his arm round Milly and was hugging her comfortingly when he sneezed unexpectedly, the violent spasm shaking them both.

"Sam, go to bed," she said. "Or it'll get a real hold on you."

"It's got a real hold already," Sam said dolefully. "I'm very bad this time, Milly."

"I'll find a couple of hot-water bottles," she said.

But Sam, loathing bed in day-time, insisted upon staying up despite her remonstrances. The next morning he was not fit to go to the office.

This was a circumstance which every member of the family hailed with thankfulness at a secret noontime conference in the second bathroom on the first floor.

3

Freshly posted that Monday morning, the hoardings of Ramsfield carried a striking announcement in scarlet lettering. It ran:

Some say they always pay
But

WHY IS BEN CORNERING ALL THE BUSINESS?

Try him for yourself

YOU'LL GET IT—OTHERS HAVE

BEN BUCKLEY
RAMSFIELD'S PREMIER TURF COMMISSION AGENT

Of the Pillings the first to see it was Nancy who, after dropping her mother near the Parish Church, had driven to Thorntons' for petrol. Three specimens were in glaring sight: on the end wall of the Vaults, at the far side of the station, and spread over the front of Fred Lumb's place of business, across Market Square.

The petrol-pump attendant heard her gasp. "And what's your father going to say to all that clustered in view of his office window, Miss Pilling?"

"Heaven only knows," she replied aghast.

Her mother's experiences were somewhat different. To begin with she had a chat with Frank Thornton's mother about the difficulties of Mr. and Mrs. Simeon Calverley, whose seventeen-year-old, sensationally made-up daughter refused to give up Mr. William Pobjoy's son, a man of nearly forty with four children.

Then Milly, pleasurably reflecting that Mrs. Thornton had been extremely friendly that morning, continued along Teazle Street past Madame Gladys Shires'.

"A really nice person," she was telling herself when, out of habit, she glanced at the window tables on the second floor of Wood's Café. The extraordinary thing then was her impression that a number of ladies leaned forward to stare down at her. This she dismissed as pure imagination, but nevertheless when cashing a cheque in the Ramsfield Commercial Bank's marble-pillared chamber, she suspected the glimmer of a smile on the lips of the cashier as politely he handed her the notes.

Further shopping momentarily forgotten, she examined her face for comically placed smuts in the mirror of her compact, and then crossed the street to Ainleys' the Chemists.

There, on the pavement, she surreptitiously inspected herself from smart hat to neat shoes; the front of her beautifully tailored suit received every attention and, by craning her head over her shoulder, so did the back.

Completely baffled, she was contorting herself anew when she glimpsed Ben Buckley's challenging statement; it was at the opposite side of Huddersfield Road, on the end of a building beyond the Theatre Royal.

Dumbstruck, she remained rooted as she read. "Oh!" she gasped at last, stamping her foot, "wouldn't I enjoy telling Fred Lumb what I thought of him."

Archie, scorching away at midday from the works of Murgatroyd Conveyors, missed what Church Street and the Ramsfield Bridge neighbourhood had to offer in this connection, but as he raced into Barnsley Road the splash of colour on the tower of the Regal Cinema caught his eye. Braking savagely, he nearly went over the handlebars of the Norton, but oblivious of the crude comments of drivers slowing down to circle round him, he remained in the middle of the road.

"Hell's bells!" he said, still gazing up. "Hell's bloody bells."

This sharp observation he was to repeat thrice more, in Roydlea, as similar exhibits loomed into view, and, as soon as he rushed in home, he knew from the expressions of his mother and sister that they were well-informed.

Immediately it was practicable, they took council together, for security reasons a bathroom housing the conference.

"Daddy will go through the roof," Nancy said.

"And to *think* that I used to like Fred Lumb," her mother said. "I could kill him."

Inspired, Nancy slapped the wash-basin. "He mustn't see them . . . ever. We've an excuse for not letting him out——"

"But a cold doesn't last for ever," Milly interposed. "Just now he's sure he's dying—you'll find Philip's just the same, Nancy. . . ."

From his perch on the lid of the lavatory seat, Archie's uplifted hand stayed his womenfolk.

"All we've to guard against is this week," he said, grinning. "They'll be covered over with new posters next Monday."

Milly was resolved. "Then he's not going out before then. I'll slip to the office and make certain that neither Harry Sutcliffe nor Margaret Berry mentions anything if he rings them up, as he will, of course."

The party broke up. At the foot of the stairs mother and daughter worriedly discussed the risk of pneumonia—their anxieties must have been heard by the solitary inmate of the drawing-room, who was huddled over a huge fire.

Tuesday passed most successfully, helped along by a parcel from Gilbert, containing presents for all; there was also a letter from Captain Crummock, reporting very favourably on him, with an intimation also that the ship would be returning to England the following month.

Wednesday offered no difficulties, although in the afternoon, when alone in the house, Sam telephoned to Ben Buckley's whose principal had eagerly been awaiting events.

The play-actor in him in the ascendant, Fred Lumb seemed not at all surprised when the young lady on his modest switchboard gave him a message to the effect that the fabulously-wealthy owner of last year's Derby winner desired a word with him.

"I've been expecting this, Elaine," he said solemnly. "I'll take . . . er . . . His Highness's call from my own room. And you hurry off just as you are to the Public Library and find out his London address. I can't ask a chap like him where he hangs out."

The risk of untoward listening-in averted, he went off with gleeful anticipation, but at the telephone, when his employer began to talk of very ordinary matters, he soon became quite nonplussed. The sparkle, however, returned to his eyes when he realized the position.

"Oh!" he said with a wealth of understanding. "So you're laid up, Sam lad. Well, I am sorry about that, and I do hope you won't be long before you're out and about again."

A few minutes later, a little affected by the sympathy so lavishly extended to him by his old friend and colleague, Sam wandered into the kitchen, where he stood in the window watching workmen who, on the Stonewood end of the big lawn, were erecting a large marquee and a canvas connecting-passage for Saturday's wedding reception.

"I'm not sure if I shan't take Fred's advice tomorrow," he murmured. "Fresh air *can* blow away a cold, as he says, and so long as you haven't a temperature it's safe enough."

Still touched by his old henchman's wishes for a speedy recovery, Sam began to think about him.

"He's done well, and before long now I'll give him a cheque for himself. Aye . . ." he chuckled, "and I'll make it a handsome one, too, for he's bound to feel silly when everyone in the town knows that Ben Buckley's is mine. By Jove, won't it be a sensation!"

Lost in sweet dreams along this line, the time passed quickly enough until Milly and Nancy came home.

That was Wednesday.

Thursday was less smooth, though nothing really serious happened, but by Friday Sam was decidedly restless, and in the early evening it took the combined efforts of the family to prevent him from assuming a policeman-like stance in the middle of Moorheaton Drive—the immediate cause was a short-circuit motor-race, a regularly occurring pandemonium of noisy cars and screaming passengers.

The argument was interrupted by a tremendous crash, the screech of tortured metal, and the tinkle of glass. From the window Archie identified the tangled pile as a Sports A.C., a British Salmson, and a Bug.

Milly was trembling. "Shall I ring up the Hospital?"

"You wait, Mother," Archie said unfeelingly. "You'd be surprised how fatheads like those escape scot-free."

Within a few minutes he returned, to report that beyond cuts and bruises no one was hurt; then he vanished into the hall, where his conversation on the telephone began on solid, business-like terms.

"I say, Frank, I can put you in the way of a couple of hundred pounds of repair work if there's a spot of commission in it for me——"

These negotiations were successful, and he was subsequently able to announce to the others that Thornton's car-ambulance would be starting out at once.

"Yes," he said, grinning, "I'll have a drop more in the kitty before long, thanks to these nitwits."

"Aye," his father growled. "And now I'll have a word with 'em. They nearly scared your mother to death."

"Oh, no, I wasn't," Milly laughed gaily. "The ideas you do get."

"Don't worry about 'em," Archie said hastily. "What about some snooker instead?"

Cunningly Nancy at once raised objections, mentioning that the central heating was now off, and was supported by her mother, who was no less sharp. They went on to such purpose that Sam began to experience a glow of gratification about their deep concern for his well-being.

"Of course, we could warm the billiards room the way you say, Mummy," Nancy agreed judicially.

"Yes, if we fetch both electric fires," her mother said, nodding. "But your father will have to wait until the chill is quite off."

That was that. The crisis came on Saturday, a sunny late spring day, when the master of the house was on the verge of wild rebellion.

CHAPTER THIRTEEN

EARLY on Saturday morning, caterers' vans began to run to and fro along Moorheaton Drive, bringing and fetching food, drink, flowers, and a small array of waiters and other helpers, who took complete possession of Stonewood

At half-past eleven precisely, the bride left home, accompanied in the hired car by her brother Jim.

By one o'clock Moorheaton Drive, in that vicinity, had been reduced to a single lane for traffic; for a considerable distance the cars of guests were parked on both sides of the street, while so many others had driven in that the paved court across the back was almost filled.

Laura Roebuck had certainly made an impressive social affair of her second daughter's wedding.

In the striped marquee, crockery clinked, glassware tinkled, and corks popped; laughter and a steady hum of conversation rose from the guests.

Compelled to leave his car down the road, Philip Illingworth was seen from the drawing-room by Nancy as he walked along the drive soon after lunch. She met and kissed him in the hall, and then whispered: "Quick . . . listen, darling."

When the couple entered the drawing-room, Sam looked up morosely.

"Here again, are you?" he said. "And what's the weather like, eh? Let's have an opinion from an independent source."

Philip frowned thoughtfully. "Rather deceptive, sir. It's bright, but there's no warmth in the sun, and though the wind's slight there's an astonishing bite in it for the time of the year."

"Is that so?" Sam grunted. "All the same, this lot have had me in cotton wool long enough and I'm off out."

"No, you're not," said Milly, as if to a recalcitrant child.

As his response so utterly lacked any conciliatory spirit, Archie jumped into the breach with the suggestion of a turn in the kitchen garden. It had the advantage that none of the wedding guests could stray there, as they would everywhere in the main garden.

"Laura would look damned silly if I ordered everybody back," said Sam, a little appeased as he was helped by Nancy and Philip into the light overcoat insisted upon by Milly. "No, of course, I shouldn't," he smiled, on glimpsing his wife's anxious expression. "I wouldn't spoil Lois's wedding by kicking up a shindy."

Accompanied by his guardians, he proceeded to the back door, where they were greeted by a most astonishing sight, a tall, slim figure racing from Stonewood towards the garage, the tails of his morning coat flying behind. Jim Roebuck's subsequent behaviour was even more amazing: he opened the door of Alderman Joseph Hirst's Daimler, put down his shoulder and pushed, the same treatment being meted out to Mr. Walter Murgatroyd's Rolls-Royce. The two cars gathered a little speed and then collided, to the detriment of the rear of one and a side panel of the other.

"Whatever . . ." Milly gasped.

As the bonnet of the Chrysler came out of the Roebucks' garage, the Pillings and Philip Illingworth were there to intercept it.

"What the devil's up, Jim?" Sam shouted.

Tense and pale, Jim slowed but did not stop as he wound down the window.

"Kate's friend, Barbara Ramsden Lister, has just rung up," he shouted. "She's in the hell of a stew and I don't wonder. Kate's at the top of Hirst and Calverley's chimney and she's lost her nerve."

Already he was accelerating, but Sam leapt forward and scrambled into the moving vehicle.

By the shortest cuts, over lumpy, stone-setted streets and uneven dirt tracks, Jim drove to the Island, his foot hard down and hand continuously on the horn.

"You were there last Sunday when Archie dared her, Uncle," he said. "Apparently she's been after both stockings *and* gloves."

They were racing up the slope eastward of Ramsfield Bridge, past an unending row of houses on one side and the Murgatroyds' textile-machinery works at the other. Men and women scattered and hurled abuse; Sam, jolted and thrown

377

from side to side, clung to his seat and braced his legs harder against the sloping floorboards.

"We'll be able to see Dodthong Mills in a few seconds, lad," he said.

They roared over the brow, beyond which they could overlook the Island as far as the canal, with Hirst and Calverley's mill alongside it. In the streets around they saw people scurrying; farther afield they noticed several groups gazing impotently upwards, towards a small figure kneeling in an attitude about which there could be no doubt.

"She's . . . she's praying, Jim," Sam said.

"And please God," said his nephew, "she'll be able to stick it out a bit longer."

With that fervent plea Sam was still identifying himself when the speeding car braked hard in the mill-yard; another vehicle dry-skidded to a standstill, that of the Superintendent of the Borough Police Force. The news of the sensational event was rapidly circulating.

Swiftly Jim slipped out of his coat and tossed it to his uncle. A coil of rope round his waist completed his preparations.

"You'll know best if we can do anything, Mr. Roebuck," the Superintendent said, "Would it be of any assistance if one of my men volunteered to follow you up?"

Incongruously clad for this undertaking, Jim paused on the second ladder up, to glance down.

"No thanks," he called out. "Three would make a crowd, and I wouldn't care for the extra weight."

Without further ado, he began to climb, watched intently by a growing throng. His foreshortened figure gradually grew less until, at last, beyond the out-bulging top of the chimney, he disappeared altogether from the sight of those standing at the foot below.

The dangerous descent was beginning, heralded by the appearance at the summit of the young steeplejack and the girl, whose bodies, closely knit together, were silhouetted against a patch of mackerel sky. Heads craned back, a crowd of more than a thousand were utterly motionless; the silence was unnatural, broken only by a mass intake of breath when disaster was feared; the click of the telephoto-lensed Press cameras, from vantage points scores of yards away, was heard distinctly by those at the chimney's base.

Rung by rung, in cautious but regular progress, with

occasional stops for rest, Jim brought Kate to safety. Tongues began to wag when the pair were down to thirty or so feet from the ground; a reporter of the *Ramsfield Reporter* and his photographer, together with three or four local representatives of more distant newspapers, pushed forward to await the couple.

Philip Illingworth had driven Nancy and her brother to the scene, and, just as Jim and Kate were swamped by the crowd, Archie began to shove forward to their rescue. As he thrust powerfully ahead he elbowed his father, who just then was pawing ineffectually at his breast pocket to replace the handkerchief with which he had been mopping his brow.

"Sorry, Dad," he said, "but I'm going for Kate. It'll be best if she's whisked straightaway home to Mother."

Sam seemed as if he could not take his eyes off his niece, then being interviewed. Straining his ears he heard her admit wanly, amid the sympathetic murmurs of those in the vicinity, that she had been on the point of fainting when reached.

"It'll be best, Archie," he said, bemused.

Archie bent his head. "I'll tell you what, Dad, this job's going to make a lot of headlines, and am I glad?"

"Why?" his father muttered.

"Because of Jim," Archie replied, his voice even lower. "Nobody will ever call him a funk after this packet. Good lord, there'll be dramatic pictures and harrowing accounts in dozens of newspapers. Everybody will know what he's done."

Sam again went off into a reverie as his son, Jim's coat over his arm, scrummed forward: a memory of Scarborough when Kate had been amused by his fears after she had climbed a tricky and quite respectable height.

"I wonder," he murmured. "But how could she be sure it was Jim who would come to her aid? H'mm! Maybe I could pump that friend of hers."

People were dispersing, and he had no difficulty in finding Barbara Ramsden Lister, who was still upset about her friend's foolishness in risking her life for a few pairs of stockings.

"We were going for a walk from Scargate across the moors to the Bradford Road, Mr. Pilling, and we came this dirty way because Kate swore it saved at least a quarter of an hour." She explained further. "And when we saw the ladders on the chimney it reminded her about the stockings."

A few moments later Sam nodded, after extracting more

valuable evidence. It was clear that during the walk Kate had talked a great deal about Jim's skill as a steeplejack, and the seed had fallen on receptive soil.

"Yes, it was natural for you to think of him as soon as you realized she was in difficulties, Barbara," he remarked. "And, as you say, it was lucky about the wedding reception, for you knew just where to catch him."

The Press were showing signs of releasing their grip on rescuer and rescued, and when Barbara Ramsden Lister ran off to join her friend, Sam wandered across the mill-yard.

"Everything fits in, and I'd lay a hundred against one," he mused. "And, by Jove, Archie's right about the headlines. I can just see 'em—'Girl prays on top of towering chimney' . . . 'Young steeplejack in striped pants and fancy waistcoat saves girl friend' . . . I'll buy every paper there is on Monday."

A few seconds later he chortled, as near to being fully convinced as was possible.

"Yes," he muttered, "this is going to do Jim some good— the little devil that she is!"

His smile was so long in dying that Nancy, chancing to glance in his direction, perceived the welcome change in his humour, which she attributed to relief about Kate. At once she squeezed Philip's arm and whispered to him; the couple then had a most important conversation during which tactics were discussed.

The authorities could hardly fail to take official action about Miss Kate Dyson's exploit: her very least misdemeanour was that of trespass on the premises of Messrs. Hirst and Calverley, whose chairman was Mr. Simeon Calverley. But the Superintendent was of the old school, a very different individual from the Chief Constable, and he and Sam, friends of long standing, thrashed the matter out. It was privately agreed between them that the culprit's fright was sufficient punishment for her; but before she was driven off in Jim's Chrysler, with Archie and Barbara, the Superintendent sternly instructed her to present herself at the Central Police Station the day but one following, Monday, at three o'clock in the afternoon.

As soon as the Superintendent, saluting smartly, opened the door of his car, Sam sauntered off, well pleased with himself. Nancy and Philip fell in with him, one on each side, Nancy clinging to his arm as she animatedly talked about the stirring events of the past hour. In this she was artful enough, with all the advantages of a pretty girl; she teased him about the adroit manner in which he had twisted the Superintendent round his little finger, and, incidentally, led him to a very secluded corner of Messrs. Hirst & Calverley's extensive properties, a stone-paved alleyway between a single-storey dye-house and a five-storey spinning mill.

"Mmm . . ." Sam murmured, glancing about him. "Yes, I think nothing worse will happen to Kate than a severe lecture for her escapade. By the way, love, you wouldn't have any ulterior motives, would you?" he continued, eyeing her. "Flattery is very nice, of course, but you've been laying it on with a trowel, you know."

This observation, and Nancy's open-eyed innocence on hearing it, were too much for Philip Illingworth, who chuckled involuntarily. As for Nancy, she fought to preserve her position and then, dimpling, surrendered wholly. But despite the lines of laughter her voice was anxiously serious.

"Daddy, we're terribly, *terribly* glad about Kate, of course, but——"

Philip was not a young man who cared to delegate an attempt upon one of the stiffer hurdles of courtship.

"Mr. Pilling," he broke in, "Nancy is trying to say there's something you could make us terribly glad about. And it's that you'll give your permission for us to be engaged."

"So that's what the manoeuvring was about?" Sam said.

As the pair drew together, many thoughts flashed through Sam's mind about the love-match, for that was what it would be. He reflected about the great wealth of the Illingworths on the one side, smiling wryly on recalling that, on the other, his own finances were supposed to be in the doldrums. And what was his duty—to remind Philip of his first disastrous mistake in an endeavour to ensure that his second marriage should not be another? But that would hurt Nancy, as the knowledge that she was not the first would always hurt her, and in this moment, one of the supreme moments of her life, he could not do it. But, as he looked at them, he felt comforted: his fears were groundless, merely those of any man with a loved daughter.

"You'll take good care of her, Philip?" he asked.

Philip's grasp on Nancy tightened; his eyes, behind the lenses of his spectacles, began to shine.

"I will, sir," he said huskily.

Radiant with anticipation, Nancy flung her arms around her father's neck. "We can be engaged, can't we, Daddy?"

Sam smiled over her shoulder at Philip. "Yes, I think you can, love," he said.

Probably often on winter afternoons, before the engine stopped for the day, this corner had seen snatched love-making between young workers there. Indulgently watched by Sam, such a thing happened again.

"Well, come on, you two," he said. "There's somebody at home who's going to be very interested in all this."

Unashamedly holding hands, the pair walked blissfully along with him, but it spoke well for both that on reaching the Alfa Romeo they were not too lost in themselves to forget that, billed throughout the district, there was a parody of PILLING ALWAYS PAYS.

Grimacing unseen by her father, Nancy took the first preventive step. "Philip darling," she said, "I don't think Daddy ought to be exposed to the full winds of your chariot."

"Lord, no," Philip remarked with concern. "Tell you what, my sweet, I'll put the hood up."

Sam laughed. "I'm not as frail as all that. If you'll just drive your hotted-up contraption a bit slower than usual——"

"Philip is the most dreadful pot-hunter and *never* drives slowly," Nancy interposed, simultaneously giving her *fiancé* a most pregnant look. "He always finds the most out-of-the-way places and practises for mountain rallies . . . and things."

As the young people raised the hood and, brilliant afterthought, placed in position side-screens with yellowing panels of soiled mica, Sam was filled with warm pleasure at this further example of forethought. Before the trip began he was very much inclined to reproach himself for his ill-humour of the past two days.

A charming young woman sitting on the knee of the young man of her choice may seem to him as light as thistledown, but to her father, fond though he be of her, the burden assumes different proportions, when he is squeezed into the bucket seat of a car driven with racing expertness round corners and over bumps and vicious pot-holes.

At the south side of Ramsfield Bridge, where Philip at Nancy's quick signal spun over the wheel to enter a dreary road alongside the river, Sam had had enough.

"Never mind any more of this 'race round the houses,' Philip," he bawled to make himself heard above the high-pitched scream of acceleration. "Turn right just here, and let's go peacefully up Barnsley Road."

"Oh, but it's such fun, Daddy," Nancy shouted.

"Not for me," Sam retorted.

She might have argued had not Philip closed an eye significantly and crouched lower, mime through which she guessed that henceforth the Alfa's speed would be such as to allow merely the most blurred impression of the passing scene.

In Barnsley Road everything went swimmingly as they streaked up the slight slope, and Ben Buckley's arresting announcement on the tower of the Regal Cinema and another succeeding it were passed in a flash. But higher up, approaching Knowlbank Road, the combination of a car cutting in from the other direction and a lengthy procession of passengers alighting from a bus going their way proved the schemers' undoing.

The hoarding cosily flanked the pavement; on it was one of Fred Lumb's scarlet-lettered posters. The line WHY IS BEN CORNERING ALL THE BUSINESS? seemed to stand out with malignant prominence.

Pop-eyed, Sam had just glimpsed this striking query when his daughter sought to draw his attention to a small building in the middle of the road. In her panic she quite failed to realize that the roof under repair was that of a gentlemen's lavatory.

"Don't you think that's a shame, Daddy?" she said, pointing. "I . . . I mean using those horrible blue slates instead of stone tiles."

One glance at her flushed cheeks was enough for Sam. Heralded by strangled, incoherent sounds, he found voice.

"When a chap's hell-bent for a spot like that he's not inclined to be critical of the artistic qualities of the place," he bellowed. "And now, miss, let's——"

Philip swallowed a laugh. "I can nip through now," he announced, his own voice queer. "Yes——"

"You pull into the kerb and wait for me," Sam roared, jerking his thumb sideways. "But first of all how many of these damned bills of Fred Lumb's are about? They're plastered all over the place, aren't they?"

Nancy achieved a series of shrugs. "Oh, those," she said. "Oh, there are a few certainly. But I don't think people notice things like that much nowadays. You know I'm sure that advertising has . . . has overreached itself."

"Go on, keep it up just as you've done all this week to make me stop indoors," Sam growled. "Oh, yes, I've tumbled to the conspiracy now. 'We'll put the hood up, Philip darling,

383

so that dear old Daddy won't catch cold.' And as for you," he was glaring at his driver, "you've been in it as much as anybody. Anyway, I've business to do, so let me out of this damned coffin."

Unceremoniously thrust from his lap, Nancy nearly came a cropper on the pavement. Her father scrambled out behind her, and started off with tempestuous strides towards a red-painted telephone kiosk farther along.

"Phew!" Philip whistled.

"Pipped on the post," Nancy said bitterly.

In the confined space of the kiosk, Sam searched through his change for coppers. Shortly afterwards he dropped two pennies into the slot, which brought him into contact with Ben Buckley's office, where the girl was so startled by a coarse and most uncivil demand that she switched him through to her employer without asking for his name.

The conversation between Ramsfield's leading turf-accountants was brief and one-sided. Fred Lumb was instructed to present himself at Glenfield that afternoon, with the minimum of delay.

Taking advantage of the sunny afternoon, the wedding guests had left the sultry atmosphere of the marquee and were strolling on the lawn and among the flower-beds when the Alfa Romeo, after describing a serpentine course amid the cars parked in the court, reached the Pillings' garage— where Archie, to whom an ill-running internal combustion engine was ever a challenge, had been bending over the Chrysler's engine until a couple of minutes before, when he was interrupted by his bosom friends.

"Oi!" hissed Frank Thornton. "Rations for the poor and needy."

"And he's industrious, too," Alec Murgatroyd remarked. "Yes, I think I can safely say that the old man and myself are succeeding in making a decent citizen of Archibald Pilling, Esquire."

The shapes of both young men were queer, their morning coats and light waistcoats bulging in the most unexpected places. But after unloading in the garage, virtually a disrobing process, they became quite normal, and a shelf took on the appearance of a well-stocked buffet, with ample champagne on the side.

"Now I see," Archie gloated. "To begin with I thought you two blokes were fresh."

"Not yet, brother," Alec Murgatroyd said.

Frank Thornton had discovered an omission which pained him. "Damn you, Alec, you've forgotten to scrounge a supply of those lobster patties," he was saying as the nose of the Alfa Romeo came into view.

Archie's grin vanished when he saw the expression on his sister's face as she was thrust out of the car.

"Strewth!" he muttered. "The balloon's gone up."

Sam was addressing Nancy. "You stay here until I've had a talk with your mother."

The Roebucks' guests were circling more widely, as Nancy noticed, among them Tony Flassati, to whose arm, laughing drunkenly, her cousin Estelle was clinging. That could be a most distressing meeting.

"Oh, Daddy, we can't stop here," she exclaimed.

"Then take Philip elsewhere, to the potting shed or wherever you prefer, and have a good laugh about how you both chose the right moment to twiddle . . . no, twist it was . . . to twist your father round your little finger."

Thanks to Archie's beckoning, Nancy was able both to avoid an embarrassing encounter and to receive much needed sustenance, but her father was unfortunate—he found his path blocked by three friends as he strode off towards the house.

"Hel-*lo*, Sam, lad," Mr. Dale Watkinson cried out. "Where have you been hiding yourself since Monday?"

Sam's eyes were bellicose. "And what of it?" he demanded. "As a matter of fact I've been laid up with a very severe chill —damn near pneumonia."

"Oh, so that's it," Mr. Walter Crabtree said, as if relieved.

"Do you know, Sam," Mr. Jim Oldfield said confidentially, "daft as it sounds, we actually wondered if those adverts of Fred Lumb's had got under your skin."

Dale Watkinson and Walter Crabtree were abruptly parted, by a pair of arms opening out in breast-stroke motion.

"Nobody's got under my skin," Sam snapped. "And to hell with the whole boiling of you."

Watched with frank curiosity by many people, he continued to Glenfield, where his entry was so tearaway that Kate, sitting by herself, nearly choked over the tea she was drinking.

"Well," Sam glowered, "got over your frightening experience?" To her alarm he leaned so far over the table that their faces nearly touched, his a close-up of protruding veins and red-tinged eyes. "You little fibber," he growled. "Do you think I haven't guessed what you were up to? You were acting, weren't you?"

The shock made her tremble. "Yes, I was . . . but promise me," she continued imploringly, "that you'll never tell Jim or anybody. *Please*, Uncle."

"Deceivers!" Sam laughed unpleasantly. "That's what all women are from birth. You're one . . . your cousin Nancy's another . . . and so's your Aunt Milly. And where *is* your Aunt Milly? Enamelling the gas-fire in the second-best spare-room or distempering the cloakroom?"

The suggestions were so novel and unexpected that Kate, forgetting her own fears, stared wide-eyed at him.

"She's only just gone out of here, with a teapot," she replied. "I expect she's gone to the conservatory, Uncle."

"Oh, that's her other outlet when she's in a turmoil," he grunted. "She'll be refreshing one of her beefsteak begonias."

This concluded the conversation between uncle and niece. Watched speechlessly by Kate, Sam left the kitchen.

Depressingly often throughout that week Milly vaguely remembered Burns's lines: "The best-laid schemes o' mice an' men gang aft agley," and never was she more conscious of them than on the Saturday afternoon when her husband left the shelter of his home for streets in which loudly-compelling advertisements must catch his eye. And so, oppressed still more on hearing of Kate's rashness, she spent a wretched hour until Archie and Jim brought the culprit home. That brightened her, but not for very long.

A great believer in cutting for the promotion of healthy growth, she was nipping off a few seared leaves when Sam entered the conservatory. Very deliberately he closed the door behind him.

"I've still more news for you," he announced. "Nancy and Philip are engaged."

Sheer pleasure drove out more forbidding thoughts. "Oh, I *am* delighted," she exclaimed. "Where are they? I must . . ." Her words petered out. "Aren't you pleased, Sam?"

His tone was ironical as he remarked that Nancy had just taught him how she took exactly after her mother.

"And as for her ability to hoodwink a man—well, you and she are as alike as two peas in a pod."

Sharply Milly pushed a flower-pot into a safer position. "What do you mean by that nasty remark?"

"I know all," Sam retorted.

"Who do you think you are . . . Henry Irving?" she asked. "How do you mean you *know all*?"

"About Ben Buckley's advertisements," said Sam, taking half a dozen turns along a length of coco-matting before halting to deliver his conclusions. "I've never been so hurt in my life," he continued. "While my reputation was being torn into shreds you've pretended to fret about my health—yes, there was a regular traffic all day long to feel my forehead. And why?" He laughed hollowly. "For you own comfort, so that you needn't be inconvenienced if I did carry on just a little about Fred Lumb."

This unfairness quite roused her. "Nothing of the sort," she said. "All we wanted was to prevent you from being upset by something you couldn't do anything about."

"I'll show you whether I can or not," he said, his lip curling back. "Let me tell you I've ordered Fred Lumb to come up this afternoon."

From then Milly began to worry about him. "*Ordered!*" she said.

Sam's attitude was Napoleonic. "But that's only the beginning," he said, gesturing grandly. "To-night I shall tell Archie that as soon as he's competent, he can have eight or ten thousand to buy an interest in a sound little engineering company. And he'll have a new car, of course, next week— any kind he cares to name. And, speaking of cars, I'm ordering a Rolls limousine for you from Thorntons' on Monday, and as soon as it's delivered there'll be a chauffeur to take you out shopping whenever you wish."

Sick with anxiety, Milly abruptly seated herself on a stool, her head whirling.

"And I haven't forgotten Nancy, either," Sam resumed, warming up with excitement. "We'll give her a wedding that will make to-day's look like one in a back street. And for a wedding present she's going to have a house a good deal better than Philip and Estelle had, expensive though that was. What do you say to that?"

Fighting down horror, Milly smiled grotesquely. "It's lovely, but . . . but never mind now, dear," she coaxed him.

Sam had the urge to unburden himself. "I'm going to have Ramsfield talking about me thirteen to the dozen for days on end. And do you know what'll start everybody off? *When they learn who I am.*"

"And . . . and who are you?" Milly faltered.

Sam tapped his chest. "I'm Ben Buckley."

After another frightened glance at his flushed face, Milly made up her mind. "Sam dear," she said as she got up shakily, "for my sake, for all our sakes, you must take care of yourself."

"I'm all right," Sam protested.

To his surprise he found himself being pressed down, forced to sit in a wickerwork chair.

"Of course you are, dear," she said, her eyes swimming. "But I want you to do something to please me . . . and that's to sit quietly here until I've rung up Dr. Lister Fox."

Sam gaped. "Good lord, I've done without him so far this week. What on earth could he do for me now?"

"He . . . could give you a sedative to calm you down," Milly said. "That's all you need, so you mustn't worry."

"A *sedative!*" Sam exclaimed.

For a while, quite astounded, he stared at her, irritably scratching his head. Then, smiling, he hoisted himself out of the wickerwork chair and, taking her hands, held her so that she faced him.

"So you think I've gone off my rocker, love," he said. "Well, before long you may be even more sure about it, because I've a very strange confession to make to you. Now listen, Milly . . ."

He then gave her a full account of the deception from beginning to end, and, as the story developed, her woebegone expression slowly vanished to be replaced by the most profound stupefaction. In itself that was comical enough to Sam, but he laughed outright at the unexpectedness of her first remark.

"And to think how I've put my nose in the air whenever I've met Fred Lumb's wife," she gasped. "I'll never be able to look her in the face again."

Sam chuckled. "She'll understand."

She began to assert herself. "So she's known all about your game, has she? Which is more than your own wife was allowed to."

Scenting stormy weather, Sam attempted to mollify her. "If you'll be fair, Milly, you'll admit that sooner or later you'd have let something slip."

"A nice opinion you've got about me apparently," she retorted in high dudgeon. "Of course I can keep things to myself when it's essential."

Sam pinched her cheek. "Except when that soft heart of

yours is touched. If you'd been aware of the real situation you'd have soon been helping Archie and Nancy out, with a few pounds now and then."

"No, I shouldn't," Milly declared, though not with immense conviction. "Not when it was for their own good."

He lifted her chin. "Now, come on."

She smiled slightly. "Well, I might," she confessed.

Quite unconscious that from then onwards she began to grow troubled again, Sam joyously outlined grandiose schemes for the future, only to be brought up with a nasty jar on realizing he was meeting opposition. Zestful anticipation chilled, he promptly lost his temper.

"Why can't I make a splash?" he demanded. "Haven't I suffered long enough the sneers of those who always sneer at a chap who's had a financial reverse?"

Milly grasped his arm. "You can't, for the children's sake, Sam."

To do him justice, Sam understood exactly what she meant, but he was too stubborn to concede it.

"What harm would it do Archie and Nancy to find out we were almost as comfortably off as ever we were?" he snapped. "They've shown they've both got backbone, which is what mattered."

"It'll do all the harm in the world," Milly urged. "Oh, Sam, at the bottom of them they're proud of how they stood up to the change in our circumstances, but if they learn that their sacrifices haven't been necessary it wouldn't be the same to them . . . it *couldn't* be."

Sam refused to admit there was a fragment of truth in his wife's plea.

"What sacrifices have they made? You talk as if they'd been living on dry bread ever since."

Milly shook her head. "They've made sacrifices all right, Sam, and I don't mean being short of money and so on. There's other things they've had to stick out, and did stick out, but it's hard to bear when you're young and the world's been your oyster."

Sam's fist, crashing down, shook a range of plant-pots. "Aye, and it's been hard to bear for an old codger like me to be set down for the fool he isn't, especially when he hasn't been backward beforehand in letting everybody know how smart he is. Oh, yes, that's my weakness, and I'm not blind to it."

Her lips trembled. "Oh, Sam, you're grand, so don't run

389

yourself down," she said, nearly crying. "I used to be worried to death about the children, and you've done something with them I hardly believed was possible. But you'll spoil everything if you do as you say you will . . . say you won't . . . please, Sam dear."

It was the moment of crisis as they confronted each other, Milly pale and beseeching, and Sam, angrily red, bent on carrying out an intention of which he was ashamed.

"And so you expect me to go on being the laughing stock of Ramsfield?" he asked passionately.

"All I hope just now—is for you to think things over, and not suddenly take any step you might regret," she said.

Furiously he turned from her. "There's no thinking needed," he shouted as he marched off. But at the door he spun round. "And that's final, Milly, absolutely final."

The quietness of the conservatory seemed strange. In that silence Milly could hear the faint sounds of his footsteps, and the thud as he went outside.

Still simmering about a situation which, with aggravating insistency, the voice of conscience told him he could do nothing to ameliorate, and appreciating the imperative need for a period of consideration, Sam had hurried down the ravine, through the kitchen garden and the orchard. Climbing the wall beyond he had then taken a path which ran behind the grounds of the houses in Moorheaton Drive. This brought him to his goal, Penny Lane, along which buses from town came at intervals. Here he knew he must wait if he were to be sure of gaining for himself a respite, that spell of time necessary for wise decision.

Once, in his ill-humour, he groaned aloud. "Of all the bloody fixes to be in . . . this is the day I've been waiting for for months, and there she's got to put doubts in my head."

Far too annoyed to admit, even to himself, that he was not being fair to Milly, and certainly too chagrined at the moment to care, he began to promenade within sight of the bus stop, cheerfully feigning to be out on an afternoon stroll when he met anyone but otherwise looking extremely disconsolate.

His disturbing reverie was rudely interrupted when, at the extremity of the to-and-fro patrol he was taking, he encountered a couple of people on the bend: a man of about forty, very precise in appearance, and a tall and slender young woman whose shapely figure might have been seen to greater advantage had she been attired in a style less restrained and ladylike.

"Why!" Sam exclaimed, pulling up in surprise. "Why, if it isn't——"

Shocked by the suddenness of the meeting, Hilda Schofield flushed painfully. But the rush of vivid colour ebbed away almost as swiftly as it had come, leaving her noticeably pale, the pallor even more intense than was usual with her. Breathing unevenly, she introduced her *fiancé*.

"Well, and so you're getting married, are you, Hilda?" Sam said. "And when is it going to be?"

Lips unsteady, pointed chin with a tendency to quiver, she seemed hardly able to speak just then. Fortunately her companion did not perceive this, and, equally fortunate, he proved to be of a voluble nature. From him Sam learned that the wedding had been arranged for the Saturday of Ramsfield Thump.

"Right, and my very best wishes to both of you, and I hope you'll be happy," Sam said heartily, taking out a notebook. "And I might as well tell you that I shall be sending you a very nice present."

The bridegroom-to-be smiled. "That's *very* kind of you, Mr. Pilling."

Hilda Schofield's dark eyes were on Sam and, so long as he did not look at her, she watched him constantly, longingly, as if she wished to revive and strengthen a picture she would never really forget.

"Kind be hanged." Sam, dismissing unnecessary courtesies, waved his hand after again being profusely thanked. "I'll tell you this, my lad, Hilda was one of the best secretaries a chap could have, and if I can't express my appreciation of what I owe her—well, it's a poor affair."

They parted soon after this, shaking hands all round.

"Good-bye, Hilda," said Sam. "I'm very glad I've seen you again, and all good luck to both of you."

For this once, though fleetingly, she met his eye. "Good-bye," she whispered. Then, a startling change, she smiled brilliantly at her *fiancé*. "Come on, darling," she said.

Tightly linked together, Hilda Schofield almost ostentatiously parading the wealth of her affection as she clung to her future husband's arm, and chattering to him with a vivacity out of keeping with her character, the pair moved off along the road.

Sam, frowning slightly, stared after them, recalling the

expression in her dark eyes before she had turned away.

"Anyone watching 'em would think they were a very devoted couple," he muttered. "But I'm not so positive as all that that she's as happy as she might be. Well . . ." a prolonged sigh escaped him, "well, life isn't a bed of roses and we all have our troubles, and maybe she has hers. I know . . ." he wound up bitterly, "that I've got mine."

Back to his own acute disappointment, gloomy that in all probability he must deliberately rob himself of a triumph he had yearned about for many weary months, Sam again began to amble along Penny Lane.

Some distance away, as yet unseen by him, two vehicles were approaching, a Corporation bus and a more ancient piece of machinery. The latter, belonging to Thorntons' Taxi-Hire Service, was a vintage Rolls-Royce, but it did not lack impressiveness because of its age; the old-fashioned coachwork and solid metal fittings were beautifully polished, and the upholstery inside the capacious body was still in prime condition.

Immaculately dressed, in no manner detracting from the dignity of the equipage, Fred Lumb sat on one of the rear seats. In Penny Lane, however, just beyond the sharp bend in the middle, his consequential pose was interrupted by a gleeful smirk, and hurriedly he rapped on the glass division with a malacca cane. As instructed, the chauffeur slowed, and the car rolled silently to a standstill behind an individual who was scowlingly scrutinizing the passengers alighting from a bus. This watcher whipped round on hearing a squeak as a window was wound down.

"How do, Sam," Fred Lumb remarked, nicely patronizing.

Sam eyed the gleaming conveyance and its occupant. "Keeping your colours flying, I see," he observed.

For the highly-intrigued chauffeur's benefit, Fred spoke very clearly. "I got up by the swiftest means available, as I could tell by your voice what sore straits you were in. My words, and you must be to have come out to meet me."

Spluttering, Sam invited his former manager to saunter along the road, but when they reached a place out of earshot of Messrs. Thorntons' driver, he seemed uncertain how to begin.

"Well, I gather I've touched you up with that advertisement, Sam." It was left to Fred Lumb to re-open the conversation. "I suppose this meeting of ours is for you to tell me the game's off? And haven't I been wreathed in smiles, because I reckoned that within an hour or two I should be free of the affair."

"Why?" Sam gaped. "Why should you want to be free of it?"

People were passing regularly along Penny Lane, and many of them glanced at the pair whose business feud was common property in Ramsfield.

"Well . . ." Fred Lumb murmured as he carefully lighted a cigar, "I'd expected to have some fun, and there's no fun in flogging a dead horse."

"There's been fun all right, but you're the only one who's had it," Sam said bitterly. "And who's the dead horse?"

"Who could it be?" Fred remarked. "You see, I'd always hoped you'd tackle me in my own coin. Ah, well," he sighed, "maybe you were smart enough to know your own limitations."

"Are you inferring I couldn't match you?" Sam snapped.

Elderly shoulders were shrugged. "The proof of the pudding's in the eating, isn't it? You've preferred not to attempt it."

"If I did, I'd make rings round you," Sam growled.

"With all respect, talk's very cheap, Sam," Fred Lumb pointed out blandly. "Anyroad, the opportunity's gone for testing that, I assume."

"I don't . . . I haven't decided," Sam replied.

He fell silent again, perplexities plainly visible in his expression; and in the end he told his old companion and friend about Milly's entreaties.

Fred was most sympathetic, but there is no doubt he also brightened enormously. "Looks as if I shall have to remain in command at Ben Buckley's for the present," he said.

"Well, I can't rush myself into a decision," Sam said. "That's why I'd to intercept you before you got to the house . . . Archie or Nancy or anybody could easily have smelled a rat."

In his element again, Fred nodded. "Aye, and they still will if you and me stand confiding here much longer," he said. "Anyhow I'll fill in a bit of time somewhere while I conjure up some excuse for being in this locality. But . . ." he winked, "you can trust me to pull that off, Sam lad . . . oh! oh! Yes."

With upraised cane he signalled to the chauffeur and, taking with him a strong odour of eau-de-Cologne, climbed into the limousine which, a few seconds later, moved off, although not in the direction of the town.

Meantime, at Glenfield, there was the most acute anxiety upstairs, though life downstairs was proceeding in a very jolly vein. Archie was teasing his sister outrageously about her engagement, and convulsing Kate with an estimate of his despair had she tumbled from Hirst & Calverley's chimney.

The laughter evoked no response in the heart of his mother who, worried to death by his father's absence, patrolled steadily between front and back of the house, pausing briefly at one window before moving along to another with a different view.

"Where can he have got to?" she murmured. "And he was so mad when he left as to be capable of doing something really rash."

The paintwork on a linen cupboard attracted her interest, but while semi-professionally feeling the surface with a finger-tip she thought of a very different matter.

"And what he'll say about that I can't imagine," she muttered to herself. "But he'll have to be told . . . yes, he will."

For the next few minutes, from Nancy's room, she was blessed with a little distraction. The Roebucks' guests were massing round a car to which a lively party of young men were tying an assortment of footwear. Then the bride and bridegroom appeared, with the majestic Mr. Law Watkinson and the no less majestic Mrs. Law Watkinson, both of whom were reported to be most disappointed with their son's match. Augustus Firth and Bee Hirst also captured her attention, as it was being remarked that their engagement was an unduly long one for a young man and woman with wealthy parents.

After the departure of the bridal pair, Milly became ever more apprehensive. "I'll have to go out and try to find him," she decided at last.

It was a resolution from which she shrank when so many wedding guests were about, the thicker-skinned of whom, if they caught her, would inevitably inquire why she had not been to her niece's wedding.

"Perhaps he's smoking a pipe in the greenhouse," she was saying to herself when she glimpsed him on the court below her. His back to her, Sam went steadily on towards the garage, which he entered by the small door in the main one.

"Thank goodness," Milly said with relief.

She would have been with him sooner had not the letter-box clicked as she reached the bottom of the staircase. A letter lay on the highly polished tiles of the outer hall, and within seconds she was eagerly slitting the envelope. Less than two minutes later she was hurrying along the hall, past the baize door, through the back passage, and then outdoors.

Her joy was forgotten when she saw Sam. He was sitting on an old box, a brooding, dejected figure surrounded by broken deck-chairs, tennis equipment, and junk of every description. As she quietly closed the door behind her, his foot thrust against the axle of an old perambulator, sending it careering against the end wall, from which it slowly returned.

"Oh, Sam, I . . . I can guess what you've decided," she said, the lump in her throat intolerably painful, knowing so well what the restraint meant to him. "You're not letting Archie and Nancy, or anybody, know about your trick, that's it, isn't it?"

Smiling, Sam invitingly patted the box. "There's just room, love, so sit down and we'll have a nice talk."

She wrinkled her nose distastefully. "Not on that horribly dirty thing," she declared. "And you're changing your suit as soon as you go in."

"It'll dust off, but anything for peace," he said, laughing. "Yes," his expression suddenly became grave, "I'm leaving things exactly as they are, because you're dead right, love— it'd be foolish to tell them. But I'm a lot more cheerful about it than you imagine."

"Sam, dear," she gulped, "you needn't act with me."

Sam chuckled. "Would it suit you better if I burst into tears? Oh, no, I'm not pretending to be in a seventh heaven, but all the same I'm honestly looking forward to one thing, to do with Fred. Would you believe it, love, but the old devil has really got it into his head that he's smarter than me. And aren't I agog to teach him a lesson?"

This gay determination to make the best of a bad job so affected Milly that, resolved not to let him down, she averted her head to hide the tears springing into her eyes.

"Yes, it will be fun for you, darling," she said. "Though, of course, with you owning Ben Buckley's, you could stop all these stunts of his, couldn't you?"

"What!" exclaimed Sam. "Why, he'd never let me live it down if I did. Besides," he shook his head in rebuke, "it wouldn't be sporting. And so long as he keeps within the advertising appropriation we've agreed on I can't complain, good lord, no."

She couldn't help laughing. "Sorry, dear."

Sam nodded. "And now I'll let you into a secret . . . the profits of the combined business so far this flat are nicely up on the same period last year, so we're not completely crazy. This public rowing between me and Fred is attracting quite a lot of new custom. And it'll attract more when I begin to warm his kettle up—to date, as you know, love, it's me who's always been at the receiving end."

"Yes, you give him what-for," said Milly.

Sam was smiling broadly now. "Good old Fred," he murmured. "This Guy Fawkes stuff has really gone to his head . . . I've seen him, by the way, so he won't be turning up to spill the beans."

"I . . . I *am* happy, Sam dear," Milly said. "What with Archie and Nancy being so different, and . . . and. . . ."

Sam stretched out his arm. "What about me casting an eye over whatever that is?" he asked. "Oh, yes, I'd noticed you were clutching something."

"It's from Gilbert," she said. "And it *will* please you, dear."

Together, Milly stooping, they read their younger son's letter, both laughing at the passage in which Gilbert gave chapter and verse of a profitable book he had been making on the ship's daily run—until this business-like enterprise had been forbidden by the Old Man, as he disrespectfully called his captain. He also breezily announced his intention, on returning home for good shortly, of taking Archie's place in the firm, "to pull Dad out of the mire."

Sam roared with delight. "A chip of the old block, eh? By George, but this has been worth waiting for."

"Isn't it wonderful, Sam darling?" Milly said huskily.

"And don't you dare think I shall be doing any repining after this," Sam said. "What we've done is to pull it off with all three of 'em."

"*You* have, you mean," Milly insisted. "Oh, yes, you have."

"Well . . ." said Sam. "Anyhow, I wouldn't have done it if I hadn't been sure that you'd take it like a trooper when the day came for me to tell you the truth . . . as you did. Yes, love, this just about puts the seal on everything."

Milly's voice changed quite extraordinarily. "There's still something else, Sam."

He glanced up. She was swallowing occasionally, and, trying to speak, made several false starts. But he was not frightened until she blurted out:

"I've been to see the doctor, Sam."

"Lister Fox?" said Sam nervously. "Why, love?"

"I had to," she replied.

Sam vigorously attempted to reassure her and himself. "Now look here, dear, Lister Fox is all right in his way, but when all's said and done he's only a G.P. in a provincial town, and chaps like him can be wrong. What you want is a good specialist, and I shall arrange for you to be examined by the best there is."

She was shaking her head and smiling. "Oh, Sam, it's nothing of that sort. It's only that I'm having a baby."

Sam sprang up so quickly that he lost his balance, and bumped into the steel tommy-bar of the vice bolted on to the well-appointed work-bench fitted up by Archie.

"You're having a baby!" he exclaimed, ignoring the pain. "And however did that come about?"

Milly blushed. "On that trip to London."

"Well . . . well, I'm damned," Sam muttered.

She pouted. "Is . . . is that all you've to say?"

"It's . . . it's just that it's so unexpected, Milly," he explained.

"It took me a bit of getting used to," she confessed. "But I don't mind now."

A grin was dawning on Sam's face as he took her into his arms and kissed her fondly. "I'm thinking of the others, with a baby sister or brother."

"Archie," Milly giggled. "You can't even guess what mad things he'll do with it."

With an exuberant shove Sam sent the perambulator off on another trip. "Milly love, this is going to be fun of another sort. And another thing," he chuckled, "do you realize we're doing what I tried to kid you I was after doing: starting a new family. A caution, isn't it?"

For the next few minutes they animatedly discussed this fresh burden of parenthood. During the talk Sam had a most disquieting thought.

"Was Lister Fox sure it would be all right? I mean you're not as young as you were by a long chalk."

She turned indignantly on him. "You didn't talk as if I were an old woman when we were in London, or behave like it. Licentious . . . that's what you were."

Far from resenting this charge, he appeared gratified.

"Ah, well, there's life in the old dog yet," he said, but then became more serious, remarking that this piece of news did make a difference in another direction. "You know, Milly, you can't keep on slaving away at housework now, and when the baby comes along—well, we're not doing everything on a shoestring. But I'm reckoned to be tight for money. How are we going to explain away a maid or two and a nurse for the baby? For we're having all of them."

Milly laughed. "Oh, that's easy, dear. You'll have to pretend the business is doing better . . . that'll be child's play to you after all you have done."

Deep in thought, Sam frowned. "I'm not sure if you haven't given me an idea . . . yes, maybe you have. More money, sensibly speaking, would be helpful to launch our three properly . . . well, I've got plenty of it, and I'm wondering whether, in addition to my battle with Fred, I couldn't *appear* to be making a lot in some other direction."

"Still after rousing Ramsfield?" Milly said, thoroughly amused.

"Not at all," said Sam austerely. "All I'm contemplating is providing. . . ." Then he grinned. "Well, maybe so, love."

They were joking about his weakness when the small door of the garage was opened by Archie. With him were his sister and Kate, and Jim and Philip.

"And what are you two doing in here, Uncle?" Kate inquired.

"Ah!" Sam, staring rather hard at her, wagged a finger. "That's a secret. And, Kate love," he continued, "I'm one of those chaps who can keep a secret to myself."

Kate was rewarding him with a grateful smile when Nancy asked why the party was being held there.

"Bailiffs soon coming to seize the family pile?"

"Not until Monday," her mother said.

Archie groaned and covered his ears as for the third time, out of habit, his father sent the squeaky-wheeled perambulator on its short outing. To any ardent engineer's soul a lack of oil ranks high in the lists of indictable crime.

"Why *must* you do that, Dad?" he said.

"Oh, I'm just getting my hand in, lad," said Sam.

This jocular remark had important and immediate consequences: Nancy, a young woman newly engaged to be married and thinking it applied to her, coloured painfully at the unnecessary vulgarism and looked perceptibly distressed; while her mother at once began edging towards the doorway.

"Good gracious, I shall be losing my head if I'm not careful," Milly declared, in a voice that was a trifle high-pitched.

"Something I've forgotten in the house, and I must run off. Of course it has been a topsy-turvy afternoon, hasn't it?"

Waving vivaciously over her shoulder, her back to them all, she fled out of sight round the jamb of the door.

"What on earth . . ." Sam started off, and then thought better of it. "Aye," he resumed, "I reckon I'd better go in myself . . . I've strict instructions to change before I sit down anywhere in the house . . . that mucky box I've been sitting on."

As he went out Nancy and Kate were eyeing each other, while Archie, lips pursed as if he were about to whistle, closely scrutinized a couple of tyres hanging from a rafter overhead.

Undeviatingly, without hesitation, Sam tracked down his wife to precisely the place he expected, their bedroom. She was in a fine fury.

"Whatever possessed you to make that remark about the perambulator?" she stormed. "About getting your hand in, I mean. It was just as good as telling them I was having a baby. Why ever did you do it?"

Sam smiled ruefully. "To tell you the truth, Milly, I wasn't even thinking about our . . . our addition. It just slipped out."

Complete disbelief was in her eyes. "It's an extraordinary coincidence, isn't it?"

"Not a bit," said Sam, opening the clothes-closet. "Because it's just the sort of smart-Alec joke any chap playing about with a pram might come out with. As a matter of fact, poor Nancy thought I was hinting at being a grandfather."

Milly softened appreciably. "You don't think they'll have guessed then?"

"Not an earthly," said Sam stoutly, as he took off his coat. "That is, unless you've given something away yourself."

Unexpectedly she giggled, but clapped a hand over her mouth and jabbed towards the floor on hearing voices below.

"I might easily have," she whispered, eyes dancing. "You see when Dr. Lister Fox's receptionist rang up one evening about my appointment, Archie answered the phone."

"And how did you get out of that?"

Milly smiled. "I spoke to her, of course, but afterwards I made an awful fuss to Archie, complaining how people are so careless these days."

"Careless!" Sam ejaculated. "What *do* you mean?"

She blushed. "Not what you do." When her confusion passed she developed quite a prideful air. "Oh, I said to

399

Archie: 'How in heaven's name could anybody mix up Sam and John Arthur? They're so different.' "

"And *now*," emphasized Sam, "it's as clear as a bell."

She reacted strongly. "You are dense sometimes, Sam. Don't you understand I made out there was a mistake, that the message was for Mrs. John Arthur Pilling—you know, Pillings' the sports goods shop, where you bought that idiotic rowing-machine."

"Brilliant, love." Sam chuckled. "Yes, after that, you needn't fear you've given anything away, not an inkling. Of course," he went on, teasing her, "if we hang about here much longer they might begin to wonder."

She acknowledged his humour with a bright nod, but nevertheless the bare possibility caused her to scurry to the dressing-table where she worked swiftly with powder and puff. Very shortly afterwards they were companionably descending the stairs, discussing the repainting of the linen cupboard.

The drawing-room door was open and so, for the last six steps into the hall, Mrs. Sam Pilling even more energetically outlined her plans for treating gold scroll-work on a green background of egg-shell finish.

The party in the drawing-room were amusing themselves with the supplement of a dictionary, which gave Christian names and their significations. Unfortunately neither Nancy nor Kate was listed, but those for the men were more comprehensive. Gilbert: "yellow-bright, famous," James: "a supplanter," and Samuel: "heard of God," which raised a roar of laughter.

Archie, "extreme boldness," was grinning wildly as he pressed his cousin Jim, the reader, for further revelations, but Kate, whose head was also closely over the book, anticipated him.

" 'Philip,' " she cried, " 'a lover of horses.' "

"Internal combustion 'uns," Archie hooted.

"It's on the right lines," Nancy said, laughing loudly. "Speed-merchants with flying scarves and charioteers with flailing whips."

Convulsed to a degree the circumstances hardly seemed to warrant, seemingly none of them were aware of the couple in the doorway. Milly's face depicted a wide range of emotion.

"Now then, what's up?" Sam inquired.

He glanced at them pleasantly, a man ostensibly delighted

that young people could so enjoy themselves beneath his roof. In turn he was eyed in all innocence, by Archie, nearly flat on his spine in a chair, and by Nancy, blooming with happiness, who was sharing the curved piano stool with her *fiancé*. Kate and Jim were crowded at one end of the large sofa, and Sam's gaze rested on her longest, with perplexity, for she looked different to him: much more a young lady than a schoolgirl. Had he known it there was no mystery about this; her own clothes soiled by the afternoon's exploit, she was wearing a tweed skirt of Milly's and a soft cashmere sweater belonging to Nancy—these ladies had also given her a new hair-do, and, under instruction from both, she had used lipstick and powder to telling advantage.

"Well, I don't remember quite how it started, sir," Philip Illingworth said, in his grave vein. "We got to talking about——"

"Yes, how did we, Philip darling?" Nancy intervened, her forehead screwed up quite unnaturally. "Isn't it funny how one starts discussing the most extraordinary things?"

Jim, changed into flannel suit from sadly damaged striped trouser and pale grey waistcoat, had apparently abandoned the wedding reception. "Anyway, what it led up to was the fantastic names parents sometimes inflict on their offspring," he said.

"You should hear what Scipio says," Kate giggled.

From a prone position, Archie addressed his remarks to the ceiling.

"As an engineer of some repute, I favour more rational methods," he said. "For instance, wouldn't it have been simpler if I'd been Pilling 1, Nancy: Pilling 2, Gilbert: Pilling 3, *and* . . . er . . . so on?"

Milly's peal of laughter startled everybody. "The ridiculous things you silly creatures talk about!" she exclaimed, smiling dazzlingly before beckoning to her husband, her behaviour that of a very lively matron. "Anyhow, Sam dear, will you come into the study while I remember? It's a bill of Ainleys', which I'm perfectly certain we've paid?"

"Ho! Ho!" Sam murmured. "Ainleys' the Chemists, eh? This may be interesting."

He stayed behind long enough to comment to Archie upon a certain client's account, at the business, which was already under investigation. The gentleman in question was employed by the firm mentioned.

When Sam went into the study, Milly, statue-like, was

standing in the window gazing into remote spaces. This immobility ended when she heard him come in.

"They've guessed," she said.

"The woman who was never wrong," Sam said.

That fired her. "You tiptoe into the hall and listen at the drawing-room door," she said. "*Then* you'll discover what they're talking about."

"A shocking suggestion," said Sam coldly. "Really, I'm surprised at you, Milly."

For this, he received a hoydenish push, which sent him a few feet in the desired direction. "It would only be to prove my words, and not a nasty sort of eavesdropping," she declared. "Now off you go."

And so Sam started out on the journey, a very short one.

The drawing-room door was partially open, and through a slit he was able to obtain a comprehensive view of the occupants. They were strangely silent apart from Kate, who was being shaken by Jim, himself grinning broadly; she had stuffed a handkerchief against her mouth but this did not stifle all her gurgles. Philip Illingworth's eyes were crinkled with mirth, and Nancy, her face burrowed into his chest, was heaving uncontrollably. And Archie, in the same position as before, almost on his back, clapped his hands steadily but never allowed the palms to meet, the sole sound the tinkle of his cuff-links.

The observer, having digested this, withdrew as quietly as he had come, grinning almost as broadly as his nephew.

"Just what I expected, the young limbs," he muttered.

Milly was all ready for him when he entered the study. "What did I tell you?" she said. "Of course, it isn't so important, but when a woman has grown-up children and suddenly she finds she's going to have a baby, she does feel a fool."

"Interesting," Sam said. "But they never so much as mentioned you or a baby."

Her mouth opened. "Honestly?"

"Honestly," Sam replied, a twinkle in his eye as he affectionately patted her hand. "But I don't think you'd find it embarrassing even if they did know. They're a nice lot, love."

She looked up at him. "They have guessed after all, haven't they?"

Sam nodded. "I'm pretty sure, Milly," he said.

For a few seconds she stood quite still, thinking of her son and daughter, her daughter's husband-to-be, and of her nephew and niece. Then, slowly she began to smile as slowly she shook her head.

"Yes, you're right, Sam. They *are* a nice lot," she said softly. "No, I shouldn't mind about them."

"Of course you wouldn't," said Sam. "Now I've a suggestion to make. What about us two sneaking off together for a walk down the ravine. It's a lovely afternoon, and though we seem to have been on the go ever since lunch with one thing and another, it isn't tea-time yet."

Milly glanced at her dress, a very pretty yellow one. "Yes, it would be nice, dear," she said.

"Right," said Sam.

Her arm in his, they crossed the paved court to the garage, acknowledging such wedding guests as were near, before disappearing into the winding path to the ravine, whose depths were lighted up by sunshine filtering through the trees. At the foot of the defile they turned left along the rock scar, where Milly sat on the handkerchief Sam spread for her, and he squatted down on an upturned tub.

Overhead they could hear the chatter and laughter of the Roebucks' guests, while before them, fringing the low side, the orchard stretched charmingly. Even the buildings, dotted about, utilitarian though they were, were not without attractiveness, well-cared for and nicely sited.

"I'm not surprised you often read here, dear," said Milly. "It's so peaceful and secluded. We're lucky, aren't we? In so many ways ... especially now."

"We are," Sam agreed. "Yes, by Jove! And don't forget, love," he went on solemnly, "we're going to be further blessed, aren't we?"

Milly had always been prone to blush, and did so again. Then, very spiritedly, she was declaring that she had not the slightest intention of allowing herself to be teased, when she stopped and cocked her head.

"That's Fred Lumb's voice, I'm certain," she said, bewildered.

"Fred Lumb!" Sam ejaculated, looking at her with eyes in which comprehension quickly dawned. "He'll be up to something, love," he continued. "He gave me a sort of hint that he'd be covering up why he was in Moorheaton and ... well, maybe it's going to be at my expense. Anyhow, we've a seat in the front row of the stalls even if we can't see anything. But we can listen."

Beforehand, however, Sam made a reconnaisance as far as the end of the rock face, to the ravine, that is. He returned to Milly with the news that Fred Lumb was in the grounds of The Turrets, and from there was conducting a conversation with a party in the vicinity of the sundial at the outer corner of the lawn.

Earlier, a well-dressed gentleman had wandered round The Turrets, peering into windows, examining woodwork and the condition of the pointing between smooth-faced blocks of stone. These activities had been interestedly watched by four people, two of whom had recognized the prowler as Fred Lumb, the proprietor of Ben Buckley's.

"I say," said Mr. Septimus Firth as he stared across the ravine, "he's never contemplating buying that spot, is he?"

Mrs. Firth and her friend, Mrs. Thornton, both of whom had been familiar with The Turrets when it was last occupied, began to speak of upkeep, how heavy it would be.

"Yes, I'll bet," agreed Mr. Simeon Calverley. "If he is, he must be coining brass, and we know at whose expense that'll be."

"It's a licker, isn't it?" Mr. Firth murmured. "What a smack in the eye for poor old Sam if his former manager moved in next door, and into a house more than twice as big as his own."

Simeon Calverley had obtained the result of the Jubilee Handicap over the Roebucks' telephone. "We'll have a word with him," he said.

His jovial hail carried far, certainly to guests chatting in the vicinity of the marquee, and, as quite a lot of hilarious laughter followed, many of them, scenting fun, began to saunter that way.

"Well, Commander III has pulled off the big event at Kempton," Mr. Calverley was shouting. "What do you think of that, Fred?"

The conversation was being conducted at a range of about twenty-five yards. Fred Lumb had come down to the boundary wall of The Turrets, which reached shoulder height.

"Remember he's trained by Elsey at Malton, Mr. Calverley," Fred Lumb remarked gravely. "And when a Yorkshire horse is sent down to London, it isn't to gawp at Piccadilly Circus with a straw in his mouth."

"What price will you offer us blind on his next outing . . . seven to one?" Septimus Firth chipped in. "To a tenner."

404

Fred Lumb coughed. "There's such a thing as professional ethics, Mr. Firth," he said. "And I hardly consider it fitting to rob a fellow bookmaker of a client when that client's standing where he is, in his present bookie's private garden."

Simeon Calverley bellowed with laughter, and, further lively exchanges across the little tree-lined valley producing the same result, the gathering was quickly augmented, until at least fifty or sixty persons were there, with streams more heading towards them. The whole point of the jollity was to find out whether or not Fred Lumb was considering house-purchasing.

This tone changed disastrously when the bride's grandfather joined in.

Mr. Sykes, attired much less sombrely than usual, had already had one skirmish that day, with his daughter, about the extravagance of the wedding, which was far greater, he asserted, than he had been given to understand it would be. Moreover, throughout the week, at Chapel meetings and elsewhere, including interviews with the printers and the bill-posting firm, he had railed about the offence to moral decency as represented by Ben Buckley's flaming advertisements. And so, when he noticed a tonsured-looking head behind The Turrets' boundary wall, he promptly resumed the crusade in vitriolic terms.

"Half a mo," said Fred Lumb, putting on his dashing grey hat again. "How am I corrupting young people? I'm not pretending that bookies are angels, but they do supply a need, and they work at a much slighter margin than a skinflint like you would consider. Yes, by Christopher, when you go in for a kill you select a right 'un."

Ezra Sykes found breath with difficulty. "I don't go in for the sort of kills you chaps do, choose how," he said, jerking his thumb in the direction of Glenfield. "There's one of your kidney in yon house who's just legally swindled a widow out of a thousand pounds—my own daughter."

Wholly in the dark about what was meant, Fred Lumb hit back tellingly. "You'd better not talk about swindling widows, you."

Ezra Sykes's top set dropped as he opened his mouth too wide. "Are you hinting," he re-started on gaining control once more, "that I've ever done owt contrary to the laws of either God or man in conducting business transactions?"

A denunciatory arm stretched out. "What about that row of cottages you own at Low Scargate?" Fred Lumb thundered. "How did they become yours, tell us that . . . and when you've told us, let's hear your ideas as to why old Mrs. Gledhill, who owned 'em, finished her last years in the Workhouse."

For the moment the eyes of enraptured spectators were fixed on Mr. Sykes who, veins protruding alarmingly, struggled to produce a searing, unanswerable reply. But then many glances shifted slightly, to Mrs. Allan Oldfield, blue-eyed and babyish-looking, whose exceedingly smart clothes had excited the comment of those who knew her circumstances. With quite a possessive air she slipped her white-gloved hand under Ezra Sykes's arm.

"Don't worry yourself any more, dear," she simpered. "It isn't worth it, Ezra, it isn't really."

Mr. Sykes sought to keep his pleasure within bounds. "Eh, I'm noan so sure about that, Phyllis love."

These signs of a budding romance naturally electrified the womenfolk. Meantime Septimus Firth, endeavouring to bring about a more harmonious atmosphere, resumed his earlier conversation with Fred Lumb.

"Anyway, Fred," he said, "let's be hearing what you're doing in there if you're not buying?"

Poker-faced, Fred Lumb disposed of that. "Nay, how could I have got the brass so quickly as to afford a palace like this?"

Mrs. Gainsway-Sinkinson was a relative of the Watkinsons, and had attended the wedding with her husband who, with no love either for Sam Pilling or Fred Lumb, was delighted by this opportunity of paying off old scores. He began, with withering sarcasm, by referring to the glowing advertisements of the individual across the ravine. Then he entered upon a damning indictment of Sam Pilling who, he declared, had feathered his nest to the detriment of his widowed sister-in-law.

"I have Mrs. Roebuck's word that she knows nothing whatsoever about it," he added. "Of course it's a good stroke of business for Pilling, this sly commission which he has not disclosed, but the whole thing stinks in any decent chappie's nostrils."

There was much head-turning and eyebrow-raising among a crowd of over two hundred as the full sense of this unsavoury charge was grasped, but Sam was not without his defenders, and one of them, a well-known personality of the district who bluntly declined to believe the statement, was listened to intently.

Colour ebbing and flowing, Captain Gainsway-Sinkinson did not appreciate the verbal hiding he received from this gentleman, a man of middle height with an air of authority about him.

"But dash it all, Crowther old man," he remonstrated, nervously fingering a toothbrush moustache, "Peter Entwistle told me——"

"That may or may not be," Mr. Simjoss Crowther said coldly. "But if you have any gumption, which to me has always been debatable, you will be careful about repeating this tale."

Broad smiles greeted this observation, which seemed as if it would end the incident. But the lone figure in the grounds of The Turrets took up the cudgels for the accused also. Loyally, realizing how much harm had been done to Sam already, Fred Lumb set out with all his heart and strength to depict his antagonist as the shadiest of customers.

"You've got your knife into me and Sam Pilling because we won't have your business, for reasons quite a number of folk know," he bawled. "Aye, you, Gainsway-Sinkinson . . . but if you'd any decency in you you'd remember that if it hadn't been for Sam's clemency you'd have been black-listed by every bookie there is . . . yes, and warned off every race-course in the land."

Laura Roebuck, who had been bidding farewell on the drive to a party of early leavers, began to run across the lawn. She had had her worries that day, worries quite apart from those which are normally expected to be the lot of the person responsible for a considerable social undertaking—there had been the breeze, not too serious she believed, with her father; then she was annoyed with Estelle, through whose connivance Tony Flassati had been present without having received a formal invitation; and, behind the façade of the cool and charming hostess, she simmered with fury every time she remembered Captain Gainsway-Sinkinson's account of her brother-in-law's infamy.

But, until now, she had had every reason to preen herself about the smoothness with which the function had gone. It would be utter tragedy if, in the closing stages, the affair were ruined by a vulgar disturbance. Her lips momentarily compressed, she recognized the elderly man beyond the boundary wall of The Turrets, the cause, she had not the slightest doubt, of this deplorable incident.

As she pushed forward, Captain Gainsway-Sinkinson, livid, was replying to his traducer.

"It's a damned lie, you . . . Lumb, you," he shouted.

Mrs. Roebuck reached him, and, mistress of herself, smiled at him and at the sea of faces around.

"Don't you think we might . . . er . . . circulate, and forget about that unpleasant creature over there?" she suggested easily. "I mean, why pander to rogues of that type by bandying words with them? It merely gives them an importance they don't possess, don't you think?"

Fred Lumb stuttered. "Hey! I heard you. You guard your tongue in future, Mrs. Roebuck, and less of your talk about rogues."

"Bookmakers!" she scoffed. "Really, quite the scum of the earth, aren't they? Scum *perfectly* willing to do *anything* for money, even to robbing their own . . . yes, even to robbing their own, as I'm afraid I have learnt to my cost only this afternoon. And now, shall we . . ." Smiling again, she waved her hands in a shooing gesture.

At their hostess's bidding the throng began to disperse, the majority of the ladies gladly, in the hope that, as the ranks thinned, she might see her father at the other end of the lawn, where he was strolling arm-in-arm with a widow known to all. Judging by Laura Roebuck's demeanour that day it was thought she had not an inkling about the tender affair.

Two people, silent and very still, were sitting in the Pillings' kitchen garden, at the foot of the rock face. Sam's cheeks had lost their ruddiness and his expression was pathetically defeated; Milly was very pale, and every now and then she clenched and unclenched her hand.

In the distance they could hear the excited chatter of the Roebucks' guests, but no longer was there rancorous discord over their heads. It could have been so peaceful—the pleasant outlook, the amusingly demanding chirrup of a hen chaffinch, the cadences of a thrush perched on an upper branch of a laburnum.

Sam stirred. "Well, love, shall we go home," he said. "Or would you prefer to wait until all that lot have left . . . they'll soon be off now, I should think."

"No, let's go now, Sam darling," said Milly, rising quickly as if she yearned for action. "What I'd like to do," she continued fiercely, "is to go on to the lawn and saunter about with you in front of everybody."

Sam smiled wanly as he took her arm. "I married a spitfire, didn't I?"

"Oh, but something *must* be done," she urged as they turned up the ravine. "We can't have people thinking you've done Laura down, Sam."

"I've no option, not without telling about Maggie's baby," he said. "And . . . well . . . that would be betraying Clem's trust, wouldn't it?"

"Yes, I suppose it would," she gulped, lips quivering. "But we can't have your name trailed in the mud."

"Those that matter won't believe it, and the others don't count," said Sam. "It'll soon be forgotten anyway."

She shook her head miserably. "You know that isn't so, Sam. Oh, I don't mind for myself, dear . . . it's you I'm thinking about. You've done all sorts of things in your life, to build the business up, but you've never done anything . . . anything rotten."

"Well, love, I've still got good friends," he said. "You heard Simjoss Crowther and one or two others chiming in for me. No, I'm not friendless."

Milly rubbed her cheek against his shoulder. "Of course you're not, Sam darling."

There was a fund of love and affection in Sam's eyes as he put his arm round her waist.

"Milly, whatever else, I never want you to forget one thing," his voice deepened. "And it's that what matters most to me is you and the children and home, and in the long run I don't give two hoots for anything else. Oh, yes, you may say I'm wrapped up in the business, as I am, but the other is what really weighs with me, nothing else."

She glanced at him, unshed tears in her eyes. "All right, Sam," she said softly.

When they came out of the winding path by the garage there were few people at that end of the court, though at the other a fairly large crowd had gathered round Alderman Joseph Hirst and Mr. Walter Murgatroyd. Together with their chauffeurs, these gentlemen were standing near a Daimler and a Rolls-Royce, and the principal object of each owner and driver seemed to be to blame the other party for damage to these vehicles.

Nearer, Jim Oldfield was staggering forward, with an arm entwined around Mr. James Wainwright's neck.

"Hallo, Mrs. Pilling . . . and Sam, old cock," the box manufacturer cried out. "I say, I hope neither of you will bother your heads about the . . . excuse me . . . the Staff Captain's bloody silly tale. But I've news for you, and I've been celebrating. Do you know, Sam, I've every reason to believe that I'm going to be rid of that stepmother of mine."

"Be careful, Jim," James Wainwright cautioned him.

Mr. Oldfield attempted to focus on the lawyer's face. "James," he hiccoughed, "is it true that Hildred Pickersgill is suing you for big damages, and that——"

"Will you keep your mouth shut?" James Wainwright said violently.

In other circumstances this might have been amusing, but, though Sam and Milly were grateful for the drunken man's encouragement, their cares were too onerous for them to do other than nod acknowledgement.

Indoors, totally unconscious of what had occurred, a communal tea-making was in lively progress in the kitchen, all the young people taking part.

But Milly went at once upstairs, and Sam wandered into the drawing-room, where from the window he stared towards the town in the hollow below.

He sighed heavily. "Yes, up to now I'm the chap who was a bit too clever . . . but from now I shall be the chap who twisted his widowed sister-in-law."

Sunlight shaded one side of the slender spire of the Parish Church. "Poor old Clem," he mused sadly. "Well, I've kept faith with you, lad, and it's my damned smartness, and not your fault, that I've landed myself in the mess I'm in. If I'd been content to allow Jim to pay Maggie . . . but, of course, I had to be a slick 'un and prise a commission out of Entwhistle—and, by God, he's open-mouthed, if ever a chap is."

Restlessly he began to pace between the radiogram and the entrance to the conservatory.

"Yes, I'm ingenious, that's it, and I always have been, maybe too much so," he admitted to himself. "But no amount of ingenuity is going to get me out of this."

For a brief space, perched on the arm of a chair, he reflected about the might-have-been which had vaguely occurred to him when in the garage with Milly, some step he might have taken *that* summer to electrify Ramsfield and also serve more personal ends. As always when cogitating about some novel scheme, his eyes kindled . . . but quickly the new spark died.

"It's just a waste of time even thinking about it," he

murmured. "Because even if I made another fortune, real or imaginary, I should be pursued by that thousand pounds —it wouldn't be enterprise and hard work that had done it . . . it would be sharp practice and underhand tricks. Yes, my cuteness with Entwhistle, and the fact that I can't explain what I was doing it for, has settled my hash for good and all."

Rising, he again meandered to the window, his glance now steadied on the tower of the Regal Cinema. Without field-glasses it was impossible to read the posters displayed on it, but one was scarlet, and he guessed what it was. But, as a roar of youthful laughter rose in the kitchen, he nodded, and smiled faintly.

"Well, whatever else, Sam lad," he told himself, "you've done one thing all right. What you've got in the back of the house there is worth . . . worth all the travail . . . and now just another piece of advice to you, my good fellow— no more of your blasted moping."

A split second's hesitation, and then he walked with jaunty step into the hall.

Milly was coming down the stairs, eyeing the various bowls of flowers below her: golden trollius, pale yellow tulips, and rather gaudy doronicums.

"Hallo, love," he called out, adding in a whisper: "Something's just hit me on top of the head . . . fancy you and me with a baby on the way. Can you believe it?"

Milly laughed. "Just another Sam Pilling stunt," she said.

"Yes, it could be," Sam said, grinning. "Yes," he went on much more thoughtfully: "Yes, it could, couldn't it?"

"No, it couldn't," Milly said firmly.

Jim and Kate were bringing the trolley through, neither as yet seeming in the least inclined to go home, although the Rev. Dyson had been fully informed about his daughter.

"Tea's ready, Aunt Milly," said Kate.

Nancy bustled into the hall with a footstool. "To put your feet on, Mummy," she explained briskly.

In the drawing-room, Archie also saw to his mother, placing her chair just as she liked it, and assisting her to sit down. Then, in an incredible bass voice, he remarked tenderly: "Little Mother."

Blushing vividly, Milly glanced at Sam. "What shall we do with them?"

Sam chuckled. "Oh, they'll soon tire."

It was a jolly meal, interrupted frequently by Jim's many

411

visits to the telephone. In some unknown manner friends and acquaintances had discovered where he was, and many rang up to congratulate him upon his rescue of Kate. This traffic grew so regular that, after his return to the drawing-room on the fifth occasion, Philip solemnly escorted Nancy to the piano, where she played *My Hero* from *The Chocolate Soldier*.

"Oh, they're all lovely, Sam dear," Milly said about three hours later when the house was strangely silent. Jim had taken Kate home to Highthwaite Road, Nancy and her *fiancé* had also gone out, and Alec and Frank had called for Archie. "No, I don't mind their teasing a bit."

"And it's done very nicely," said Sam, smiling. "Anyhow, what about a turn in the garden?"

And so Sam and his wife, each trying to cheer up the other, wandered outdoors, their first call at a tulip bed, where Milly's dire suspicions were confirmed—the men setting up the marquee *had* driven in stakes.

About nine o'clock the Alfa Romeo returned, much earlier than usual. As soon as she saw her daughter walking across the lawn Milly knew that something had happened. Nancy was gay enough, but when not on guard there was quite unmistakably anger in her eyes.

It was not until they were all walking towards the house that Milly found out the cause, deliberately loitering behind with Philip while Nancy, holding her father's arm, went ahead.

"Philip, I want you to tell me something," she said to him. "When you and Nancy were out, was she upset in any way? . . . I think it would be about her father."

Philip Illingworth nodded. "Yes," he said gravely. "She was."

"I thought so," said Milly.

When she got inside she began thinking about some late tea. "We might as well make it straight away," she said. "But we won't bring a cup for Archie—he'll not be home for ages yet."

In this she was wrong. Her elder son arrived at ten minutes past ten, with a red and bulbous nose and an air of suppressed fury. No one inquired into either.

At ten minutes to eleven Philip got up to leave. "Good-night, Mrs. Pilling, 'night, Archie," he said. "And good-night, sir. Er . . . by the way, you won't be fit for golf to-morrow, but what about a round to-morrow week?"

Sam twisted in his chair. "It's a very pleasant suggestion, Philip, and I'll be delighted to discuss it with you again," he said, a slightly grim smile on his lips. "Yes, a very good idea, lad. Anyway, come for lunch to-morrow, if you're not already doing so, which I suspect you are."

"Daddy!" Nancy said, laughing.

Her farewell in the hall took an appreciable while, and it was not until ten minutes past eleven that she returned. When she was closing the drawing-room door behind her, the front door bell rang, and, fully expecting her young man had come back for something, she skipped out again. A few moments later she popped her head in.

"It's Jim, Archie," she said. "He wants a word with you."

At a quarter to twelve Sam stirred. "What are Archie and Jim doing? And where's Nancy? Why didn't she come back?"

There was no need for Milly to attempt a solution to this, for Jim appeared just then, his cousins behind him.

"I'd like to have a talk to you and Aunt Milly, Uncle," he said.

Milly had noticed her nephew's grave face. "Sit down then, and make yourself comfortable," she said.

Jim Roebuck did not begin all at once, but his opening remark made up for any delay. It had an overwhelming effect on both his uncle and aunt.

"You've what?" Sam exclaimed.

"I've told Nancy and Archie about Father and Maggie," Jim said quietly. "Not because they'd ever believe you were capable of such a dirty trick as collaring that commission for yourself—but because they've a right to know."

"Well . . ." Sam was nearly speechless.

Jim glanced at them. "Moreover this tale has to be quashed from to-morrow onwards, and it can be," he continued. "Mind you, I'm not pretending harm hasn't been done already . . . but if it's denied at the source—from our end, the Roebuck end, I mean—I reckon it's got a good chance of dying a natural death before long."

Milly had taken out a handkerchief. "Oh, Jim, none of us will ever forget this. But . . . but. . . ."

"I think I know what's on your mind, Aunt Milly."

They were all watching him, noting every fleeting expression on his thin face. "It's Mother, isn't it, Aunt Milly?" he went on. "Well, I've told her everything. And from now on she'll explain that it was all a tragic mistake on her part—and she's pretty good when she gives her mind to things . . . as she will . . . she's too terrified about scandal not to do."

Sam, too restless to sit, got up and stood with his back to the fire.

"And what will she say, Jim?" he asked.

"What I've told her to say, Uncle—that I've known about the commission from the beginning, which is true, and that you gave me every penny of it, which in effect is true."

"Why are you so sure, Jim, that she'll do this?"

Momentarily Jim Roebuck's lips tightened. "Because she now understands beyond any doubt that if she doesn't . . . I shall make sure everybody who matters knows what that thousand pounds was used for."

The room was very silent, and it was Jim who ended that silence, by telling them how he had worried since first hearing the tale that evening.

"What I've done I haven't done hastily, Uncle Sam," he went on. "And to be honest I should never have done it, even for you, if it hadn't been for one thing—I was quite certain it wouldn't break Mother. She . . ." he finished painfully, "she was never passionately fond of my father—it couldn't hurt her like it would some women."

Tears were in Nancy's eyes. "Oh, it must have been hard for you, Jim dear, and I'm awfully, awfully sorry. But I can't help being glad for Daddy . . . it would have been so terrible for him."

Archie recrossed his legs impatiently. "Wish I'd heard about this sooner. I'd have lammed a few bastards once or twice more . . . legitimately."

"You've been fighting again," Milly declared. "Don't imagine you've deceived me by sitting sideways."

"About my misappropriation of money, Archie?" Sam inquired—adding to this, on receiving a short-tempered nod: "Who was it with and where?"

"In the George bar," Archie replied succinctly. "With Boothroyd Gee, a colleague of yours when you were a director of the Hornets, and a couple of his pals. And if it weren't damned well too late I'd trek off to root out any other similarly misguided blokes. Still, there's always another day."

"Now, Archie," his mother started off.

"Well, I think that's about all," said Jim, "and so I'll get home."

"There's no need to hurry, Jim," said Milly.

"No, I won't stay, Aunt Milly," he replied, smiling faintly.

"So good-night, all. I . . . I don't know whether you'll think I've done right, but I haven't any doubt, none at all. It seemed to me I'd no choice, and I'm glad I was so certain that what I was doing was *absolutely* right. Anyway, good-night again."

Archie saw him out and then returned to the drawing-room. No one had spoken in his absence.

"Well, I don't know what to say about this," Sam murmured.

"I damned well know what to say, Dad, and it's that Jim's done the proper thing," said Archie. "No bloke should be wrongfully stained as you would have been for your natural. Yes, too bloody true he's done right—apologies, Mother."

"And do you think for a moment, Daddy, that Uncle Clem would have ever allowed it to be thought that you were a shark nobbling their money?" asked Nancy. "Uncle Clem was decent and honest, and he just wouldn't if he could pop down and do anything about it. And to me he's still decent and honest despite this baby. He'd an *awful* time at home."

Milly was quietly crying. "You're all forgetting the most important thing of all," she said, swallowing. "Jim hit on it when he spoke of—well, some women's hearts would have been broken by it, but . . ." she shook her head, completely sure, "but Laura's won't."

"She's a hard nut," said Archie. "By God, aye."

"Oh, I am glad," Milly said through quivering lips. "But all this doesn't mean you're at liberty to use such dreadful language, Archie."

Sam was wandering about the room as if in some doubt as to what to do with himself.

"Well, after this packet I think I'll fetch a cigar from the study," he mumbled. "Maybe it'll soothe my nerves."

He went out, along the hall and into the study, where for a time, perfectly motionless, apart from his lips which moved now and then, he stared blankly at a calendar on the wall. This intense preoccupation was brought to a close by a tickling sensation, when he knuckled his eyes.

"Whatever next?" he muttered, horrified. "I know I'm a baby who everlastingly wants to show off . . . but now I'm a cry-baby also. Good God! I'll have to hide it somehow."

Many years before, for a few weeks only, he had taken snuff, and so, seized with an idea, he snatched open the drawers of the roll-top desk, rooting through the contents until he found the box, still almost full. From it he took an enormous pinch. Thrice he sneezed violently.

"That's done it . . . a genuine reason for reddened eyes," he remarked to himself. "Ingenuity, that's it, and you're the boy for it, Sam lad."

On the way back he sneezed once more in the hall, and again in the entrance to the drawing-room, a terrific paroxysm.

Milly, alarmed to begin with, then recognized the small pewter box in his hand.

"Sam," she expostulated, "you're never dreaming of taking that filthy habit up again, are you?"

"You'll explode, Daddy," said Nancy.

Archie murmured: "Then we'll be scraping bits of the old man off Ma's cherished wallpaper."

Vision blurred, Sam Pilling looked towards his own: at Milly and Nancy, smiling at him from the small chintz-covered sofa on which they were sitting, two pretty and very charming women; and at Archie, grey-eyed, square-jawed and grinning.

Deep feeling welled up in him. "Here I go again," he said.